The Trular Chronicles

Children of Elium

The Trular Chronicles
Children of Elium

LIS JANLEE

THREADWING
PRESS

Cover design, interior formatting, and editing by
Alisa Russell

Printed in the United States of America
ISBN: 979-8-9939520-0-0
First Edition

For Kevin, Natalie, Ben, and Katie
my favorite crew

For Mom and Dad
because you believed I could

Trust Yourself
-Lorna Occlen

Part One

1

Betham stood silent. The oranges and pinks streaking across the sky made the village almost beautiful. On any other evening, the girl named Behler, who lay hidden in the tall weeds just at the edge of the village, might have paused to take in the sight, but not this evening. *This* evening she hid and watched the Gorlog who stood guard outside a small depot on the outskirts of the village. She'd seen him around many times. He was easily recognizable thanks to the large scar that ripped jaggedly across his missing right eye. While she waited for the day to give way to the night, she daydreamed about different ways the guard lost the ugly orb, and she smiled slightly as each way was more horrific than the last.

Gorlogs were despicable creatures. They had a tough, gray hide covered in hundreds of sharp, coarse hairs that could pierce a human's skin. They lumbered about with bulky bodies, smashing and crashing through whatever may lay in their path. This particular one's hulking frame took up the entire doorway behind it. Behler tried not to gag when it snorted and a large string of saliva slipped from its gaping mouth, trailing unbroken from its puffy lips to the ground. It wiped and slurped green globs of snot from its oozing snout.

"Gross," she said to herself, happy to be upwind of it. She knew from experience it smelled like rotten eggs and pig kak. All the Gorlogs did.

She could have overlooked a lot of the physical ick if they'd had an ounce of decency toward any other living thing.

Her attention was diverted when she caught movement out of the corner of her eye.

"Kak!" she cursed as she watched Dax, a boy just a bit older than her, walking down the path and heading their way.

The guard wasn't remotely aware Dax was approaching. Gorlogs weren't the highest quality guards, but they were cheap labor, happy to be paid in meat and ale.

The boy was carrying a wooden bucket. Behler knew he was heading to the river to collect water.

"Why are you taking the main path?" she whispered.

Most villagers believed the Armigoth's guuns had contaminated the well at the center of the village. Anyone who drank much of the water changed. They become angry – or sad – or just empty. Once those types of feelings became strong enough, it was easier for the Armigoth to take hold.

No one *really* understood what the Armigoth was *exactly*. Behler had heard from others that it looked like a giant summer storm that never went away. But it was no summer storm, and it brought no rain. It only brought destruction to everything it touched.

It was still centered to the north, at Kilgen Castle – but it spread a little more every day.

In Betham, villagers often snuck to the river for water. Dax must have thought he could get by the Gorlog without trouble. He was probably right; Gorlogs usually didn't give a kak about much except where their next meal was coming from.

As soon as Dax rounded the curve by the depot, though, the Gorlog jumped and shouted, "Stop right there! What do you think you're doing?" It drew a stubby sword from its belt and pointed it directly at the boy's throat. Startled, Dax dropped his bucket. Behler tensed, but then the Gorlog started laughing. "Rik ta yuna," he said in his native tongue. *Clumsy moron.* "What are you doing here?" It demanded but didn't wait for an answer before it grabbed Dax by the nape of his neck and forced him to his knees.

Dax let out a little cry. "My mother needs water," he explained, his voice meek and pitiful. Behler's heart leapt as she watched the scene unfold.

"Water?" The Gorlog snarled. "Your *mother* needs water?" He taunted and released him. "Drink out of the well then, *yuna*," He leered down at the boy, chuckling, then walked over and lifted his leg high and brought its foot crashing down onto the bucket, shattering it into splinters. The guard walked back over toward Dax then leaned down so that his face was just above the boy's head. "How can you get water without a bucket, *yuna*?" Another string of drool fell from its mouth and across Dax's cheek – Behler had to grab the tall grass around her to keep herself from leaping out from her hiding place and challenging the Gorlog then and there.

She was completely wrapped up in the scene unfolding on the road, so when a rustling came from behind her she nearly jumped out of her skin. It was only Mathias, though, and she had been expecting him.

She looked back to see him crawling toward her through the thick grass. Once beside her, he sat up on his haunches. When he saw what was transpiring on the road, he glared at her with his best stern impression and gave his head a quick shake. He knew exactly what was going through her mind.

"Don't. Do. Anything," he ordered.

Dismissing him, Behler looked back toward Dax. "If it goes near him again, I will."

Mathias shook his head. "No, you won't."

"What if it tries to kill him?" she whispered harshly.

5

"Bale. It's a *Gorlog*. You know they don't kill anything." He made a face of disgust as he looked through the weeds at the ogre-like guard. "Except maybe my appetite."

"I don't care about your stomach right now, Mat" Behler snapped. She kept her eyes on the giant pig of a creature. "Something's different about this kakweed." She turned and looked at her best friend. "He just shoved Dax down. Hard."

Mathias cocked his head to one side, contemplating the situation. "Yeah, I've never seen one do that...*BUT*—" he continued quickly, "Shoving him to the ground is a lot different than actually trying to kill him."

She pointed toward the broken bucket remains. "He smashed his bucket," she said, as if that changed everything.

"Oh, I see." He nodded. "We *should* kill him then." He rolled his eyes.

Behler still refused to yield. "We're just going to knock him out anyway. What does it matter if we do it now or wait?"

"The whole point is that no one else will see what we're up to," he reminded her. "Dax can't know we're here."

"If that pig makes one more move toward Dax, I'm going to do it." She picked up her bow and started to place the arrow's notch on the string.

Mathias sighed. "If he escalates any more, I'll create a distraction, okay?"

She thought about it for a moment then said, "Okay," she reluctantly agreed.

"What's going on here!?"

Behler stiffened. The voice that had demanded that answer was one she knew well, but her heart still sank when a little old woman from the village came from around the back of the depot.

Tilda.

This plan was not going well.

The Gorlog growled. "None of your business old woman," it snarled. "Move on,"

Tilda looked down at Dax, then back up at the guard. It was hard to tell what the guard was thinking under the layers of fatty skin covering its face.

Behler whispered to Mathias, "Something is definitely wrong with that Gorlog."

Mathias nodded. "Maybe he has rivertick fever." Behler shot him a dirty look. Only dogs got rivertick fever. "I'm serious," he insisted. He wrinkled his nose. "They're barely more than animals anyway."

Behler raised an eyebrow. "Good point."

"Release this boy," Tilda said, her voice small but steady.

Behler's heart was pounding in her chest. Tilda had been like a grandmother to her since she'd been small. She wasn't surprised the feisty woman had stepped in, but she was terrified for her.

The Gorlog had still been leaning over Dax. It straightened and faced Tilda. "Move on, old woman."

The cold, uncharacteristic hatred in the Gorlog's voice had Behler gripping the arrow in her hand. If she let it fly now, there'd be no hiding. She'd be revealed to Dax and Tilda, and that was not part of the plan. Still, she wanted to put that arrow straight through the guard's heart – but that was wishful thinking since the arrow she carried would only penetrate the Gorlog's thick outer layer of skin. There was no way she could get it all the way to its heart, plus she wasn't exactly sure where the thing's heart was anyway.

She assumed it had to have one – somewhere.

Just as the tension on the road seemed to reach a breaking point, Samuel came from the same direction Tilda had only moments before.

"It's a party now," Mathias said in a low voice.

Samuel was one of the only people in the village who knew Behler and Mathias were hidden and waiting. He looked from Tilda to Dax who was still on the ground. "Enough of this," Samuel said in a loud voice. He looked squarely at the Gorlog. "Enough."

The Gorlog's demeanor changed and his body language indicated he was backing off.

Tilda walked over to Dax and helped him up from the ground. She started guiding him back toward the village center.

As Samuel turned to walk away with Tilda and Dax, he looked over his shoulder and said, "I'll be watching you, Gorlog."

"I'll be quaking in my boots, human." He made a sound that must have been laughter, but there was nothing happy about the noise.

Tilda stopped and turned back to face the Gorlog. Without a word, she spat at his feet. That only made the Gorlog laugh and wheeze even louder.

Mathias scanned the road. "No one's coming and the light is almost gone. Shoot that son of a pig."

Behler smiled and pulled the arrow back until the bow's string was taut. She took aim with the arrow tipped in greet nettle root – strong enough to knock a Gorlog out cold.

"Goodnight," she whispered, then let the arrow fly.

2

Behler scanned the room inside the depot. "Look at all of these," she spoke with an air of disbelief. The collection of weapons ranged from swords and daggers to pitchforks and scythes. Horde guuns had taken away anything that remotely resembled a weapon when they'd invaded Betham the previous summer.

Behler and Mathias had given up their weapons along with everyone else, or at least it had appeared that way. There was a group of rebels that both Behler and Mathias were part of strewn throughout the villages. They were kept secret from just about everyone in Betham and beyond and had managed to hold on to some of their weapons. The guuns knew about the rebellion and were always on the hunt to find anyone who was a part of it, so Behler and her fellow fighters had to blend in with everyone else in the village. It was hard to know who could be trusted on any given day, and even those who could be one day could be an enemy the next. The Armigoth could turn just about anyone at any time.

"Let's get these to the black house," Mathias said. He looked around the small room and sighed. "We'll get Kellum and Meela to help us, before the Gorlog wakes up or a Horde guun comes to relieve him."

An hour later, Behler and Mathias were sitting in the middle of another small building. This one was tucked in the side of a rise far on the northeastern outskirts of the village. The one room house, called the black house by the rebels for the black ash that coated its walls, had long been abandoned and forgotten. The Gorlogs and guuns were unlikely to find it thanks to some eerie legends about the woods surrounding it.

Piled in the middle of the black house were the swords, small daggers, bows, arrows, countless axes, pitchforks, and pretty much anything else from the village containing a blade. Most of the Betham rebels were gathered around, all waiting for their leader Lorna to speak.

She was also Behler's aunt.

Lorna gave her niece a stern look. "You closed up the depot – no sign you'd been there?"

Behler tensed at the condescending question but tried not to reveal her resentment in her voice. "Of course," she answered. She held up the arrow she'd retrieved from the Gorlog's hide. "No evidence of us there left behind." Even if the guard figured it out, it would never tell. The Armigoth officers only tolerated a certain amount of incompetence, and allowing the rebels to retrieve the weapons would mean execution for sure.

Lorna's shoulders visibly relaxed. "With these weapons and those we already had, we can arm those left in Betham willing to fight with us...if it comes to that."

Her second in command, Rogan, asked. "Do we know how many townspeople are still with us?"

Lorna's brow wrinkled. "Our last estimate was around thirty, but we can't know who may have turned."

Across the room, Meela's chair squeaked as she shifted her weight. She was only a couple years older than Behler and stayed to herself. Meela looked around the room. "I think our neighbor may be falling under the influence of the Armigoth. He's been acting strange lately."

Her mother, Ria, nodded. "Along with a few others who live near us."

The sniveling boy in the group, Kellum, muttered something to Meela beside him. She gave him a slight nod.

Behler's jaw tightened. Meela was too kind. The rest of people Behler's age had long ago stopped bothering with Kellum – years of whining complaints and his need to be the smartest one in the room had seen to that.

When they were younger, Behler had felt bad for him and had tried to befriend him many times. But when he paid her kindness back with hostility, her sympathy for him quickly dwindled. She often wondered how he and his uncle, Broty, could possibly be related. Not only were they physical opposites – Kellum being tall and lean with jet black hair while Broty was a blond bear – but Broty was so jolly and fun. Kellum – he was not.

Rogan, shaking his head as if vexed, said. "We may not be able to wait much longer. Some things are still so far out." Behler thought she saw Rogan's eyes dart in her direction and she shifted uncomfortably. She didn't like eyes on her, for any reason. "We should take back this village now."

Mathias shifted in his seat, and Behler knew he was feeling his anxiety. He hated it when his father questioned Lorna.

Everyone looked to their leader, who had her head down. Behler could tell she was weighing every option they had. Finally, she looked up. "No. We have to wait. As painful as it is to see our friends and neighbors fall to the Armigoth, the risk is too great." Rogan started to speak again, but Lorna held up a hand. "Drawing attention to this village is too dangerous."

Rogan sighed and sat back in his chair. It was obvious he disagreed. "Part of our duty is to protect the people here in Betham. The more that are lost to the Armigoth, the stronger the shadow gets."

"Yes!" Lorna snapped, sharp enough that the entire room lost all its air for a moment. "But at this point, we know our top priority. We must protect that. You all know the longer we can wait, the better."

Behler noticed a couple other sets of eyes glancing at her. *What the – ?* She wiped her nose in case something was hanging out of it.

Lorna sighed deeply. "I don't like sitting around letting Varek take more of our neighbors any more than the rest of you, but we don't have a choice at this point."

The room was silent. Behler's mind wondered. Varek was the Armigoth in human form – although Behler wondered if he'd once been a human like the guuns she saw in the village. They were human...but not quite as human as they'd once been. For Behler – fighting a Gorlog or guun – she could handle them any day and any time. But the thought of fighting Varek with the power of the Armigoth within him made her anxious. Varek was ruthless. And the Armigoth, well she knew the Armigoth slithered into a person and changed them, possessing them and turning them into shells of who they'd once been. She couldn't imagine how they'd ever defeat Varek *or* the Armigoth.

A dull thud hit the side of the black house, low and flat. Every head snapped up. Lorna stood and quickly extinguished the fire, placing everyone in complete darkness. Behler grabbed her kintar, the rebels' version of a short sword but made of better steel than typical Elium swords. She would've preferred her bow, but the kintar would have to do.

She heard Rogan slowly move across the room toward the door. When he opened it, dim gray light reached halfway into the room. A low whistle came from somewhere outside.

Rogan's outline was discernible in the dimness, and she could visibly see him relax. "It's Dalen," he whispered to the room, then whistled the call back.

With the outline of the door clearly visible, Behler waited to see Dalen's silhouette. A moment later there were two shadowy figures blocking all the light.

"Help us," Dalen said breathlessly.

"Who's that with you?" Rogan asked in a hushed tone.

"It's Sam," Dalen said. "He's injured. Badly."

There was the sound of shuffling feet then the door shut. The fire was re-lit, but when the firelight touched Sam's face, Behler wished it hadn't been.

Samuel's cheek was torn, his chest gashed open, blood soaking into the fabric.

Behler's stomach twisted. Not just from the gore – but from the question she didn't want to ask: what could do that to him?

"Was it the Gorlog from the weapons depot?" she blurted out, surprising everyone – most of all, herself.

Dalen looked up at her, confused. "Why do you think a Gorlog did this, Bale?"

Behler felt her cheeks flush and cursed herself for speaking up. "Mathias and I saw Sam confront it earlier," she said quickly.

"The Gorlog was acting strangely before Behler knocked him out," Mathias explained. "Sam had a confrontation with it." Behler could have hugged him for drawing some of the attention off her. He knew she hated it.

Dalen shrugged. "I just found him like this outside the pub."

Rogan was carefully examining Samuel. "I've never seen wounds like this before. If it was the Gorlog, we've never seen them attack someone like this."

"As the Armigoth and Varek grow stronger, things will continue to change," Lorna said. She turned to Anilin. "Bring me the canteen." Behler grabbed her own canteen and started to hand it to Lorna, but her aunt dismissed her and Anilin gently stepped in front and handed Lorna a canteen with something etched into it: a beautiful, intricate set of swirls and lines.

"Matti, hand me a cloth from that pile over there." Anilin pointed.

Mathias reached for a piece of cotton that had been torn into a strip – a bandage for any future wounds.

"Here, Ama." He handed his mother the cloth.

Lorna took the cloth from Anilin and soaked it with water from the odd canteen. She touched it gently to Samuel's wounds. "I'll tend to Sam. The rest of you take these weapons to the bunker in the forest. We can't trust the black house will be safe for much longer. They will be getting more desperate to find us, and will get bolder in their attempts to flush us out. Ghost stories won't keep them away when they get desperate enough." She turned to Anilin. "Will you stay and help me?" Anilin nodded and knelt next to Samuel with another wet cloth. Lorna looked around the room. "Once you're finished, return home – all of you. Matti, stay with Bale."

"I'll make sure she gets home," Mathias said – as if Behler was a child.

She had to bite her tongue to keep from saying something she knew she'd regret. Lorna was constantly treating her like some helpless thing, always making sure someone escorted her home. But this wasn't the time or place to say anything. Not with Samuel lying bleeding on the floor.

She grabbed as many bows and arrows as she could carry then silently crept out into the night.

3

A hidden training ground lay about three hundred paces into the forest, tucked beneath the dense canopy. Even though the thick foliage provided cover, torchlight was limited as an extra precaution. Behler and Mathias were just turning to head back to the village when Rogan stopped them.

He looked at Mathias. "Be careful getting back to Lorna's house. The village has never been more dangerous. Stay with Behler until Lorna returns."

"I will," Mathias said. He rolled his eyes as soon as his father turned his back. "As if I don't know that," he muttered as soon as Rogan was out of earshot.

"Stop your whining," Behler hissed. "They have you watch over me like I'm a child. You're only a week older."

He shrugged. "I know. But it makes them feel better knowing you're not alone." His mouth curled into a devilish grin. "Want someone older? They could always send Kellum."

She rolled her eyes and didn't bother responding.

They moved back in the direction of the black house, but before walking out from the cover of the trees, they turned and headed south, remaining hidden in the shadow of the forest. They'd be able to stay hidden until they were only a few yura lengths from the door of Lorna's and Behler's house. Other rebels lived closer to the center of the village, but Lorna had made sure that she and Behler lived close enough to the forest that they could escape into it quickly if it came to that. No one except the rebels ventured into the trees anymore. Over the years, villagers who had gone more than a hundred paces into the forest returned with stories of ghostly whispers, dark shadows that darted in and out, demons with glowing eyes, and paths that were there one minute and gone the next. Some people just never returned at all. After the invasion of Betham, officers in the Horde refused to believe the stories. They knew that rebels used the forest as a refuge, so they sent scouts in to try to find them. The first scouts had returned battered and bloody days later unwilling, or unable, to speak about what had happened to them. But the Horde was determined and sent in even more guuns. Those men and women never returned, so the Horde finally stopped trying.

All the children in the village were afraid of the forest, and Behler had been no exception when she was younger. She had hated living so close to the ominous place and could never understand why Lorna wanted to. That is until she was ten when Lorna took her by the hand and walked her past the training circle. Behler's fingers trembled in Lorna's grasp – her feet dragging as they pushed deeper into the trees. Every step made her want to run back home. But Lorna kept walking with stoic determination.

When they reached a clearing Behler had never seen before, Lorna kept down and looked straight into Behler's eyes. "Listen."

Behler shook her head. "I don't want to."

But Lorna insisted. "Just sit and listen."

Behler reluctantly sat down and hoped she wouldn't hear anything. She closed her eyes to avoid seeing any dark, shadowy figures lurking about. It wasn't long, though, before she did begin to hear hushed whispers. She threw her hands up over her ears, but Lorna took them away.

"Listen to them, Bale," she said gently but firmly. "They aren't going to hurt you."

Behler's heart was pounding so loudly in her ears that she couldn't hear anything else for a few moments, but eventually she calmed down enough to hear the whispers again. She had to listen carefully to hear the voices that were more like music on the breeze than ghosts or evil spirits.

Lorna sat down beside her. "Our family carries a gift. We call it the Deep Thread – or thaelic in the old language. It runs through everything and connects us. Sometimes we can hear it with our ears; but often, we hear it more with our hearts and minds."

She ran a hand along the forest floor. "The Thread runs through this forest. Through the Arbiran Trees. This place is special. The Arbirans are special. The forest and Arbirans protect us." She looked up at Behler. "Don't be afraid of either, but respect them." A shadow passed over her expression. "You should only come to this part of the forest. Don't go any farther unless your life depends on it."

For some, that exception might have sounded like a hollow threat to hammer the lesson home; but for Behler it was a real possibility. They were hiding in Betham because Varek wanted her dead.

Behler agreed at the time to her aunt's rule, and for a while, she'd even obeyed. But one day, after Lorna had forbidden her from going on a scouting mission that Mathias was allowed to go on, she broke her word and defiantly went deeper into the forest.

She only went one hundred steps beyond the training area before she stopped and sat down next to an impressively tall tree that stood out amongst the others. The tree's trunk flared at the base, its roots reaching like fingers clawing free from the soil. Its bark was smooth and creamy white, entirely free of knots. When she looked closer, she saw delicate patterns in the surface—like fingerprints, swirled and ancient. There were similar looking trees growing throughout the area, each with different swirling designs imprinted on their trunks.

After that day, whenever she needed space to breathe, and when she could slip away unnoticed, Behler would return to the forest. Always the same twenty-three steps. Always to the same tree. When she was touching the tree, she could feel the Deep Thread and hear the Arbirans speaking to her. Most of their language was a mystery to her; but the more she listened, the more she understood. Images would appear in her mind, and she knew what they were saying. And even though the images were often disconnected and confusing, something about them felt familiar - like the tickle in the back of your mind when you're trying to remember a far-off memory that's just out of reach.

The forest and her Arbiran were her secrets, ones she didn't even share with Mathias.

They reached Lorna and Behler's small house without seeing another living soul, not even a guard. Normally, by that time, many of the Gorlogs could be heard carousing in the center of the village with off-duty Horde guuns.

The silence was unsettling.

As soon as they were inside the house, Behler said, "I'll start a fire."

"I'll find something to eat." Mathias headed for the basket of biscuits left on the table from breakfast.

"How can you eat?" The memory of Samuel's wounds was still fresh, and the thought of food was completely unappealing to her. She tried to busy her mind by focusing on getting the fire going. Mathias came and sat down beside her and held out a biscuit. She shook her head. "I don't want anything."

"You should eat," he said, moving the biscuit closer to her.

"Stop being annoying," Behler said, although not with much conviction.

"I'm not." He took a bite. "I'm being overprotective." He annoyingly emphasized the last word.

Behler rolled her eyes. "Well stop."

Mathias smiled. "Only if you eat."

Behler glared at him, then yanked the biscuit from his hand just to shut him up. She took a bite, but it tasted like sand. Her stomach churned. All she could see was Samuel's blood, and she knew she wouldn't be able to eat any more.

Mathias ate two more biscuits while she gazed into the fire trying not to see Samuel's face. When he stood and walked across the room to get some water, she started to ask him to bring her some too, but she stopped when he turned back around. He was already holding a cup for her.

She took it and sipped some. Mathias annoyed her to no end, but he also knew her better than anyone in all the world. It had been hard for her to keep her treks into the forest a secret from him; but she knew if he knew about it, he would probably try to talk her out of ever going back. She even thought there was a good chance it was the kind of thing he would tell Lorna about. He was protective, and he was getting even more so as time went by. Since people had started going missing after the contamination of the well, he'd been almost unbearable.

"We should've brought a chicken back with us," he said, referring to the hens they had cooped in the forest. Behler eyed Mathias for a minute until he noticed her and stopped stuffing his face long enough to say, "Whaa...?" around a mouthful of biscuit.

She started to say how insensitive it was to think about slaughtering a chicken while Samuel was injured and bleeding, but then just sighed and said, "Nothing." She was tired of watching Mathias eat, so she closed her eyes and tried to think of anything besides Samuel's face. Of course, the more she tried not to see it, the more the image burned in her mind.

4

The next few days appeared uneventful, but it was clear something sinister was happening around them. The Gorlogs staggered through the village, their pupils blown wide, their limbs twitching. They lashed out at anything that moved. Behler had to wonder if maybe they actually *did* have rivertick fever. The Horde guuns were even worse. They had never been shy about being mean and aggressive, but they at least had let those in the village go about their daily lives in relative peace. Now they were becoming vicious and randomly violent. A couple of days after Samuel's attack, Behler witnessed one of the most vicious of Horde officers, a fierce-looking woman named Eun, tie a man to a post and whip him all because he tripped and fell in her path. Mathias had to, once again, keep Behler from intervening in the attack. Eun sounded as if some savage beast was screaming through her as she struck the man again and again.

"If we step in, she'll have us arrested," Mathias said, holding her elbow gently. "We can't fight if we're in some prison camp somewhere."

If only a prison camp was their biggest threat.

The air was heavy, as if the presence of the Armigoth had gotten so strong and so dense that it was starting to be a part of the very air they were breathing, like an invisible toxin seeping into their lungs.

It had been nearly two weeks since the raid on the weapons depot, and if anyone knew it stood empty, no one was speaking about it in the streets. Even

Dalen, who ran the pub and who sometimes caught wind of things thanks to grog-induced loose lips, hadn't heard anything.

Behler had yet to see the Gorlog with the scar over its eye though.

The sun was just beginning to make the day hot when Behler and Mathias decided to head to the river to collect water. On their way, another loud commotion in a plot of larger homes where Horde officers had taken up residence caused them to deter and check it out.

They snuck around a corner of one of the houses and found three men in officer's jackets fighting. All three were bleeding from various wounds, and none showed signs of stopping. Two of them wore green lieutenant jackets, while the third wore captain blues. The man in blue took out a dagger and began slashing at the other two. Wounds began opening on their cheeks and hands. Then one of the lieutenants grabbed the captain's wrist and twisted. The bone snapped, and the captain cried out. His cries were cut short as the other lieutenant grabbed the knife and plunged it into his chest.

Quietly, Behler and Mathias backed away from the scene, but before they could make their way out of the village, they bumped into Dax. His terrified eyes were a clear indication he'd witnessed the fight as well.

"Get out of here, Dax," Behler said before she and Mathias continued. "Go straight home."

He nodded, eyes as wide as tea saucers, and slipped around a corner.

Once on the road outside the village boundaries, Mathias said, "What the hell was that?" He shivered and shook his head, as if trying to shake the image out of his memory. "Maybe it's a good thing. Maybe they'll all just kill each other and save us the trouble."

23

Behler shuddered. "There is nothing good about what we just saw." She looked at him. "They just killed their captain. They're out of control."

"Never thought I'd miss the way they used to be." Mathias said. "They used to be downright civil compared to that back there." He tried to chuckle, but it came out too strained.

An amberly tree stood near the road about halfway between the village and the river. They paused next to it and checked their surroundings before Behler leaned over and found a rope hidden in the grass. She pulled and a wooden lid rose up, revealing a large wooden box with six water buckets hidden inside. She grabbed two and closed the lid.

"Here." She handed Mathias one of the buckets.

The road went up over a small rise. At the top, the river and entire countryside from Betham to the borders of the desolate Serilons would unfold in front of them.

Mathias sniffed at the air. "Do you smell that?"

Behler inhaled a few short whiffs but didn't smell anything. "No. What do you smell?"

Mathias sniffed again. "Dead fish, I think."

Behler sniffed again. "Yeah, I do smell it now."

When they cleared the rise, the source of the smell became clear. Hundreds of fish lined the banks, dead and rotting. Behler and Mathias stood wide-eyed and speechless, but it wasn't the sight of the fish that was leaving them staring and disbelieving. The once beautiful flowing waters of the river were now mixed with some sort of black, bubbling ooze.

"What the kak?" Mathias muttered.

Behler looked down at the water bucket she was still holding and dropped the useless thing onto the road. It rolled off to the side and into the grass.

"The sons of pigs poisoned it," she said. Tears welled up in her eyes. "The well wasn't enough. They had to ruin this, too." She wanted to yell and scream, but most of all, she wanted to look away, but she just couldn't force her eyes to focus anywhere else.

Finally, Mathias said, "Let's go take a closer look." He was still holding his bucket.

Behler nodded but didn't say anything, just started to walk toward the stone bridge that had spanned the rushing waters the day before. As they approached, the smell got much worse, and along with the rotting fish, there was another smell – an acrid smell that burned the back of their throats.

The river barely moved. The black sludge was so thick it seemed to pin the water beneath it, suffocating the current. The black tar-like substance shimmered slightly, as if it were alive. It clung to the dead fish like leeches.

Behler bent down and picked up a stick then stuck a dead fish with it. The fish split open at the touch and black goo oozed from its body. Behler gagged. The ooze shimmered faintly in the light, as if breathing – alive in a way that made her skin crawl.

They walked along the riverbank silently. Then, a few yura lengths from the bridge, Mathias tapped her arm and pointed. He was looking at a deer laying next to the river.

"It's injured," Behler said and took off toward the animal.

"Bale, wait!" Mathias called out, but she ignored him.

She was still a few paces from the deer when she could tell that it wasn't injured. It was dead. Her heart sank as she took the last steps, sinking to her knees next to the young animal. She started to reach out to touch its neck.

"Don't!" Mathias grabbed her hand. "The poison might be lethal even to the touch."

Mathias' gaze moved back to the toxic river then up the hillside on the other side. When Behler followed his gaze, she saw what had filled his eyes with rage and finally made him drop his bucket. Countless animals lay dead or dying in the tall grasses.

"Why would they drink the water?" Mathias asked.

"What else are they going to drink?" Behler pointed out. "It hasn't rained in a while. They were desperate."

"Let's get out of here." Mathias touched her shoulder.

She looked back down at the deer. "They've killed all these innocent animals."

Mathias leaned over and grabbed her inner elbow. "They'll kill anything in their path. Destruction is all they want. All the Armigoth wants."

Behler stood, eager now to get away from it all, and they walked most of the way back to the village in silence. Finally she said, "We have to tell the others right now. Whatever that black stuff is, there's a reason for it. And taking away the river, it's all the start of something bigger."

"Yeah," Mathias agreed.

They stepped off the road at the edge of the village and started heading in the direction of the forest while they still had the cover of the tall grass to conceal them. Lorna and the others should be at the training circle there this time of day, so they made their way around the village as quickly and quietly as they could. It soon became clear they could have run screaming and not have been noticed. Not a Gorlog or soldier was in sight. Where violence and mayhem had ensued earlier, now there was only eerie silence.

They made their way through the forest to the training circle and found Lorna standing off to the side talking to Dalen. Rogan was slowly going through some exercises with Samuel who had made nearly a full recovery in the two weeks since his attack.

They all listened as Behler and Mathias told them of their discovery of the river and dead animals.

"We have to build a dam," Lorna said. "We can't let more of the poison make it downriver."

"The Horde will just destroy it," Dalen objected.

Lorna shook her head. "Still, we have to try. Send Ivan and his engineers. Have them build it just north of the fork. Maybe the Horde hasn't poisoned the west river and those downriver can still be saved. Once it's built, tell them to stay there to defend it."

Rogan rubbed the stubble on his chin. "The villagers will have no choice but to drink from the well."

"How much water do we have in our supplies?" Lorna asked.

"We still have fifteen barrels," Rogan answered.

Lorna ran the numbers through her head. "That's good. That should last until we can get more. We'll distribute it tonight, discreetly...but only to those we know we can trust."

Behler stiffened. More? Where was there more? The river was poisonous. If the barrels ran dry, then what?

It took a moment to realize Lorna was speaking to her. "...don't want you and Mathias going near the river again."

Behler nodded, but the words didn't sit well. The river was her safe place, and the kakweeds had tried to take it away from her. Now Lorna was, too.

As they turned to go, she glanced back through the trees, toward the distant river, violated solely to hurt those who dared to stand up against the Armigoth. Something cold and deep opened in Behler's chest, and she started to understand how people could get swallowed by that icy anger.

5

The riverbanks had been one of Behler's favorite places to sit and enjoy some peace. Sometimes Mathias would sit with her, and that was okay, but usually she preferred to just be by herself. She loved the sound of the water rushing by in the rapids. She would sit under a large grizzleberry tree and watch the rushing water for hours, sketching birds and other animals she spotted.

Now, she sat looking at the black sludge that was the only thing left of her beautiful river. It had been three days since she and Mathias had first discovered the river's remains. Lorna had gone with Anilin to check on the dam's progress, so Behler took the opportunity to defy her aunt's order to not return to the river.

Mathias sat next to her. She hadn't been able to avoid him on her way out of the village, and it was the only way she could avoid him telling Lorna. He'd gotten very hard to avoid ever since they'd witnessed the fight between the Horde officers.

"I loved it here," she said angrily, snapping a twig she'd been twirling around in her fingers. The attack on the river felt like a personal attack, which made her feel helpless, and she hated feeling helpless.

"Me too."

She looked at him, irritated at his presence for the sole reason that she was just angry and irritated in general. "Thanks for coming along, Magnus," she sneered, using the of a spy from their childhood storybooks. He gave her a dirty look and she returned it with a sardonic grin.

"I'm no spy, Bale," he snapped angrily.

She turned back to the dead river, ignoring his uncharacteristic anger. "What happened to all the animals and stinking fish?" There were still some fish lying around, but not nearly as many as there had been.

"Don't take your bad mood out on me, okay?" Mathias held his angry gaze for a while longer then looked back at the riverbed. "Animals wouldn't have eaten the fish, not with that stuff coming out of them. Same goes for the other animals." He shook his head as if trying to clear it. "It's getting strange around here. That's for sure. I swear the Gorlogs are getting bigger."

Lying back, Behler closed her eyes and tried to imagine the river still flowing by. She tried to hear the sound of it as it moved over the rocks.

She stopped when she realized it was just depressing her more and studied the leaves above her instead. "I've never wanted a grizzleberry so much in my life," she said, eyeing the dark purple berries overhead.

Mathias snorted. "You don't even like them," he pointed out.

Behler shrugged off his logic. "I want one anyway."

Mathias looked up into the tree. "Grizzleberry with just a touch of black goo poison."

Behler twisted her head and eyed him, annoyed. "You don't know that it affects the tree way up here."

"Be my guest." Mathias stood up and went to grab a low hanging branch.

"Don't!" Behler sat up. "I don't want you dying a slow death from some Armigoth poison just to prove a point."

"Aww." He clutched his hands together under his chin as if flattered. "I didn't know you cared so much."

Behler rolled her eyes. "I just don't want to try to explain it to your parents...or to Lorna why she's down one rebel."

He laughed and plopped back down next to her. She managed a small grin in return. Then she lay back in the grass and stared up into the leaves. The sense of loss around her—the poisoned river, the ruined land—pulled her thoughts to the greatest loss of all: her parents.

"Tell me about them again," Behler said softly. "The stories your parents told you."

Mathias hesitated, even though he knew exactly who she meant. "Who?"

"My mother and father."

She always asked the same way—like the memories were borrowed, like she was hoping this time they'd feel more like her own.

All she'd ever been told was that they'd tried to assassinate Varek when she was a baby. They'd failed. They were captured. Killed. Afterward, Varek learned they'd had a child and vowed to hunt her down – make an example of her. That was why she lived hidden in Betham, why Lorna kept them so close to the forest's edge.

"Everyone says they were the best rebels in the resistance," Mathias said – the same way he always did.

Behler sighed and plucked a blade of grass. She lifted it to her lips, then tossed it aside, thinking better of it. "Yeah, I know. But what were they really like? Lorna won't talk about them."

Mathias scratched the back of his neck—an old habit she'd learned to read. It meant he was uncomfortable. Hiding something.

"They had to be brave," he said. "To do what they did."

"That's not what I asked."

"It's not like I was around to meet them either," he scoffed.

She didn't push further until finally she asked. "Do your parents ever talk about them?"

"Sometimes," he said. "Not much. They knew them. They were friends – I think."

She lay back in the grass again and stared at the blue sky above. "I wonder if Varek even still remembers me," she murmured. "Lorna acts like he's got my name written in blood somewhere, but it's been more than sixteen years."

Mathias scoffed, too quickly. "He remembers. You're a symbol of everything he's trying to destroy," he said, meeting her gaze. His voice was steady, but his hands fidgeted in the grass. "He hasn't forgotten you."

Behler frowned, studying him. "That almost sounded like you know for sure."

"Maybe I do," he said, then forced a half-smile. "Maybe I just pay more attention than you think.

She raised an eyebrow. "Doubtful."

Behler sat up and glanced at the ruined river. "Maybe you and I should start coming with—"

She froze.

A Gorlog was walking along the riverbed, heading their way.

Behler grabbed Mathias' arm and yanked him down into the tall grass. The creature hadn't seen them—yet.

"What is it doing?" Mathias whispered, even though it was still far off.

Behler shrugged. The Gorlog was hunched over, using a long walking stick to prod the sludge like it was searching for something. It kept moving closer, never looking up.

"Hurry up already and do whatever you're doing," Behler muttered. The hot grass was itchy, and her nerves were tightening with every step the creature took.

The Gorlog came into full view, just a few strides away. It jabbed its stick into the muck, hit something, and bent down to dig it out. With one oversized hand, it wiped away a layer of caked mud.

"Is that a fish?" Behler asked.

Mathias groaned. "I think so."

"What's it going to do with—" She cut herself off as the Gorlog let out a gurgling laugh and bit the fish in half. Thick black goo oozed between its fingers, and it eagerly licked it off.

"You've got to be kidding me," Behler muttered.

The Gorlog finished the fish and began searching for another. It was close enough they could see its skin was mottled with what looked like tumors. As they watched, the tumors roiled under the surface as if about to burst.

"Vlocking kak," Mathias cursed under his breath. "That's what's turning them," he said, his voice tightening with realization. "The poison doesn't kill them, it makes them...*vicious*." He was transfixed by the grotesque scene in front of him.

Behler reached up and grabbed his shirt, pulling him back down. "Quit looking, kakweed. Or you're going to puke."

"I don't think I'll be able to eat for a week," he said, groaning again as the Gorlog slurped down another fish and licked the black slime off his hand.

Behler snorted. "Yeah right. C'mon, let's get out of here."

He nodded. Together they belly-crawled through the tall grass until the riverbed was out of sight behind them.

Back at the water's edge, the Gorlog continued to feast—one rotting, oozing fish at a time.

6

The next day, Lorna's most trusted scout, Frawna reported back to the black house. Behler overheard Frawna and Lorna speaking inside as they waited for others to join them.

"When we couldn't reach you, we thought the worst," Lorna said.

"I know," Frawna replied, her voice tight. "I thought the same. Something is wrong. I couldn't find the Thread at all. Could one man do that? Break the Thread?"

Can others use the Deep Thread? Behler thought. Lorna had led her to believe it was just their family.

"He's not just a man any longer," Lorna pointed out. "He hasn't been for a long time."

"Eavesdropping, are we?" Mathias' voice nearly made Behler scream and punch him in the face.

She felt her cheeks flush. "No!" she said too quickly. "I just didn't want to interrupt."

Mathias laughed. "Sure." And he walked in.

Once everyone was settled, Lorna stood. "What news do you have, Frawn?" Her attention snapped back to the room. "I tracked a group of Horde officers north to Blighton Pass where they met with an Okinar council. I think Varek is trying to convince them to fight for him."

Lorna nodded. "We always assumed he'd try." Lorna said

"If he's recruiting the Okinars, he'll go for the Desharet prisons soon," Rogan grumbled.

Lorna looked at the younger people in the room, hesitating on Behler. "There are prisons hidden to the southeast that house the Sulimar: a vicious race that makes the Gorlogs look like puppies." She pursed her lips in the way Behler knew well. Her aunt was mentally working through something. "The most dangerous events will begin soon."

Behler saw Rogan glance at her before he said, "Things seem to be escalating quickly now. I think it's time for some of us to move to a safer location."

Behler was sure he was talking about her, but what sort of safe location was there? The forest was their only safe place. Is that what he meant? And if the war was about to break out, she didn't want to run off in hiding and miss it. Her eyes flicked to Lorna as she worked up the courage to ask, "Shouldn't we all be preparing to fight these Okinars and these Sulimar prisoners?"

Lorna nodded. "We all need to be ready for whatever is coming."

Rogan sat up straight, "Lorna, you know the risk," he said a bit more sternly than what the conversation called for.

"Of course I do. I'm not going to risk everything we've worked for," Lorna replied as if she were tired of the conversation.

Behler turned to Mathias and whispered, "What risk?"

Mathias shrugged and tried to look clueless, but she could tell he knew something.

"Maybe Mathias and Behler should go into the forest. They're the only ones here underage," Kellum suggested.

Behler's eyes shot open. Her jaw dropped and she stared at him, disbelieving he had the nerve to say such a thing. She turned to Mathias, expecting him to be as outraged as she was at the thought of being sent into hiding because of their age, but for some reason he kept his eyes focused on the floor.

"Lorna," she spoke and could hear her voice shaking. Her fear of speaking in front of the others choked her words.

Lorna held up a hand to silence the room, and Behler felt the tears well up in her eyes. "Keeping her close ensures our protection over her."

Her? *HER*?

It was all about her.

Rogan stood up. "Keeping her here any longer only further endangers her along with the rest of us. Our focus needs to be on the battle, not on protecting her any longer." Behler sat up a little. Protecting her? She didn't need protection. "It's too soon for her to fight and you know it. She's not ready. She must wait until it's time."

Behler was livid. Her heart beat so hard that she could hear the blood pumping in her ears. "I can take care of myself," she managed to say. "Besides, Varek probably has forgotten all about me." She couldn't manage to say anything else without her voice rising to an obnoxiously high pitch as she tried to contain her anger.

Rogan made a sound that resembled a laugh before he finally turned to her and acknowledged her presence. "No, child, you can be sure he has not. You must leave before any battle takes place. You are not ready yet. Through no fault of your own, mind you."

Child? CHILD? Rogan's harsh words took Behler's breath away. She looked around the room, searching for someone to meet her eyes, but found only averted gazes and set jaws. Why did it feel like everyone was suddenly against her?

Lorna's face was pinched and tight. She pressed her fingers just above her eye the way she always did when she was working through her thoughts. "Rogan, please just shut up." She looked at her niece. "Bale, there are some things we need to talk about."

Behler barely heard her aunt's words. Maybe Rogan was right. Maybe she *wasn't* ready. Maybe they had all just let her believe she was. The raid on the weapons depot – was that just them throwing her a bone so she'd feel like she fit in with the other rebels? Her throat tightened. She'd thought she was being trained for something real. But maybe she'd just been kept busy—kept quiet—until it was time to be moved.

She wasn't a fighter. She was a liability. A secret. A burden.

Behler's heart was pounding in her chest in a mixture of anger, anxiety, and bewilderment. She looked again at Mathias for support, but he was still going out of his way to avoid eye contact. Lorna walked over and put a hand on her shoulder as if she sensed the storm going on inside her niece. It was an uncommon sign of affection from the stoic woman, especially with all the others around to see it.

Lorna looked around the room and took a deep breath. She straightened her shoulders to stand a little taller. "I know all your concerns. Everything will be worked out by dawn," she said calmly. "Matti, come to our house tonight after we leave here."

He nodded.

Lorna's words satisfied the others, at least for the time being. The rest of the meeting was spent discussing strategy and how they could try to get word to the guards at the prison and what they could do if the prisoners were set free, but Behler barely heard any of it. Her mind wouldn't quit racing over the questions burning through her brain. Why was everyone suddenly so eager to get her into the forest? She's always imagined it as a last resort and only if Varek indeed found her. And why were they all suddenly acting like she was completely incompetent? The more she thought about the latter question, the more she convinced herself that she really had just fooled herself into thinking she was a good fighter. The thought was beyond embarrassing; to think everyone had been in on a secret that she was just discovering.

Finally, the meeting ended. Before everyone left, Lorna said, "We'll meet tomorrow at dawn. Bring anyone you trust who will fight with us. We'll set up a camp in the training area."

Then they began leaving in groups of two and three.

Mathias walked over to Behler with a strange look on his face. It was an odd mixture of guilt and relief. She expected him to offer to leave with her, and she really wasn't feeling like venturing anywhere with him, so she turned away. He leaned down and whispered, "You'll know everything soon. Just trust me."

Before she could ask what he meant, he gave her shoulder a quick squeeze and turned away.

"I know you have many questions for me," Lorna said almost immediately. "I promise you, I'll answer them all, but first we need to go home. There are things there I need to give you, and we can talk there."

Behler nodded begrudgingly. She didn't like the idea of having to wait, but it was clear she didn't have a choice.

"Let's go. There's so much to do." Lorna extinguished the fire, then moved across the room and opened the door. The door creaked slightly, but in the dark, it felt loud enough to be heard across the village. She peeked outside then quickly slipped out the door with Behler trailing close behind. There was no moon, leaving the world around them cloaked in a blackness so deep it felt one could reach out and touch it in places.

Somewhere nearby a crooner bug was chirping. It could have been the only sound in the entire world; the village was as silent as death. If they hadn't just been with fourteen other people, Behler would've believed she and Lorna were the only people left in the village, maybe the world. An image of each of the other rebels disappearing into thin air as they stepped out of the door formed in her mind and she quickly forced the unsettling thought away.

Despite the apparent lack of guards or soldiers, Lorna still went straight to the edge of the forest to use it as cover, and the two of them became nearly invisible in the darkness; nothing more than two shadowy figures slightly blacker than the darkness surrounding them. Soon they had moved out of earshot of the crooner bug, or maybe it had simply quit its song for the time being. The silence was heavy and claustrophobic, and Behler silently urged the little bug to start again.

A twig cracked in the forest nearby, and they both immediately froze in place. Behler's eyes had adjusted enough that she could see her reach out and touch the trunk of a nearby tree as if to steady herself. Behler held her breath, straining to hear any movement or sound.

Another crack of a twig made her jump, and she scrunched up behind the closest tree. Her fingers ran up the bark, and she felt how smooth it was and knew it was an Arbiran

Truuulaaar, she heard in a drawn-out whisper spoken as if through the leaves around her. It was the same whispers she'd heard before, next to her tree.

The Deep Thread.

The image of something giant in the sky flashed in her mind, but it was too shadowy to tell what it was. Could the Deep Thread put images in her head too?

Lorna turned and motioned for them to move onward. Behler took her hand from the smooth tree and followed her aunt who was suddenly moving much faster and with less caution.

As soon as they were inside their small home, Lorna went straight to a chest in the corner of the small living area.

"I think something's coming..." Behler began.

"I know." Lorna's eyes were wide, and she was breathing fast.

"What's a Trular? Is that what's coming?"

Lorna flinched. "That's a long story. I'll explain everything soon enough, but Rogan was right. It's time for you to leave Betham. Mathias will come and take you somewhere safe, tonight." She was speaking quickly and with a sense of urgency. She opened the chest and pulled out all its contents as if they were of no concern to her. She reached into the chest and Behler heard a loud click. The sides of the chest fell away from each other and landed on the floor. In the center was a handle that Lorna grabbed and lifted. The remnants of the chest lifted like a door and revealed a space beneath it. Lorna got down on her hands and knees and reached inside.

Behler said. "I want to stay and fight."

"You heard the Arbiran. Something is coming and you don't want to be here when it arrives. Varek has found us, and has sent it here," Lorna said quickly.

"But what's coming?"

Behler cut off her words when Lorna stood up holding a short staff, about half as tall as Behler. At one end was an oval head covered in spikes. The opposite end had been carved so that three claw-like prongs elegantly extended out.

Behler had heard about the weapon but had never seen one. She didn't even know they existed anymore. "That's a draka," she said in disbelief.

Lorna smiled a little. "It's your draka." She tossed it across the room and Behler caught it squarely in her hands. The wood was smooth and worn, as if many hands had gripped it before hers. "It was your grandmother's."

Behler looked up. "You should have it then." She held it out for Lorna to take it back.

Lorna held up her hands and shook her head. "I have one of my own. That one is meant for you."

Behler stared down at the weapon. "I thought these were all destroyed years ago."

"We couldn't risk using them, not even in the training circle. Rebels like us are the only people in all of Elium who use drakas. If we were somehow discovered with them then the Horde would have surely figured out who we are."

"We're Trulars, aren't we? Rebels and Trulars are the same."

"For the most part," Lorna agreed quickly. "Now, go, we'll talk more as soon as you are packed up." She bent down and pulled out a satchel. "Go grab your bow and kintar."

As usual when her aunt was around, Behler did as she was told. She knelt down in her makeshift bedroom and removed a board from beneath her cot and pulled out her favorite bow. Her fingers curled around the weapon's familiar shape. She held it close for a moment, remembering the last time it had truly saved her life...

It was the summer just before her thirteenth birthday, long before the Gorlogs and the Horde had invaded. She'd been on the western river trail, hunting with Mathias, when she'd fallen into the flooded river still rushing from the spring rains. She was a strong swimmer and was able to get herself out of the river eventually; but as she was making her way back home, she realized she was being stalked by a kindurbeast. She first heard its call soon after she'd made her way out of the river. Then, around noon, she caught a glimpse of it out of the corner of her eye. It circled her for hours, and she silently wished for Mathias to find her before the kindurbeast struck. Finally, the animal leapt out on the trail in front of her. Its massive shoulders were hunched and covered in long silky hair the color of corn silk. Its muscular back legs were long and lean, made for leaping. Kindurbeasts weren't the best of runners—but they didn't need to be. The animal had just stood staring at her, panting and occasionally baring its large front fangs. It was sizing her up, and she knew it. Finally, it had lunged at her and she let the first of three arrows loose followed quickly by the second and third. When it fell, she couldn't take her eyes off of it. Its fur was matted in blood around one of the arrows lodged in its chest. She stood watching its side rise and fall, its breath labored from the arrows that had punctured its lungs. The creature had wanted to make a meal of her only moments before, but she couldn't help but feel remorse. She took a step closer, careful to stay clear of its back claws that were as long as a man's hand. Livestock often had fallen

43

prey to claws just like those, and there had even been bears found with the tell-tale wounds of kindurbeast claws. She knew she was lucky the first two arrows had slowed it down enough for her to shoot the third.

She sat down next to it, its eyes tracking her every step, and for reasons she didn't know, she reached out to touch it. It growled at her, feebly, but soon it was too weak to even do that.

"Shhh." Slowly, she reached for it until her fingers touched the wiry fur on its side. Her hand sank down until she felt the body hidden beneath. She sat with it until it died, unable to let it die alone.

Mathias found her there not long after, still seated in the mud beside the beast. He never told anyone about the tears on her cheeks—or how they had mixed with the kindurbeast's blood.

Remembering how she felt as she watched the animal die made her wonder if maybe what everyone seemed to be saying was right. Maybe she wasn't cut out for war.

She stood up and walked back out into the main room.

"Here, take this." Lorna shoved a satchel into her arms. "I don't know how much time we have but I'll try to tell you as much as I can."

A moment later, a piercing cry ripped through the night. Behler put her hands up over her ears to try to block the painful sound.

"What was that?" she asked after it had stopped.

Lorna's face was a mix of fear and worry. "They're already here." She looked up at Behler. "Varek has the dragons. That's what the Arbiran was showing us." She grabbed Behler's shoulders and looked her squarely in the eyes. "Whatever happens, you must get into the forest and to safety. If you have to, go alone. Just keep heading east. Understand? You'll find where you need to go."

"I can help you!" Behler insisted, already anticipating that Lorna intended to keep Behler out of whatever fight was to come.

A woman's scream tore through the night. "My daughter! Please help us! They've taken her!"

Lorna held tightly onto Behler's shoulders. "Bale, you have to go, now! There are things you don't understand. Please just promise me that you'll get to the forest, one way or another." Lorna's face looked desperate, so Behler nodded. Lorna pulled her close and hugged her then quickly pulled away. "I love you." She gave her one last look and then slipped outside. The night was still dark enough that Behler lost sight of her almost immediately.

Stunned into silence by her aunt's last words, Behler finally was able to whisper, "I love you too." Lorna was too far to have heard.

The silence that had fallen back over everything was unnerving. Something was out there—lurking, watching.

Another scream pierced the dark. Behler's grip tightened on the satchel.

I promised her I'd run.

But she couldn't. Not with people screaming.

She slung the bow across her shoulder, grabbed an arrow from the quiver on her back, and slipped into the dark.

Once outside, she turned toward where she thought the scream had come from. She'd expected not to be able to see anything in the darkness, but instead she saw the flickering glow of flames.

"Lorna! Lorna, where are you?" she asked in a hushed voice.

Suddenly a rough palm covered her mouth as someone grabbed her from behind. Whoever it was had hit her with such force that they both went sprawling to the ground. When her body hit, she lost her grip on both the bow and arrow but was already reaching for the draka her aunt had handed her minutes before.

A hand grabbed hers. "Bale, it's me."

She exhaled sharply.

Mathias.

7

"Matti!" Behler hissed. "What are you doing?"

"Shh." He pressed her bow into her hands and tugged at her arm.

In the flickering firelight, she caught sight of something strapped across his back.

A draka.

She heard the flap of giant wings just before a wrenching cry ripped the night apart again. Behler dared to look over her shoulder, and there, in the light of the fire, she saw it silhouetted in the glowing flames. A dragon.

Stories were told about them, but there hadn't been one seen in the Midowlands for a hundred years. Behler stood frozen for a moment, unable to believe what she saw; but then it cried out again, and the sound snapped her back to her current situation. The dragon swooped down toward the roofs of the nearby buildings close enough to the flames that she could see the fire reflecting in its emerald-green eyes. Its body was long and lizard-like, but its wings—thin, fleshy membranes stretched tight over bone—resembled those of a cavernbat. They spanned the rooftops, covering three houses, maybe more. It opened its mouth, and Behler covered her ears. But, instead of the ear-splitting sound erupting from its throat, fire spewed out. Four more roofs went up in a blaze, and as if pleased with its accomplishment, the dragon flapped its giant wings once, rose in the air and cried out again. The fire illuminated its snakelike belly covered in iridescent golden green scales.

Mathias roughly grabbed her arm. "Come on!" He yanked on her. "We have to get to the forest."

"But the fire!" She pictured dry branches catching like tinder, fire racing through the canopy.

"Trust me." He didn't wait for a response, just pulled roughly on her arm.

Just then, a piece of a roof came hurtling toward them. Behler turned in time to see it silhouetted in the flames behind it.

"Look out!" She screamed, pushing Mathias out of the way just before the large chunk hit them.

The impact knocked her backwards, and Mathias lost hold of her arm. Behler fell to the ground, hitting her head hard enough to make her see stars. After a few moments, she rolled over onto her stomach and pushed herself up onto all fours. Her head felt like she'd drunk far too much grog the night before.

Then she heard the wings again, right over her head. She looked up in time to see the dragon land only a few yura lengths away from her. Visions of her being engulfed in flames flashed through her mind.

But the dragon held its fire. It eyed her curiously, and for a moment, Behler felt a familiar pull to it, just as she had with the kindurbeast so many years before. Behler saw the dragon wore a large metal collar around its neck, and within the collar was a large purple jewel. As if it was waiting for her to see it, the jewel began to glow. A strange tug pulled at the back of her mind—deep and aching. Suddenly, a soul-wrenching sorrow welled up inside her and tore a sob from her chest. She clutched at her heart, as if it were breaking. At that same moment, the dragon roared—but the sound twisted, shifting into something else. A cry. One that echoed the pain she felt.

"Behler!" Mathias pulled her up off the ground and ran toward the forest with her again.

As soon as they were under the cover of the forest's canopy, Behler planted her feet. "I have to find Lorna." She tried pulling her arm from Mathias' grip.

He turned and faced her but didn't let go or even loosen his hold. "Bale, that thing is here for you. We have to get further into the trees."

"It could have killed me, and it didn't," Behler argued.

"Yeah, you're welcome," he snapped.

Chaos was quickly breaking out in the village behind them. She could hear more people screaming and crying out for help. She knew soon her own home would be engulfed in the fiery blaze.

"Matti!" Kellum yelled from beside Behler's house. She and Mathias turned to look. Kellum was carrying a torch, and they could see that his left arm was badly injured. It hung limp and his sleeve was covered in blood. He ran to them then, panting a little, told them, "The Gorlogs and Horde are attacking. They're taking all the girls. Killing anyone who gets in their way"

Mathias' tight grip got a little tighter on Behler's arm, and he pulled her a few more steps into the forest.

"Stop it!" she shouted at him.

"We have to get to the training area," he said without stopping. She could hear Kellum's steps right behind her.

"Go back for Lorna, Kellum!" she screamed desperately.

Without stopping, Mathias yelled, "No, Kellum! Come with us!"

Every step they took only made Behler angrier. Someone needed to go help the others.

When they finally reached the circle, they could still easily hear the chaos they'd left behind. The fire had grown large enough that they could see an orange glow in the sky above them through the treetops.

"Wait here," Mathias ordered.

She pulled her arm roughly out of his grip and scoffed. "No, I won't."

"Yes, you will." His voice was sterner than Behler had ever heard it. He didn't quite look like himself either.

"You're going to have to stop me," she challenged.

Mathias stepped toward her so he was only inches from her face. Quietly and firmly, he spoke, "I will tie you to that tree if I have to, but you are staying in this forest."

Behler staggered backward a step; his tone was so unfamiliar to her. Shocked, she stayed quiet. Mathias breathed in deeply. When he spoke again, his voice was a little softer. "You have to stay here, Bale. Don't you get it? They're taking all the girls because they're looking for you."

She noticed Kellum standing off to the side. "They aren't looking for him!" She turned on him. "Why did you come with us?" she sneered. Fear for her aunt amped up her anger. "You should be back there – fighting!"

He looked at her as he ripped off a sleeve and made an impromptu sling with it, tying it using his teeth and one good hand. "I did fight. Broty and I fought the Gorlogs that were trying to take the girls from the house next to ours." His voice sounded different too. If she'd closed her eyes, she didn't think she would've believed it was coming out of Kellum's mouth. Gone was the nasal, whiny voice and instead he sounded confident and strong. "I fought and watched Broty die,

and then I fought some more until some Horde scum tried to take my arm off."
He gritted his teeth as he pulled his limp arm into the sling.

Behler faltered and took a step back. "Dead?" Kellum nodded angrily. She
stood staring at him a moment longer then, "Broty's dead because my parents tried
to kill Varek years ago?"

"Bale," Mathias said gently. "That's not why this is happening."

She looked at him. "Well, that's why they're taking the girls...to get to me."

Mathias nodded. "Yes, that's true...but not because of anything your parents
did."

"What are you talking about? Of course it is." She looked from Mathias to
Kellum, who was busying himself with his makeshift sling. Her eyes went back to
her best friend. "What do you mean?

They all flinched as the dragon's shriek came from above.

"We don't have time for this," Kellum said, stepping between Mathias and
Behler. He looked at Mathias. "Give me your canteen. I'm going back to help the
others."

"Don't be stupid," Mathias said. "With that arm, you wouldn't last five
minutes. But you're right, we don't have time for this." He glanced at Behler, then
looked back at Kellum. "Make sure she stays here. If none of the others get here by
dawn, move on." He looked over at Behler and smiled. "I'll see you soon."

She didn't believe him, and the look in his eyes showed her he wasn't sure he
believed it either. He walked away, but when he got to the edge of the circle, just at
the point where darkness swallowed up the torch's light, he turned one last time.
"I'm serious, Bale. Stay in the forest." Then he looked at Kellum. "Sit on her if you

have to but keep her here." He looked back at Behler once again, and a smile touched the corners of his mouth. Then he turned and was gone.

Behler stood staring defiantly after her friend. Her gaze eventually fell on Kellum. "I swear, if you sit on me, I will shoot an arrow through your butt."

She turned and walked away before he could respond. When she felt she'd put enough distance between them, she leaned into a tree, wishing she could just melt into it. Angry tears burned in the corners of her eyes as she clinched her fists hard enough for her nails to dig painfully into her skin.

8

Mathias had been gone for five minutes when Kellum called over to her. "Do me a favor, would you?" He turned so she could see the draka strapped to his back. "Take my draka out of its holder so I can sit. I can't reach it with this arm."

Behler hastily wiped any lingering tears from her cheeks. She didn't respond to him, just walked over and pulled the draka out. Kellum turned around and she handed it to him. "Thanks." He dropped the draka on the ground. A purple stone was clasped in the claw at the end.

"What's the stone for?" Behler asked, not sure she *actually* cared.

"For fighting," he said as he sat down. "And other things."

"What, do you just bludgeon the other guy with it?"

Kellum snorted a bit. "Not exactly."

He didn't elaborate, and Behler didn't care enough to ask more.

For the next hour, they both sat and endured the sounds coming from the village. If Kellum hadn't been sitting there with her, Behler knew she would've broken her promise to stay in the forest at least a dozen times since Mathias had left. Mercifully, the sounds were fading, although that just created a whole new set of worries to endure.

Behler noticed her satchel lying on the ground next to her, and she considered opening it just to take her mind off other things, but she didn't want to look through it with Kellum nearby.

"I wish there was a way to find out what's going on back there," she said just to fill the silence, but Kellum's gaze was unfocused as he was lost in his own thoughts. "Kellum?"

He looked up at her, a little startled. "Huh? Oh, sorry. I was just...thinking."

"I wish we could know what's going on back there," she repeated.

Kellum nodded. He looked as concerned as Behler felt. She stood up, placing her satchel's strap across her body, and started pacing. Nearby was an Arbiran with the smooth, cream-colored bark. She walked over to it and touched it, wondering if she would hear any more whispers as she had earlier with Lorna.

"They don't always talk to us," Kellum said. She turned and looked at him. He got up and walked over to a Tree near where he had been sitting and placed his hand on it. He closed his eyes and whispered something. After a few moments, he shook his head. "They're not in the mood to speak I guess." His expression turned curious. "Did Lorna tell you about the Deep Thread?"

She nodded. "Yeah. But she said it was just our family. Is it all of us? All...Trulars?"

Kellum laughed. "Trulars, huh? She told you more than we knew." His lips curled in a pleased grin. "Good for you. Yeah...yeah, it's all Trulars."

Behler was sure of it now; Kellum's voice was absolutely different. He sounded stronger and sure of himself but not in a cocky way. She must've been eyeing him suspiciously because he gave a small, uncomfortable laugh. "What?"

She narrowed her gaze. "You seem...different."

He laughed again and sat down, leaning against the tree he'd just been touching. "Not really. You're just seeing another side of me."

"Well, I think I like this side better."

54

Kellum smirked and his eyebrow arched over his right eye playfully. "Yeah, me too."

"So why would you ever act any other way than this? You've always been so...so..."

"Obnoxious?" Kellum finished it for her. "It was an act. The Horde wouldn't suspect a whiny little kid is a Trular."

"I don't really understand what a Trular even is."

His face scrunched up funnily. "Yeah, maybe we should hold off on all that until Lorna or Mathias come back."

Behler ignored Kellum's protests. "We're Trulars. We're rebels... different than Elians living in the village." She spoke the words out loud as if speaking them might help to make them more real. She looked at an Arbiran nearby, clearly discernible by its smooth bark and unique marks. "And we can speak to trees, and they can speak to us."

"Watch out calling them trees," Kellum chuckled. "They'll give you the silent treatment for such an insult... but yeah, we speak to them and they speak to us."

"The trees don't like for us to call them trees?"

He blew a piece of hair out of his eye. "They're not really trees. Arbirans are an ancient race that happen to resemble trees."

"Why do they talk to us but not others?"

"I think we're just the ones who know how to listen." He coughed and cleared his throat. "I really think we should wait for the others."

"Kellum, please." She caught herself before she started sounding too whiny. "We just fled into a forest because a dragon is in our village destroying it trying to find me for reasons beyond what I have apparently been told." The words spilled out of her. "I think it's time *someone* started telling me what the vlock is going on." She paused, then added, "Besides, what else do we have to do to keep our minds off of everything?"

He rubbed his one good hand over his face then nodded. "I'll tell you as much as I can."

"Lorna's not going to beat you for telling me," Behler said, noting his nervousness.

He laughed. "No, it's not that exactly. Lorna knows it's time for you to know everything."

A loud dragon cry came from the direction of the village and made them both jump. After her nerves had settled, Behler said, "Tell me why they won't let me fight."

He shook his head. "We can't risk it. You're too important."

"Important? What do you mean?"

"Kak!" Kellum said frustratedly as he roughly ran his fingers through his hair. "This is why I shouldn't be the one talking to you about all this." The torch started to flicker and dwindle. He motioned toward her satchel. "Open up your satchel."

"Why?"

"I'll show you."

Curious, Behler pulled the satchel's strap from around her body and opened the flap. She blinked to make sure her eyes weren't playing tricks on her. There was something glowing faintly inside. She reached in and found the source of the glow. It was a stone like the one in Kellum's draka, only blue. It looked as if liquid was swirling around inside it. "What *are* these? They are so beautiful."

"They're isari stones. They were given to us a long time ago." He looked down at the stone in his draka, and it began glowing as well. "One of those *other* things I said they're good for is providing light." He scratched his head. "We brought them back with us the last time we went home."

Behler's expression tightened. "Home? What do you mean? Betham?"

He winced. "I am so bad at this." He exhaled sharply and rubbed his face again. With a deep breath, he continued, "There's a village in the forest – Ardin. Technically it's our actual home." He picked up a small pebble and rolled it around in his fingers. "It's where we'll be heading at dawn...when the others get here." His voice dipped at the end, like he could make it true just by saying the words out loud.

"A village. In the forest."

"Hidden deep inside. Only those of us who belong there can get to it. It's the base for all the Trulars here in Elium's Midowlands. As you've figured out, we're different from the people we've lived next to. Our people were chosen to be guardians. We are born to protect others." He looked up at the leaves of the Arbiran. And..." he smirked, "Trees talk to us."

Behler felt the corners of her mouth lift and she was surprised when she almost laughed. "The fire, though, are we sure it won't spread into the forest?"

"Arbirans have their own special abilities. They won't allow the fire to spread."

Silence fell over them. Questions swirled in Behler's head while Kellum wrestled with what he wanted to say to her next. "Bale," he finally began. She flinched a little at his use of her nickname. "I really think you should know," he roughly rubbed the back of his head. "Uh – your mother is there...in Ardin. Alive."

All the air was sucked out of Behler's lungs and the world started spinning faster. "What!? What are you saying?" Her mind struggled to comprehend what Kellum had just told her. "You're saying my mother's not dead?"

Kellum nodded sympathetically. "Yes, that's what I'm saying."

Confusion muddled her thoughts. "Why did everyone tell me she was?"

"If you believed it then everyone else would too. It would make it harder for Varek to find you."

"But why's he even trying to find me? If they're still alive – or at least my mother – did they even try to assassinate him?"

Kellum cocked his head to the side. "Not *exactly* – at least not your mother."

"Then why did he just send a dragon to try to kill me?" She could hear the desperation creeping back into her voice again.

"It's...complicated. I really think you should wait and let Lorna or your mother tell you."

Behler scoffed. "Lorna has had my entire life to tell me and she didn't. And I don't even know my mother. I know *you*."

He looked surprised. "And you'd rather hear it from me?"

Behler shrugged. "Like I said, at least I know you." She eyed him a little suspiciously, "Or at least I thought I did."

Kellum chuckled but didn't say anything for a minute. Finally, he said, "Mathias and I have talked about telling you everything so many times. He had to bite his tongue every time you brought up anything about your parents. He said it wasn't his place, but I think he was just afraid of what Lorna might do to him if she found out he'd told you too much."

"You and Matti...talk?" Behler almost had more trouble accepting that than she did about her mother being alive.

Kellum nodded. "Sure."

"Talk like... friends?"

Kellum snorted a bit. "Sure."

She scrunched her brow. "I find that hard to believe considering how he treated you."

He laughed, and the sound was the first joyful thing Behler had heard in a while. "Oh, he enjoyed that, believe me."

"He enjoyed terrorizing you?" Her mind pivoted – "Yeah, that does sound like Matti."

Kellum ruffled his hair through his fingers. "All part of the act. Matti's favorite part if you ask me." His mouth turned up into a crooked smile. "He's actually a pretty good friend." He paused. "Actually, one of my best friends."

Her stomach turned so hard she thought she might puke. Matti—her Matti—had what? Bonded with Kellum over staged torment? Shared inside jokes? Maybe even secrets about her? How could he be her best friend? Had he ever been? Or was she just... there? Convenient? His duty to watch over?

Her throat tightened, and a queasy heat rose in her chest. She had to look away. She wasn't even sure who she was mad at—Kellum for saying it, Mathias for doing it, or herself for caring so much.

Kellum saw her distress and realized what he'd done. "He was one of *my* best friends. I wasn't *his* best friend," he said reassuringly. "I just didn't – don't – have many friends..." he trailed off.

She had to gather herself. "Can you at least tell me where that dragon came from? I thought those died out a long time ago." She wanted to talk about anything other than Mathias.

He shook his head. "They never died out. They live in the north, in the Black Hills mountain range. Some of the rebels thought that Varek would try to use them, but others didn't think he'd ever be able to control them."

"It had a collar around its neck with some sort of stone that glowed..." she stopped. "Kind of like these," she gestured to the purple and blue glowing stones.

Kellum nodded. "It *is* a stone like ours, only twisted because of the Armigoth." He studied her for a moment. "Have you ever seen the Armigoth?"

"Pfft! As if Lorna ever let me get anywhere near it."

"Be grateful for that," Kellum said. "The sight of it feels like the saddest sadness you have ever felt."

Images of people she'd known walking through the village like the undead, empty inside, echoed in her memory.

She sorted through questions in her mind until she found one that felt safe to ask. "Why didn't we all just live in this Ardin village if it's so safe?"

"To keep you safe, they had to keep you separated from... someone." He stumbled a bit on the last word, his voice tightening at the edges like he wasn't quite sure he should say it.

"Separated from who?"

Kellum looked at her. The glow of the isari stones cast shadows across his face. He took a deep breath. "From your twin brother – Fenn."

In a matter of minutes, she went from being an orphan to having a mother and a twin brother. It felt like everything Kellum told her was a sucker punch to the gut. All she could manage to utter was, "I need some space," before she stood up.

As she walked away, one of the Arbirans shimmered faintly in the corner of her eye. A single leaf drifted down and brushed her shoulder—like a hand trying to offer comfort.

Behler picked up the leaf and held it to her cheek. It was soft and cool on her warm skin. The coolness from the leaf spread, soothing the confusion and rising angry heat.

9

It had gotten chilly when the sound of a Hunter owl woke her. She'd fallen asleep unintentionally, and it took her a moment to get her bearings. She was a little surprised when she saw that Kellum had covered her with a cloak. Her isari stone was sitting next to her, still glowing.

She was alone.

"Kellum?" she called out softly.

There was a rustling behind her, and she quickly jumped up and ran for her bow. She took aim at the point in the forest where she'd heard the sound. "Kellum?" she asked cautiously.

"It's me," he said before coming into view.

He stepped into the light. "Where were you?" she asked.

Kellum held up a canteen. "Getting water." He gestured toward her bow. "Want to lower that?"

"Oh – right." She relaxed and put the bow back down on the ground. "How did you see where you were going out there? It's pitch black."

"The Trees can luminesce."

"Glowing Trees? No wonder people are afraid of this place." She looked around. "No one's come yet?"

He tossed her the canteen. "No."

"Is it close to dawn?"

"No. You weren't asleep very long."

Her heart sank wondering where Lorna, Mathias, and the others could be.

After a few minutes she asked, "Is your arm alright?"

Kellum looked down at his arm in his makeshift sling. "It'll be fine."

Another couple of minutes passed quietly, and the silence made waiting unbearable. Behler tried to think of something, anything, to say that would fill the silence. "I'm sorry about Broty. I liked him. I always thought you were lucky to have him as your uncle."

Kellum frowned and then shook his head. "Thanks, but he wasn't really my uncle. He was my father's best friend. He stepped in to watch over me when I volunteered to leave Ardin." His mouth turned up into a sad smile. "He sacrificed a lot to look out for me."

"I'm so sorry," Behler repeated. She let the moment have the silence she felt it deserved. "You volunteered to leave Ardin?" she asked after a long pause. "You've been in Betham for as long as I can remember. Since we were both so small."

Kellum nodded. "I understood enough back then to make the choice." He smiled but a dark cloud passed over his face.

"The choice for what?" she pushed gently.

Kellum shrugged. "To be a guardian outside of the forest. To try to keep the people outside of the forest safe."

Behler sensed he meant her, but she didn't press any further. Instead, she opened the canteen and took a drink. The water inside was cool and crisp, and as she drank it she felt her head clear.

"The water's special," Kellum said, noticing the change in her. "We call it aji."

"Where did you get it?" She took another drink.

"The Arbirans. They take in ordinary water and make it...different. It's what lets them glow. We gather the water from the condensation on their leaves here in the forest. In Ardin, there is a well that's tapped into their underground root system that transports the water."

"And you collected enough water from condensation to fill this canteen?" It seemed highly unlikely in the short time he'd had to collect the water.

He smiled and shrugged. "I asked nicely."

Behler almost laughed, but happiness seemed selfish given everything.

Kellum held his hands out for her to throw the canteen back. "Aji helps our bodies more than normal water. It can heal our wounds and give us energy. It can bring us back from *almost* dead. It can make dark moments seem a little less...dark." He took a big swig from the canteen. "It'll help this arm heal up pretty quickly."

Behler remembered the canteen from the night Samuel had been injured. "It's the water they gave Sam when he was hurt," she said, and Kellum nodded.

"You've had it before – I'm sure. We always had a supply in Betham."

Somehow, the world felt much clearer and her thoughts more organized than they had just a few moments before. She looked around the circle and her isari stone caught her eye again. It flashed bright for just a second then returned to its normal glow.

Kellum clapped. "Nicely done!"

Behler looked back at him, confused. "What's nicely done?"

He gestured toward the stone. "You did that."

"Did what?"

"You made it glow brighter."

"How'd I do that?"

"The Deep Thread. Thaelic is what connects us with our stones. When you hear the Arbirans, have you ever noticed you can kind of feel a tug in your chest?"

Behler thought about it then nodded.

"That's the Thread," he continued. "In the beginning, you'll have to focus a little more, but after a while, you and your stone will form a connection called sama. It's the Deepest Thread. Eventually, your stone will respond without effort – just like catching something without thinking." He threw the canteen back and she instinctively threw her hand up and caught it.

Behler looked at her stone. "Why couldn't we have at least used them in the forest while we were training?"

"We couldn't have them when we were younger. As you can see," he gestured toward the stone, "you weren't even trying and it's glowing. If anyone ever found one, especially if it was glowing, they may have figured out who we were. We couldn't risk having them and accidentally making one glow...or trigger any of the other things they can do. You *definitely* couldn't be around them."

"Why?"

Kellum laughed a little. "Well, there is a ceremony we all go through called an ilari ceremony. We're placed in the middle of several isari stones. Normally we go through it when we're twelve, but Sera anticipated that might be a problem – so she had it done when you and Fenn were one.

"Usually one stone will glow, showing it's bonded with us – for life. That's what normally happens, anyway." He smiled, clearly amused at the story. "That's not what happened at your ceremony. When they put you down in the middle of the stones, they all glowed. They just chose the one that glowed the brightest." He chuckled. "Fenn doesn't like that story so much. About half of them glowed for him, which is still pretty amazing." He scrunched up his face. "Fenn lets things get under his skin. The story of the stones really gets to him."

65

Behler's stomach turned. Did her brother already resent her? She was quiet for a few minutes, digesting everything Kellum had said.

"If my mother is alive, what about my father?" she asked even before the question had fully formed in her head.

A shadow crossed over Kellum's face. "He disappeared just after you were born. I'm not sure what happened." He fidgeted. "I think that's one reason they made sure to keep you a secret from everyone for so long. They didn't know what happened to him, and Varek has ways of getting information out of people."

Behler assumed he meant some horrible means of torture, and she'd rather not talk about that at the moment. "But why was I a secret? Why did Varek want to kill me if my parents didn't *really try* to assassinate him?"

Kellum shook his head, as if trying to sort something out. "You *are* a threat to him. Both you and Fenn are, and Varek *has* been looking for you. That's why you were kept hidden. Your mother sent you to Oryn first. It was the safest place at the time. When it looked like Oryn wouldn't be safe anymore, they made new plans. They sent me to Betham with Broty a little while before you and Lorna moved there. I was six, and you were four. They wanted someone a little older to watch out for you. Someone who could blend in with others our age. Matti wasn't quite old enough yet."

Behler raised an eyebrow. "If you were supposed to watch out for me, why were you such a pain?"

He shrugged and smiled crookedly. "Being nice wasn't necessary for my job." He ran his fingers through his hair again, waiting to see if his joke would fall flat. Behler gave him a small, polite smile. He grinned, a little awkwardly, then continued. "Yeah, I volunteered, but I missed my family – a lot. I barely knew Broty back then and I was just mad at the world. So, as we got older, Lorna and the others realized that if people knew we weren't friends, I would be more likely to hear any negative things that could affect you, so they decided it worked out for the best if I kept being a pain to you."

"Well, mission accomplished. You were a pain in the ass." Kellum laughed and did a mock bow as if he'd completed a performance. Behler took a few sips from the canteen before sighing. "My entire life has been a lie," she said sadly.

"Not the parts that really matter. Your friends really do care about you. You are an amazing fighter. And as for me being the obnoxious jerk, I only had to fake that a little. So, you know, that part of your life definitely wasn't a lie." A mischievous glint sparkled in his eye.

She chuckled again. "Thanks."

As they settled back into silence, the breeze began rustling through the leaves overhead a little louder. Behler listened to see if there were any whispers hidden within it. Nothing.

"I hope they get here soon," she said and wrapped the cloak around her shoulders.

"Are you cold?" Kellum closed his eyes. "Just think about being warm."

"I don't think that will help."

"Just do it," he said without opening his eyes.

"Fine." Behler closed her eyes too and thought about lying in the field on a summer day, feeling the heat of the sun on her face. It wasn't long before she felt real warmth on her cheeks. Her eyes shot open, thinking the fire had somehow reached them. Instead, her isari stone had changed from glowing the light bluish white color to a deeper blue and it was warming the air around them.

Kellum opened his eyes. "Yep. You're going to be fine."

Wide-eyed, Behler said. "Just fine at what?"

Closing his eyes and settling back in as if he were ready to go to sleep, Kellum chuckled. "Knowing you, everything."

She looked over at him, but his eyes stayed closed. He had an annoying smirk on his face.

"You're a real kakweed, you know that?" she mumbled.

His smile broadened, and he opened one eye to look at her. "I told you I wasn't faking much."

Behler grunted, but as she settled down and closed her eyes, the warmth from the stone on her face brought a small smile to her lips. She still had many questions. Kellum hadn't answered why Varek was after her, but her brain felt like it was a churning pool of chaos – despite the aji. Questions and answers would have to wait.

10

The sound of birds chirping awoke Behler a few hours later. The light from the dawn wasn't able to completely break through the thick canopy overhead, but she was just able to make out the gray of the early morning sky through a few small openings.

There was still no sign of the others, but the acrid scent of ash had reached them. Kellum busied himself collecting more water for their canteens. He brought back some berries, and they ate those along with some fish jerky he had found in a basket within the weapon's cache. Behler knew he was stalling—hoping, just like her, that the others might still appear.

But after eating and gathering up all their things, much slower than they really needed to, it became clear that they couldn't put it off any longer. The dread Behler had been feeling tightened in her stomach, and suddenly the simple breakfast wasn't sitting so well.

Finally, Kellum said, "We should go."

"Maybe we could go take a look at the village. Maybe it's all clear."

"We can't risk it. Varek isn't going to give up easily. He somehow knew you were in Betham, or he wouldn't have sent the dragon. He won't leave until he's positive you're not there."

"What if he tries to follow us into the forest?"

"The Arbirans won't allow it." He shoved the last of the fish jerky in Behler's satchel. "We have to get to the others. They need to know what's happened."

Behler wanted to shout – NO! She wanted to go back to Betham. To wait. To do anything but follow Kellum to some strange village in the woods. He anticipated her objections and quietly said, "We promised Matti."

"I only promised I'd stay in the forest. We could wait a little…"

"Bale," Kellum interrupted.

His use of her nickname caught her off guard. She exhaled loudly. "Okay."

Betham was likely ashes now anyway. She had nowhere else to go.

She stared back at where her village was only the day before. It had been small and falling apart, and ever since the Horde had invaded, greatly overcrowded, but it had been home – the only one she'd ever really known. Her only memories of her time in Oryn were vague, and probably more the products of stories Lorna had told her than actual memories. Betham was also where she'd left everyone she loved in the world.

Kellum touched her arm—hesitantly. The unexpected contact made her look up. "They know the way," he said. "Maybe they're already there." He bent down and picked up her bow then handed it to her. "Come on, let's go."

She nodded. Her head felt like an ocean of information had been sloshing around in it for hours, and it was finally moving into the numb stage. She welcomed the cool emptiness. It was better than feeling…at least for the moment.

Kellum walked up to one of the smooth-barked Trees and gently placed his hand on its trunk. Above them, the leaves began to rustle, though no wind stirred the air.

"Shawshara ahshiwae," he whispered softly.

The limbs and bigger branches above started to creak and moan like old bones waking from a deep sleep. Behler braced herself as the sound intensified. She half expected to be crushed by falling tree parts.

But she wasn't crushed. Instead, the Arbirans began to move. They pulled their roots from the earth and stepped into a line. Their roots weren't quite roots at all, but more like legs. It seemed impossible that such short roots could support the Arbirans' large size.

Between where the Trees now stood, the forest shimmered. The space between the two lines of Arbirans seemed to fold and ripple, as if viewing the forest through water. A swirling tunnel opened like a corridor made of light and liquid.

Kellum looked over at her. "This is how so many people have gotten lost in the forest over the years. The Arbirans can create paths for us to walk, free from the trees and underbrush that would slow us down – or they can create paths that lead to nowhere." He glanced at the shimmering tunnel. "This path will lead us to Ardin."

"But how..." Behler started.

Kellum's eyes twinkled a little as he said, "Just had to ask nicely." He smiled, but it looked as bleak as Behler felt. He glanced back in the direction of Betham and hesitated. "We should go," he said. She knew it was more to himself than to her. He turned and started walking, and she had no choice but to follow him. She couldn't keep her head from turning back toward Betham one last time, then she turned and began walking away from everything she'd ever known... though, she realized, what she'd known hadn't been much at all.

11

The pair had been on the path for only a few minutes when a quiet whooshing sound made Behler turn and look. Behler could still see their campsite where they'd stayed the night before. It should have been much farther away by then. Looking through the tunnel from within, she could see the forest passing by as they moved. Curious, she leaned around Kellum who was leading the way and looked to see what lay ahead of them. The opposite end of the tunnel was clearly visible a few liyura away.

"I thought you said the village was deep into the forest," she said, pointing to the tunnel's end.

"It's the tunnel," he explained. "It's like it scrunches the distance visually, but not physically."

Behler curled up her lip. "Physically would have been nice."

Kellum chuckled. "Definitely."

They fell into a comfortable silence. Behler watched the forest's wavery images pass by through the water-like sides of the tunnel. She dared to reach out and touch the side, expecting moisture, but all she felt was a pleasantly cool space.

They didn't speak again until around noon, when Kellum blurted out, "I'm hungry."

"Wow, you sound like Matti," she chuckled. "Do you want some jerky?" She started to open her satchel.

"Maybe," he said, but appeared distracted as he surveyed the ground outside the tunnel. "I was hoping to find something else, though. Let's just keep walking. If I don't see any soon, we'll settle for jerky."

"Any what?"

Distracted, he said more to himself than to her, "I know the patch is around here some...there!" Kellum said excitedly, pointing into the forest to their right. "Come on." He stepped out of the tunnel without waiting for her.

Behler hesitated, fearful of breaking through the strange wall. "What about the tunnel?"

"Don't worry. They'll reopen it for us." He smiled a reassuring smile. "Come on, it's okay." He held out his hand. "It's fine."

Behler reached through the wall of the tunnel and felt the chill again, and then she felt the muggy summer heat on her fingers. Kellum took her hand and gently pulled her toward him. She held her breath as she stepped through, and the chill of the tunnel wall felt good.

Kellum let go of her and walked toward a small clearing. "Here." He opened his arms wide and said, "Our feast awaits."

She saw they were standing in a large patch of the biggest mushrooms she had ever seen. "Mushrooms?" she asked dubiously. "All this for mushrooms?"

Kellum plopped down on the ground. "Not mushrooms," he said and picked one. "These are nihras."

She wrinkled her nose. "They look like mushrooms. How do you know they aren't poisonous?"

Kellum looked at her as if she'd just asked the most ridiculous question he'd ever heard. "Because they're not." He took a big bite. "Trulars have been eating these for years," he said, talking around the chunk of nihra. He gulped it down. "They make a great stew with them in Ardin."

Behler sat down next to the edge of the patch. Cautiously, she picked one closest to her. Her hand wouldn't even go all the way around the stalk. "What do they taste like?"

Kellum shrugged as he took another bite. He was holding the nihra like a giant chicken leg. "Meaty," he said around another mouthful.

Behler's stomach growled, demanding to be filled with anything edible, even if it did look like a giant mushroom. "Traitor," she mumbled to her midsection, and took a nibble.

It was pretty good.

She took a little bit bigger bite. It tasted a little like cold lamb, a rare treat in Betham – practically unheard of since the Horde had taken over the village.

Kellum smiled. "Told you." He said smugly.

"They're okay," she said, trying to sound as unimpressed as possible.

Kellum laughed at her and took another bite.

She studied the forest around them with childlike curiosity. Green plants with three giant teardrop shaped leaves grew all around them. The plants were about as high as her knees and were plentiful here, but Behler had never seen them, even during her rare outings away from Betham.

A carpet of tiny white flowers blanketed the forest floor. She noticed they seemed to grow where the sun's light was able to reach them. Pollinators were buzzing happily around them, flitting from one to another.

She and Kellum ate their fill and chased it down with more aji. Kellum even found some wild grapes to finish off their meal. It felt like a feast, and Behler felt a pang of guilt for enjoying it.

Her guilt yanked her mind back to reality. She wanted to be prepared when she walked into this new village, Ardin. "What's my mother's name?"

Kellum swallowed the grape he'd just popped into his mouth. "Lorna never told her?"

Behler shook her head. "She'd barely say anything about them, and I was always too nervous to ask."

His brow creased. "Sera. She's a lot different from Lorna. My brother, Luke, knows her better than I do. He's best friends with Fenn, so he's at their house a lot. And he and Fenn have gotten into plenty of trouble together." A hint of annoyance had crept into his voice.

She was just swallowing a big gulp of aji when she also gasped at the news that Kellum had a sibling. She coughed and hacked as it went down the wrong pipe. Once she recovered, she asked, "You have a brother?" In her mind, Kellum had been a loner for so long, the idea of him having a brother was nearly as extraordinary as her having one.

Kellum nodded and his expression tightened. "Yeah. He's fifteen…just a little younger than you." He looked at her with a flat expression, as if deciding whether he should share anything else personal with her. He must have decided to risk it, because he continued, "I have a half-sister too. She's eight. Her father, Marcus, is a guardian. He's somewhere – out there," he made a gesture that indicated he meant outside the forest. "Just like we were."

A half-sister? "What happened to your father?" She cringed internally as she heard her own voice ask such a blunt question, but she couldn't think of a graceful way to take it back.

Kellum's flat expression seemed to give way to something else. His green eyes darkened, and the corners of his mouth turned down. "He died right before Luke was born."

"I'm sorry."

Kellum shrugged. "I don't remember him very well."

"Still...I'm really sorry." She picked a white flower and smelled it. It smelled a bit like stinky feet. When she looked at Kellum, he was laughing a little.

"We call those fool's flowers. Only a fool would smell them."

Behler coughed. "You could have warned me." She dropped the flower back on the ground.

"Oh never." He waved off her suggestion with his good hand. "Everyone needs to smell it at least once. It's like a Trular rite of passage."

"Well, glad I survived that one." She watched the bees and other insects flitting around the flowers and had to wonder about their sense of smell. "You keep calling us guardians."

Kellum nodded. "It's the closest Elian word to what we are. Our people have been guardians against the Armigoth for centuries. We called ourselves rebels in Betham just to blend in. To other Trulars, we call ourselves Revalars."

Behler ate another grape. "It must've been hard living away from your family."

Kellum knelt down and picked a couple nihras, giving one to Behler. "Put it in your satchel. They're even better once they've dried." He popped a grape in his mouth. She thought, for a moment, he was ignoring her, but then he said, "I spend time with them. Sometimes hunting trips and scouting missions were actually trips to Ardin." He shrugged. "It's been okay. The Deep Thread has helped...until recently."

"What do you mean? The Deep Thread has helped?"

Kellum looked at her for a moment – his face blank as if he was confused by her confusion. Then he realized Lorna hadn't told her everything about thaelic. "We can use thaelic to speak to each other – from pretty much anywhere. Or at least, we could. Something has happened to it – but only the Threads between Trulars seem to be broken." He stretched as he stood up, raising his arms above his head and twisting his neck side to side.

Behler remembered the day Frawna had returned – when Mathias had accused her of eavesdropping. That's what Lorna and Frawna had been discussing that day.

Kellum continued, "I think - we think - Varek has figured out a way to block us from speaking to one another. It's made it easier for him to move the Horde around since the scouts can't contact us as quickly."

Behler shoved the nihra into her satchel. It was so large, it barely fit inside. "If we all have this ability to speak to each other using the Deep Thread, how could Varek block all of us from each other?"

Kellum had already started walking back toward the path. He shook his head. "That shows you how powerful the Armigoth has gotten. The death cycle as Lorna calls it. When there is only death and destruction left."

Behler grimaced and nodded. "She does have a way with words."

Kellum laughed, and Behler felt their shared connection for the first time in her life. "Yeah, well, hopefully we can stop the cycle this time."

Behler wasn't sure what he meant but was drowning in too many answers he'd given as it was. She didn't ask him to clarify.

The two walked back to the space where they'd exited the tunnel. The passageway appeared again and they continued on their way. Soon, the sun had risen directly above them, making the path even brighter. The coolness within the tunnel remained, and for that, Behler was grateful.

She was deep in thought when Kellum quietly said, "I know I joked about being a jerk, but I want you to know that I really am sorry for how I treated you."

She was taken a little aback. The day before she would have never believed Kellum was capable of saying something so sincere. "I didn't treat you very well either."

He shook his head. "You could've been so much worse to me. Matti enjoyed playing the role of my bully because he knew it wasn't real, but you didn't know. You could've easily joined in, and you didn't. I earned what I got from people a long time ago. It started when we were so young and I just didn't understand. I hated Mathias for having both his parents there, and then I resented you both for how close you were to each other. Then, when I got older, I resented everyone." He shrugged. "Mostly myself for creating my own misery."

"Matti should've tried to make me understand." Her words were clipped short. She'd been trying to ignore the nagging in the back of her mind, but it was getting harder to do so. She felt sick thinking about how Mathias was supposed to be her best friend, yet he'd known all these things about her and had hidden them from her their entire lives. He had known Kellum was not the annoying prat he pretended to be yet had let her continue to treat him badly – at least she had some pretty mean thoughts about him.

"Nah," Kellum brushed her words away. "He couldn't. Besides, things got easier for me when I was thirteen. Broty took me on a scouting trip to the north. It was the first time I saw the Armigoth. You could barely see Kilgen castle for the black fog that covered everything." He raised his hands up and moved them across the canopy, as if remembering how the cloud had covered the sky over the northern lands. "I'm sure it's not *fog*, really, but I'm not sure what to call it. You could see wisps moving away from it, like tentacles slithering – trying to gain more ground. I don't know how anything could survive living within that...darkness. Broty told me if the darkness spreads, it will choke the life out of all Elium and then just keep spreading. That's when I knew that all our sacrifices were worth it – when I knew that what I was doing actually mattered. It made all the other stuff more bearable." He grunted slightly. "It's pretty stupid, Varek trying to take over everything just so he can help destroy it, but he can't help it. When the Armigoth gets inside you, all you can do is destroy."

"So he *was* a man before – like the guuns that have become really dark," Behler

Before Kellum could answer, something whizzed by Behler's face and struck his cheek.

"Ow!" He touched the red spot that was already visible.

Behler grabbed for her bow, but Kellum took her wrist and shook his head. "Poppy!" he called out, obviously annoyed. "Come on Poppy, I know it's you. No other Kribble can throw like that."

There was rustling in the forest that was followed by some muffled squeaky grunts.

"What is that?" Behler whispered. She heard the bushes rustling as whatever was hiding within them moved closer. " I thought we were hidden when we're in the tunnel."

"Not from everything in the forest." He rubbed at the red welt. "Poppy, come in the passageway and meet my friend." The underbrush continued rustling. Behler kept her eyes peeled for whatever was moving within. "It's okay. Look." He pointed down at a bush that was just on the edge of the tunnel wall. "Hello, Poppy."

Behler followed his gaze. At first, she didn't see anything. If she hadn't seen the rock hit his face, or heard the rustling and grunts, she would've thought he'd gone crazy and started talking to shrubbery. It wouldn't be the craziest thing she'd seen in the last twelve hours. Then two huge eyes blinked at her. They were nearly invisible, reflecting the greenery around them like a kinjo bird changes its feathers to blend in with its surroundings.

The little thing must've believed it was safe to venture out, because it soon stepped into the passageway. It was only about three feet tall and had the coloring and markings of the bushes it had been hiding within. Then, the color changed, and the creature was pure white.

It smiled at them. "'lo," it squeaked.

"You know, you don't have to throw a rock at me," Kellum said, rubbing his cheek to emphasize his point. "You could just say hello."

"You speak 'bout dark cloud. You speak 'bout evil one." It pointed an accusatory finger at Kellum. "Throw rock to stop you."

He nodded, then, looking at Behler, he said, "Behler, meet Poppy. She's a Kribble."

Behler looked down at the tiny creature. "A kribble?"

Kellum shrugged and rubbed at the red spot on his cheek. "They're kind of a Trular thing, too."

"Hello," Behler said to the ball of fluff.

"'lo," the little thing squeaked again then looked back at Kellum. "Stop bad talk," she said sharply, though it didn't have quite as much force as it would've had if her voice hadn't been so much like a child's. "Don' like it. Talk in A'din," she demanded. "You will bring dark."

"That's not how it works..." Kellum began.

Behler could see the little creature was trembling, out of fear or anger, Behler couldn't tell. "We promise," she piped in. "We'll wait to talk about it until we get to Ardin." Poppy smiled up at her broadly. Her teeth resembled a cat's, only a little less lethal looking in the fangs. "Me'a like B'ler." She looked at Kellum and gave him a dirty look then smiled back up at Behler long enough that Behler started to feel a little uncomfortable. Then, with a couple blinks of her big eyes, her fur changed shades again to match the forest. She darted through the liquid-like wall and vanished back into the underbrush.

"That was...strange," Behler said once the little creature was gone.

"Encounters with Kribbles usually are," Kellum chuckled. "That one was actually one of the least strange visits I've had with her."

"Um...she's a talking ball of fur who threw a rock at you."

Kellum rubbed his cheek. "Yeah," he chuckled and then turned and began walking again. "That's pretty normal."

Behler stared back into the forest where Poppy had disappeared. If she'd had any doubts before, that little creature was proof that her definition of normal would never be the same.

12

Overhead, the sky was beginning to grow dimmer through the small openings in the canopy. Evening was setting in.

Kellum looked over at her. "There's a cave nearby. We'll stay there for the night."

"Not in the tunnel? Behler had gotten used to the perceived safety the tunnel provided, although safety from what exactly, she wasn't sure.

"The Arbirans need to rest, too. Besides, the cave will be nice and cozy."

"How much farther is the village?"

"We'll reach it by dusk tomorrow."

Behler looked at the end of the tunnel. It looked so close. Then again, it had looked that close since they'd started walking. She tried not to think about the difference between what her eyes saw and what reality seemed to be, because when she did, her head started swimming.

Just a few minutes later, Kellum led them out of the tunnel and down into a ravine. "It's right down here." He pulled some green brush away and revealed a narrow opening. He turned around. "Grab your stone and think about something bright." His purple stone lit with lavender-colored light. Behler reached into her satchel and felt around for the stone. As she pulled it out, she tried to think of the brightest summer days. The stone answered with a bright blue light. She followed him into the narrow crevice which opened into a comfortable sized cave. "Here, put your stone down next to mine." He placed his draka down in a ring of rocks placed on the cave's floor. Behler put hers right next to his. "Make sure they're touching," he said, settling down and gently testing his arm.

She moved her stone close enough to his that the sides touched. "Now what?"

"Think about something warm again and focus on your stone. Feel the tug of the Deep Thread." Kellum's stone deepened to a dark purple that was almost black and Behler could feel warmth coming from it almost immediately. She sat down and imagined the hottest of summer days next to the river, and just like before, the stone glowed brighter and began producing heat. "They're stronger when you put them together. We should be nice and warm all night long."

Behler was physically and mentally exhausted, but despite her fatigue, she found herself wanting to go back outside just in case Lorna and the others passed by. "Are you sure we should stay in here tonight?"

As if reading her thoughts, Kellum said, "If the others head this way, they'll know to stop here." Behler nodded, satisfied that what Kellum said was true. "I'm going to get some sleep," he said. "Rest and aji...that's the best medicine," he chuckled as if he'd said something funny. He had taken his sling off and Behler could see he'd regained a good amount of movement already. "Get some rest." He laid down on his side with his back to the light.

Behler sat for a few minutes, watching the swirling light of both isari stones. They were more hypnotizing than the flames of a campfire, and soon she was falling asleep. Her eyes fluttered shut. When they opened again, the cave had dimmed—the stones' light now just a faint pulse. The air was still warm.

She had the distinct feeling that something had awoken her. She rolled over and saw Kellum was still asleep on the other side of the cave. Her stomach rumbled, demanding food. "I'm as bad as Matti," she muttered to herself. She sat up and reached for her satchel. As she pulled out the nihra, two small leather pouches fell out. She took a bite of the nihra then opened the flap on one of the pouches. A needle and spool of white thread were tucked in along with a small note. The letters were written in a hand similar to Lorna's, but different.

bakram thread

"Bakram thread? What the kak is bakram thread?" she cursed quietly.

As she picked up the second pouch, she could hear the jingle of coins inside and could tell there were quite a few by the weight of the pouch. She dumped it out and twenty gold coins fell into her hand along with a necklace. On the chain was a large amulet encrusted with tiny orange, white, and blue stones. She ran her fingers over them then realized they were in the same positions as the moons and constellations during the first days of autumn when both moons would be in the sky, traveling together – the Iskaara Festival would happen under that sky. Her birthday would as well.

As her fingers traced over the stones, they began to glow. "Isari stones?" she whispered. The glow faded as her fingers moved away. At the bottom of the amulet was an empty teardrop-shaped space where another stone once had been. She took another bite of the nihra then tucked the coins back into the pouch. Twenty gold coins was a small fortune in Betham. Lorna was secretly a wealthy woman. That must explain their occasional hearty meals that seemed to come out of nowhere. Instead of putting the necklace back in the pouch, she put it around her neck and tucked it inside her shirt. As it touched her skin, the amulet gave off the faintest warmth. She was just reaching back into her satchel when she heard a rustling outside the cave. She froze and listened. A crunching of leaves made her heart start pumping adrenaline throughout her body. She scrambled across the cave.

"Kellum," she whispered harshly, shaking him without being mindful of his injured shoulder.

He rolled over. "What is it?" he asked, immediately awake and alert.

She put her hand over his mouth. "Listen," she whispered.

They sat frozen, listening. Finally, Kellum gently took her hand away from his mouth. Behler blushed, not even realizing she hadn't moved it. "It was probably just an animal."

"Yeah, probably," she agreed, but there was something about the sound that didn't sound like an animal.

"No—no. Let's just both get some rest," she said, shaking her head. She'd been sick of being treated like a child back in Betham and didn't want Kellum to think she needed any special treatment now. "I'm sure you're right and it was just an animal. I'm just a little jumpy."

"Okay," Kellum agreed. He lay down and rolled back over then waited for Behler to do the same. When he was sure she was asleep, he stood up and walked outside of the cave, just to make sure no uninvited guests had found them. "Poppy?" He scanned in the dark, wishing he'd brought his isari with him. "Fenn?"

The forest was silent except for the occasional normal night sounds. When he was satisfied, they were alone, he went back into the cave. As he sat back down, he noticed something glinting on the ground nearby, so he reached over and picked it up. It was a knife.

Delicate letters were etched into the hilt and embossed in gold. To my Fenn, Love Anika

"Anika?" Kellum whispered.

The name didn't ring a bell. Anika wasn't a Trular. He wasn't surprised; Fenn had always kept his secrets close to the vest.

He turned the knife over in his hand. The gold had worn thin in places, as if someone had rubbed the letters over and over.

Kellum smiled faintly. "Figures," he muttered.

He chuckled and tucked the knife into his waistband. Seems his old friend had a new friend.

13

At dawn, Behler and Kellum slipped out of the cave, both eager—though for different reasons—to reach Ardin.

Behler noticed Kellum no longer had his arm in the sling.

They walked all morning, barely speaking, comfortable in the silence. Behler was nervous about what awaited her in the village, especially her mother. Kellum stayed quiet to avoid bringing up anything that might stir up more questions. He wanted to tell Behler everything he could but knew her mother should be the one to do it. They didn't even stop for lunch, just munched on nihra as they walked. Late in the afternoon, Behler turned when she heard a thumping on a tree. She thought it sounded like a longbeak, and those were one of her favorite birds to watch. Their long red tail feathers, short and spiky red head feathers, bright yellow breast and black back made them the most joyful looking animal she'd ever seen.

Behind them, the forest towered above them. But Behler had never noticed a downward slope in their hike.

"Is the village in a valley?" she asked.

Kellum nodded. "It makes it easier for the Arbirans in the village to protect us. If there's ever a threat nearby at night, they create a veil that covers the entire area. It's like this passage in a way, only above us."

"And you said some can see through it."

"Only Kribbles that we know of."

"Why them and not others?"

He twisted his mouth and gave a light shrug. "They protect the forest. They and the Arbirans are like a team."

"That cute little thing?" How could a ball of fluff protect much of anything?

Kellum stopped and turned. He smiled and raised an eyebrow. "Remember all those stories of shadows moving and ghosts rustling around – demons' glowing eyes?"

Behler laughed hard. "That little thing is responsible for terrifying everyone?"

Kellum was smiling and it made his eyes crinkle and sparkle. "Her – and her clan. But don't let those innocent eyes fool you – if you cross her, she'll show no mercy."

Behler was still smiling and chuckling when they started walking again, but as they moved on, she thought back to those sharp looking teeth and Poppy's ability to change her appearance. Behler made a note never to cross a Kribble.

Just before dusk, Kellum turned and smiled. "We're close." He looked up toward the sky. "Ashiwae erhana." The tunnel vanished, and they were standing in the middle of a normal forest path. "Hear the creek? It flows from the lake at the center of the village." He stopped and pointed ahead of them where Behler could see the end of the trail. It was like a doorway leading to another world – her new world. She could see the fading light of the day illuminating the village, though they were still too far for her to make out anything. Her heart started pounding.

She tried to picture the village, but her imagination could only come up with jumbled images. "What's this place like?"

"Different from Betham – in mostly good ways. There's plenty to eat and a special area to train and workout. And the beds...you have no idea how good you are going to sleep here." He looked up at the sky. "Let's wait for the sun to set. It will be less likely for someone to notice us if we wait 'til dark."

"Why do we need to worry about being seen? Aren't we welcome?"

Kellum laughed loudly. "Yeah, we're welcome. So much so that I'm afraid they'll overwhelm you if they see you."

Behler laughed, thinking he was making a joke – only he didn't laugh, or even smile.

"I'm not kidding," he said stone-faced.

"But why..." Behler began.

Kellum held up his hand to stop her. "Let's just get to your ama's house without being see, then you can ask all the questions you need." He sat down on the edge of the path and took out his canteen. "Here, have a drink," he offered.

"Thanks," Behler said and took a gulp. The special water within worked quickly on her nerves and queasy stomach.

Once she'd had a few gulps, he reached for the canteen, and Behler watched as he chugged the rest of the water, as if his nerves were tauter than hers.

It didn't take long before the opening ahead went dark along with the sky overhead. The first stars started to twinkle above them.

Kellum took and deep breath and stood up. "It should be okay now."

She followed him to the end of the trail and then stood there, staring at a village like none she had ever seen before. She knew Betham had been in poor shape, but this place made Betham look absolutely pitiful. It even surpassed her vague memories of Oryn when he was a beautiful, wealthy village. Most of Ardin's buildings were clustered along the far side of a broad lake. The still water reflected the village and sky like a sheet of glass. Around the lake stood a dozen or so Arbirans, with amberly trees scattered between. Behler caught the faint, sweet scent of their fruit drifting on the air.

At the south end, a wide creek split from the lake and disappeared into the forest. A mill stood near its edge, its wheel turning slowly in the current.

Betham had had a mill a long time ago. She had forgotten all about it until then.

There was one main road paved with bricks encircling the lake. A well-worn dirt path made a larger circle that, Behler assumed, circled the entire village. A beautifully crafted wooden bridge spanned the water, giving passage for travelers on either of the village's roads.

Behler could see Ardin's homes and buildings were larger and nicer than those she'd grown up with in Betham. They were well-maintained and in good condition.

Six watchtowers were placed strategically around the village.

"This place is...unbelievable," she said in awe.

Kellum smirked. "I know. Down at that end of the lake," he pointed toward the north end, "there's the masonry, smithy, laundry house, and warming house for growing crops in the winter." He handed her the hooded cloak he'd placed over her that first night together. "Wear this. The night is chilly. No one will think anything of it." He put his own hood up.

"Where are we heading?"

"There." He pointed at a house straight across the lake. It sat right off the bricked road. Lamps were burning in two of the windows. Kellum stepped out of the forest and Behler followed.

They walked around the south end of the lake. They crossed over the arched bridge and with each step, Behler's breath quickened and her heart pounded harder. They walked silently. Occasionally, they would hear children yelling back and forth, running home for the night. As the two of them rounded the lake, Behler could see that there was a very large building back off both roads. Fences enclosed two large, grassless areas.

They passed by homes with large wooden doors that looked very heavy. The light from inside glinted off flawless glass in every window. Inside one house, she glimpsed a man carrying a tray of food, smiling and laughing about something Behler could only imagine.

And then, they were standing in front of her mother's impressive looking home.

Kellum took her hand and squeezed it. Touching him was still very strange. "Ready?" he asked.

She gave a nod, grateful that she had him by her side despite how odd that still felt. He let go of her hand then walked up a short stairway leading to a wooden porch on the front of the house. Behler stayed by the side of the road. The wooden planks creaked under his weight and Behler cringed, feeling like everyone in the village would hear it. Then he was at the door and knocking.

The door flew open a few seconds later.

"Kellum?" Her voice was like Lorna's, only lighter.

"Hi Sera. There was an attack in Betham."

"Oh no!" She threw her hand up over her mouth. "Is she with you?" she asked anxiously. "Is Matti okay? I thought he would bring her."

Behler struggled not to stumble back as her mother spoke her best friend's name.

Her mother knew her best friend.

Her best friend knew her mother.

Kellum nodded. "She's with me." Behler saw his head tilt just a bit, as if checking to make sure she was still there. Then he stepped aside, and the lamplight spilled out of the doorway and onto Behler. Just like that, Behler was looking at her mother. Her mother was looking at her.

"Behler!" her mother said breathlessly. She ran out of the door, and Behler thought she was going to hug her. Instead, Sera stopped short and gently grabbed both of her shoulders. "Thank goodness you both made it out." She looked over at Kellum then back at Behler. "Please, come inside."

Sera gently held Behler's arm and pulled her into the house. Behler looked at Kellum as she passed by him. He gave a small smile and nod and followed them in, shutting the door quietly behind them.

Inside, the house was even more impressive. The floors were all smooth, polished wood. A large table sat in the room to the right with a bowl of fresh fruit sitting on it. A doorway led from the room with the table into what looked like a kitchen. To her left was a large sitting area. Intricately carved chairs with overstuffed cushions sat around a beautiful woven rug. Red, greens, purples, and yellows swirled around the rug, so deep and bright that it was as if the threads had been dyed that morning. A fire blazed in a large fireplace next to a wooden bench covered in more cushions with designs as bright and vibrant as those on the rug.

"Please, come sit." Sera let go of Behler and walked into the room where the chairs waited. "Are you hungry? You must be."

"We're okay," Kellum said. He brushed past Behler and gently touched her arm with his fingertips. She took it as a sign to follow him into the room. He sat down on a chair near the fire, so Behler sat in the one closest to him. "Have any of the others shown up?" He asked. "Lorna? Rogan? Without the Thread, I feel completely blind."

Sera shook her head. "No. No one."

Kellum nodded. "Is Fenn here?"

Sera's face changed for just a split second, almost imperceptible, but Behler saw it. But then she regained her composure. "No. He's been gone for four days with no word. I normally wouldn't worry, but now without thaelic…"

"I'm sure he's fine. You know Fenn. He's always needed space when things get rough. I'm sure he'll be back before the autumn equinox and the ceremony of Iskaara."

Sera looked over at Behler. "You know what Iskaara is?"

Behler nodded. "When both moons are in the sky at the same time."

"Every seventeen years, the smaller moon travels right in front of the larger, and it's always three days before the autumn equinox." Sera continued."

"Yes," Behler said. It was common knowledge in Betham. "Everyone celebrates Iskaara. We have a festival during whatever season Iskaara happens in." She glanced at Kellum. "At least we did—until the Horde came."

Sera gave a small nod. "Iskaara is a special time for *everyone* in Elium."

Then Sera and Kellum exchanged a look—brief, but unmistakable.

There was something hidden within their words.

Something that Behler knew was going to change everything.

.

Part Two

14

Sera insisted they eat and rest before they continued talking. Behler didn't have much of an appetite but was too polite to argue. When her mother served them warmed meat and potatoes along with a delicious bright green juice drink, Behler had to admit it all smelled great. She took a sip of the juice, and it made her tongue tingle delightfully. She snorted a little at the sensation.

Sera chuckled. "The juice is from the fruit there in the bowl called yulit," Kellum told her. "The elders brought it with them from our homeland. The trees grow around the lake."

They ate at the large table while Sera busied herself elsewhere in the house. Behler appreciated her mother staying clear and giving her some space. When they were done eating, Behler turned to Kellum and reluctantly said, "You should go home." The idea of being alone with her mother, who was still basically a stranger, was not pleasant, but she would feel guilty asking Kellum to stay away from his own family even longer.

Thankfully, Kellum said, "No, I'll stay tonight. It's late anyway."

It wasn't late at all. She tried not to look too happy or too relieved that he was staying.

Sera stepped into the doorway. "How are you both doing?"

"We're fine, thank you," Kellum said, patting his stomach to compliment the delicious meal. "If it's not a bother, I thought I might stay here tonight. I don't want to risk going out again and having someone see me. That would raise *a lot* of questions, and I thought we might want to ease Behler into meeting everyone." He glanced at Behler and smiled crookedly. "Not have a stampede at your front door trying to get in to meet her."

Behler's brow wrinkled as she gave Kellum a questioning look. What the kak was he talking about?

Sera smiled. "You can sleep in the loft. You both must be pretty tired after your journey." She turned to Behler, "I'll show you your room if you'd like."

Behler had a hundred questions, but exhaustion was winning. "Sure." She forced a smile and got up then walked with her mother down a dimly lit hallway toward the back of the house. Kellum followed behind them.

A small table sat on the bottom of a set of stairs, which Behler assumed led up the loft where Kellum was going to sleep. Five oil lamps sat on the table, along with some matches. Sera lit two of the lamps and gave one to Behler and the other to Kellum. He said good night and started up the stairs but turned back halfway up. His eyes met Behler's, and she knew the question he was silently asking. Was she okay? She gave him a small smile and nod. He smiled and nodded back then disappeared into the loft.

She followed Sera down the hallway to the back of the house where it met another hallway. Three doorways led into three bedrooms, and a door off to the right led outside. Sera walked over to the bedroom door to the right and opened it.

"This is your room," she said. "I've kept it ready just in case you needed to come home."

Behler walked past her into the room and realized Sera had literally meant *her* room. The room smelled faintly of amberly flowers and clean linen; the warm lamplight flickered across polished wooden floors. A large bed sat against the far

100

wall, draped in a quilt so intricate it looked like a piece of artwork. A starburst pattern unfurled at its center in shades of moss green and muted gold, tendrils of color spiraled outward like the threads of a web. At first glance it seemed abstract, but as Behler's eyes adjusted, she caught subtle details hidden within the design — Arbiran leaves, faint outlines of drakas and laurenth blades, and delicate stitching that formed curling glyphs. On the floor at the foot of the bed was a small chest that looked identical to the one Lorna had opened the night of the attack in Betham.

A window on the right-side wall was tucked behind heavy curtains. A dresser with three heavy looking drawers sat along the wall, and next to that hung a large, framed mirror. The only mirrors Behler had ever seen were small ones that could be held in one hand, and even those were so expensive in Betham that very few families had one. This mirror was bigger than she was. "That's beautiful," she said, motioning toward it.

Sera gave a nonchalant smile. "The elders here like to keep busy." She walked across the room to a large oil lamp sitting on a small table next to the bed. She lit it, and the room was immediately filled with more warm, flickering light. A smile touched the corners of her lips as she opened the table's one drawer. She pulled out something small and neatly folded. "This was your blanket when you were just a baby. I made one for you and Fenn both." She patted the blanket and smiled a little. "Yours is in much better shape than Fenn's. He carried that blanket around all day every day when he was a small boy. It got so ragged and torn, and no matter how many times I washed it, it just wouldn't come clean." She sighed. "I should've sent yours with you when you left, but I was selfish and wanted to keep it here with me." She held it up to her nose. "You only used it for a couple of days, but I could still smell your little baby smell on it. It made me feel closer to you."

Behler felt uncomfortable. She stood awkwardly and looked around the room, trying to look much more at ease than she felt.

Sera placed the blanket on the bed, then took the few steps over to the dresser and opened a bottom drawer. She rummaged through some things that appeared to be clothes. "Here it is." She pulled out a long sleeping gown. "I hope this fits. I think it will." She held it up. "I made it for you last winter." She looked down into the drawer. "I've been making things for you for months now, knowing you'd be coming home soon."

"Thank you," Behler said, taking the gown when her mother held it out for her. It was very soft and surprisingly lightweight. She wasn't used to sleeping in anything so nice.

"It will keep you warm in the winter and cool in the summer." From atop the dresser, she grabbed a white pitcher with numerous figures delicately painted around its base. There was a bowl with similar artwork. "I'll go get some water. I'm sure you'd like to wash up a little."

Behler nodded and smiled, feeling too aware of her own face. After Sera left, Behler's eyes scanned around the room. Besides the bed, dresser, and small table that held the large lamp, there was an oversized wooden chair with a large cushion just like the ones in the front room. Along the inside wall was a huge armoire. Behler wondered what was in it, if anything, but she was too tired to explore. She heard the comforting sound of Kellum's footsteps above her and wished she could go upstairs and talk to him. Instead, she walked toward the bed but caught a glimpse of herself in the mirror. It had been a very long time since she'd looked at herself in anything besides a rippling, watery reflection. Her dark, wavy hair was tied back, and her face was streaked with dirt. She looked older than the last time she'd seen herself. She groaned when she saw how filthy her clothes were.

Sera returned with the water and brought a glass along with it. She placed them both on the dresser. She fussed with the pitcher and the basin for a bit then without turning around, said, "I've thought about what I would say to you every day since Lorna walked away with you. Now," she sighed deeply, "...now it all seems empty and not enough." Her voice caught in her throat, and she gave a quick cough to clear it. She turned to face Behler. "I'm so glad you're here. I've missed you more than I could have ever imagined. My only comfort was knowing you were with Lorna. I knew you were safe, and I knew she loved you."

Hearing a stranger talk about Lorna felt wrong. "I hope she's okay," Behler managed to say around the lump in her throat.

"Lorna's one of the strongest people I know." Sera stood quietly for a few moments then said, "I'll let you get your rest. I know you have countless questions, but those can keep until morning. For now, you should get some sleep." She smiled then left the room, quietly shutting the door behind her.

Behler pulled off her clothes and washed up. She pulled the nightgown over her head, and the material was the softest thing she had ever felt.

She walked over to the bed and collapsed into it. It felt like what she imagined a cloud would feel like. It made a slight poof as she landed and formed a nest-like cradle around her. She laid there, staring up at the ceiling – not really thinking about anything, just feeling numb.

She welcomed the numbness.

It was so much better than confusion and pain.

15

Despite her exhaustion, or maybe because of it, Behler slept poorly. Her mind wouldn't stop long enough to find1 restful sleep. In one dream, Lorna fought a kindurbeast with her bare hands. In another, Mathias was attacked by a massive lizard wearing a collar. She was relieved when daylight finally crept through the window.

She put her feet on the floor, felt its chill, and pulled them back onto the bed and under the sheet. At some point during the night, she'd kicked the heavy quilt off, so she reached down and pulled it back up to just below her chin. The room looked different in the daylight. The lamplight the night before had softened the edges around her, but daylight showed every detail – every line and every corner. The sight of it made her stomach hurt. This wasn't her room – her room was in ashes.

Footsteps walked across overhead. Kellum was awake and up. She heard him move around some more before his footfalls moved down the stairs. His muffled voice said something then Sera's voice spoke in return.

She turned toward the window and thought of Lorna. Where was she now? Was she safe? The knot in Behler's stomach twisted tighter. Frustrated tears threatened, and though part of her wanted to stay under the covers forever, she forced herself up.

Her clothes from the night before were still in a heap. She assumed there were clean ones in the dresser, but rummaging through drawers in a stranger's house—

especially her mother's—felt wrong even if this was supposedly her room. She pulled on her same dirty clothes. After having the soft nightshirt against her skin, her own clothes felt irritatingly rough and itchy. Her boots, she now saw, were caked with dried mud. She winced, imagining the mess she might've tracked in the night before. She left the boots and walked to the door in her socks.

The hallway was dim, and her socked feet made no sound as she stepped forward. At the table, Kellum and Sera were speaking in hushed tones. She hadn't meant to eavesdrop, but then—

"Behler doesn't know much," Kellum said.

"I know," Sera replied. "Lorna and I spoke often about when and how to tell her. Especially lately."

There was a pause.

Then Sera spoke again. "She was happy in Betham—or as happy as she could be. We didn't want her to carry the burden until she had to. Fenn has carried it much of his life, and it's changed him. You've seen it."

"I have," Kellum said softly. "Especially lately."

"Ever since we told the other Trulars that Fenn had a twin, all anyone talks about is Behler. Everyone has their own idea of who she's supposed to be. Fenn feels... second-class now. The people here have known him, but she's a mystery."

"They are going to be so impressed by her," Kellum said.

Despite everything, the words made her stomach twist in an entirely different way.

A chair creaked.

"Thank you for getting her here safely," Sera said. Her voice sounded thick with emotion.

"I'll do whatever needs to be done to protect her."

Kellum saying he'd protect her still made the world feel tilted and off, but it was also starting to feel like something else. Comforting, maybe. She could take on a kindurbeast but taking on whatever was happening here in this new village – that was something else she wasn't as confident with.

The quiet that followed made Behler consider revealing herself. But her feet didn't move.

"Maybe Fenn went south to one of his caves or the old ruins?" Kellum offered. "Did anyone check?"

"Luke went last week, but there was no sign. The forest is vast. He could be anywhere... though I hope he hasn't gone beyond it."

"He's smarter than that," Kellum replied.

"Smarter, yes – but you know he doesn't always do the smart thing."

The sound of a chair scraping back made Behler nearly jump out of her skin.

"We've put it off long enough," Sera said. "It's time to tell her everything... but how do you look someone in the eye and say, you're the key in defeating the Armigoth? You are the hope for us all."

Behler's chest tightened. So that's what all of this was. She wasn't just a lost daughter or a hidden twin. They thought she was some sort of weapon; one they'd sent away for safekeeping and put into an invisible cage until she was *ready* - as Rogan had so annoyingly put it.

She turned and slipped back down the hall, nearly running to get away from Kellum and Sera's conversation.

She'd heard enough and didn't want to hear any more.

16

Behler's eyes scanned around her room, frantic to find anything to help her calm her racing brain. She walked over and opened the heavy curtains then cracked the window. The crisp morning air immediately made her feel a little better. She gazed out into the village through glass so clear it was like looking through nothing at all. Any windows in Betham that had glass in were merely to let in some daylight. The glass was so bubbled and pocked, looking through it was pointless.

When she turned back toward the room, she spotted her satchel lying on the floor where she'd dropped it the night before. She grabbed it and sat down on her bed then flipped open the flap. She pulled out her isari stone and what was left of the nihra along with the two small pouches she'd discovered the night in the cave. She placed everything aside and reached back in. Her fingers brushed against a rolled piece of parchment. As she pulled it out, she could see it was a manuscript, folded up and tied tightly within a piece of leather. She untied the string and rolled open the documents inside. It was a star chart with the same constellations that were on the amulet around her neck. She absentmindedly rubbed the stones in the piece of jewelry. She didn't notice their faint glow.

A small piece of paper fell out onto her lap. It was a letter from Lorna. The scrawling flow of the letters bumping into each other was unmistakable.

Bale,

I'm sorry I couldn't always be the person you needed me to be. I'm sorry for all I had to hide from you. Ardin is a wonderful place. Enjoy it. Train. You'll be ready. But be cautious. The Armigoth can change even those we love. Trust yourself.

Lorna

Lorna wasn't one for saying she was sorry very often. This had to be some kind of record.

Someone knocked on her door.

"Behler?" her mother's voice came, muffled through the wood. "Are you awake?"

Behler started to put everything back in the satchel then changed her mind. "Yes. Come in." She stood up and stuffed the necklace down the front of her shirt then smiled politely as Sera walked into the room.

"Good morning," Sera smiled back. "Breakfast is almost ready if you'd like some." Her eyes fell on the bed. "A letter from Lorna?"

Behler nodded, picked up the paper and handed it over.

Sera read it, smiled then handed it back. Her eyes moved down to the star chart. "The night sky when you and Fenn were born. It will be the night sky for your next birthday as well." Her gaze returned to rest on Behler. "After we eat, we'll talk."

Behler wanted to confront her about what she'd overheard but was afraid her exhaustion and nerves would quickly escalate any conversation, so instead, she nodded and stood.

Her mother looked at her for a moment, making her feel very self-conscious. "If you'd like, there are clothes in that armoire that will fit you. I can wash yours and you can put them back on as soon as they're dry."

Behler looked down at her dirt-streaked clothes. In Betham, clean was a relative term. "I wouldn't want to bother you with these." She stepped toward the armoire but paused. The clothes inside looked nothing like what she was used to—intricate patterns, soft fabrics, all far too nice for just another day. "Maybe... you could help me?"

Sera smiled. "Trular women traditionally wear a luka." She touched her own. "Men wear a moktole. Lukas are just a bit longer and split at the hips so we can ride more easily."

She continued pulling clothes from the armoire. "Most of what we wear is made from bakram leather and wool."

"A bakram?" As in bakram thread? The pouch she'd found in her satchel.

Sera nodded absentmindedly. "Animals we raise here. The wool's nothing like the itchy stuff from Betham."

She handed over a neatly folded stack of clothes. "I ran a bath for you if you'd like to soak for a minute. It'll do your muscles good after your long hike."

Behler's stomach lurched a bit. A bath? In what? How deep? "Maybe I shouldn't take the time—"

"Take the time," Sera cut her off gently. "Everything else can wait just a bit longer."

Sera led Behler down the hallway to a small door she'd barely noticed before. Inside was a large bronze tub suspended over a fire pit. A pipe fed water into the tub, and red coals glowed beneath it. Steam curled lazily from the surface.

"You can dry off with those there," Sera pointed at a stack of thick towels. Behler hadn't seen a towel in years. Sera handed Behler a comb made from some sort of bone. It was polished so it shone. "You can keep that," she smiled. "It's yours." She put a hand on Behler's arm. "Just come out when you're done."

Sera closed the door behind her. Behler had been anxious about what her mother meant by *bath*. Bathing in the river had once been a treat, but after her near drowning, going very deep into the river was out of the question for her. But this…this wasn't a rushing river. This was something close to paradise.

She threw off her clothes, eager to get into the warm, clean water. Her toes touched the surface. Gently, she eased herself down until she was sitting on the bottom of the tub. The water came up to her chin. She pulled her hair out of the loose bun and carefully tilted her head back to get her hair wet. She ignored the tug of fear in her chest as she felt the water pull at her, the weight of her hair trying to pull her whole head under.

She stayed in the warm water longer than she'd intended, unready to face whatever was on the other side of that bathroom door. Eventually, she reluctantly pulled herself out of the water and went through the pile of clothing. Sera had discreetly placed some undergarments in the middle of the stack. Slightly embarrassed, Behler put them on and then slipped into the rest of the clothes. The pants were lightweight and snug but didn't restrict movement at all. In fact, they almost felt like a second skin. The simple white top had sleeves that stopped right at her elbows. It was loose and flowing, allowing for easy movement. She quickly ran the comb through her tangled hair until it slipped through easily and then tied it back up.

She stepped into the hall. The smell of breakfast made her stomach growl.

As she turned the corner, her eyes met Kellum's. Although she was fully dressed, she suddenly felt completely exposed in her new clothes. She shifted uncomfortably.

For just a moment, she thought she saw Kellum's eyes widen, but then his face relaxed. "Good morning," he said.

She scooted the chair out across from him and sat down. "Good morning."

Sera arrived with a steaming mug. "Our tea's a little strong," she warned. "Let me know if you'd prefer something else."

Behler sipped it—and winced. "It's... good," she coughed.

Kellum laughed. "Try adding honey," he suggested, handing over a small pot.

The honey transformed it. She gulped it down and refilled her mug.

"Aji water?" she asked with a half-grin.

Kellum smiled. "Of course."

They were just settling in when the front door burst open and a small girl dashed inside.

"Avenly!" Kellum yelped in surprise.

"I knew it was you!" she squealed. "And when I saw the lights on upstairs – I *really* knew it!" She swung her arm across her body to emphasize how much she'd known it.

She was Kellum's sister, no question. Same dark hair, same bright green eyes.

"You can't just barge in," Kellum said.

"It's Sera's house. I come here all the time," she said, shrugging.

Sera laughed. "She practically lives here."

"Especially since Fenn disappeared," Avenly added.

"Avenly!" Kellum scolded.

Behler couldn't help laughing. She liked the girl already.

"You're Behler, aren't you?" Avenly asked breathlessly.

Behler's head tilted to the side. Kellum's warning about others in the village recognizing her seemed plausible now. "Yes," she said hesitantly.

"I knew it!" The girl looked ready to explode from excitement.

Kellum gently grabbed her by the shoulders and turned her to him. "Did you tell anyone else we're here?"

She rolled her eyes dramatically. "Of course not! I'm not a yuna."

Kellum's jaw looked as if it were going to drop off his face. "Where did you learn that word?"

Avenly shrugged. "Luke and Fennix."

Behler chuckled. "Why are you so excited?" she asked the little girl.

Avenly stared at her. "Because you're Behler."

The way Avenly was looking at her, Behler felt *she* must be the yuna. "So?" she frowned.

"Because you and Fenn are going to save us. The foretelling says so. We've all been waiting for you to come before Iskaara, and now—you're here!"

Behler blinked. She looked at Sera. Then Kellum. "What foretelling?"

Avenly looked shocked. "You don't know the foretelling?"

"No," Behler said. She tensed the muscles around her mouth. "But I think I really should."

A soft knock at the door made everyone stop and look.

Sera rose. "Yes. It's time. I asked one of our elders to come help us explain."

She opened the door, and an older woman stepped inside. Her thick, silvery curls framed a warm, weathered face. She wore a flowing yellow luka and carried the calm presence of someone who had seen much – and knew more.

"Hello Nelly." Sera said and embraced the woman as she entered the home.

"Sera, I'm so glad to see you," the woman said before turning to Behler. "And I'm even happier to see you, dear girl." She smiled and it was the kindest and most genuine smile Behler had ever seen. "Shall we get comfortable? There's much to talk about."

Without waiting for an answer, Nelly headed for the sitting room.

Sera poured another cup of tea and followed. Kellum and Avenly stood, waiting for Behler.

She rose too, but before following, she grabbed her mug and chugged the rest.

She had a feeling she was going to need every drop of aji she could get.

17

Behler sat down in the large chair directly next to the fireplace. Avenly jumped up from where she'd sat down and crammed herself into the chair next to Behler.

"Why don't you scoot over and give Behler some space," Kellum suggested.

Avenly gave him a dirty look and didn't budge. Looking up at Behler, she asked, "Can I sit here?"

Behler smiled. "Yeah."

The little girl grinned up at her then turned to her brother and wrinkled her nose and stuck out her tongue. Behler looked away to hide her spontaneous smile and tried her best to swallow her chuckle.

Sera handed the older woman the cup of tea then sat down in the chair next to her.

"I'm Penelope," the woman said, "one of the elders here in Ardin. But everyone just calls me Nelly," she said with a wink and a tinkly laugh. She took a sip of the tea. All eyes were locked on her except for Avenly's whose kept darting back to Behler.

"I'll begin at our beginning. We are Trulars, and we are guardians of all that is – the Anarsari." She held her hands up toward the ceiling. "There are so many lands outside of Elium – countless worlds beyond the one you've known. In fact, we aren't of this world. We Trulars come from a world called Arda. Centuries ago, our people were brought together by the High Guardians to protect everything and everyone from the evils that rise, the strongest of these being the Armigoth. Our ancestors were given the ability to use the power of the Embera, the Armigoth's opposing force. That ability has been passed down each generation, allowing us to be more powerful than others."

"Tell her about the special drink," Avenly interjected, only to have Kellum quickly shush her.

Penelope smiled. "Okay, little one. The High Guardians gave our ancestors a special drink that carried the Embera's powers within it. Because of the trust between our ancestors and the High Guardians, that power has been passed down generation after generation – never fading."

"What was in the drink?" Behler asked.

"It's a mystery," Penelope shrugged. She continued as if her answer was sufficient enough. "The High Guardians also put doorways on each world so we could travel throughout the Anarsari. As far as we know, we are the only kind that can activate these doorways. We, the elders, came to this world many years ago through one."

"So you lived on a different world before?" Behler asked. The thought of multiple worlds was hard to wrap her head around. The thought that she was looking at someone who had come *from* another world was even more difficult to comprehend.

"Yes, everyone of my generation was born on Arda. Your parents' generation and yours – you are all children of Elium." Penelope smiled, but her eyes didn't seem as joyful. "So," she continued, "the Armigoth only wants to destroy, as you know, but it can't destroy on its own, it must choose a living thing as a host – like a parasite." Her brow wrinkled. "And just like a parasite, the Armigoth eventually destroys its host. Because of that, it's always trying to find those strong enough to withstand the toll it takes. Most hosts last a few years. Maybe ten if they were strong

115

and healthy to begin with. Sometimes, though, the Armigoth finds someone who can survive for decades. When that happens, both the host and the Armigoth become incredibly powerful, like we are seeing here with Varek."

Behler felt as if she were listening to some story told to children instead of a history lesson. She glanced at Kellum, but his expression was even and flat. It was clear he'd heard the story before.

"Nearly two centuries ago," Penelope continued, "on Arda, there was a Trular named Olgum. No one knows exactly what happened, but Olgum started acting strangely. We had already been fighting the Armigoth's darkness for generations on other worlds, so our people recognized what was happening fairly quickly. He had fallen under the Armigoth's influence.

"Once he knew the Revala was on to him, he fled Arda. The Revalars gave chase. He eventually led them here, to Elium. This world is so full of such various creatures and races, it's unlike any others our people ever protected. This is where Olgum found the Sulimar. They were the Horde and Gorlogs of his time...only so much more vicious.

Penelope paused. "Our best guess is that Olgum survived the Armigoth for 150 years. Having lived out with Elians your whole life, that may seem impossible. Another gift we were given was the gift of very long lives. But, also, the Armigoth prolonged Olgum's life – if you can call it life. When the Armigoth finds a good host, it won't release it until the body is completely wasted...and our bodies seem to be well equipped to withstand whatever the Armigoth puts it through.

"Nonetheless, at some point, his body was too wasted to continue. We aren't sure exactly what happened, but there was a period of time where the Armigoth's power did wane." Her hands glided gracefully down, illustrating her point. "We believe that is when it was looking for a new host. It found Varek."

"So, he was a man – *is* a man," Behler said, more to herself than anyone else in the room. "But not just a man anymore." Just like Lorna had said to Frawna that day in Betham.

Sera sighed heavily. "Unfortunately, Varek is a former Trular, just like Olgum."

Behler's eyes widened. "He came through with you?"

Penelope shook her head. "He was with the first of the Revalars to come through chasing Olgum. We aren't sure why he fell to the Armigoth – only that he did."

The room fell silent, and Behler sensed everyone was letting her work through what she'd just heard. Finally, she leaned toward Penelope and said, "So if the Armigoth keeps using Trulars to become so strong, maybe it would be better if our people just went away."

Penelope nodded as if she understood, but then said, "Whether or not we existed, the Armigoth still would, and it would ravage the Anarsari if there weren't people like us to keep it at bay."

Behler stayed silent for a while as her mind processed the fantastic story she'd just heard. Finally, she asked, "And what do I have to do with this?" Behler pressed. "What's this foretelling Avenly mentioned?" She felt the little girl squirm at the mention of her name.

Penelope continued. "Our ancestors were told about a world with two moons just like the fire and water moons here in Elium. We had scouts searching for it for generations, with no luck. But when our Revala, our most elite guardians, followed

Olgum here, they discovered the two moons during their second cycle, when Iskaara occurred. They believed this had to be the land where the foretelling would be fulfilled." She paused and took another sip of her tea.

"The foretelling said two children, born under the two moons, would become as powerful as anything that has ever been and who would be able to bring balance to the Anarsari, destroying the Armigoth. That's you and Fennix. Together, you both will bring balance back to the Anarsari."

Completely dumbfounded, Behler looked from Kellum to Sera. "Just the two of us?"

"Of course not." Sera reached out and touched Behler's knee gently. "You will lead the rest of us. We will all fight right by your side."

Behler couldn't quite wrap her head around what the two women were telling her. But then it hit her like a ton of bricks. They expected her and her *missing* brother to defeat not only Varek, but his entire Horde army...oh, and the entire Armigoth while they were at it. Her head started to swim. "You can't be serious!" she said quickly and louder than she'd intended. Sera pulled her hand away. Behler looked over at Kellum. "This is ridiculous." Her eyes pleaded with him to agree with her. When he stayed silent, her eyes darted between Sera and Penelope. "I'm not a leader. Lorna never let me lead anything in my life." She looked at Kellum again. "You know I'm not a leader."

His head twitched just a bit. "Except, you are. Lorna knows that, and she should've let you lead more so you could see it in yourself." His bold, defiant words targeted at Lorna left her feeling even more confused

Penelope sighed. "Yes, Lorna is quite pig-headed. Her sense of responsibility for you and the fulfillment of the foretelling led her to make choices that were a bit too overprotective, but we had to allow her to do as she saw fit. After your incident in the river and the kindurbeast, she and others like Rogan were quite scared of letting you out of their sight. And she did have pressure from some of the elders to keep you better protected."

Behler's insides twisted a little at the realization that this stranger knew about her encounter with the kindurbeast. She took a deep breath. "Kellum..." but she didn't know how to finish what she'd begun to say.

She wanted to talk to Mathias.

Except – her heart sank as she realized he must believe this insane idea too...along with every other rebel she'd ever known.

Not rebel – Trular? Revalar?

Kak! She didn't know.

What she did know was that she was alone.

18

Penelope stood. "I'll excuse myself so you can have some time with all this," she said gently. She turned to Sera. "Get this young woman some more tea, Sera. Her nerves are more than rattled." She gave Behler one more, brief smile, then headed out of the room. Sera followed behind her.

"Behler, are you okay?" Kellum asked softly.

She scowled at him despite his tender tone. "I can't believe you believe this. You know me...at least better than these people do. You know I'm not some savior sent to destroy the Armigoth." Her face became hot and she began to hear her heart pounding in her ears. "I was just beginning to think you were someone I could trust."

Kellum flinched as if she'd punched him. "You can," he said, the hurt evident in his voice. Behler immediately regretted her hateful words.

She slowed her breathing and calmed her frazzled nerves. "I'm...I'm sorry," she stammered. Her stomach hurt and the room spun slightly. It was all too much – the idea that she could have some vital part in defeating the Armigoth. She thought she was going to be sick, but then she felt Avenly's little fingers softly on her hand and a feeling of calm washed over her. Behler looked down.

You're going to be okay, she heard Avenly's voice in her head.

That wasn't possible. The Deep Thread was broken...wasn't it?

The air in the room thickened, at least that's how it felt in Behler's chest. "I don't understand what you think is going to happen to me that will make me capable of fighting something so powerful." She fended off hopelessness and the feeling of defeat. "Lorna wouldn't even let me go on scouting missions."

Sera walked back into the room, carrying a cup of tea just like Penelope had suggested. "Behler, I know how all this must sound." She walked across the room and handed Behler the cup. Steam lazily swirled up and around Behler's face as she took a sip. Sera had added just the right amount of honey.

After a few large sips, she asked, "Why didn't Lorna tell me any of this?" She could feel tears stinging the corners of her eyes.

Sera sat back down in her chair across from Behler. "We didn't want you to feel any different than anyone else in the village. We didn't want you to stick out. And the less you knew, the safer you were."

Behler let those words sink in. She let them mingle with everything else until the dread she was feeling was slowly replaced with a simmering anger. She was angry for being dragged to this village when she should've been out fighting and helping the others. She was angry that these people thought she was some sort of weapon that would lead them out of the darkness. She was angry for being lied to her entire life.

"Well – you all failed at me not sticking out," she said flatly. She looked over at Kellum. "We were all out of place in Betham. I just never knew why. We've spent our entire lives trying desperately not to stick out so the Horde wouldn't catch us – or me."

Kellum looked at her with those unsettlingly confident green eyes. "Believe me, it would've been even harder if you'd known everything. You would've carried that weight around with you all the time, and it would've changed you."

Behler wished Lorna was there in the room. She wanted to scream and curse at her. She took another sip of her tea and a deep breath before speaking again. "You made a choice for me when I was too young to make one for myself," she said, measuring each word. "I understand that." She stared at the floor, afraid that if she met Sera's eyes, she would lose her nerve. "But when I got old enough to understand, you, or Lorna, or Penelope, or my best friend, Mathias 'kakweed' DeBran – *anyone* should have told me the truth." Her measured words were quickly disintegrating into anger, but then she realized she'd just cursed in front of Avenly and quickly shut her mouth, afraid she may let something else slip.

"You might be right," Sera admitted, seemingly unphased by Behler's spicy language. She sat upright, her jaw set in a very familiar way. "But we had to make a choice, and we did. It's in the past, and we can only move forward now. There is much to do, and the time grows shorter every day. You *must* be ready for whatever is to come because it's coming for you whether you like it or not." Her words were harsh but spoken gently.

For the first time, Behler could see how Lorna and Sera were sisters. Their ability to speak bluntly when needed seemed to be a family trait.

The anger drained from Behler. She was too overwhelmed and too tired to hold on to it. "How could I possibly fight the Armigoth? It's stronger than any of us...no matter what you think makes me special."

Sera leaned closer. "The foretelling says that on the first night of Iskaara, when the second moon returns to the sky and travels with the first, you two will gain abilities beyond any of the rest of us."

Behler looked at her mother closely. "What kind of abilities?"

Sera shook her head. "We don't know for sure."

Behler sat quietly for a while. She leaned over and rested her elbows on her knees and held her forehead in her hands. "This...this is a lot." She looked up with weary eyes. "Are you sure Fenn and I are the ones that the foretelling was about?"

"Yes," Sera said with absolute certainty. "As your mother, I could feel your Threads before you were born. I felt something was special – and knowing you were twins, I just had a feeling. But I kept it to myself. I didn't even tell the others I was expecting twins. You weren't due until weeks after Iskaara, so part of me thought it was just wishful thinking on my part. But then, you were born four weeks early under both moons. And you each have shown signs of being special since the day you were born." She leaned over and started to reach for Behler again then pulled her hand back and rested it in her lap. "I know it's a lot. It's more than a lot."

Behler nodded but didn't say anything. The room was silent, and she sensed they were all waiting for her to speak again. Finally, she said the only thing that kept repeating itself in her own head. She looked at Kellum. "I'm not ready for this."

"You're more ready than you think. And you'll get *more* ready each day," he said. "I'll be right by your side to make sure you do."

Behler shook her head. "Iskaara is in six months." Time felt far too short and it just wasn't fair. Maybe if she'd known earlier and had more time to prepare. Looking over at her mother, she asked, "Why did you send me away in the first place? This village seems like the safest place for me to be. Why not keep me here with you and Fenn? Why was it so important to keep us apart? Why the secrets?"

"Because we didn't want anyone knowing you were a twin. We didn't even want our own people knowing Fennix was a twin in case they were captured and tortured for information." A line cut across her forehead for a moment as if

123

recalling a painful memory. She quickly recovered from whatever had troubled her and continued. "As Trulars, we had no idea which generation the twins would arrive in. We weren't even sure Elium was the right place the foretelling was about. When I became pregnant and realized the timing would be so close to Iskaara, I had a feeling. Others did too, and my instinct told me to be careful. When I realized I was pregnant with twins, I knew the danger that created for you both. I told no one except your father and Nelly about you. No one expected you to be born that night, so two nights later, we snuck *you* out of the village with Lorna and hid Fenn so no one would know his actual birthday. Eventually, we had to tell others about you so they could help keep you safe. But they were the only ones who knew – until recently. Fennix didn't even know he was a twin until he was ten. "

Behler stared at her mother, trying to process the weight of what she'd just heard. She had to wonder what choices she would make if faced with the same decisions. Would she hide someone she loved to keep them safe?

Probably.

That didn't make any of it much easier.

She stood and crossed the room to the window. The sun glinted off the lake, and for a moment, she longed to run outside and sit beside it. To let the quiet wash over her like the water.

What if she couldn't be the leader they all thought she was?

A cool morning breeze drifted in through the open window, carrying with it the scents of early summer—green leaves, damp earth, the sweetness of distant blossoms. They were all the smells of nature. But none of them smelled like home.

She didn't know if she'd ever feel like she belonged here.

She didn't feel like she belonged anywhere anymore.

19

Sera left the room once more, making the excuse of cleaning up breakfast. Behler knew it was to give her space.

"It's going to be okay," Avenly said when she looked over and saw Behler deep in thought. "Kellum says you're very strong and a very good fighter."

Behler scoffed. She looked at Kellum. "A good fighter, sure...but better than Lorna? Rogan? Broty?" She cringed even as her lips were forming Broty's name, unsure of how Kellum would react so soon after the man's death.

Kellum's expression didn't change, but she noticed the flick of his gaze at the mention of Broty. "What do you mean?" he asked, careful and measured.

"I mean how could I be the one to lead anyone when there are others so much better?"

"Stop being so humble," Kellum said with a tone that shocked Behler. "You're good and you know it. You can hit anything with an arrow from distances further than anyone I know. And after Iskaara, who knows what you will be able to do?"

Behler laughed cynically. "Will I be able to shoot a target one hundred liyuras? Cut a tree down with one swipe of my kintar? Fly?"

"Maybe," Kellum said with a raised brow and a smirk.

"Oh...if you can fly will you take me too?" Avenly said with excitement only a small child can muster.

Kellum rolled his eyes at his sister then shifted in his chair so he could face Behler more directly. "The trip Nelly was talking about, when you fell in the

125

river..." Behler's stomach twisted again. "Lorna had to answer for that. But you killed a kindurbeast...with just your bow and a few arrows...when you were twelve! Bale, that's unheard of."

Behler shook her head. "I've regretted killing that animal ever since. Some ferocious warrior I am."

Kellum's eyes changed, and something about the way he looked at her made her look away. "Kindness doesn't equal weakness. It's one of the things that separates us from Varek."

Behler had never thought about it that way. Kellum popped up out of the chair he was sitting on and slid into the seat where Sera had been seated so he could better see Behler's face at the window. "They barely even let you alone enough for you to learn what you can do. Someone was almost always watching to make sure you were safe."

She mulled over his words, unsure of herself like she'd never been before. Here she was being told she was some savior capable of defeating the greatest darkness ever known, yet she's always had guardians all around her. Her brows furrowed. "I was never alone, but where is my brother? Where is Fennix? Why is he allowed to be alone?"

Avenly did a dramatic eye roll. "Fennix is insufferable when he's stuck in the village."

Kellum laughed. "She's right. And he's not *really* alone. The Arbirans are his guardians."

Behler plopped back down in the chair next to Avenly. "I have a lot of questions, but I don't even know what those questions are yet." She closed her eyes and took a deep breath. When she opened her eyes, Avenly was looking up at her, smiling. Behler couldn't help but smile back. She looked at Kellum. "I have a draka I've never used. Want to show me how it works?"

Kellum smiled. "Sure, but I'm no expert either."

Sera cleared her throat from the hallway between rooms. "I think I can help you with that if you'd like."

Behler smiled and felt it throughout her body. A spark of a thought formed in the back of her mind. Lorna wasn't around to control her every move. For the first time since it had all started – maybe for the first time ever – she was going to take control of her own life.

20

Behler walked into her bedroom to grab her weapons. She stopped just outside the doorway and looked around the room again. Once she walked across that threshold and grabbed her draka, she knew there was no going back.

"Hello," Avenly said from behind her.

Behler jumped and turned around. "Hi," she smiled.

Avenly took a step around Behler and into the room. She slipped her hand in Behler's and pulled her through the doorway. "I'm so happy you're here."

Behler smiled. "Thanks. I'm starting to come around." It was just a tiny lie.

"I know, you're not...not yet," Avenly said matter-of-factly. "I have nishiri." When Behler just stared at her blankly, Avenly chuckled and explained, "I can feel people's feelings—and make them feel mine. But only when I'm touching them."

"Is that how I heard your voice in my head earlier?"

Avenly nodded. "Yep."

"Can others do that?"

"Yes, some can, but most people can't do it as much as I can until they get older. Some people were worried about me when I started doing it so young, but I'm fine." Her eyes twinkled. "I like being different. Don't you?"

Behler grinned slightly. "Maybe I do." She let go of Avenly's hand and slung her quiver over her shoulder, the strap crossing her chest. Her bow followed, resting diagonally across her back. Then she picked up her isari stone and draka. For a moment, she studied them, unsure how the stone could possibly stay in place.

But then she felt it—like the faint pull of magnets drawing together. She brought the stone to the clawed end of the draka, and with a soft click, it locked into place. The stone flared a sharp blue, and the draka vibrated gently in her hand.

"Very cool," she murmured, then reached for her kintar.

The quiver had a leather strap attached so that the kintar blade fit snugly through, then rested on its hilt.

"You look ready for battle," Kellum said from her doorway.

She turned and looked in the mirror. "Maybe. I feel a little better...more like myself," she admitted.

Kellum stepped into the room. "Did Sera show you your taakin?"

"My what?"

"Taakin," he walked over to her armoire.

Behler quickly slipped across the floor and put a hand on the door he was starting to pull open. "Whatever it is, I'm sure I can get it."

"You don't even know what it is."

"So tell me."

Kellum took a step back. "One night in a room of your own and you're already acting so possessive and secretive," he teased.

Behler huffed. "What is it you think I need so badly? A token?"

Kellum laughed. "A *taakin*. It's Trular armor. You'll need it...unless you're looking to get hurt, that is."

Behler raised an eyebrow at him. "I've fought you before. I'm not worried."

Kellum laughed again, louder. "Oh, but you want me to help you prepare to fight Varek. That means all rules are out. I'm not sure you know what you're getting yourself into." His eyes twinkled playfully.

Behler turned her back to him and opened the door of the armoire. "Just tell me what I'm looking for."

"That right there," he pointed over her shoulder.

She pulled out something that resembled a vest but with short, capped sleeves over the shoulders

. It was made of thin leather braided together and covered with material identical to what her clothing was made of.

"This? This won't protect me from anything."

Kellum took it from her. "Yes, it will."

"It's barely thicker than the shirt I have on."

"Trust me. It will protect you." He handed it back to her. "Just put it on."

She thought maybe Kellum was playing a joke on her. "If I put this on and I find out it's some sort of prank you're trying to pull...I will hurt you – badly."

Avenly nearly fell over laughing.

Kellum laughed, too. "What? Like shoot an arrow through my butt?" His eyes sparkled wickedly. Avenly shrieked with laughter, and Behler thought she may hyperventilate. "Just put it on." Kellum continued. "I'll meet you out in the hall." He grabbed Avenly's hand. "C'mon, kiddo, let's go."

Avenly went with him, still laughing and murmuring something about butts.

Behler was left holding the thin taakin. "I'm going to have to hurt him," she muttered to herself as she pulled all of her weapons off so she could put the armor on. She caught herself smiling when she looked at her reflection in the mirror across the room.

The others were all waiting for her in the hallway when she stepped out of her room. She breathed a sigh of relief when she saw her mother had a taakin on too. Maybe she wouldn't have to hurt Kellum after all.

"The training grounds are just beyond the stables," Sera said. She was holding a draka with a greenish blue stone. "Ready?" she asked as she grabbed the latch on the door.

Behler took a deep breath and nodded.

Sera opened the door and Behler could smell the hot summer air. The sun was just reaching high enough to shine over the treetops and chase the dew off the grass.

Avenly's hand worked its way into Behler's again, and Behler's nerves settled a little. Sera stepped out the door.

Behler inhaled the sweet smells of the warm morning, stepped out of the house and into her new world.

21

The houses in the village were built in three rows. Sera's row faced the bricked road and lake. Another row of homes was built behind Sera's, facing away so that their front doors looked toward the dirt path. The final row was built on the opposite side of the dirt road, facing it. They'd gotten nearly to the grass on the opposite side of the dirt road when they heard a voice call.

"Kellum!"

A woman stood frozen in place up the road, a basket of what looked to be laundry rested on her hip. All at once, she dropped the basket and began running toward them. She wrapped her arms tightly around Kellum and buried her head in his shoulder. Kellum returned her hug.

"Hi Ama," he said happily.

She let go and took a step back then lovingly reached up and touched his cheek. "Oh, it's so good to see you."

"You too." His smile faded. "Broty's gone. It happened two nights ago in Betham."

"Oh, sweet Broty. May he rest in Shamar." His mother kissed her palm then held it over her heart.

She turned her eyes to Behler. "You must be Behler." She took Behler's hand in both of hers. "I'm Kellum's mother, Nirain."

"Hello," said Behler. She bowed her head, a show of respect expected in Betham.

132

Nirain smiled. "It's been a long time since I've been greeted in such a way." She bowed her head in return. She looked at Sera and her smile faded. "Any word of Fenn?" Sera shook her head. "I'm sure he'll return soon, probably with a great story to tell."

Sera smiled, but Behler noticed the gesture didn't reach her eyes. "I'm sure you're right." She looked around. "We should be going. We're heading to the training fields."

Nirain picked up her basket. "I think everyone is at the stables. I heard something about it as some of the children passed by a while ago. People are trying to keep their minds off what's going on outside the forest."

Sera pursed her lips and looked at Behler. "The stables are right next to the training fields. Are you sure you're ready for this?"

Behler swallowed a lump in her throat and nodded.

"Check on your brother for me," Nirain said to Kellum. "He's been spending most of his time with the horses. I have a feeling, whatever everyone is watching at the stables involves him."

"Oh, you can bet on that," Kellum said and didn't sound happy about it.

They said goodbye to Nirain and continued on their way. They walked along the edge of the road, heading south toward the large barn that Kellum and Behler had passed on their way into the village the night before.

Sera and Avenly were far enough ahead that Behler felt she could ask Kellum a question that kept bugging her. "Why would Fennix just go into the woods and disappear? Besides being *insufferable*, I mean?" She smiled at the memory of Avenly's little voice struggling to form such a big word.

"He's done that kind of thing for years." Kellum subconsciously touched the knife from the cave, still tucked in his waistband. "He's known about the foretelling for a while and it's weighed on him. Fenn needs space sometimes." He looked at Behler. "And by sometimes, I mean a lot of the times."

"But without even telling his mother?" She couldn't call Sera *her* mother...not yet.

"Fenn's my friend and I love him like a brother...but he's got his faults."

They were almost to the stables when a sudden roar erupted followed by loud clapping and high whoops and whistles from the far side of the building.

Sera pointed at the barn. People were lined up along the fence watching something inside the enclosed plot on the other side of the building.

"What is it?" Behler asked.

"Luke," Avenly said with an exaggerated eye roll.

"Speaking of faults...my brother has a way of drawing a crowd." Kellum's face did nothing to hide his annoyance.

Avenly suddenly punched him in his side. "That's not a fault! Be nice to him."

He feigned injury from her punch then tousled her hair. "I will."

Behler didn't need nishiri to tell Kellum was lying.

The sight of the large and riled-up crowd was making Behler think twice about facing people...especially what appeared to be everyone at once. "Do you think we could maybe avoid them for a bit?"

"The training fields start there," Sera pointed beyond the stables, near the edge of the clearing just before the forest took over the landscape again. "And they go all the way back to the treeline there." She pointed in the direction directly behind the barn. The entire training area was in direct view of the side of the building where everyone was standing.

"We could probably make it into the stables without anyone seeing us," Kellum suggested.

Behler nodded, relieved. That sounded like a very good plan.

They walked so that the building shielded them from everyone's view then quickly slipped inside.

The smell of hay and animals struck Behler in the face as soon as she walked through the door. The air felt dry and earthy in her lungs.

All the stalls had windows and doors that opened to the outside, and all the windows were opened. Behler could see movement outside, but the horses blocked most of the view. Another roar from the crowd and a flash of color whipped past two of the stall openings.

"Woooo!" The rider atop the bucking horse cried out, obviously enjoying the ride and the attention.

"Luke," Kellum said through pursed lips...clearly concerned. "He's going to break his neck."

"No, he won't," Avenly objected. "He's really good."

"Being good doesn't mean he should be stupid," Kellum scowled. He looked down and noticed his little sister's wide eyes and his scowl immediately softened. "You're right, kiddo. I'm sure he'll be okay."

Sera moved over to a window where she could see outside. "He's trying to break Sabana."

"Sabana!?" Kellum rubbed his forehead. He lowered his voice so only Behler could hear him say, "He's going to do more than break his neck. I'm going to go

135

stop him." He started to grab the door to head back outside when the crowd outside let out a collective gasp. A loud thud then a horrendous crunching sound made Behler flinch.

Avenly's eyes shot wide open. "Luke!"

Kellum was out the door in an instant. Avenly would've been right on his heels if Sera hadn't grabbed her. "Kellum will take care of him," she said reassuringly.

Behler tracked the sound of Kellum's voice as he worked his way through the crowd then watched him through the stall windows as he ran toward his brother. He crouched down and gingerly touched his brother's shoulder. "Luke," she heard him say quietly. "Luke," he repeated a little louder.

Behler breathed a sigh of relief when she saw Kellum's brother move a little.

Behler turned and smiled at Avenly. "He's okay." Although she wasn't sure how okay he *actually* was.

They were so focused on listening to what was going on outside of the building, none of them heard the old man come in the back door of the stables until he loudly said, "I told that boy Sabana was cranky this morning," he chuckled. "He was close this time, though, boy he was close." The man walked casually up the aisle. When he reached Sera and Avenly, he patted the little girl's head. "Your brother's just fine. He'll get her before she gets him, you can believe that." The man turned to Behler. He had hair as white as snow and bright blue eyes that looked far too full of youth to belong to a man who must be at least seventy. He carried himself with the strength of a man much younger, yet his face was full of lines and wisdom.

"You must be Behler," he smiled and stuck out his hand. "We've been waiting a long time to see you young lady." He tightly gripped her forearm then released it. "I'm Warln. I'll be here to help you with your horse. She's right back there." He gestured toward the back of the stables.

"My horse?"

Warln smiled. "Yep. Mathias and Lorna picked her out for you last spring. I think you'll approve. Hold on and I'll go get her."

The old man walked back toward the last stall on the right. He reached up gently with his hand and Behler could just make out the muzzle of a horse as Warln's hand gently patted it. He spoke softly to the animal then he opened the stall door and stepped inside. Just a few moments later, he stepped back outside, leading the most beautiful animal Behler had ever seen. Its coat was light brown, the color of a golden wheat field in late summer. Its mane and tail were cornsilk blond.

Warln walked the horse right up to her. "Ciela, meet Behler."

Behler smiled. Gently, she took her hand and touched the horse's nose. The horse chuffed softly.

The moment between Ciela and Behler was broken when Kellum and Luke came in through the back door. Kellum was talking quietly to his brother, but it was obvious he was scolding him.

"I'm fine!" Luke said curtly, but the bone between the boy's elbow and wrist was noticeably at the wrong angle.

"This time, but that horse could kill you," Kellum scolded him.

Warln loudly cleared his voice. "Luke will be just fine on that horse, Kellum. He's going to have her broken soon enough. He brought her in from outside the forest, and she's his to break."

Kellum looked at the old man with wide eyes. "Look at his arm." He touched the shoulder of Luke's broken arm, making his brother wince.

"Take him to Zola. She'll fix him up," Warln said.

Kellum looked at Behler, and she knew he was reluctant to leave her. She smiled and nodded, but Kellum still looked torn.

"Go on," Warln said. "The sooner Zola gets a look at that, the sooner Luke can heal up and get back on his horse."

Kellum looked ready to object again but then shut his mouth. He looked at Behler. "I'll be back." His frustration at having to leave her was clear to everyone in the barn. He motioned for Luke to follow him out the front of the stables.

Warln turned to Behler. "Want to ride her? I promise she'll give you a better ride than Sabana gave Luke." He chuckled.

"Sure," Behler said. "But there are a lot of people out there."

Walrn waved off her worry. "They'll be leaving now that the show's over."

Behler turned to Sera, "We were going to do some training."

Warln turned. "Whaddya think, Sera? Does she have time for a quick riding lesson?"

She smiled. "I think a ride is just what she needs right now."

"Hooooaaah!" Avenly cheered and jumped in the air. She turned to Warln. "Can I take Cake out?"

Warln winked at her. "Just throw his saddle on."

Avenly made a sound akin to an excited Velvet Owl and ran off toward the back of the building then disappeared into a stall on the left side. Behler could hear her moving things around.

"Ever been on one?" Warln asked.

"No. By the time I was old enough, all the horses had been stolen from the village to be taken to Kilgen."

Warln wrinkled his forehead. "Old enough? Around here, as soon as you can walk, you're old enough. Well," he turned to Ciela, "let's get her saddled up. I'll show you how to get her ready." He started to grab the leather strap dangling from the bit in Ciela's mouth then stopped. "Why don't you bring her back down to her stall? Just give this a little pull and she'll follow you." He patted Ciela's neck. "Honestly, if you just let her know where to go, she'll follow you anywhere."

Behler felt a little unsure of herself as she grabbed the strap and began to walk, but Ciela immediately turned and began following her. Warln showed her how to place a blanket on Ciela's back to help cushion the saddle he placed on next. The saddle was golden brown leather with delicate details embossed on it. She recognized many of the same images she'd seen on her quilt. Behler ran her hand over it.

"It was your grandmother's, on your father's side. She was a good friend to me and my wife. I'm sorry to say she's no longer with us. She died a few summers after you were born."

Behler couldn't help but feel sad at losing someone before she even knew they existed. "What about my grandfather?"

"Obidiah is out with the Revala. He refuses to retire, but he's still got too much fight left." He smiled slightly.

"My mother's parents?"

He shook his head in response as he helped Behler up into Ciela's saddle. From there, the horse felt enormously bigger. Behler could feel the taut muscles as the horse shifted from one leg to another. She was ready to run and was only waiting for Behler to tell her to go.

"Maybe not a run just yet," Behler whispered.

The horse whinnied back.

Warln walked them out of the stall and through the large door at the back of the stables. A warm, fresh breeze rustled through Ciela's mane. Soon, Avenly rode out on a chestnut-colored horse. His black mane and tail were in dark contrast with the rest of his body. "Ready?" she asked eagerly.

Behler looked at Warln. "Aren't you coming?"

"I'll be along. You have an excellent teacher right there." He nodded toward a beaming Avenly.

"Let's go," she said. "Just kick your heels a little bit right in her side. Let your body move with her naturally." Avenly gave Cake a little tap with her heels and they headed toward the north end of the grassy field, away from the fences where some were still gathered.

Before Behler could even tap Ciela with her heels, the horse whinnied again and began following behind Cake. "Show off," she said softly. Ciela chuffed at her and shook her head so that her mane shook back and forth.

She grinned and felt the pressure of the weight of everything lift ever so slightly. And for the moment, she wasn't the embodiment of a foretelling or a secret to be kept tucked away.

She was just a girl and her horse.

22

Avenly gave Behler riding tips. It was clear, though, that with or without an experienced rider, Ciela was going to do exactly what she was supposed to do. It felt she had a sixth sense for where Behler wanted to go, Warln and Sera watched from the stable doors, but no one else had ventured back behind the building except for a group of curious children.

The open, grassy field where they rode took up the entire length of the village. Behind some of the houses were small gardens and animal coops, but at the farthest end was a cultivated field full of what looked like very tall beans. A herd of animals grazed in the grass near the crop. They resembled a cross between sheep, fluffy pigs, and maybe even a bit of cow – and they all looked as if they'd been recently shorn. Behler guessed they were the bakrams her mother had mentioned.

Avenly rode up to her. "Matti did a good job picking her out, didn't he?"

"Matti?" Only someone who knew him would call him that. "You know Mathias?

The little girl nodded. "He's best friends with Luke and Fenn."

A sharp pang of betrayal tore through Behler. *No – he's best friends with me!* This village was going to take away everything she thought was true in her life.

A moment later, Warln rode up to join them on a gray and white speckled horse. "Do you think she's ready to take Ciela for a little run?" he asked Avenly. The little girl beamed. Warln patted Behler on the back and smiled a broad, cheerful smile. "A good run can make a lot of things a whole lot better."

"Okay." Behler smiled, but her stomach churned with nerves. The ground was a long way down from atop Ciela, plus it was still upset thinking about Mathias having *best* friends that weren't her.

"Down to the kogum field and back," Warln said. "Willa and I will take it easy on you." He grinned and winked. "At first."

Without waiting for an answer, he took off at a trot, heading north. Avenly and Behler followed behind.

For a while, Behler kept pace with the others, keeping Ciela at a gentle trot. But as they got closer to the field, she grew more comfortable with a slightly quicker pace. Her balance got better, and her confidence grew. She urged Ciela into a quick canter.

Then she pushed the horse faster.

And faster.

She passed Warln. He whooped and shouted, encouraging her on.

The sound of the horses' hooves pounding the hard earth beneath them was solid and comforting.

At the large field of the tall, beany-looking crop of kogum they were dead even, so as they turned to head back to the stables, it was an all-out race. The air rushed past Behler's face and through her hair that had come loose. She could smell the grass, the plants, and the animals. And she could feel some of the hurt and anger wash away in the wind.

Ciela pulled ahead without Behler pushing her anymore, and by the time they reached the stables, Behler was actually smiling and laughing. Warln and Avenly rode up right behind her.

"See," Warln said, "a good run is all you needed. You're a natural."

Behler shrugged. "Ciela did all the work."

Warln laughed a big laugh from his gut. "You did your job. You just had to stay on."

Avenly giggled. "That already makes you better than Luke." Her eyes sparkled with the orneriness of a child, and Behler couldn't help but join in on the laughter. Warln looked past her then gestured toward the stables with a tilt of his head. She looked over and saw a handful of people gathered at the fence. Some were talking excitedly to each other. Others were smiling broadly. One was pointing and gesturing at her. Behler's heart did a little skip and a jump in her chest.

"Look back there," Warln said.

Behler looked back and saw that people had gathered all along the row of houses and buildings lining the grassy field.

Word had spread: the other twin had arrived.

23

Warln and Sera stood close by Behler's side as the Trulars gathered around. Avenly stood nearly on top of her, holding tightly onto her right hand.

"Trulars, this is Behler." Warln chuckled heartily. "I'm sure she needs no introduction. She and Kellum have made it home safely, fleeing Betham after an attack." He put his arm around her shoulders. "And for that, we are so grateful. There will be time to speak with her in the coming days. I think a lunafet is called for – to show how grateful we are for her safe return to us." He turned to her and softly said, "If that's okay with you."

Behler looked at him blankly. She had no idea what a lunafet was.

Avenly leaned up to whisper. "It's a fun party with lots of yummy food."

Behler looked back at Warln, still unsure. "Okay," she managed to say.

"Excellent. Three nights from this evening should be good. Until then, we'll let her get settled." He clapped his hands together once. "Well, everyone, I think we have some more work to do with Ciela, so feel free to watch, but please excuse us for now." He gently put his hand on Behler's back and turned her away from the group of people. She heard the crowd behind her begin to chatter amongst themselves, but they all kept their distance just as Warln had requested.

For the next half hour, Behler rode up and down the edge of the forest with Warln and Avenly. The treeline was close to one hundred yura lengths from the stables, far enough away that no one could really get a good look at her. The onlooking crowd gradually dispersed.

Warln stopped. "Let's give the horses a little break." He dismounted, and the girls followed his lead. He sat down and pulled three large, red apples from his pocket. He tossed one to Avenly and one to Behler then took a bite out of his own. "I hope that was okay back there, about the lunafet," he said. "I kind of jumped in without checking with you first."

"I'm glad you did," Behler smiled. "But what is a lunafet exactly?"

Warln smiled. "An old tradition. We gather to celebrate, to mourn, to give thanks, whatever brings us together. In three nights, you'll have a little better footing, and it'll be a good way to meet everyone."

Avenly made an excited noise and pointed toward the barn. "Kellum's coming!"

Kellum was riding up on a smokey gray horse with black splotches. The sight of him reinforced how comforting it was to have him in Ardin with her.

"How's Luke?" Avenly asked anxiously when Kellum got close enough to hear.

"He'll be fine." He hopped down off his horse. He patted the horse's side and rubbed its nose. The horse turned its head and nuzzled Kellum's neck. "Good boy, Storm." He turned and looked at Behler. He wrinkled his brow, looking very concerned. "Sera told me about the lunafet. Are you okay with that?"

Behler shrugged and nodded. "Sure."

"You sure?" he asked again, lowering his voice. "Don't let Grampa rope you into something if you're not ready."

Behler looked from Kellum to Warln then back at Kellum again. "He's your grandfather?"

145

Kellum grinned. "You couldn't see the family resemblance?" He lifted his chin up as if she would study it.

Behler looked between them. The likenesses were clear now—jawline, brows, even the stubborn tilt of their heads.

Kellum knelt next to her. "Are you really okay with the lunafet? Everyone is going to be there. They'd probably like for you to say something in front of the entire village."

"She's going to be great," Warln insisted.

Behler smiled at Kellum. "I'll be fine." She hoped.

Kellum looked at her skeptically, and she knew he didn't entirely believe her. "Well good. I didn't want you doing anything you weren't comfortable with." He stared at her a few seconds longer.

"You're becoming as overprotective as Matti."

"Maybe." He gave her a lopsided smile. "But you'll have to get used to it. You're stuck with me until Matt gets here."

He winked and turned to Avenly who was desperately trying to get him to look at a butterfly that had landed on her finger.

Behler's gaze lingered on him, still amazed by how much comfort the promise of Kellum's presence brought.

24

Avenly and Warln left to go back to the stables, leaving Kellum and Behler alone.

Kellum walked over to Storm and grabbed something out of the satchel hanging off the saddle. Behler watched as he walked back over and sat down next to her. He'd brought lunch with him, and he handed her a piece of soft bread.

She took a bite. "Mm, it's good."

"Ama makes the best bread. Here, try this." He handed her a jar full of something dark purple and thick. "Spread it on the bread." He handed her a knife.

She popped the top off the jar and smelled the contents inside. "Grizzleberries?" she asked, eyeing the jar.

"I know you hate them, just try it," he said with a grin.

She took a cautious nibble, then raised her eyebrows – delightfully surprised. "It's sweet!"

"They mix in syrup from amberly trees."

She took another bite. "The last time Matti and I went to the river, we joked about eating the grizzleberries from the tree." She chuckled at the bittersweet memory of her friend. That feeling of betrayal tingled in her stomach again. "Um," she began, "Avenly mentioned that Matti is best friends with our brothers."

Kellum shrugged. "Sure, they're good friends."

"Funny," she said, quieter than before. "I always thought *I* was his best friend." The words sounded so childish out loud, and she immediately felt embarrassed that she'd said them.

"Oh." Kellum put down his piece of bread and leaned back. "Avenly is a little girl whose entire world is what you see in this village. Matti's best friends here – in Ardin – are Luke and Fenn, but you're his true best friend." He gave her a reassuring smile. "In *all* of Elium."

Behler sighed, still feeling sorry for herself. "No." She shook her head. "How can I be his best friend when there were so many lies between us?"

"They weren't lies – not really. They were...omissions. And I promise you, if he could have told you without Lorna murdering him, he would have."

Behler shrugged, not quite ready to let go of her self-pity. "I guess you're right."

Kellum smirked. "I usually am."

Behler rolled her eyes. "Gah...sometimes you really do remind me of Matti." She leaned back and let the warmth from the sun wash over her face. It helped her feel a little better. They sat quietly while Ciela and Storm grazed a few yura lengths away. "I like your grandfather," she said after a while.

"Most people do." He picked a blade of grass and twisted it between his forefinger and thumb, tossed the grass aside, and then picked another, repeating the same process as before. "Grampa was the leader of the Revalars when they first came through the doorway from Arda. He was their leader until he was injured. It was hard for him to accept that he couldn't fight like he used to. I think that's what made him push my father to try and take his place as Revala captain. Apa wanted nothing more than to please him, but my father was never quite good enough – at least in Grampa's eyes. That's what I've heard, anyway. I was pretty young the last time I saw him." He rubbed his face roughly with his palms. "I'm sure it was true – most of it, at least. Grampa wanted his entire family to be the most elite of the Revalars. That's the reason I was in Betham. He thought it would do me good to be out there. It was our family's duty – making those kinds of sacrifices." Kellum's voice grew quieter. "I'd give just about anything to fight by his side now. But," he sat up, "it's too late for that."

When he didn't continue, Behler carefully asked, "What happened to him?"

Kellum dug his heels into the soil in front of him. "He died on a scouting trip to Kilgen. He and nine others were trying to find out if there was a way inside the city walls. They planned to get close enough to Varek to assassinate him."

So, there *was* an assassination attempt. "What happened?"

Kellum bit his lower lip and his shoulders rose slightly as he took a deeper breath. "The plan failed and almost all the Revalars were executed in their sleep, including my father."

"I'm so sorry." Her words felt empty compared to what she wanted to say to him.

Kellum tried to shrug it off. "I never really knew him, so it's hard to feel sad about it." He looked up at her as if sizing her up.

"What?" she asked, squirming a little under his gaze.

"Your father, he was there too."

"Yeah? So, he really was going to try to kill Varek?" It took her a moment longer to realize what Kellum was saying. "What happened? He escaped?"

"He left the group to come back here. It was the night you and Fenn were born."

149

"Oh, Kellum…" she reached out and touched his shoulder.

Somewhere in the grass a crooner bug rubbed its wings together, calling to its mate. Soon, in a different area of the field, the mate called back.

Kellum traded the blade of grass he'd been holding for a stick that had found its way into the middle of the field. "I want to get something off my chest," he said. "I was angry with you when we were little for pulling me away from my family. It was easy to be obnoxious around you because of how I felt. My stupid kid brain was mad that your father was still alive and mine wasn't, all because of a twist of fate. And then you started trying to be nice to me. At first, it just made me angrier with you, but as I got older, I realized it was no more your fault than it was mine. We were both trapped there in Betham because of our families' decisions." He snapped the twig. "I wasn't being completely honest when I said I chose to leave Ardin all on my own. Grampa pushed for me to go, and I just wanted to please him. That wasn't your fault.

"When I understood that, that's when I started feeling differently about you. But by then… you were done with me." Behler started to object, but he smiled and held up his hand to silence her. "It's okay. I don't blame you. You should've been done. Like I've said, I was a jerk."

Behler chuckled. "And now here we are."

"Here we are." He laughed. "No one planned on that, that's for sure. It was supposed to be Matti."

"He's lucky he's not here. I'd kick the kak out of him for keeping this all from me." The two of them laughed loudly, but then Behler thought about him out there, most likely fighting, and her mood immediately turned sober. "At least I hope he is," she said softly. "Lucky, I mean."

Kellum stopped laughing. He exhaled deeply and looked up at the sky. "Me too."

Behler didn't want to let her thoughts linger so she quickly said, "Let's do some training. Kintars."

"Gladly," Kellum said, welcoming the distraction.

After putting Ciela and Storm away, the rest of the day was spent running through familiar routines with their kintars. Sera showed them both a few moves with the draka, and by the time the sun was setting, each was breathing heavily and covered in sweat. Behler's muscles were pleasantly sore.

"Not bad," she said to Kellum as they packed up to head home.

"Yeah," Kellum said, squinting into the sky as he took a big drink from his canteen. "Next time I won't go so easy on you."

Behler raised an eyebrow, grinning at his cheekiness. This Kellum was someone she could really get used to.

25

After the sun had set that night, a group of elders gathered in the Great House. Sera, the only second generation Trular in attendance, and Warln sat at the end of a large wooden table. The top had been worked until it was smooth and without splinters. The grain of the wood ran beneath a coat of a thick, clear sheet of treated amberly tree sap, flattened under pressure until it was as crystal clear as glass and hard as stone.

"We must think about what we will do if none of the Revalars return." Penelope asked. "We don't know what happened to the group in Betham, and we haven't heard from the other scouts in days." She glanced over at Sera. "We don't know where Fenn is," she said gently. "We can't put all of this on Behler's shoulders."

"Certainly not," Warln agreed. "She can't fulfill the foretelling alone."

"Fennix will return," Sera said confidently. "You all know him. You know he needs space and time."

An old man with a large scar across his forehead and a missing ear cleared his throat. "What if he doesn't this time? I'm sorry to be so blunt, Sera, but there aren't a whole lot of us here in the village who can fight. Most of us here in Ardin are old and broken or too young to carry a sword. We must prepare as if we have no one coming back to help us. We need to start thinking about what to do if the foretelling isn't fulfilled." He coughed to clear his throat. "We could return to Arda."

"And let Elium fall?" Penelope snapped. "That doesn't sound like you, Shael."

He shook his head, forcefully. "Of course not. We could bring back help."

The room fell quiet. They all knew the risk in that choice. Time passed faster on Arda. Five hundred years had gone by there. No one had come through the danari in decades. Arda's status was a mystery.

"Fennix will return, Shael," Sera repeated, her rising blood pressure making her voice shake.

Vira, Kellum's great aunt, sat at the opposite end of the table as Sera and Warln. "The village is full of the elderly and children – and injured Revalars. We can't win this battle alone...not even if Fennix does return."

"My group from Betham and the other Revalars are out there fighting." Kellum said from the doorway. He didn't like the idea of them meeting this way, in secret. It felt like he was betraying Behler, but that's also why he stayed so that he could be her voice...and her informer if he needed to be. "I'm sure they're out there. And Fennix will return – soon. He's always taken his role in this seriously, no matter what he portrayed to others."

Kellum glanced and caught his grandfather's gaze. For a fleeting moment, he thought he saw respect in the old man's eyes.

Vira shook her head, the doubt clear on her face. "Without thaelic, we just don't know what is happening, with Fenn or with anyone else."

"No, we don't know what's happening." Warln agreed. "But that also means that we don't have any reason to believe that the Revala has been defeated."

"But the Armigoth and Varek must have grown stronger if we can't find the Deep Thread," Shael pointed out.

Everyone in the room had their eyes on Warln. "Yes, that seems to be the most obvious explanation," he said. "But that doesn't mean the Revala isn't still out there putting up a fight. We can't become so discouraged that we become hopeless. We all know that will lead to nothing good." He took a deep breath as he gathered his thoughts. "Behler and Fennix will turn seventeen in a few months. The Armigoth and Varek may be growing in strength, but the twins will do the same. We've seen it with Fenn and those in Betham reported the same in Behler. I believe everything is beginning to happen quickly and we must be stronger than we ever have been before. Losing thaelic is probably just the start of things to come. Our mental fortitude will be put to the test as much as our physical strength. Now, let's think about some *strategy* since we don't know about the Revala."

"We could send a messenger to Halaanvail. Perhaps they will fight with us," Vira said.

"Would they?" Shael asked.

"They would," Warln said confidently. "If they knew that to not fight would mean their own doom. If it comes to it, we will send for them, but not yet."

Penelope nodded. "We're safe here in the forest. Even from the beast they've brought from the north. The Arbirans will cloak us. I agree with Warln to go ahead with what we've always planned. The Revelars will come." She looked at Sera. "And we will believe in Fennix's return."

"We're safe," Warln agreed, "But we still need to have a plan if the village is breached. Children and the injured should have a place to gather where they can leave immediately."

"The stables," Penelope suggested. "They will need wagons and supplies that can easily be stored there."

"Agreed," Warln said.

"Someone will need to work with Behler. Teach her the Trular ways," Shael said.

"I'll do it," Kellum said quickly.

"Kellum," Warln said, "your years in Betham have taught you a lot, but not everything."

"We've trained together our entire lives," Kellum argued.

Warln shook his head, holding his hand up to stop Kellum's words. "Precisely why she should learn from someone else now."

His grandfather's comment cut deeply. Warln might as well have punched him in the gut. "She's just been thrown into a world she barely understands. At least give her something from her past she can hold on to for now. That's me." Kellum had rarely stood up to his grandfather, but this felt as if he were standing up for Behler more than for himself.

Warln studied his grandson's face for a few moments, pleased that Kellum was becoming such a leader. "You may be right," he finally conceded, "You *should* work with her. But we will also assign others to train her in the Trular ways. The more people she learns from, the stronger she'll become." He let his gaze linger on Kellum. "That doesn't make your role any less important. It just means you're not alone in carrying it." His gaze went around the room. "We may be old and broken, but we still can go a few rounds in the circle."

A few of the older Trulars around the table chuckled quietly and nodded. Warln's forehead wrinkled. "Friends, we've been too complacent, relying on the Revala to fight this war. This will be the battle to stop the Armigoth's spread, and we *all* must be willing and ready to fight. We know what will happen if it's allowed to spread through a danari."

A few of the Trulars shifted uncomfortably in their chairs. It had been many years since they had seen any real battle. Warln looked back at Kellum. "And if that means you and Behler teaching us a few things, that's all the better."

An awkward silence settled over the group, each mulling over their own thoughts. Finally, Penelope said, "I think everyone should spend more time in the circle in the coming days."

Warln turned back to the table. "Agreed. We'll start tomorrow. And we should include children who are old enough to carry a bow or kintar, even if they aren't of age yet. They need to know how to defend themselves – if it comes to that."

Kellum turned and stepped outside. His nerves were shot after the interaction with his grandfather, and Warln's last comment only made it worse. Thinking about Avenly having to defend herself – he hadn't ever thought about that before. He'd fallen into the same trap as others in Ardin, believing it would always be a safe place.

As he stepped into the cool night, a crooner bug was somewhere nearby chirping methodically. Stars reflected in the clear water of Abawon Lake. The eldest Arbirans stood nearby, silently watching over the lake and the village. The large Arbirans in the village, along with the nearby well that contained the village's aji supply, were the epitome of how life in Ardin was so much different than his and Behler's had been. The smaller, younger Arbirans near Betham could only provide them with small amounts of aji at a time. The Trulars had hauled barrels of it from Ardin whenever they could, but they still had to ration what they had, saving it for times like when Samuel was injured.

He looked across the lake toward his mother's house. His brother and sister were there, sleeping. Luke had been treated for his badly broken arm and collarbone then ordered to bed. Avenly had such an exciting day she'd barely made it to bed after dinner before passing out.

They were his family and he barely knew them. At least he didn't know them in the ways that really mattered. He threw a small pebble he'd been rolling between his fingers into the pond and heard the *blurp* as it hit the water. There was no veil over the village tonight, and the stars and the moon were bright enough that he could watch as the rings moved out across the lake.

Kellum sat there in the peace and quiet with the sound of the insect behind him. He wasn't sure how long he'd sat there before the meeting door flung open and everyone started filing out and into the night.

Across the village, Behler sat up in bed, jolted out of sleep by a terrible dream. She didn't remember most of it as she sat up in bed panting and trying to catch her breath. But the feeling she'd had in the dream still lingered, as if she'd pulled it out of the dreamworld with her. There was a lone image she couldn't get out of her mind – cold black eyes staring at her full of hate. And there'd been something else: voices speaking is raspy whispers all at once. They spoke over each other, so it was impossible to tell what they were saying.

She pulled the covers up tightly under her chin and shivered as if the whispers were right in her ear. Goosebumps popped up all over her arms and legs and she instinctively pulled the covers over her head as if she were a small child terrified of the dark.

Even the soft sheets and comfortable bed couldn't keep her from missing her Betham home.

"Lorna," she whispered. "Where are you?"

26

Behler's bad dream clung to her long after she got out of bed the next morning. That, along with the feeling of dread in the pit of her stomach, was making the sunny morning feel gloomy and oppressive. Eager to get out of the house and into the sunshine, she jumped up from the table as soon as Kellum walked through the front door.

"Ready?" She asked but didn't wait for an answer before she grabbed her bow and headed for the door. Feeling the smooth wood of her bow in her palm made her feel a little better. She was happy that she hadn't left it in the small chest Warln pointed out in Ciela's stall. He'd told her most everyone left their weapons in them, so Behler had put everything except her bow and a handful of arrows inside. She noticed Kellum had his as well.

At the training fields, a good-sized group – a couple dozen at least – was mingling about, gearing up and preparing to train. Some had their drakas, some had kintars, and some had bows. Warln was busy setting out bales of hay and other targets for archery practice. He had his own bow sticking out from the quiver on his back.

"Sera mentioned that we'd have company today, but I didn't expect this," Behler said. She could already feel her nerves starting to flutter in her stomach.

"It's good. They need to be ready," Kellum said. He turned and looked at her. "Just do what you do."

Luke was mingling among some other boys, all of them with kintars. He was still nursing his arm a bit, but he had far more use of it than he should have – all thanks to aji and whatever treatment he'd received.

Behler pretended not to notice people's glances in her direction, but occasionally she'd catch someone's eye and she'd give a slight smile and nod. She knew they were all just waiting to see just what she could do.

"Might as well start with what I know," she mumbled to herself.

She headed over to the archery targets, and Kellum followed close behind. Warln nodded to her as he adjusted the last target then began walking back toward where she and Kellum stood. The soft murmuring from the gathered groups behind her fell silent, and she didn't need to turn around to know all eyes were on her.

Reaching back, she pulled an arrow from her quiver. She ran the feathered tip through her fingers. Their silky texture calmed her nerves and steadied her breathing. She took in her surroundings. The slight breeze rustling through the trees was coming from the south. The target was twenty yura lengths away.

She placed the arrow in the bow, pulled back the string so that her hand rested just at her cheek. Most of her brain forgot about the eyes glued to her back. She exhaled and released the arrow and an instant later it struck dead center in the target. She reloaded and aimed at the next farther target. After hitting that one and the next just as easily, Kellum said, "I'll be right back." She turned to ask him where he was going, but he was already jogging toward the stables.

She quickly turned back toward the archery targets to avoid making eye contact with any of the onlookers. She grabbed another arrow, shot it and grabbed a fourth. She'd lost track of how many arrows she'd gone through by the time she felt Kellum brush past her carrying some sort of strange contraption. It looked like a crossbow, a few of the guuns carried them – but this one was too large and heavy to be of any use on a battlefield. Some kind of catapult hybrid, she thought. He also had a large canvas sack slung over his right shoulder. She could tell by the way he was walking, whatever was in the sack was very heavy.

"What is that?" she asked cautiously.

He didn't answer but had a sly smile and a twinkle in his eye. "You'll see. Just be ready with an arrow."

He proceeded to walk out to stand next to the archery target nearest the forest's edge. He dropped the large sack to the ground and started fiddling with the crossbow-like apparatus. He reached into the bag and pulled something out and then placed it in the device. Finally, he stood up and looked toward her, giving her a slight nod to show her he was ready. She pulled another arrow from her quiver and loaded it into the bow.

Kellum raised the cumbersome machine and pointed it upward then yelled, "Fly!" He pulled a lever, and his body slightly lurched back as a brown object flew into the sky.

Behler pulled the bow up and aimed quickly. She released the arrow and the sound of it slicing through the air was like music.

She'd judged the speed and height of the flying object perfectly. The arrow struck its mark just as the target reached the highest point in its arc. Sand and seeds spilled out of the split material. A grin spontaneously stretched across Behler's face.

It had been a long time since she'd hunted the quailings in the fields outside Betham, but her body had remembered, even if her mind had forgotten.

Kellum motioned to her, holding up two fingers. She nodded and readied her bow. This time, two targets flew from the device. She quickly aimed and fired, reloaded and fired again. *Thwack, thwack.*

Kellum repeated it, only with three targets. Behler hit them all. Behind her, hushed murmurs rippled through the crowd. They were all looking at her, but she didn't care anymore. She was having too much fun to mind.

When she hit four targets, the crowd behind her cheered her on.

When she hit five, the crowd hooted and clapped. Someone let out a long whistle. Another called out, 'Did you see that?' The small crowd, which had gathered silently, erupted into clapping and a few shouts of amazement.

Kellum continued shooting targets into the sky, trading up how many he would do at one time. Finally, Behler was out of arrows. She dropped her bow and began walking out to the field to track down the fallen targets along with her arrows. Kellum did the same.

"Nice job," he smiled.

Behler shrugged and smiled. "It's kind of my thing."

They walked toward another of the fallen sandbags. Casually, Kellum said, "You should work with everyone here, teach them what you know."

"I don't know anything," Behler said quickly.

Kellum stopped and looked at her as if she'd said the most ridiculous thing he'd ever heard. "Don't be stupid. You know plenty."

Behler glanced back at the group to make sure her audience was out of earshot. "I don't know enough to *teach* them anything."

"There isn't a person here who could do what you just did. I've never seen anyone shoot that many targets out of the sky," Kellum said softly but firmly.

162

"Plus, you know we have a much better idea of what we're up against. *We've* lived with the vlocking Horde – not them." He tipped his head behind him, toward the group of onlookers. "We should at least try to motivate them, and you are their best inspiration. Now's not the time to be modest. Step up and accept who you are." He bent down and grabbed the sandbag. Sand trickled out around the shaft of the arrow lodged in the bag. "Besides," he smiled, "being humble doesn't really suit you."

Her mouth dropped open in genuine shock. "When have I ever bragged?"

Kellum chuckled. "Out loud? Never. But you carry yourself in a way that..." he paused.

"That what?" Behler's voice rose as she tried to decide if she was going to be offended or flattered.

"That shows you know you're one of the best."

She rolled her eyes, and stifled a grin – not offended, but maybe slightly embarrassed. Glancing back at the crowd, she shook her head. "I don't know how to be a leader. I've never even thought about being one." Lorna had been so overprotective of her over the years that most of her daydreams had been about being on her own and making her own decisions. As a leader, she would be making decisions for herself and everyone else.

He handed her an arrow, but as she went to grab it, he didn't let go. He looked her in the eyes. "You can be a better leader than Lorna was because you feel for other people in ways she never could."

Behler stared at him for a moment. "If I can be half the leader she is, I'll be happy."

Kellum gently grabbed her elbow. "Bale," he said softly, "think about that dragon and the fire. We knew how bad it had gotten and even we were barely ready for what came. Those people," he gestured toward the crowd again, "they aren't ready." He let go of the arrow and stood up taller. "Besides, it's what Lorna would do."

She stared at him for a moment, knowing he knew that he'd just pulled a card she couldn't ignore. "Fine," she said, "but I'm not doing it alone. You're helping me."

Kellum smiled and gave a quick nod. "Deal." He extended his arm out so they could shake on it, grinning widely the whole time.

"Sometimes I really miss the guy you were back in Betham...you know, the one who never spoke to me." She tilted her head slightly. "Matti never made me be the leader."

Kellum laughed loudly. He bowed. "And you're welcome, my captain."

Behler, still holding one of the leaking sandbags, let a handful of sand fall into her palm then she hurled it at Kellum's feet. "Kakweed," she said, unable to contain her laughter.

Kellum dodged the sand, laughing right along with her. They quickly remembered they had an audience, so they gathered all the remaining arrows and sandbags. As they did, Behler wondered to herself what Lorna would say about her being a leader and a teacher. Would she be proud, or would she say her niece still wasn't ready?

27

Over the next two days, Kellum and Behler worked with every Trular strong enough to hold a weapon. During down times, Behler was quick to jump on Ciela and ride through the field and around the village. In the evening, when everyone else had gone home, she and Kellum worked together. He was such a better fighter than she'd ever seen in Betham. He was strong and fast, and she loved sparring with him. Lorna had good reason to send him on so many missions.

The night of the lunafet Behler found herself wishing she could stay in the training circle with him instead of going home to wash and dress for the dinner. At least she had started to make some friends through her training. And quite a few of the Trulars she'd worked with she'd already become quite fond of. Maybe the dinner would be bearable.

"Are you going to say anything tonight?" Kellum asked as they gathered up their weapons and gear.

Behler shrugged. "I guess I probably should. I just wish I knew what. I'm not one for talking to crowds."

Kellum chuckled. "I know."

She glanced up at him, wondering how he knew about her fear of speaking in front of people.

The sun was setting below the treeline, and the sky was just beginning to show signs of dusk.

She sat down and stared up at the sky; nostalgia tugged at her heart. "Do you miss home?"

"Yes...but I guess maybe I just miss the people. There wasn't much of the village left to miss since the guuns took over."

Behler remembered the sight of the poisoned river. "No, there wasn't," she agreed.

"After the Horde invaded, Meela, Dax and I used to go into the caves in the hills outside the village," Kellum said, smiling at the memory. "We'd swim in the little pool next to the cave and just get away."

"I didn't know you were friends with Dax."

"He's a nice guy. His brain just works a little differently, that's all. We took him with us once on a whim, and he just kind of always ended up there with us."

"I'm glad. I always worried about him."

"It was just something to do to get out of the village and to get away from..." he looked at her guiltily, "everything."

"Everything? What do you..." she stopped when his guilt seemed to settle in deeper, etched across his features. "Do you mean me?" She was laughing, but the thought stung a little. She wouldn't have been surprised to learn that Kellum had tried avoiding her, but she'd always thought Meela was a friend. And Dax...he'd have no reason to avoid her – would he?

"No, no," he said quickly. "It wasn't you we were trying to get away from. It was just...all of it." He looked at her. "Sometimes I just couldn't stand listening to the others talk about you and planning your future for you. I wanted them to tell you what was going on. It got frustrating to sit and listen to it, especially when they wouldn't really let me, or Meela, or Matti add much to the conversation." He raised his right eyebrow at her. "You must've wanted to get away from all of it too."

She thought of her spot next to the Arbiran. She remembered all the times she'd tried to sneak away without Mathias spotting her. She shrugged. "I guess."

He laughed loudly. "I saw you roll your eyes more than a couple times when Lorna made Mathias watch out for you."

Behler laughed. "I was hoping I wasn't that obvious."

"I hate to tell you," he chuckled, "but Lorna had meetings about what we'd do if you decided to run away."

"What!?" She was mortified at the thought. "I wouldn't have left Lorna and any of the rest of you."

He laughed. "Maybe not, but there were times you were thinking about it."

"Well...," she stammered, "I wouldn't have ever *done* anything about it." She paused. "So, what were you going to do if I had left?"

"Use the Deep Thread to find you."

"How would you have done that if I didn't even know what it was?"

He shrugged and shook his head. "You didn't need to. We would have found your Thread and waited for you to be asleep. We could have spoken to you, but you would've just thought it was a dream."

Behler was horrified. "We can just hijack a person's mind at will with thaelic?"

Kellum looked shocked. "No, no. You can only speak to people in thaelic. Besides, we would never have done that unless *absolutely* necessary. It would've been a violation since you've never been taught how to use it."

A chill ran up the back of her neck at the thought of the cold, cruel eyes she'd seen in her sleep.

Maybe instead of a dream, it would feel like a nightmare.

28

Behler dipped her toes into the bath. The water was hot enough that she had to ease herself in, gradually letting her body get used to the temperature, but once she was submerged, it was glorious. In Betham, baths had to be in the river ever since the wells had been spoiled. Behler had always cautiously waded in and washed carefully, using buckets of water to wash. Even before the wells were spoiled, baths weren't quite what they were here in Ardin. A large basin of water and a cloth were about all they had.

This Ardin bathing experience was still so new to her. She decided to push herself a little and dunk her head completely in the water. She breathed deeply to calm her nerves.

"It's completely fine," she told herself. "Don't be a baby." She scooted down until she felt the tug of water on her hair. "It's fine," she repeated and took a deep breath and went under.

It's fine.

She stayed below the surface until she could no longer hold her breath, then resurfaced and wiped the water from her eyes. "Completely fine," she said, but didn't go back under again, even when she washed her hair. A few minutes later, her mother knocked softly at the door.

"Behler?"

"Yes?"

"I put some clothes out for you there next to the tub. If you'd prefer something else, just let me know."

Behler looked over and saw a charcoal-colored dress folded neatly on the shelf. She had never seen fabric so pretty. "Thank you. They look perfect."

"Take your time," her mother said. "We don't need to be there for a while."

Twenty minutes later, after scrubbing the dirt from her face and hands, she stepped out of the tub and wrapped a towel around her. She picked up the dress and held it up. It shimmered slightly from silver threads interwoven into the weave of the material. Beneath the dress was an elaborate comb for her to place in her hair. It was made from white, iridescent stones and looked like a white loola flower with small green leaves extending away from it. It was beautiful, but she had no idea how to put it in her hair without it looking like she'd just stuck it on her head.

She combed her hair then pulled the dress over her head. The neckline was wide and sat right on the bony part of her shoulders. The bodice of the dress was form-fitting then just below her waist, the dress became free and flowing. It stopped mid-calf, very different from the longer dresses women wore outside of the forest.

"Shoes," she said. She couldn't wear her boots with something so pretty.

Just then, another knock came. "I can help you with your hair if you'd like."

Behler opened the door. "Thank you, and I'm not sure what to wear on my feet."

Sera smiled and pulled her hand from behind her back to reveal a pair of simple, black leather slip-on shoes. "I used your boots to figure out the size. Henry made them for you."

Behler smiled at the especially kind gesture. "Thanks."

Together, they walked into the sitting room. "Come sit by the fire so your hair can dry a little more."

Behler sat while her mother ran the comb through her hair for a few minutes. "No one has combed my hair since I was about six years old," she said, feeling a little awkward.

"Lorna and I used to do this all the time while we were growing up. Lorna pretty much hated it and just tolerated me doing it." Behler could hear the smile in her voice without looking. "I had to bribe her just to get her to do mine."

Soon, Sera put down the comb and Behler could feel her gently pulling pieces of her hair up while she hummed softly to herself. Finally, she felt her mother secure her work with the decorative comb.

"There," Sera said proudly. "I used to do Lorna's like that." She smiled and held up a small mirror for Behler to see herself.

She looked at the two braids that swept back and up into the rest of her hair. The comb was just above the nape of her neck, and it looked like she'd picked a loola flower and placed it in her hair. "Thank you. I didn't even know my hair could look like this."

"Erhana," her mother said.

"What does that mean? I heard Kellum say it once."

"It's Trular for thank you."

"Erhana," Behler repeated.

"Doa lau. You're welcome."

A knock came at the front door.

"That's probably Kellum," Behler said.

Her mother smiled and went to let him in.

171

When he walked into the sitting room and saw Behler, he stopped and stared for a few moments.

"You look," he cleared his throat, "good," he fumbled.

He was wearing a simple black moktole, opened at the neck. He wore dark pants and black riding boots. That along with his jet-black hair made his green eyes stand out even more.

"You too."

After a short pause, Sera spoke up. "You two go on ahead, I'll be right behind you."

"We can wait," Behler began, but Sera waved her hand dismissively.

"Go, go. I'll be right there."

So together, Behler and Kellum walked across the village, toward the Great House. The lunafet was taking place in the grassy area next to it.

The veil was just beginning to cover the sky. "I'd forgotten how magical the veil is at night," Kellum said.

Through the water-like ceiling, the stars shone brighter and glittered like jewels.

Behler looked up. "Why do you think it's here tonight?"

Kellum shrugged. "It's hard to tell why. Something could have happened far off in another part of the forest." He looked over at her and smiled reassuringly. "The forest is a very big place. The dragon would have a hard time finding us even without the veil."

She tried putting all thoughts of the dragon out of her mind. She was uneasy enough just thinking about being the center of attention at the lunafet. As they walked around the corner of the large building, she took a deep breath and tried to think how Lorna would act in such a situation. Her aunt would be strong, stone-faced and wouldn't allow anyone to see anything else.

Kellum had already pointed out how Behler was so much better at feeling than her aunt was.

Behler didn't know what she expected to see when she rounded the corner, but it wasn't a huge tent. Long poles had been staked into the ground and were holding up a large canopy. Beneath it were rows of long tables with dozens of chairs set at each, and the entire place smelled delicious. Some smells were familiar, while others were harder to identify. Drakas with glowing isari stones were placed throughout.

At the far end of the tent was a group of musicians playing mostly unfamiliar instruments, although some looked very much like those back in Betham. The music was lively and very pleasing. She laughed a little to herself when she noticed one man played some sort of wind instrument that was so large he'd taken off his shoes to play the lower keys with his toes.

Warln walked up and greeted them cheerfully. "Hello kids. Your seats are right up here." He put his arm around Behler and guided her to a table near the front of the room. Unlike the other tables, this one was round. "This is my wife, Sillar. Kellum's grandmother." An older woman stood up. She had long gray hair and rosy cheeks. Her kind smile reached her eyes, and Behler liked her immediately.

"Hello dear girl. I am so pleased you're here." The isari stones' light created an unearthly aura around her. Her skin barely had a wrinkle. She turned to Kellum, and her smile widened and her eyes lit up. "Kellum." She reached her arms out and grabbed her grandson, hugging him tightly. "I was wondering when I would get to see you."

"I thought I'd see you at the training fields," he lightly scolded her. He pulled away slightly so he could look her in the face.

"Oh, I'll be there. I'll be there." She waved off the topic.

Penelope stood up to greet Behler with that same radiant smile she'd had on Behler's first morning in Ardin. "Hello, again."

"Hi Penelope."

The older woman chuckled and made a face like she'd just bitten into something sour. "Oh no, dear, only my mother called me Penelope. Please, call me Nelly."

Behler smiled. She noticed there were still five empty seats at the large table. "Who else will be sitting with us?"

"Some of the elders," Warln said. "They're eager to get to know you better." He looked at Kellum. "Your seat is right here."

Kellum nodded and took the seat to Behler's right. A few moments later, Sera sat down in the chair on Behler's left.

Soon the table was full, and although all eyes were on Behler, there was something kind and comforting in all of them.

Nelly cleared her throat loud enough to get everyone's attention at the table." It may not be good dinner conversation, but can you tell us what it's like outside of the forest? Some of us haven't been outside of this village for quite a while."

Behler and Kellum looked at each other. "Well," Behler began, "the Horde has taken control of every village north and west of the forest, at least as far south as Roan. It fell last summer. I'm sure you know that." Penelope and the others nodded "Haalanvail, Brecken and Riverfork are the last villages in the Midowlands that still aren't occupied."

174

Kellum nodded then added, "The Gorlogs were getting more aggressive. They used to be more of a joke than a threat; now they're just unpredictable and scary."

Behler nodded. "Plus, the guuns in the Horde have always been willing to get violent, but recently that violence has been getting worse. I saw them fighting each other like a pack of dogs." She paused. "And now, of course, there's the dragon."

"We should've been out there..." Shael began, but Penelope reached out and touched his hand to quiet him. He shut his mouth and clenched his fist on the table.

Just then a boy just a little younger than Behler began setting plates full of food in front of each of those at the table, beginning with Behler. Some of the food was recognizable, but some of it was completely unfamiliar.

"I have never seen so much food for one person in my life," she whispered to Kellum.

There was roasted kogum with butter, purple leafy vegetables in a white creamy sauce, nihra stew that was as good as Kellum had said it was, roasted meats, and smoked fish from the lake. The spiced drink made Behler's cheeks warm, and she guessed there was more than just aji in it that was warming her up from the inside out. Her favorites were the fruit pies and custards that were brought out after the first round of plates had been cleared.

Finally, after she had finished and was feeling beyond stuffed, Warln stood and quieted the people down. "We are all here tonight to welcome Behler back to Ardin. It is up to all of us to teach her about who she is and who we are. And it is up to us to learn everything we can from her about who we are fighting out there." He placed a hand on Kellum's shoulder. "And of course, from my grandson

175

Kellum as well. They've seen firsthand what we're up against, and we can learn a lot from them both."

He leaned over so that only those at the table could hear. "Would you like to say anything Behler?"

She absolutely did not, but she gave a weak smile and stood up anyway.

"Hello," she said. Her voice shook. Thankfully, the ale had begun to calm her nerves. "I've met many of you at the field." She looked around to find familiar faces she could focus on, but that just made her notice how many people were looking up at her, so she focused on isari stones instead. "I hope those of you who haven't made it out to train will be there soon." She paused and tried to organize her thoughts so that when she spoke again, she wouldn't appear like a complete dimwit. Her mouth felt like it had too much spit in it, so she swallowed and continued. "Even though Kellum and I have lived outside of the forest, we're not even sure what exactly we're up against anymore. Something was changing, as if everyone who serves the Armigoth can't control their rage. We saw them fighting themselves – attacking villagers without any cause. When they poisoned the river, that's when things began to turn." Her confidence grew as she focused on facts and details instead of all those eyes staring up at her. "And of course you all know about the dragon. We don't know how many of the rebels, I mean Revalars, are left out there, but I think we have to prepare as if everything depends on us. And to be safe," she paused and took a deep breath, "we can't assume that my aunt and the others..." her voice started to shake a little and Kellum inconspicuously gently held her wrist that was below the table and out of view from the rest of the room. "We can't assume that they made it out of Betham," she said quickly to avoid choking up in the middle of the sentence. She took another deep breath to calm her nerves.

"I know you think that everything depends on me and my brother, but I'm telling you that we are going to need your help. Please, come to the fields for training. It's the only way we will be able to fight Varek and win."

She sat down, finished, but the room remained silent. Finally, Warln stood back up. "I expect to see all of you at the fields in the coming days. Check with your family elder for when your family is to train." He looked at Behler and Kellum. "We all will do all we can to help win this war." His voice cracked halfway through his sentence. Quickly, he walked away. Behler watched him move swiftly through the room and out of the building.

When she turned around, she saw that Kellum had been watching him too. "Is he okay?" she asked. "Did I say something wrong?"

He looked as puzzled as Behler felt. "No." He looked at her. "You were inspiring," he gave her his crooked grin. He turned to his grandmother and asked, "Is Grampa okay?"

"Of course," Sillar said, but she appeared a little flummoxed herself. She stood up. "I'll see you tomorrow," and leaned down to kiss Kellum on the cheek.

By then everyone else was getting up from their tables and moving about the room. A few walked over and patted Behler or Kellum on the back, promising to see them at training.

They both smiled and said they would be happy to see them there, but each kept glancing over their shoulder, hoping to see Warln walk boisterously back into the party.

Sillar found Warln sitting under the eldest Arbiran, the first he had placed when he'd arrived in Elium seventy years before. It was his "thinking" spot as he liked to call it. "Warln, what's wrong?" she asked.

He grunted and shook his head. She sat down next to him and quietly took his hand then waited for him to speak, knowing silence was the best strategy.

"He's had a difficult life," he finally said.

Sillar patted his hand. "We knew he would."

Warln grunted his agreement. "Listening to them both speak back there just made it a little more real, I suppose."

"Of course. You did what you had to do, just like we all did when we chose to leave Arda. Everything is as it was meant to be."

He nodded then sighed deeply. "Did you see when he held Behler's wrist?"

Sillar smiled. "He cares for her, that's easy to see." She chuckled a little. "He looks like his father, don't you think?" Warln nodded but didn't say anything. "He will be a good fighter," Sillar added. "A good Revalar."

Warln looked away, out over the still water of the lake. "He already is." He sighed heavily. "I hope he can forgive me one day."

"If he hasn't already, he'll soon realize there is nothing to forgive."

Warln looked into her eyes, and she was surprised to see tears glistening in them. "I've got such little time left to make him understand. The time I have left, it's not enough."

Sillar smiled and kissed his cheek. "You still have now, dear...and that's all any of us have. Make the most of it."

A leaf floated down from the Arbiran's lowest branch and Warln knew his old friend agreed with his wife.

29

Behler awoke the next morning exhausted thanks to another night of nightmares. As she walked up to the training fields, she spotted Kellum sitting on a bale of hay, so she walked over and sat down next to him.

"You don't look very good," he said.

"Thanks," she said miserably.

"Here, have some water." He tried handing her a canteen.

Grumpy, she snatched it out of his hand. "What is it with this water, anyway? How do trees make magic water?"

"Woah, woah," Kellum smiled. "Yikes!"

Behler knew she was taking her bad night of sleep out on him, so she took a big gulp of the water. "There. Happy?" But she started to feel the effects from the aji almost immediately. "Sorry. This whole place is a different world to me. It's overwhelming sometimes."

"I know." He gave her a gentle smile, and she knew he'd already forgiven her. She watched as he nodded toward the training circle. "I guess what you said last night worked."

Behler looked at the small crowd of Trulars that had already gathered at the circle.

Avenly walked up to them with Luke trailing a little behind. "Will you work with me on my kintar?"

Luke rolled his eyes behind her. "I told her I would, but she insists on working with *you*."

Behler smiled and nodded then grabbed her kintar. She was eager to do something to take her mind off the dream.

Avenly may have been the one to ask for help, but Luke was clearly happy to get into the sparring circle. It was the first time he had full use of his arm since he'd been thrown from Sabana, and Behler saw quickly that he was impressive with the sword. He made for a challenging partner. He was fast and strong but still lacked some of the practical skills he would need to fight a real enemy. It was Avenly's first real attempt at wielding a sword, and she was a natural. Behler taught her some of the tricks that she'd found helpful when she was smaller, like how to use her size to her advantage.

More people gradually included themselves in the kintar training. Soon, there were two dozen of them. Everyone over the age of twenty in the village was either a mother or a father. Their spouses were all out fighting with the Revala, and they themselves had fought with the Revala. They all could have easily stepped in the circle with any of the rebels back in Betham. Behler had them work with the younger, inexperienced Trulars.

Behler worked with Penelope and Shael learning how to anticipate an enemy's moves by watching their shoulders and hips. Just before lunch, she had an archery contest with a grizzly elder named Henry, the current cobbler of the village.

The elder Trulars surpassed Behler's greatest expectations. Many were still nearly as strong and as quick as the younger men and women, plus their experience was a clear advantage.

No doubt, Trulars aged well.

At their lunch break, Penelope walked up to Behler and Avenly. "Mind if an old lady sits with you?" she smiled.

Behler chuckled. "Not at all." She moved her canteen from the bench next to her. "But I'm not sure I see any old ladies around here," she said as Penelope sat down.

The older woman laughed deep and heartily. "Oh, Behler, thank you for saying that...but I'm indeed, an old woman – and proud of it. I've earned every ache, pain, and scar."

"You all are so strong and powerful compared to people I knew in Betham. In fact, I'm not sure I knew many people your age." She thought of Tilda confronting the Gorlog that night at the weapons' depot. If only Tilda had been able to fight like Penelope just had. Had the little old woman made it out of the village the night of the attack? Behler had to put the thought out of her head before her heart began to ache too much.

"It's our connection with the Embera," Penelope explained. "Just as the Armigoth can extend lives, the Embera extends ours, only in healthy ways. The Armigoth brings darkness, but the Embera... it is the light that chases away the darkness."

The phrase reminded Behler of something from her childhood. "Lorna once used the word Embera when I was really little. I remember asking her what it meant, and she told me it was the light that would chase away all the darkness."

Penelope's smile got even broader. "That is what we usually tell our children just before they go to sleep at night."

"Ama tells me that all the time!" Avenly said, excited to add to the conversation.

Behler smiled and hugged Avenly. "It's a nice way to fall asleep, isn't it?" Avenly nodded then went back to eating her grizzleberry jelly sandwich. Behler turned back to Penelope. "Lorna told me never to repeat the word. *Ever.*" She smiled at the memory that was such a vivid reminder of her relationship with her aunt.

Penelope nodded. "Elians wouldn't even know that word, so for you to have used it would have been a dead giveaway that you were an outsider."

Outsider.

That's what she'd been her entire life.

That's what she was when she walked into Ardin that first night.

She looked at the people scattered around the training yards. Warln eagerly helped a group of young Trulars master a jousting routine that Behler had learned when she was first learning the kintar. She remembered vividly going through the same steps with Lorna. Henry was out trying to beat Behler's number of flying targets with his bow. She remembered standing in the field with Dalen and trying to get more quailings for dinner than he did.

A pang of sadness swept through – she missed her aunt and the others more than ever. But there was something else, too.

There was a bittersweet happiness about it all.

These were her people.

This was where she belonged.

30

Dusk was settling in when the last of the Trulars finally left the training fields. Behler, Kellum, Warln, and Sera were the only ones who remained. Behler sat and sipped aji from her canteen while she watched Kellum demonstrate for Warln a shield-and-retreat move he'd designed.

Sera sat down next to her. "Would you like to get some work in with your draka?" she asked.

Behler could hear something in her mother's voice that made it impossible to say no. Despite her achy muscles, she nodded. "Sure."

"The draka is the most powerful weapon we have. It's going to be especially powerful for you once you've learned how to use it." She grabbed her own draka and hopped up. "Do you have yours?"

Behler's draka and stone were still tucked away in the chest in Ciela's stall. She ran quickly to the stable doors and smiled as she entered and heard Ciela give her a whinny and a chuff. She patted the horse's neck and back, and the horse's muscles twitched under her touch. Ciela shifted her weight around and tapped her front right hoof on the floor, and Behler knew she wanted to go for a run. "Sorry, girl. Not right now." She opened the chest, moved aside Ciela's blanket, and pulled out the draka underneath. The stone had fallen into a corner. Before Behler could even touch it, it began to illuminate a soft glow as if it sensed her presence. She quickly snatched it up and placed it in the draka's claw, then replaced the blanket and closed the chest.

"I'll see you later," she said to Ciela, standing and giving the horse's snout a quick kiss. Ciela gave her a soft snort and nibbled at her hair.

Behler walked out of the stable doors and saw that Kellum and Warln had finished up. They were standing close to one another, and Behler could hear their low voices as she made her way back across the grassy field. The glowing stone made her feel very conspicuous, and she mentally begged for the stone to go dark.

As she approached, Sera looked over at her and smiled and nodded toward Behler's glowing stone. "That should be helpful once the sun goes down."

"Yeah," Behler chuckled, a little embarrassed. "I seem to be great at making it glow, and kak at making it stop."

Sera laughed. "It's okay. We'll work on it. First, let's start with some basic moves. I'll teach you the first kara. It's like a dance that uses different defensive and offensive moves with the draka."

"Dance?" Behler blinked. The last time she'd even tried to dance she was dodging village boys at a summer festival years ago—and she'd tripped into a water barrel.

Sera chuckled. "Sort of. Don't worry, you'll be fine."

Behler nodded and smiled, silently urging Kellum and Warln to leave. She didn't want to make a fool out of herself by trying to *dance* in front of them too.

Behler watched, captivated, as Sera stepped through each movement of the kara gracefully. As Sera spun, her shirt billowed around her. Her braid flew out and whipped in the air like an additional weapon. Where Lorna had gotten brute strength, Sera had gotten powerful grace.

"Okay, are you ready to try?" Sera asked after she'd gone through the entire kara twice.

Behler smiled weakly and glanced back at where Kellum and Warln had stood minutes before. To her relief, she saw they had gone back to the stables. She sucked in air to steady herself, but she was fairly certain she was going to look like an oaf trying to replicate what Sera had just shown her. Her mother patiently went through each separate stance, watching her transition from one to the next. She gently corrected anything that needed adjustment, moving Behler's leg to the left or right, or repositioning her hand up or down the draka to change its balance.

Dusk faded into twilight. Both Sera's and Behler's stones glowed brightly, illuminating their silhouettes as they performed the kara side by side. From the shadows just inside the stable doors, Kellum smiled as he watched Behler perform the moves. She had the routine memorized by her second time through. Her long dark hair had fallen from the tie she'd pulled it up with, and as she turned and moved through the kara, it moved behind her like silky waves of trellin grass moving in the wind. The light from the stones made her dance even more beautiful.

"She's quite something, isn't she?" Warln spoke from behind him. Kellum had been so engrossed in the kara and Behler that his grandfather's voice startled him.

"Yeah, she is," he said quietly, his voice catching slightly in his throat. He coughed to clear it.

Warln stepped up beside him. "It must've been something growing up with her in Betham."

Kellum's stomach twisted. "You know we weren't close...by design."

"No, I know you weren't. I also know your years in Betham weren't easy. And I know you blame me for that." Kellum started to object but shut his mouth instead. Warln nodded. "Now, I am sorry you had to live away from your family, I want you to know that. But I'm not sorry for the person you've become because of it. You've become a great leader and fighter." Warln kicked at the rocks around his boot. "Most importantly, you have stepped up and become the person Behler needs right now. She needs stability and a rock. That's you. I'm proud of you, son. Very proud." Warln turned and squared his shoulders to him. "But you've got to tread carefully now. Love can make us do things we wouldn't normally do. It can change our thinking...affect our decisions."

"Love? But I don't..."

Warln held up a hand. "Take it from an old man, my boy. There's something there between you two. Just be careful, that's all I'm saying."

"But..."

Warln looked Kellum square in the eye. "Just be careful." Kellum wanted to object more but was taken so aback by his grandfather's words that he just nodded instead. "Well, I'll see you tomorrow," Warln said abruptly. He turned and quickly walked toward the front of the stables, whistling to the horses as he went.

Kellum watched his grandfather until he stepped outside the front door, stunned by the old man's pronouncement. When he finally turned back around, he found the light had completely faded from the sky, and Behler and Sera were standing close to one another, discussing something quietly. Behler's draka was leaning against her hip and the light from her isari stone softly illuminated her face.

Kellum's heartbeat sped up a little and he felt his cheeks flush. He hadn't let himself think about his feelings for Behler—not really. But now his grandfather had named it, and the truth clung to him like dew in the night air: he cared for her. More than he was ready to admit. He wasn't sure why his grandfather had said what he'd said. All he knew was that he couldn't deny it, at least to himself, anymore.

31

Behler and Sera had just finished up their final run-through of the first kara and were gathering their things to head home for the night.

"There are five karas all together. Would you like to get an early start in the morning and learn the second?"

Behler nodded. "Definitely." It was invigorating moving in such new ways.

"Each one gets a little more difficult. By the time you master the third, you'll be proficient with your draka. The fourth and fifth are challenging, but when you complete those, you will be lethal."

Behler looked at the stone in her draka. "Lethal?"

Sera nodded. "If that's what's called for. But the power of the isari doesn't work on all enemies, so don't abandon your other weapons."

Behler thought of her bow and the feel of letting an arrow loose to fly across a field. "Never," she said.

Sera paused. "Your father was the best I've ever seen with a draka." She looked into Behler's eyes, and her own eyes shifted and filled with a pained sadness. "Has anyone even told you his name?"

Behler shook her head, feeling guilty for never asking.

Sera's eyes were full of emotions: sadness, longing, love. "Brant. His name is Brant." Another sip of aji to calm her nerves, then she said, "There's something else I need to tell you. It's not because I wanted to hide it from you. It's just something very painful for me to speak about. After you were born, your father was captured when he returned to Kilgen to try to finish a mission he'd begun earlier."

"Kellum said he disappeared, nothing about him being captured."

"He may not know. Some things aren't spoken of. Your father was taken to the castle where he was tortured." Sera's voice cracked and she swallowed hard. "He was able to use thaelic to contact me, but only for the first week or so. A panara of Revalars tried to get into the castle to rescue him, but breaching those castle walls has been impossible." She sighed heavily. "After the second or third day, I could tell his mind was becoming scattered. He would fade in and out of thaelic, and his thoughts were completely disjointed." A sad smile touched the corners of her lips. "I couldn't take it anymore, and I gathered a group of my own to go for him. I tried to get as much information from him as I could about the castle and where they were holding him, but he was kept in a small, dark room and couldn't help me much. It didn't help that when he discovered my plan, he refused to speak to me for three days. He finally answered me while our group was on the move. We were already north of the forest and headed toward him. But that night, when he answered me, he was no longer the same man. Varek had forced thaelic-ren on him and destroyed his mind while he was doing it."

"Thaelic-ren?"

"It's a darker version of thaelic. It can be used to enter a person's mind and control them or manipulate their thoughts, and it can only be done by the strongest of us."

"Like Varek."

Sera nodded. "Unfortunately, yes. That's how he found out about you and Fenn. He was trying to get your identities when…" she stopped.

"What?" Behler asked carefully.

"Your father shut down his mind before Varek could find out. It worked, but it came at a high price. It was as if his brain couldn't quite get started back up again. I heard from your father one more time afterward. He was lost, physically and mentally. They'd tossed him out to let him wonder, at least that's what I could gather from him. I'm sure they thought he wouldn't survive on his own in that state." Her brow crinkled, and the light of the isari stones cast strange shadows across her face. "He kept repeating the same things over and over to me."

"What did he say?" Behler felt as if she were prying, but she had to know.

"He said he was lost and I could feel his fear. And," she paused, "he kept repeating your name and your brother's over and over again." Sera sighed. "We searched for him for nearly a month, but there was no trace of him. But there was something strange about that last conversation we had. It was as if we were standing in a deep fog, but I could see a symbol all around us, as if it were drawn on the air itself." Sera knelt and laid her draka down so the isari stone shone on the ground. With her finger, she drew a symbol. "This was what I saw."

Behler knelt beside her mother. Tracing the outline with her finger, she asked, "Do you know what it means?"

Sera nodded "It's a symbol from an isolated tribe near the coast. I hope that maybe he's there, with them. But they aren't known to welcome outsiders." She looked at Behler, and the shadow cast across her face from the isari stone made her look haggard. "He was the first to hold you, after the midwife. He even gave you your name. A behler bird is a legendary animal from stories told back in Arda. Did Lorna never tell you the story?"

Behler's brow crinkled as she tried to bring the memory forward from the deepest parts of her mind. "I remember a story about a bird saving a mouse from a falcon."

"Yes," Sera's voice lit up with a grin. "That's one of the stories. That one was always your grandfather's favorite to tell us when we were children."

They walked back to the house in silence listening to the night sounds around them. A soft rain began to fall and Behler inhaled deeply.

Just before they were to step through the back door of the house, Behler asked. "Do you think he made it somehow – to the coast?"

"I don't know. I hope he found peace, whatever happened to him."

32

Behler was plagued by the nightmare again that night – but if it was someone tormenting her via thaelic, which she was becoming more certain that it was, they underestimated her threshold for where fear turned into anger. Thaelic-ren was a whole new terrifying possibility, and she knew she had to tell Kellum. She wasn't sure how to face it on her own.

Sera looked tired at breakfast – so exhausted that Behler contemplated suggesting they put off learning the next kara. The only thing that stopped her was thinking about getting to the fourth and fifth karas quickly. She was anxious to learn how to master her isari stone.

Just then thunder ripped through the sky and rattled the windows.

"Looks like we're going to get wet this morning," Sera said, looking out the window and sipping her tea. She looked utterly miserable.

Behler was just getting ready to ask her mother what was wrong when another rumble of thunder rattled the windows.

"I wonder how many will show up in this," Behler thought aloud.

"Hopefully just as many as if it were sunny." Sera looked out the window. "War doesn't wait for the weather."

She'd mumbled the last part, but Behler could already see the dark circles under her eyes beginning to diminish. The aji tea was working its magic.

"We should get going if you want to learn the second kara before the others show up," Sera said, sounding a little better.

Behler smiled and drank down the last of her tea.

The rain was coming down in sheets, and by the time the two got to the stables they were as wet as if they'd jumped in the lake on the way to the training area. They walked around the side of the stables and saw Kellum already in the circle, performing the first kara and completely oblivious that he had an audience.

His taakin lay on a bale of hay next to him, and his shirt was soaked through. It clung to him as he moved the draka around and twisted his body into the different positions, Behler could see the sinewy muscles outlined on his arms, chest, and back.

They stopped and watched him quietly, until he had completed the kara.

"Very good," Sera said when he was done.

Kellum shrugged off the compliment. "I'm rusty."

"Let's shake that rust off, then." She turned to Behler. "Why don't you both go through the first kara together? I'll watch you both and help where I'm needed."

Behler nodded. At least if Kellum was doing it, he wouldn't be able to watch her so easily. "Sure, if that's okay with Kellum."

He chuckled. "I need all the practice I can get."

Thunder rumbled around them as the two walked out to the center of the circle. "The storm's kind of nice," Behler said as she inhaled the smell of the rain.

Kellum laughed and looked up to let the rain fall on his face. "Yeah, bathing while you're training is extremely convenient."

Behler smiled and winked at him. "Well, it is helpful in keeping *you* from smelling up the village."

For a split second, Kellum's smile vanished. He blinked a couple of times as if he'd been struck, and then he smiled again and raised an eyebrow at her. "I suppose we should hope for rain all the time then."

Behler smiled back at him but saw how his years in Betham hurt him much more than he let on. Her heart ached knowing she'd helped to contribute to his misery.

Those days were over. She depended on him now, and she hoped that by confiding in him about her dreams, that would show him just how much.

They spent the early morning going over the first and second karas. Behler quickly learned the second, and Kellum remembered it after just a couple run-throughs. They had both nearly mastered it by the time everyone else started to show up.

"Tonight, we'll work on the third," Sera said. "When you have got a good handle on it, we'll start with the fourth and fifth."

Kellum nudged Behler a little. "The fourth and fifth are fun." His eyes twinkled playfully. His black hair was drenched and water dripped down over his face.

"So I've heard," Behler said, feigning indifference. She was ready to learn how to make her isari stone do what she actually wanted it to instead of it seeming to act with a mind of its own, endlessly tormenting her.

Around mid-morning the rain finally let up enough that Behler no longer had to squint to keep the water out of her eyes. She was happy that everyone who was supposed to attend the morning training showed up, along with a few extras. Everyone was even in good spirits despite the soggy weather.

By lunch, the clouds parted to allow the sun to dry everything and everyone out. Behler made sure she and Kellum sat off from everyone to eat their lunch so they could talk. "I need to talk to you about something."

Kellum swallowed his food and turned to her. "Okay. What's up?"

Behler was nervous to share her thoughts, but she had to speak them out loud even if it was just to get them out of her own head. "I've been having strange dreams, only I'm not sure they're really dreams at all."

Kellum leaned in a little closer. "Tell me about them."

"There's not a lot of details. All I can remember when I wake up is that I was surrounded by darkness, but I can always tell someone is there with me. I can feel someone watching me. Sometimes I can see eyes looking at me, just a shade lighter than the darkness around us. The rest of the face is fuzzy, but something about it feels...almost familiar. I thought maybe it could be someone – maybe Fenn – trying to reach me...but it feels like whoever is behind those eyes hates me. I'm worried it could be Varek. Maybe he's trying to use thaelic-ren."

Kellum pondered the idea. "It could be, but usually to use thaelic-ren, the two people have to be touching – but, I would say that anything is possible at this point."

Behler focused on the apple she was holding. She rubbed at it with her thumb, feeling its waxy skin. A green apple – her favorite. "Is there a way I can keep the dream from happening if it is thaelic or thaelic-ren? Some way I can block whoever it is from getting in my head?"

"Sometimes when I don't want to be bothered, like if I'm going to nap or just want to have some quiet time without even feeling the pull of the Thread, I picture my mind as a locked room. I imagine a heavy wooden door with multiple locks in my mind, and I picture it slamming shut and locking." He chuckled. "Pretty dumb, but it usually works. I think you should try something like that. Something you can lock up and keep safe. Tonight, before you fall asleep, imagine every detail of it, and fall asleep with the image in your mind."

Behler took a few bites of apple, trying to enjoy it despite the grim topic of conversation. "I hate that I can't use thaelic but someone else might be able to get in my head."

"You've never even tried it before, not with another Trular." He studied her face for a few moments. "Maybe you should try."

"Really?"

"Let's just see what happens." Kellum shifted toward her and put down the piece of cheese he was eating. "Close your eyes and imagine the person you want to talk to. Reach out with your mind. Picture a rope reaching from you to them."

Behler closed her eyes and pictured Mathias' face. Then she imagined a rope stretching from her chest to wherever he might be. "What now?"

"Focus on your breathing. And here," she felt Kellum's fingers gently touch her wrist. "Put her finger here and focus on your heartbeat. It helps to keep your mind centered."

Behler put her finger on her wrist, but in the end, it didn't help. When she opened her eyes, Kellum asked, "Did you feel anything?"

She shook her head. "No." The disappointment she felt was clear in her voice.

Kellum picked up his piece of cheese again and put it between two chunks of bread. "It's okay. It's difficult to reach out to someone the first time you try it. Usually, the first time we use thaelic, another person initiates it."

Behler thought of those eyes staring at her in her dream. "I hope it's not Varek and just a run of the mill nightmare."

Kellum nodded sympathetically. "Me too."

Behler took a sip from her canteen. She looked over at Kellum. "What do I do if it is?"

Kellum swallowed down a bite of cheese and bread. Then with a wicked grin and glint in his eye, said, "Tell that kakweed to get the vlock out of your head."

Behler had just taken a sip of water, and when she laughed, it came shooting out her nose...which just made her laugh even harder. Kellum laughed, but apologized for making her laugh, which made them both start laughing all over again.

They were still laughing when the light around them changed. It was as if someone had put a giant lens in front of the sun and amplified the light. Both of them fell silent as they watched what looked like a giant sheet of watery glass form overhead.

"It's the veil," Kellum whispered. "I haven't seen it during the day in a long time."

All around them, people stood up from where they'd also been eating lunch, looking around with the same confused expression Behler and Kellum had.

"It's probably nothing, just like it usually is at night," Kellum said – but no sooner had he said it than they heard the sound of the dragon's fleshy wings. *Thuwat. Thuwat. Thuwat.*

Behler's heart leapt up in her throat as her mind was instantly back in Betham. "It's found us," Behler whispered, terror threatening to take over her entire body.

Kellum held up his finger to his lips. "No," he whispered, "it's searching." He turned toward the closest group of people and motioned for them to stay calm.

Thuwat. Thuwat. Thuwat.

"It can't see us; the Arbirans have hidden the village," Kellum whispered.

And then it was there, above them. It was the same dragon from the village. Behler recognized it easily. She silently begged every living thing in the village to remain still, despite the veil's protection.

Thuwat. Thuwat. Thuwat. A second dragon trailed behind the first.

She held her breath, expecting the dragons to spot them through the veil, but to her relief both dragons continued on as if nothing below them was of interest. Minutes after both dragons flew overhead, the village was still eerily silent.

Slowly, everyone started moving around again. People murmured and moved a little slower for the rest of the day, as if walking on eggshells just in case the dragons made another flyover. The veil stayed overhead for an hour after the dragons flew over. Although the episode was scary and more than a little worrisome, Behler also felt it was a gift. Now the Trulars in the village had seen the fearsome creatures that had destroyed Betham. Their sanctuary may not be as untouchable as they thought.

33

After the flyover from the dragons, Behler and Kellum suggested everyone keep a set of weapons in their homes as well as in the stables. It seemed a logical step after seeing how close danger had come.

With Fennix still missing and the threat of the dragons more tangible, Behler felt fueled by the thought that she may face serious threats without him. Each day, she stayed in the training circle until late into the night trying to perfect the third kara. It was far more difficult than the first two, requiring her to move her body in ways she never thought possible. Her muscles ached each night, even after a hot bath. Finally, a week after she first started it, she had the third kara mastered, and the very next morning, she was at the training fields with Sera before dawn, eager to start to fourth.

Sera held up her draka and looked at the stone. "Using your isari stone is a little like using a piece of glass to focus the light of the sun. Instead of sunlight, though, you are focusing Embera's power. It's all around us. You'll get better at it over time, but to begin with, it's easiest if you have a word or phrase for each of the things you want your stone to do. For example, if you'd like your stone to glow, you could say light. If you need warmth, you could say heat, and so on. Sometimes it may take a while to find the right word that works for you. The isari stones often respond to our native language much better." She leaned over and picked up her draka. "Aluma!" she commanded, and the stone began to glow brightly. "Aluma means light from a fire in our old language. Your turn. Close your eyes and imagine you're in a dark room. You can't see a thing, and all you want to do is light up that place. Feel all your energy running through your hand, into the draka, and through the stone. Now, give your command."

"Aluma," Behler said, and even with her eyes closed, she could see a change in the light in front of her. She opened them to see her stone glowing brightly, bright enough that she had to squint her eyes to look at it.

"Good." Sera smiled.

"How do I control how bright it is?"

"Concentrate. Close your eyes again if you need to."

Behler did and imagined the stone was part of her mind. She tried to ease it down into a dim glow.

"Good," her mother said again.

Behler opened her eyes, and the stone was noticeably dimmer.

"What's the Trular word for off?" Behler asked, giggling.

Sera laughed, too. "Uhret."

Behler looked at her strone. "Uhret, vlock-it," Behler laughed. "Would you please just uhret?"

The stone flared as if teasing her then went off.

Behler and Sera both erupted in soul-healing laughter.

When Sera could talk again, she said, "Now, let's try some others." She looked over at a bale of hay. She lifted her draka and said, "Sho." The bale of hay rose a couple yura lengths above the ground as if it suddenly became weightless. "Ahmei," she said, and the bale moved across the ground. "Shuka." The bale fell back to earth.

Behler tried the commands on the same bale. For about half an hour, it simply sat there, mocking her. But finally, it started to wobble a bit, then rock to and fro. Finally, it lifted off the ground enough to see daylight beneath it.

"You'll get better as you practice. Eventually, you won't even need to say the words out loud. It will be a split-second thought in your mind, and your stone will do what you want it to. The next command I'm going to show you is probably the most valuable of the skills you can use your stone for. It's a shielding command. It can protect you from regular weapons, and it can also protect you from becoming like that bale of hay over there. It blocks other stones from working on you. The command is indar. Here, try to make me lift off the ground like the bale." Sera walked away a few steps then turned and faced her.

"I don't think that's a good idea," Behler hesitated.

"I'll be fine." Sera gave a reassuring nod.

"Okay." Behler took a deep breath then said, "Sho."

Sera immediately held up her draka. "Indar!" Behler could see something nearly invisible burst out from Sera's stone, like the wave of heat off a flame. Seconds later, she felt a strong breeze pass by, only it felt like it had passed right through her. "Good. We'll practice that one later. Let's continue to practice the others for now."

They spent the morning practicing the commands. They would begin the fourth kara that night. Soon, it was time for others to join them for the day. They sat down and sipped from their canteens while they waited for others to join them.

"There's one more crucial thing to know. The isari stone will sometimes need time to rest, I guess that's the best way to put it. Focusing all that energy through it, the stone risks injury if pushed too far. And remember, some enemies aren't as affected by the energy of our stones as others. The isari won't always be enough. When our stone isn't enough, we fight with our other weapons like the shadow wants our soul."

Behler grinned. That was something Lorna would've said.

She touched her stone and thought *aluma*. The isari glowed, soft and steady.

She smiled again, pleased with herself. Being proficient at weaponry was one thing. She'd been around those sorts of things her entire life. But making a stone perform such amazing things – well that felt like something else entirely.

When the time came, she *would* fight like the shadow wanted her soul, and maybe, just maybe, she'd be able to leave some scars before the shadow took it.

34

Every day for the next week, Behler practiced the fourth kara with anyone who would get in the circle with her. At first, she used a stuffed dummy to practice the more dangerous isari commands, but eventually she felt comfortable going up against some of the more experienced Trulars. The kara was like the previous ones only in that it also had steps to learn and body movements to master. The rest of it was based completely on the power of the isari stone. She improved a little each day until Sera finally said, "You're ready to learn the fifth."

"The fifth kara is a little....uh....a little more *intense*," Sera said. Behler and Kellum stood with their drakas at their sides. Luke, who had asked to join them as soon as he learned what they were working on, stood on Kellum's other side. "Kellum, have you ever learned the fifth?"

"Yes, but it's been a long time....and I never really mastered the commands. There was never enough time during my visits here." Although he tried to hide it, Behler could hear the sadness in his words.

Sera turned to Luke. "What about you?"

"I've practiced it a few times with Fenn."

She looked directly at Behler. "This is where our stones become truly lethal." She turned and directed her isari stone at a melon sitting on a bale of hay. "AAH!" she cried out. A beam of blue-green light shot from her stone into the melon, shattering it into mush.

Behler's eyes shot open wide, and she looked over at Kellum who was smiling.

He chuckled. "I'd forgotten how impressive that is."

Sera turned back to them. "Now just imagine that as your enemy's head," she chuckled and Behler grimaced at the thought. "It doesn't have to be quite so dramatic." She turned to a second melon and shot another beam of light at it. The melon didn't move, and the only sign that anything was different was the perfect circular hole burned completely through it.

"How do you keep it from burning through everything behind your target?" Behler asked.

"Practice," Sera smirked. "Okay, let me demonstrate the fifth kara." She started to begin then looked back up at them. "You might want to take a few steps back. The last move packs a bit of a punch." They all took five very big steps back so that they were clear of the training area, and Sera began. The graceful and elegant moves of the kara were now in stark contrast to Sera's blasting through the melons that had been placed on each of the bales of hay on the circle's circumference. After she'd obliterated the last one, she jumped, spinning in the air, and brought her draka down hard. As it struck the ground, she shouted, "*Kahto*!" A burst of energy erupted from her isari stone—like the shield command Behler had seen before, but larger. The wave ripped the dirt from under Sera's feet and shot outward. In an instant, it struck Behler, Kellum, and Luke, knocking them all backward.

Behler looked over at the guys, her eyes wide.

"Remind me never to spar with your ama," Luke smirked. He brushed dust and dirt off his moktole.

Behler laughed uneasily as she stood up and brushed off her own share of dirt.

"Ready to give it a try?" Sera asked.

Behler gave her mother a crooked grin. "Um, sure." She'd been anxiously waiting to learn this kara, but now part of her wished she could go back to the simpler, less fruit-smashing ones.

Over the next two hours, long past sunset, numerous melons and squash were blown to smithereens. Three bales of hay caught fire, and an overzealous *kahto* command left them all covered in dirt and a decent-sized crater in the center of the circle.

Sera was chuckling as they all packed up for the evening. "You'll all get it, don't worry. You just need to have confidence in yourself that you can control the energy from the isari stone. And like I said, that just takes practice."

Behler chuckled as she brushed some of the dirt from her hair. "More for some of us than others." She wickedly eyed Luke.

"What?" he asked too innocently. "I meant to do that." They all laughed, and Luke joined in. He looked over at the crater at the circle's center. "Yeah, I should probably get here early tomorrow and fix that."

"I'll give you a hand," Kellum said. He sheepishly eyed the training circle. "I need to replace a couple bales of hay myself."

Sera and Behler laughed even harder at them. "It just comes with it," Sera said. "Broty burned down an entire barn when he was learning."

Behler and Kellum stopped what they were doing and burst into joyful laughter as they imagined their old, burly friend as an inexperienced boy.

The group headed off the field. When they neared the stables, Luke said, "I'm going to check on Sabana."

"I'll come with you," Kellum said. "I need to make sure Storm has some fresh hay and water."

They said goodbye to Sera and Behler and walked through the stable doors. Sillar stood waiting for them.

"Gam!" Luke said, surprised to see her.

"Hi boys," she said with a slight smile. "I was hoping you would come in before heading home." Her right eyebrow rose impishly. "I was watching you out there." She smiled wryly. "I think you both should keep practicing." She chuckled then her face became serious. "I need to talk to you boys."

Kellum and Luke looked at each other then back at Sillar. "About what?" They both asked at the same time.

Sillar sighed. "Your grandfather."

"What's wrong with him?" Kellum asked immediately.

Luke turned to him. "What makes you think something's wrong with him?"

Kellum kept his eyes on his grandmother. "There is something, isn't there?"

Sillar nodded. "He has lidic disease." Her expression was calm and gentle— the kind worn by someone who's had time to make peace with the weight of bad news.

Both boys stood speechless for a few moments.

"But how do you know?" Luke asked desperately. "He seems fine."

Sillar walked to him and took his hand in hers. "The symptoms start slowly, He has shown them." She sighed. "His father had it before we left Arda."

"But..." Luke started. "But..."

"Is that why he's been so different lately?" Kellum asked, thinking of the exchange they'd had in that very spot.

Sillar nodded. "But it's not a symptom of the disease. It's simply that the disease has made him...realize what's important."

"How long will he be…okay?" Luke stammered.

Sillar lovingly touched Luke's arm. "No one knows. It's different for everyone. He'll slowly become weaker. His mind and body will deteriorate, and it will continue until he can no longer walk and won't recognize us."

Kellum closed his eyes. He didn't want to imagine his strong and commanding grandfather in such a way.

Sillar clasped her hands together and took a deep breath. "Well, enough of that dismal talk. I just wanted you both to know. He's fine for the time being with just occasional symptoms popping up, so don't go moping around like he's dying tomorrow. You know he would be furious about that." Luke and Kellum stood silently. "Boys?" she said, firmly.

"Okay, Gam," Kellum said.

"Okay," Luke echoed softly.

Sillar put a hand on each boy's cheek. "He's fine," she said reassuringly. "But you both deserved to know."

"Thank you for telling us." Kellum said.

"Now, both of you get home and get some rest. You'll need to get out here bright and early if you want to practice the fifth kara without wounding or maiming half the village." She winked then turned and walked away.

Both boys stood frozen in place for a few moments before they silently went about checking on their horses and tidying their stalls and weapons. Later, as they walked home, Luke finally broke the silence.

"Do you think he'll still try to fight as part of the Revala?"

Kellum rubbed his eyes. "Lidic disease can progress extremely fast out of nowhere. He could endanger himself and everyone else." He looked up through the veil that had formed while they were in the stables, each star shimmering brightly. "But, yes, I think he'll still try to fight anyway."

"So, what should we do?"

Kellum scoffed. "Not let him."

Both boys fell silent and remained that way the rest of the way home. They knew that not letting their grandfather do something was like saying they wouldn't let the sun come up.

Somehow, the sun always managed to find its way into the sky.

35

It had been nearly four weeks since Behler and Kellum arrived in Ardin. Each day that passed brought her birthday closer, and her thoughts began to dwell on what changes may be about to happen to her. There had been no word from the Revala, and returning scouts had not been able to locate them. The scouts did bring back news, though, and it was grim; the darkness of the Armigoth reached nearly to the northernmost edge of the forest. Behler and Kellum climbed up one of the guard towers every day to check its progress.

And her sleep was still plagued by the dream. The image of the locked door helped sometimes, but not always. It had gotten bad enough that she dreaded lying down each night.

Kellum could see the heaviness of the foretelling starting to weigh on her, much like it had on Fennix. "Let's take the horses for a run," he said one evening after they'd finished up with training.

"It's getting dark," Behler said.

"That's okay. The veil will make it bright enough for us." The veil had been appearing overhead more often as the Armigoth crept closer. "I want to show you something."

They went inside the stables and saddled up their horses then met back outside.

"Here," Kellum motioned for Behler to hand him her draka. She watched as he slipped it into a slot she'd never paid much attention to before. It allowed the draka to lay flat against the right side of Ciela's body with the stone end resting just at the horse's shoulder. Kellum looked at her and smiled smugly.

"Convenient." She pulled herself up into the saddle. "Where are we heading?"

Kellum pointed toward the north end of the field. "That way."

"Great!" She smiled and tapped her heels into Ciela's side while Kellum was still pulling himself up into Storm's saddle.

"Hey!" She heard Kellum cry out as she rode off.

"Aluma!" She cried out, laughing as she went. The stone lit up brightly enough that she could see many yura lengths ahead of her and to the sides.

Soon, Kellum caught up with her, and she could see his attempt at an angry scowl in the light of his isari stone. Too bad he couldn't keep from laughing as he rode past. She chuckled again, letting him pass since she wasn't sure exactly where they were heading anyway.

He headed straight for the treeline on the northeast corner of the village, near the kogam field. The trees were getting close quickly.

Up ahead, Kellum's isari stone flared, and the approaching Arbirans immediately began to rise out of the ground, pulling their shallow roots out of the ground. Trees slid apart, forming another passageway through the forest. The fluidity of the tunnel shimmered and sparked as they sped through, and the reflections of the stars above made it appear they were racing through the sky.

A few minutes into the forest, Kellum slowed Storm to a quick trot then to a walk.

Behler rode up so that she was directly beside him. They rode for a few more minutes in silence, the only sounds coming from the forest around them muffled through the tunnel walls. That's how she heard it before she saw it. At first it was such a low sound, she wasn't sure if it was anything at all, but it steadily became louder and stood out more from the other sounds around them.

"Ashiwae," Kellum said softly. The tunnel around them disappeared.

The muffled sounds immediately grew louder until it sounded like rain hitting the roof during an early spring shower.

Kellum motioned for her to look up ahead. She could see a natural clearing at the end of the path. A minute later, the horses stepped into the open space. The large fiery moon reflected in a large pool of water just in front of them. The sound of water splashing over large falls was so loud, she felt it deep in her bones. To their right, at the bottom of the pool, a smaller waterfall led into a large creek that, following a bend, disappeared into the forest.

Behler had never seen such a waterfall before. She looked at Kellum, but he was looking out over the water, a peaceful expression on his face. The veil over Ardin didn't reach this far out. She looked up and took in the sight of the night sky and the blanket of stars that twinkled, unobstructed, above.

"It's like...it's like the river," she said, her eyes welling up at the memory. "The way the water moves." She closed her eyes and inhaled. "The way it smells."

Kellum's eyes were twinkling. He knew he'd done well. "Want to go for a swim?" He slid down off his horse and started taking his boots off before waiting for an answer.

"A swim?" She hadn't gone for a swim since the day she'd fallen into the river. "I...I don't think so."

"Don't worry. I'm right here."

"It's just..." she began. "I haven't swum since..."

"I know. But I also know you used to be a great swimmer." He smiled. "C'mon." He winked at her...or at least she thought he did. She couldn't be sure because he immediately took off running toward the water.

She stayed put on Ciela, irritated that he couldn't have just let her sit there and be peaceful for a bit.

He let out an excited cry as he leapt into the water.

"Yeah...peaceful," she muttered. Reluctantly, she got down from Ciela. "Am I really going to do this?" She asked the horse who just nickered at her. "Yeah, but you're not afraid of the water." She chuckled and patted Ciela's forehead.

Slowly, she walked toward the shoreline.

"Come on! Get in!" Kellum called up to her.

She slipped her feet out of her boots. "I don't even know how to start to get in. I'm not just going to jump in like you did." She inspected the bank for a place where she could easily wade into the water.

"Okay highness," he teased and tilted his head toward the smaller falls. "There's some rocks over there past those reeds. Just don't twist your ankle."

Behler walked across the bank past Kellum's draka and crumpled clothes. She realized the crumple was his shirt and pants. Her head snapped up and she looked at him with wide eyes. "Are you naked?" She'd heard of people doing that in the river in Betham but would never have dared.

"Oh my... NO!" Kellum looked as embarrassed as she felt. "I've got my shorts on."

"Okay. Good," she said. Her cheeks were as hot as forge coals in the smithy. She wished she could melt into the reeds and disappear.

Instead, she made her way down to the water, then slipped only her socks off. She'd be swimming fully dressed.

Thankfully the moon and their isari stones provided enough light for her to see clearly, and the rocks weren't too treacherous. They were all worn flat and were heavy enough that they didn't shift under her weight, but she still took each step carefully in case they were wet or covered in moss.

Finally, her feet were in the water and safely on the bottom of the pool.

"Now, just walk toward me," Kellum urged her. He had swum closer and was standing so that the water came up to his chest.

The bottom of the pool felt strange on her feet as her toes sank into the soft silt. It was slightly distressing not being able to see what she was standing on. After a few steps, though, she began to feel more at ease. The spongy bottom became strangely soothing. She continued to walk until the water was up to her belly button. Her lightweight pants clung to her and felt slightly heavy, and she understood why Kellum had thrown his off. She stopped, still a couple yura lengths from him.

"Come on," he urged again. "You used to love this, remember?"

She did remember. In the summer, she and Mathias, along with countless other children from the village, would cool off by swimming in the river during its lazy, meandering dry season days. "Come on," Kellum encouraged her gently. "You'll still be able to put your feet down and touch. And I'll be right here."

"Alright." She took a few more steps and the cool water around her came up to her chest, just at her armpits. The pressure of the water on her chest suddenly felt like a vice gripping her and she panicked. She tried to back out of the water, but her feet slipped out from under her on a slick rock. Her head went under.

Frantically, she tried to find traction with her feet, but her terror was preventing her brain from telling her legs what to do. Then she felt Kellum's hands grip her and pull her out.

She clung to him as she coughed and hacked and gulped air.

"It's okay," he said soothingly. When she continued to sputter and gasp, his voice came again, but with a firmness she couldn't ignore. "Bale, it's okay."

Finally, her feet found some footing, and she was able to stand on her own.

"I just...I just panicked," she stammered.

"Yeah," he chuckled in a reassuring way. "I saw that."

She realized she was still gripping onto his arms and had her head buried in his chest and took a step back. "I'm okay now. Thanks."

He looked at her for a moment then said, "You've got to get over this."

"Yeah, yeah," she nodded. "I know."

"Let's try something else." He moved toward her. "Remember when we had floating contests to see who could float the longest?"

She smiled. "Sure."

"Remember how I always kicked your butt?" He smiled.

"What!? No way!" She laughed and splashed water at him.

He ducked, laughing, and said, "Oh I most certainly did."

"No way," she repeated.

"Fine. Let's see who can float the longest," he challenged.

"Right now?"

"Right now." He took a step toward her. "Turn around." He gently grabbed her arms to guide her so that she was standing perpendicular to him.

"What are we doing?" she asked suspiciously.

213

"Just trust me. I want you to lie back, and I'm going to hold you up until you feel safe."

Behler was skeptical. "Okay," she said finally. "No tricks."

Kellum nodded and placed his right hand over his heart. "I promise." He moved his hand from his chest and held it right between her shoulder blades. The gentle pressure of his hand made her feel a little more confident. Slowly, she leaned back, and the pressure from Kellum's hand increased under her weight. She felt her hair hit the water, get heavier as it got wet, and pull slightly at the rest of her head. She stood up quickly. The feeling of being pulled down by her own hair nearly made the panic rise within her again. "Sorry, sorry," she said quickly.

"It's okay," Kellum smiled. "I'm not going to let you go under."

Behler took a deep breath, trying to steady herself and her nerves. "I know." She took one more big breath then began to lean back again. She felt Kellum's hand providing more and more support then the tug from her hair. Finally, she was leaning back far enough that her feet were trying to come up off the bottom. She started to panic again and her body tensed.

"Trust me," Kellum said gently.

She looked up at him. "I do."

Their eyes met, and there was an understanding that passed between them; she wasn't just talking about swimming. She let her feet come up off the bottom. Kellum's right hand stayed in the small of her back, and his left hand was just at the back of her knees, helping to keep her legs straight.

"Perfect," he said. Her hair floated around her, framing her face. Her pale-yellow shirt almost glowed in the light from the bright moon directly overhead. "When you're ready, I'll move my hands away."

She glanced at him. She was starting to remember how it felt to have the water hold her up. To be part of it and feel nothing but peace in it. Hesitantly she said, "Um, okay. Just don't go far."

"I won't." He crouched down and moved his hands down deeper in the water, so they weren't supporting her but were right there if she needed them. He laughed a little and said, "Don't hold your breath. Relax. Enjoy it for vlock's sake," he teased.

"I *am* enjoying it," she smiled. The coolness of the water surrounded her, and it felt like her worries and the stress of being who she was were floating away with the water, down the second waterfall, and away into the forest. "I'm good. You can step away."

"You sure?"

"Yeah, I'm sure."

Kellum stood up. "Good, because I'm going to kick your butt... again." He laid back and floated beside her. They stayed like that, letting the current slowly move them as they gazed up into the clear sky above. Eventually, the current had pushed them close enough together that their hands were brushing against each other as they bobbed up and down in the water.

Neither of them made a move away from the other.

The current slowly moved them close enough that their hands were nearly right on top of each other. Kellum took her hand in his own and wove his fingers between hers.

Both their hearts were beating loud enough that they thought the other would be able to hear it.

A few minutes later, the current pushed them until they were nearly ready to go over the second falls. Reluctantly, they both let go of the other's hand and stood up.

"Should we call it a draw?" Kellum reached out his hand to shake on it.

"Sure." Behler grabbed his forearm in agreement. "For now."

They walked toward the shore, Behler following behind Kellum. She almost ran into him when he suddenly stopped. "What's wrong?" she asked immediately.

"Hang on." He bent over and reached into the water. When he pulled his arm back out, he was holding an iridescent eltip shell that changed colors depending on how the light hit it. He held it out to her and she accepted it. "So you remember you can do anything you want, even when you're scared."

She smiled. The gesture was ridiculously sweet, and she tucked the shell in the inner pocket of her luka.

They both got out of the water and walked back to the horses in silence. As they made their way back through the forest, both kept their horses at a slow pace, each wanting to prolong their time together just a little while more.

36

Behler got back that night and crawled into bed, so content that she forgot to even worry about what dreams may await her when she fell asleep. She'd dozed off remembering how Kellum's fingers had felt intertwined with her own. It was a peaceful night until she was suddenly jolted out of sleep by loud voices yelling across the village.

She jumped out of bed, threw on her clothes and her boots. She grabbed her weapons and walked out her bedroom door. She met her mother in the hallway, who was already fastening her own weapons' strap around her body. Sera had a befuddled expression, and Behler knew her own expression was probably a reflection of her mother's.

They stepped outside the front door to see a group of elder men and women talking excitedly. Warln and Penelope were both in the group.

"What's going on?" Sera asked them.

"We don't know for sure. The Arbirans alerted Shael that someone is coming."

Warln looked at Behler. "He was sleeping at his campsite, so some of the Arbirans outside the village warned him."

"The old fool can't sleep in a bed," Penelope added.

Warln raised a bushy, white eyebrow at her. "A fortunate thing for us tonight, Nelly."

"Well, it would've been nice if they'd told him *who* was coming," Penelope curtly pointed out.

Kellum and Luke ran up to the group.

Kellum leaned over and asked, "What's happening," in Behler's ear.

"Someone is coming through the forest," she answered in a hushed voice so that both boys could hear.

"Shael believes they're coming from the northwest, through the passage," Warln explained.

"What passage?" Behler asked.

"It's a swath of land where nothing grows except trellin grass," Henry said. "Bad ground maybe."

"Cursed ground," Penelope interjected.

Henry swiped his hand, dismissing her comment and exhaling through his lips. "Just old tales, Nelly."

She shrugged him off, obviously not going to change her prerogative any more than Henry was.

Warln seemed used to the bickering, because he just continued on as if they hadn't said anything. "It's so well hidden you'd never find it unless you knew it was there." He looked in the direction of the passage. "It must be the Revala."

Behler's heart leapt in her chest. Lorna! Matti!

She forced her hopes down, afraid how much the disappointment would hurt if it wasn't them. "How close to the village does this passage reach?" she asked, preparing for the worst in her mind.

"If they could make it to the passage," Warln said, "they can make it to the village."

Penelope pointed to the northeast tower. "The tower there overlooks the entrance. We will set archers there," she suggested. "Just to be safe."

"Kellum and Behler are our best archers, along with you and Henry." Warln said.

"We'll go to the tower." Kellum said.

"We'll set up a perimeter on the ground behind you," Warln said.

"If it's not the Revala," Sera said, "Nirain and I will take the children to the south and make our way to Halaanvail."

Warln gave a quick nod. "They'll be gathering at the stables. Go there and send anyone who can fight up to our line. If anyone but the Revala walks through that clearing, we'll send up a red flare. Once you see that, don't wait, just take them and leave. Take the wagons for the youngest and those who can't ride. Avenly and anyone else who has a horse should take them. There is a chest of food and supplies in Willa's stall. Take it."

Sera nodded. She took one last look at Behler then took off for the stables.

Behler looked at Kellum. "Let's go."

He nodded and, along with Penelope and Henry, they sprinted to the tower. It was built so that its floor was at the same level as the top of most of the buildings in the village. Behler grabbed her draka just to feel the worn wood in her hand. If arrows began flying at them, she was happy that they all had their isari stones to shield them.

Once on the tower, it felt like time slowed down until it stood still. They sat, quietly, waiting to see if they could hear the telltale sounds of hoofbeats. Behler was irritated that no one had mentioned the passage. It seemed like something she should've been told if she was indeed a leader.

"You should've told me about the bad ground, or whatever it is," she whispered to Kellum so that Penelope and Henry couldn't hear.

"I hadn't even thought of it since we got here. No one really worries about it because it's so well hidden. Like Warln said, no one could find it if they didn't know about it."

Penelope shushed them and raised her hand. She'd tilted her head down as if she heard something. Behler's heart was pounding in her chest. She couldn't quash the hope that Lora and Mathias would soon walk into the village.

A few moments later, they all heard it. It was quiet at first, like distant thunder, but as it grew louder and more discernible, they could hear the distinct sound of horses thundering toward them. Lots of horses. Twenty? Thirty? It was impossible to tell.

Behler looked at Kellum, and the way he looked back at her made her reach out and touch his forearm. He immediately slid his hand up so that he could take hers in his own. They stood staring at the forest, waiting, and gripping the other's hand tightly.

Then they could feel the earth vibrating through the framework of the tower.

Behler and Kellum let go of one another and took a position along the railing next to Penelope and Henry. Each of them readied their bows. Light reached the opening at the edge of the treeline, and all four pulled back on their arrows and aimed. As the first horse crossed into the open field, Behler's breath caught. Her fingers were tightening on the string, the arrow ready to fly.

Then Kellum's hand clamped around her arm.

"It's Rafe!" Henry said. "Shadow take me, it's Rafe!" He laughed as all the nervous tension left his body.

"They've returned!" Penelope said in a voice an octave higher than her usual one. She grabbed Henry's arm. "It's Rafe and the others." Her smile was as wild as her eyes.

"Yes," Henry said flatly, his scraggly brows puckered. "I believe I just said that."

Behler straightened up and looked down. In the light of a glowing isari stone, she could see a large, ruggedly handsome man with mocha colored skin. From the look of his scruffy beard and longer locks, he'd been out of the village for a long time. He looked up at them with fiercely intense eyes. He dipped his head to them, crossed his right arm over his body and placed his fist over his heart. Kellum and the other two returned the gesture. Behler was still trying to figure out who he was.

Others on horses were filing through the entrance. As more filed in, she searched for faces she knew. Lorna, Mathias, Samuel – any of them.

Finally, there was a familiar one. "Meela," she said and pointed her out to Kellum. And right behind Meela – Mathias. Relief washed over her so quickly that she felt dizzy. Rogan, Anilin, and Dalen were behind him. Behler's heart soared. They had made it.

"Look," Kellum pointed. "There are others from the village with them."

He was right. Regular people from the village had joined up with the Revala. Behler recognized entire families. She was sure some were seeking protection while others had joined the fight.

Penelope gasped and covered her mouth with her hand. Her gaze was locked on something below the tower.

Behler looked down to see who or what the elder woman was looking at. There was a younger man on the left and a white-haired man on the right. She knew who the younger man was before he even looked up at her, but when his eyes met hers, she gasped just as Penelope had only moments before. She'd seen eyes like those before, staring at her hatefully.

"It's your grandfather and..." Kellum began.

Behler finished the sentence for him.

"Fenn."

Part Three

37

The Great House was overflowing. Fifty-three Revalars had returned to Ardin along with twenty-three Elians (eighteen adults and five children) and two Trular scouts who had left Ardin only a couple days earlier. Warln quickly took control of the room.

"Quiet! Quiet!" He said gruffly. "Our Revalars have returned, and we have plenty of questions, but we can't ask them all at once. Plus, I'm sure they are tired and in need of rest and a good meal – I'll let them decide what order they take them in." Behler saw some of the Revalars smirk at his comment. He turned to face the bearded man who was so obviously the leader of the Revala. He wore a cloak made from the blond fur of a kindurbeast over his shoulders despite the season. "It does our hearts so well that you all have made it back to us."

Behler could barely focus on anything the old man was saying. Her mind kept racing in circles, her thoughts moving so quickly that they kept tripping over one another. Where was Lorna? Why wasn't Lorna there? She looked at Mathias to try to make eye contact, but he wouldn't look at her, amplifying her fears. Kellum stood close by her.

In a hushed voice, he said, "Don't panic. We don't know anything yet."

Behler nodded, but the word 'yet' echoed in her ears. She couldn't calm her racing heart.

"Rafe, would you like to say a few words?" Warln asked.

The man nodded. He uncrossed his arms, and when he spoke, his voice was as powerful as his appearance. "The black cloud of the Armigoth has spread. It reached the edge of the forest a couple weeks ago, but it seems to be unable to penetrate the forest's boundary. We hope the Arbirans can keep it from spreading here. I've sent Aeron and Uri to stand watch to the north. Armigoth troops were gathering, and I want to keep an eye on them. Warln has told me about your encounter with the dragons. We believe they've been scouring the forest for the village. Frankly, I'm surprised you've only encountered them once." He paused as if to collect his thoughts. "We've suffered casualties in the weeks since the Betham fire. We've lost fifteen Revalars in total since then. First, with the fire at Betham, two were lost – Samuel and Broty.

Behler bowed her head. Samuel was gone too. She heard Kellum curse under his breath.

"The following days we fought Horde guuns just to the north of the village. They had taken many of the girls from Betham that were around the right age, so we took back as many as we could. Even those we were able to save had already endured horrendous torture as the enemy tried to get them to tell who and where Behler was." Rafe's jaw clenched. "If they'd known, they would've told. No Elian could withstand thaelic-ren." A murmur rippled across the room. "Yes," Rafe continued. "Varek still has use of thaelic-ren, and it does work on Elians, to an extent it seems. Varek has grown extremely powerful."

Behler looked up at Kellum, whose eyes mirrored her own concerns.

"We lost eleven in skirmishes here and there," Rafe continued. He went on to name the Revalars who had died. Behler held her breath and didn't look up.

"...Tomas and Garret," Rafe finished. He hadn't said Lorna's name.

226

Behler watched as Trulars around the room clutched each other and cried for lost loved ones. But Rafe still had two names to reveal.

"The final two lost were killed in a raid on our camp just last week. We were ambushed at night. Zander was on watch, and he died protecting the rest of us. If he hadn't gotten to the alarm, we all may be dead." Across the room a woman, Behler guessed Zander's mother, gasped and gripped the man next to her. Rafe continued. "Because of Zander's bravery, we only lost one other that night." Behler looked at Mathias, who finally looked back at her. When their eyes met, she knew what Rafe was going to say. Her breath grew shallow. Her pulse quickened to a frenzied pace and the room began to spin. When her vision blurred, she instinctively reached out for Kellum's hand. He took it and squeezed it. Rafe's voice sounded like it was underwater now—too slow, too loud. And then..."Lorna died protecting those girls. She saved them."

Behler's weight was suddenly too much for her legs to support. She slumped, but Kellum was there to keep her from falling. She let out an involuntary whimper.

"Come on," he said quietly, and guided her out the nearby door.

The cool night air hit her like a wall.

"He didn't say it," she insisted.

"He did," Kellum said gently.

"No!" She pushed away from him, anger giving strength back to her legs. "She's the best fighter out of all of us. SHE CAN'T BE GONE?" she yelled and cried at the same time.

Kellum reached out a hand to touch her cheek.

"No!" She pushed his hand away. "Don't look at me like that!"

"Like what?" He asked softly.

"Like you pity me," her voice cracked and tears were about to spill from her eyes.

"I don't pity you," Kellum said. "Bale, I loved her too."

Behler froze at his words. White hot fury shot through her body. "YOU DON'T SAY THAT! Don't you ever say that! She was all I had. My own mother didn't want me, but Lorna did." The tears stung her eyes and made her vision blurry.

"You know that's not true." His voice was gentle, but his words made her angrier, nonetheless. When he reached for her, she stepped back.

The door to the Great House opened and Mathias stepped outside. The sight of him only made Behler more furious, and she turned and began to run. She didn't know where she was running to, only that she had to get away from – everything, especially the place where she'd found out her aunt was gone forever. Ciela and the comfort of the stables beckoned her. The Revala horses would be brought there later, but she could hide in Ciela's stall, and no one would bother her there.

She hoped.

Despite the growing distance between her and the Great House, her tears threatened more until her eyes could no longer contain them. They began spilling out onto her cheeks, and the lump in her throat rose higher until it escaped as hiccupping sobs.

She finally reached the stables and ran back to Ciela's stall. The smell of hay and straw enveloped her and muted the world outside. She threw open the stall door and collapsed into the thick bed of straw strewn about the floor. She cried until she thought the sobs would rip her in two. Ciela bent down and nuzzled her in the crook of her neck and on the back of her head. When Behler turned her head, Ciela's nose was cool on her hot, red cheek.

Lorna. She's gone. She couldn't bear to utter the words. Ciela whinnied and put her nose down close to Behler's face. She puffed a little air through her nostrils softly onto Behler's cheek. "How am I supposed to do everything that I'm supposed to do without her?" she whispered.

Ciela shifted her weight and shuffled her body around. Behler felt her moving around and looked up to see her raise her front leg then lean forward until her knee was resting on the floor. Soon, the horse had gotten herself down so that she was resting on all fours right next to Behler. Ciela rested her head on the straw and let out a big sigh. Behler reached out and rubbed the horse's velvety snout and ran her fingers up and down in the shorter hair across her face. She stayed there with a hand constantly on Ciela and cried softly until exhaustion brought welcome numbness. Later, she heard the stall door latch open and close quietly. She didn't need to look up to know it was Kellum. She didn't open her eyes as she felt him lie down beside her, and she kept them closed as he put a hand on her shoulder.

Her body shook and rattled with the aftermath of her sobs, and Kellum rubbed her arm gently. He was close enough that she could feel the rise and fall of his chest against her shoulder blades. She focused on his breathing and tried to forget about everything else. Soon she finally escaped into a deep and dreamless sleep. Her mind, so tired and overwhelmed, finally allowed her to escape into blissful darkness where, even when the Revala horses were brought into the pen just outside the stables, she didn't hear a thing.

38

"Bale," Kellum gently called to wake her. The sun was up and everyone would be gathering in the training field within the next few minutes. "C'mon Behler, get up."

Behler opened her eyes. They were tired and felt swollen after so much crying only a couple hours earlier. "I can't."

"Yes, you can," he said patiently. "Everyone is going to understand how you're feeling, but I don't think you'll be happy later if you let them see you like this."

"Like what?" She felt numb to everything. Let the Armigoth take her. Let Fennix fight it by himself. She didn't care.

Behler started to lie back down, but Kellum grabbed her firmly by the shoulders. "Don't," he said firmly.

"Don't what?" she snarled.

"Don't lie back down for starters," he said sharply. "Here." He held up a canteen. "Drink it."

She pushed it away. "I don't want your vlocking magic water. Just let me be."

"Drink it." He pushed it toward her lips.

She sneered at him, but he just continued to stare at her and hold the canteen in her face.

"Fine," she finally said, and grabbed the canteen roughly from him. She took a sip then dropped the canteen.

Kellum picked it back up. "More." He held it up for her to take again.

She snatched it out of his hand and gulped every last drop of the water down out of spite. To her chagrin, her tired and swollen face immediately began to cool. Her aching joints quit screaming at her, and her head cleared. The only thing it didn't improve was her broken heart.

"Better?" Kellum asked.

Behler handed him the canteen. "Not really," she said miserably.

"Here." He pulled another canteen out from behind him. "Wash your face off. It'll make you feel better."

She did as he told her without another fight. She sighed and swallowed the lump in her throat back down before it turned to tears again. "What am I going to do?" she asked miserably.

He took the canteen from her and took a drink. He'd been resting on his haunches and now fell back on his butt. His arms rested on his knees. "You're going to do just what Lorna trained you to do."

"I don't know how to live in a world that doesn't have Lorna in it."

Kellum was silent for a few moments then said, "If you don't fight now, everything Lorna did, her entire life since you were born, will have been in vain. I know you don't want that to be her legacy. Her legacy should be that she raised the woman who saved Elium and kept the Armigoth from spreading to the entire Anarsari. Don't you think so?" Behler hung her head and didn't respond. "If she were here," he continued, "She'd be all over you right now to get out there and learn all you could from the other Revalars. She'd literally be pushing you out there to meet Fenn and start training with him...and if that didn't work, she'd carry you out there on her shoulder. She'd want you to be ready the night Iskaara starts. Now honor her by doing what she set you out to do." His tone left little room to argue.

Behler stared at him for a moment then said, "There is no way you are the same person I knew in Betham. How did I not know?"

He shrugged. "You weren't supposed to know."

"Or I was just stupid."

Kellum shrugged and smirked. "Maybe." Behler was astonished when the corners of her mouth turned up into a slight smile. She wouldn't have believed it was any longer physically possible for her muscles to do that. It still felt like someone had ripped a hole through the top half of her body, but she felt like she could at least stand up and take a few steps. Kellum reached his hand out to her. "Let's go shoot some sandbags out of the sky."

She nodded, grabbed his hand and stood up. She picked up her weapons and had just turned to walk out of the stall when Kellum turned back around with a strange look on his face.

"What?" she asked, but then she saw *him* standing in the doorway of the stall.

Mathias gave her his crooked smile. "Hello, Bale. Can we talk?"

Kellum started to walk out the stall to give them privacy, but Behler quickly said, "It'll have to wait. We were just heading out to work on some archery." The thought of talking one on one with Mathias was just too much for the time being.

"Okay. I'll walk out with you," he said, determined.

She nodded and walked out. When they stepped out the back doors of the stables, they saw that most, if not all, of the Revalars were already gathered at the field, inspecting weapons and going over gear. Tents and other temporary shelters had been put up sometime during the night.

She felt their eyes on her, sizing her up – possibly even more than the others had a few weeks before. She imagined them all wondering about this girl who would help defeat the Armigoth. This was the girl they had fought to protect? This was the warrior they'd lost so much for?

She spotted Rafe quickly. He was still wearing the kindurbeast skin. His long locks of black hair and beard had been shaved short since she'd seen him the night before. He had spotted them too and was walking across the field to meet them. As he approached, Kellum reached out a hand. The two men grasped each other's forearms firmly.

"It's good to see you, Kellum," Rafe said. He smiled and it changed his entire face. The man turned to Behler. "Behler, I'm sorry about Lorna." He extended his hand out to her, and Behler grasped his forearm just as Kellum had. Rafe held tightly to her arm. He bent down and touched her forehead lightly with his. It was an Elian gesture reserved for times of mourning. "She spoke of you constantly. She was very proud to be your aunt."

Behler gulped down the lump in her throat that had spontaneously regenerated and nodded, blinking away tears. "I'll miss her very much," she managed to say.

"She wanted you to have these." Rafe held out Lorna's draka and a dagger in an elaborately decorated sheath. Behler took them and held it tightly in her hands.

All the things Behler had been mad at Lorna about now felt trivial. She nodded at Rafe. "Thank you."

"She wondered about how you might be doing here." He looked around. "It looks as if you are doing just fine." He turned back to the Revalars who'd been watching intently. "Rest. Go visit your families," he announced loudly. "We don't know how long we might have here." He turned back to Behler. "There's much to discuss. Can you meet with me at the Great House in an hour?"

"We'll be there," Behler said, making it clear that Kellum would be joining her.

Rafe turned to Kellum. "I've sent Marcus to try to recruit others from the far west. Will you tell your mother?"

Kellum nodded. "I will." His mother would be disappointed that her husband hadn't come home with the rest of the Revalars.

Rafe said a quick goodbye and walked back toward the dispersing group of Revalars.

Behler turned to Mathias. Anger rose instantaneously in her gut. "How did she die?" she asked hotly.

Mathias wasn't rattled by her tone. "You heard Rafe. She died saving those girls."

"How?" Behler repeated.

"Bale," Kellum said gently and touched her arm, which she just shook off.

"I wanted to tell you about Lorna alone, not in front of everyone," Mathias said quietly, hoping to diffuse her temper.

"Then why didn't you?" she spat angrily.

"I didn't have the chance," he pushed back.

Behler lowered her chin, a gesture she did when she was at her angriest. "Like you never the chance to tell me the truth in Betham?" she sneered.

"Bale," Kellum said in a sterner voice. She felt his hand brush against hers but ignored it.

The gesture didn't go unnoticed by Mathias.

She took a step towards her oldest friend. "If I'd been there, I could've stopped it. You made me stay in the forest." She clinched her teeth and locked her jaw. "Now, how did she die?"

Behler's hand gripped her draka, and the isari stone flared with a burst of indigo light, catching Mathias in its glow. She hadn't meant to do it. But there was a part of her wanted to burn everything down.

"Bale," Kellum stepped in front of her to look her square in the face. "Don't. It's not Matti's fault."

Behler looked up at him and the look in his eyes snapped her out of her anger, if only slightly. When she looked back at Mathias, he was eyeing both her and Kellum suspiciously.

Mathias glanced back at the crowd then quietly said, "Rafe has been fighting for so long, he's forgotten how to be sensitive...if he ever knew how to be in the first place. If I could've gotten you away from the others and alone, I would've told you. I swear it."

Kellum noticed others were still watching them. "Do you still want to work on archery targets?" he asked Behler.

She nodded.

Kellum turned to Mathias. "You up for it?"

Mathias nodded. "I don't have a bow. I lost mine in Betham and I haven't been able to replace it yet."

"Warln has extras in the stables," Kellum said. "I'll run and get one of his." He glanced at Behler and gave her *"cool it"* look then turned and sprinted toward the building.

Mathias watched him until he was out of earshot then said, "It seems like you two are getting along."

Behler almost slapped him at the insinuation. "What do you mean by that?" she snapped.

"Nothing." Mathias held up his hands defensively. "It's a good thing. That's all. I wasn't sure how you two would be when I left you with him that night."

"It was supposed to be *you*," she said scornfully.

Mathias looked down. "I know. But you were safe and I had to go back. Kellum was too injured to help the others, but I knew he could get you here safely." He paused. "I thought we'd be right behind you."

Behler looked at him. The image of him running back into the burning village replayed in her mind. She felt betrayed when the anger she felt subsided. Anger made the hurt quieter.

"What happened when you went back?" she asked, softer.

"We used our isari stones to fight off most of the guuns. We fought until dawn, arming any Elians who had stuck around and were willing to fight."

Behler swallowed. "How did Sam die?"

Mathias shook his head. "The dragon."

Behler's stomach sank. She looked down as a tear slipped out and down her cheek.

Mathias cleared his throat, and she knew he was trying not to choke up. "We were able to get through the night and by the next morning, the Revala had arrived. The Horde and Gorlogs got out fast after that."

"What about Fenn? When did he join you?"

"Just before we rescued the girls. Just before Lorna..." he trailed off.

Behler scoffed. "I thought the Arbirans weren't supposed to let Fenn out of the forest."

Mathias shrugged. "Fenn is very determined."

Insufferable popped into Behler's head. "So, you traded one twin for the other – your *best* friend I've heard," she added out of spite then immediately regretted it.

Mathias gave her a familiar look. "Don't be stupid. You're my best friend. Nothing has changed that. Fenn and I are friends, but I've spent most of my life with *you*."

Behler scoffed. "Yeah, lying to me."

"Bale, it wasn't lying...not exactly. And you know why I had to." His voice sounded sad and tired.

She started to say he should've told her anyway but stopped herself. She was too exhausted to argue anymore. "How did she die, Matti?" she asked again.

"Does it matter?"

Behler nodded. "It does to me."

Mathias took a deep breath. "She got the girls into a cave. It was tiny. Barely big enough for them all to fit. She stood at the entrance and held off the soldiers with her isari stone and bow. We were trying to get to her, but the Horde got between us somehow. An archer was hiding near the cave and got a lucky shot in before Lorna knew what was happening. It weakened her, so she wasn't able to keep her isari shield up for very long at a time. When we finally got to her, she had seven arrows in her body."

Behler gasped and covered her mouth with both hands. Tears filled her eyes.

"She'd used the last of her energy to collapse the cave entrance, protecting those inside. It was the last thing she did."

Behler hung her head. Knowing the truth made a difference, but it also made her heart ache even more. She looked up into the sky until she regained some composure. She wanted to kill the guun who had killed Lorna.

"I'm really going to miss her," she said eventually.

"Yeah, me too."

She looked out over the field to avoid looking at him. "It's good to have you back," she muttered, and it felt like she'd thrown off a heavy blanket from her shoulders, especially realizing that Rafe could have just as easily said Mathias' name instead of Samuel's.

He looked over at her, squinting from the sun. "It's good to be back." He gave her his typical crooked smile again. He looked up and saw Kellum walking toward them, carrying the bow in one hand and some arrows in the other. "And I'm glad you and Kellum are friends now. He's a good person."

Behler simply nodded. She wasn't about to admit how much Kellum meant to her. "I know."

As she watched Kellum approaching, she knew that things would never again be like they had been in Betham, and that was okay.

39

So much had changed since the last time they had been together that the three young Trulars couldn't help but feel an uncomfortable awkwardness. Fortunately, target practice gave them something to focus on, and soon enough they were more at ease. Shortly after they began, Luke showed up and it was obvious he was eager to see Mathias. He joined their group without asking, although no one minded.

"Has anyone seen Fenn?" he asked.

Everyone shook their heads. "Not since last night," Mathias said. "I think he went to his house after we left the Great House."

"Hopefully on his knees begging for Sera's forgiveness," Kellum said. "She's been worried sick."

"Ha!" Luke scoffed. "You'd think she'd be used to it by now after all we've put her through over the years."

"Don't you mean what you three put her through?" Kellum asked. "I was always the responsible one in the group."

"Responsible, boring...same thing," Luke said and Kellum shot him a nasty look.

Soon, they set down their bows and headed toward the Great House. The sun was already hot and quickly warming the ground beneath them. The training field had become overly crowded almost as soon as they'd started target practice. People were eager to mingle, train, and to learn all they could of Varek and the Armigoth. Behler was sure some of the Revalars were trying to find out about her as well.

"Anything I should know before I walk through that door, Matti?" Behler's unease about the meeting grew with each step toward the Great House.

"The Horde has gotten stronger in just the past two weeks. They are like a completely new army. Something's changed. We were right about the Gorlogs. They've become violent and bloodthirsty. They'll kill anyone they come across. We've even seen them kill Horde guuns. It's as if they've completely lost their minds and are killing anything that's breathing. The Gorlogs couldn't get enough of that kak in the river. Also, the Okinars *are* coming from the north. They are probably south of the mountain range by now."

Behler remembered that day in the rebel house when Frawna had reported back about the Horde soldiers meeting with the Okinar council. The memory was painful now that Lorna was gone. "What about the dragons?" she asked, trying to force her mind on to something else. "How many have you seen?"

"At least two. They've set fires in all the villages, pushing everyone out to either starve or surrender and join the Horde. But we know much more about them now. Baret is an elder who came to Elium as a Revalar but really just wanted to study the plants and animals of a different world. He decided we needed to know more about the dragons, so he traveled north to study them. The females are the most vicious, and the males rarely leave the breeding grounds. They live in an enormous cave system in Black Hills. Baret tracked at least twenty of them. Normally, they just want to be left alone. They're fighting for Varek either against their will or out of fear. The one we saw in Betham, she's smart, not just some animal. Kak, she's smarter than any Gorlog I've ever seen. And we know that there are other Horde troops there trying to capture more."

240

"So why don't they just burn everything? We couldn't stop them," Behler said.

"Their ability to make fire only lasts for short periods of time. They must have a store of fuel, and when it's gone, it takes time to build up enough to make more fire. Baret thinks they have a vulnerable spot, just where their heads meet their necks. He saw one attack another over turf – it went right for the other one's neck." He knelt down and made a quick sketch of a dragon in the sand. "Right here." He pointed at a spot where the dragon's neck met its body.

"Where's Baret now?" Kellum asked.

"He went back north for more observations."

"Sounds safer than around here these days," Luke muttered.

They stopped walking as they approached the Great House, as if stepping through the threshold would change everything all over again.

Behler looked at the door. Mustering her strength and courage, she said, "Well, let's go," and walked boldly through the doorway and into the large room, feigning confidence she wasn't sure she had.

Rafe, Rogan, and Warln were standing at the front of the room. Sera and Penelope were sitting and talking quietly to themselves. And across the room Fennix stood with the old man that Kellum had said was her grandfather.

Fennix looked up at them when they walked into the room. When their eyes met, a chill went up Behler's spine. His eyes looked a lot like the eyes she'd seen in her dreams, but she had to admit, there was much more to his eyes than those that had haunted her. They were full of life and depth. She could see sadness and determination in them. Perhaps what was most unsettling, though, was she could see a reflection of herself in them.

241

The same fire. The same storm. The same burden.

40

Rafe immediately pulled Behler off to the side, away from everyone. "I want you to know that I appreciate everything you've done in this village since you arrived. The people here had gotten a little too comfortable, so to see them recapturing some of their Trular heart does me well, and so much of that is because of you."

The praise made Behler feel awkward. "Warln did a lot to get everyone to the training field."

Rafe nodded. "I know he's been an important part, but you have been the inspiration behind it all. Seeing your drive and your spirit has touched our people in a very important way."

Behler continued feeling uncomfortable, especially when she looked over and saw her brother watching them. "I'm sure that having Fennix back will help them just as much."

Rafe turned and looked across the room. "Yes, I'm sure it will." He motioned for her brother to come join them.

Behler's heart began to beat faster. She was about to meet her brother face to face. What could she say that didn't sound absolutely absurd? If she was confident, would he think she was arrogant? If she wasn't, would he think she was weak?

"Hello," her brother said casually. Up close, his jawline and brows reminded her of Lorna's, and her heart skipped a beat.

"Hello," she said. He reached his hand out to grab her forearm, and she extended her own to return the gesture.

"I'm going to go discuss something with Obidiah," Rafe said, "before we go any further with our discussions." He walked off without waiting for either of them to respond.

Fennix watched him walk away. "He really needs to work on his people skills." He turned back to Behler. "I've heard a lot about you." He had a slight smile on his face, but Behler couldn't read him. The smile didn't quite reach his eyes.

"If it's from Mathias , you can only believe about half of it," she quipped.

Her brother laughed, and finally the smile reached his entire face. "Yeah, most of it came from him, although I think to say only half of it was true is being modest." He stopped laughing. "I'm really sorry about Lorna." He was looking at her intently, studying her face. "I didn't know how much you look like our mother." Behler self-consciously touched her cheek. Fennix looked around the room. "So…saviors of all that is…not much pressure or anything," he said cavalierly. He laughed when he looked at her and saw the surprised look on her face. "Haha! Nobody's quite put it like that, huh? Well, no surprise there – nobody really has a clue what to say that would really matter." Behler looked at him questioningly, not sure what he really meant. He smiled cynically. "Nobody really *understands* the foretelling around here. They just know that we're supposed to be the ones who defeat the Armigoth. Everyone dances around the details because they don't really know them. The foretelling doesn't spell out every detail. That's the beauty of it, I guess. Who knows, maybe we'll transform into kindurbeasts with dripping fangs." He made his fingers into makeshift fangs and made a face that nearly made Behler laugh.

"Ones that can fly," she joked, remembering her own comments that first morning in her mother's house. She started to chuckle but stopped herself. Her brother's hostility was coming off him in waves, but she didn't sense it was directed in her direction.

He continued. "People have always just talked about the foretelling – guessing at most of the details but never really knowing. So many of them have just been waiting for us to save them." He looked at her, tilting his head to the side slightly. "Everyone does seem to have come around since you've gotten here, though."

"Oh...I don't think it's anything I've done," she said quickly. "They all realized that they needed to prepare...especially without knowing if the Revala was still out there." And if you were still out there, she added to herself.

Fennix shrugged. "Believe me, just your being here has stirred something in them I've never seen before. Some of the elders decided they were too old to fight quite a while ago, and the men and women who were left behind to care for the children and injured all felt so safe here that they took it for granted."

"Not being able to use thaelic scared them a lot," Behler pointed out. "Of course, when the dragons flew over, that helped motivate them," she added wryly.

He nodded. "Dragons tend to have that effect." He rubbed the back of his head with the palm of his hand. "It's been difficult for the Revalars without having the Deep Thread."

"Sera has been pretty worried since she couldn't use it to communicate with you."

His expression didn't change. "I needed to get out of the village. With my birthday – *our* birthday – coming up and Iskaara getting closer every day, I needed some air."

"Outside of the forest?" Behler pressed.

Her brother's face shifted, and for a moment he looked like Lorna when she didn't want to answer a question. "I, uh, was trying to help a friend but I couldn't get to them. The vlocking Horde. I ran into Lorna and the others when they were rescuing the girls. If Lorna had her way, I would've been right back here with you, but I argued my case with Rafe and convinced him to let me stay. After the raid where we lost Lorna, though, Rafe nearly sent me packing. He would have if he hadn't decided to bring the Revala back here."

Kellum, Mathias, and Luke walked up. "I was beginning to wonder about you," Kellum said as he greeted Fennix.

"Why?" Fenn scoffed. "You know me? I have to get out of here sometimes."

"Yeah, speaking of which," Kellum handed him the knife he'd found in the cave. "I believe this is yours."

Fennix smiled crookedly. "Thanks, I was looking for that."

"Who the kak is Anika?" Kellum teased.

Fennix noticeably stiffened. "Just a girl."

"An Elian girl?" Luke asked.

"Yeah, I guess."

Behler felt an odd feeling rush over her. Sadness maybe.

A ripple from the previous night's grief?

Kellum's grin faded. He clearly caught the shift in Fenn's voice. "Your mother was pretty worried about you," he said, gently nudging the conversation in a safer direction.

Fennix shrugged off Kellum's comment. "I think she's pretty used to it by now."

246

Behler cringed at her brother's callousness.

The group fell silent for a few moments. Luke finally asked, "So what happens now?"

"Rafe thinks it's best to hunker down here as long as possible," Fennix said.

"But what about all the Revalars still out there? They need as much support as we can offer," Behler said.

Mathias and Fennix shared a look.

Mathias sighed. "There was something Rafe didn't tell everyone yet. There is only one other panara of Revalars left out there that we know of, and it's lost quite a few people over the past couple of weeks."

Behler gasped audibly and Luke and Kellum bowed their heads.

Luke looked up, rubbing his face with his palms. "There aren't enough of us to fight."

"I don't think Rafe plans on us fighting this alone," Fenn said.

"What do you mean?" Behler asked.

Kellum thought back to what Rafe had told him. "Marcus is trying to get help from the west."

"Riverfork?" Luke asked.

Kellum shook his head. "A little farther west," he said with a raised brow.

Luke shuddered. "Amsha?"

"Amsha!" Behler said. "To get the cannibals?" Stories of the Niyan cannibals had been as prevalent in Betham as the ghost stories of Gaharan Forest.

Mathias shrugged. "I'm sure Horde flesh tastes just as good as any."

Behler looked at him with disgust. "I can't believe you just said that."

Mathias shrugged. She looked at Kellum for support, but he was trying desperately to hold back a smile.

"Nah," Luke piped in. "I have a feeling they would taste pretty bitter."

Everyone looked at him speechless, then Fennix started laughing – and soon all the guys were chiming in. Behler just shook her head and raised an eyebrow then turned around so no one would see her smile.

Behler hadn't talked to Sera since they'd learned of Lorna's death. She sat down at the table where Sera and Penelope were still talking quietly.

Sera gave her a small smile and placed her hand gently over Behler's. "I'm sorry about Lorna."

Behler returned Sera's smile. "I'm sorry too."

They sat quietly for a few moments until a voice from behind Behler made her jump.

"Hello." Behler turned to see her grandfather standing there. The old man smiled. "Behler, I've waited so long to meet you."

Behler stood and reached out her hand to grasp his forearm, but he ignored her gesture and took her in his arms and held her tightly. After the initial shock of the unexpected embrace wore off, Behler relaxed and hugged him back. "I was so happy to find out I had a grandfather," she said once they let go of each other. "I've spent most of my life thinking I only had Lorna." Her words caught up with her, and she nearly choked up again.

"I'm glad I lived long enough to see the woman you've become. Your grandmother would be so proud." Obidiah looked around the room. "I have to say, it's good to be home in general."

"Obi, were you there when...?" Sera began.

"Yes. Rafe was right when he said she saved all those girls. She and Zander saved us all that night." Obidiah looked down. "I don't know how the jackals got so close without us knowing."

Behler saw Rafe motion for Obidiah to join him again. Her grandfather said his goodbyes and walked away. Behler watched him go. He had a slight limp but otherwise walked straighter and stronger than any man his age should.

Behler looked at Sera whose eyes were now red and swollen. In no shape to comfort someone else, she was relieved when Rafe stepped aside from Obidiah and loudly said, "Friends, let's speak."

41

"Our numbers aren't great," Rafe began. "Those of us who arrived last night are some of the only Trulars left outside the forest, aside from those in Halaanvail."

Behler looked over at Kellum. "Halaanvail?" she mouthed, but he just gave a slight shake of his head.

Rafe continued. "I have sent Marcus and Sy to Amsha to ask the Niyan clan to help us."

Luke grimaced across the room. "But what about all the, you know, eating their enemies problem?"

Warln laughed. "The Niyans made up those stories themselves."

"I believe they'll fight with us," Rafe continued. "They know us and trust us; plus, they know the Armigoth will spread to their lands if we don't stop it." He looked at Fennix and Behler. "I'd like you two to go and ask the Desharets to join us in this fight. They are the ones who brought the foretelling to us, so I think they'll respond to you. The Horde hadn't crossed into their lands at our last scouting report, so I feel it's safe for you to travel there...and absolutely necessary."

Words from what seemed a lifetime ago echoed through Behler's head. "Varek will go for the Sulimar," she said, as if repeating the echo aloud.

Everyone looked at her. She swallowed over a lump in her throat and stood up a little straighter. "Lorna and Rogan were talking about it. If Olgum used the Sulimar, Varek will want them, too." She didn't know how she knew this to be true, but she did.

Everyone looked from her to Rafe, waiting for his response. "Then you need to get there first." His words weren't harsh, but confident and reassuring. He continued, "Once you have the Desharets, meet up with the rest of us at Riverfork. We'll regroup there."

"You'll have to find the Desharets first," Warln added. "They're hidden underground—somewhere in the Anover Mountains past Galvinar. Ask for Riv once you arrive."

"There are Arbirans outside the forest – past Galvinar?" Luke asked.

"To watch over the Desharets," Warln explained. "Provide them with aji."

"I'd like Kellum, Mathias, and Luke to go with us," Behler said.

"Meela, too," Fennix added.

Rafe nodded. "This is your mission. Take with you anyone you wish." He looked from Behler to Fennix. "Soon enough, you both will be telling me my missions."

Fenn scoffed. "Never." He glanced at Behler then back to Rafe. "When do we leave?"

Rafe exhaled. "Ideally, you would leave after Iskaara, but I'm afraid we won't be able to wait that long. If we get word that the Horde is on the move toward Galvinar, we'll have to move. Behler, Warln has told me he can see you get stronger every day. I've seen the same in Fenn. Even if we can't wait for Iskaara, you two are already forces to be reckoned with. Spend as much time together as you can. It can only help with whatever is to come.

They both nodded.

"Very well," Warln said. "Why don't you all get back to the fields? We'll see you there in a bit."

After the young Trulars had left, Warln turned to Rafe. "Do you think it's safe to send them?"

"No," Rafe said, "but are there ever safe choices in times like these? We have no choice. We need the Desharets, and they'll only come with the twins."

Warln knew Rafe was right, but he was still worried. He had sacrificed too much to lose everything now.

They all had.

That night after training was done, Behler made an excuse and walked home alone. She wanted time to herself to process the past day and a half. She found her way to the oldest Arbiran and sat down beside it, leaning against its trunk. A flock of ducks were just making their way to shore, trailed by a line of tiny ducklings. It reminded her of a song she'd heard long ago, when she and Lorna were still living in Oryn. She tried to remember how it started.

"The willows are weeping, the ducks sleep on the pond," she began singing softly. "And you know that I love you in this world and far beyond. The sheep are grazing, and the cattle are asleep, and my dear little child, dream well and do not weep." She thought that was how it went, and even if it wasn't, her version sounded nice in her ears. She closed her eyes and started humming the tune.

The leaves above her began to rustle, and she thought she could hear a soft melody on the wind. Then, from above, a small white flower fell and landed delicately on her lap. She picked up the tiny little blossom then turned and placed her palm on the tree.

Erhana, she heard in the rustling above, and she smiled because she knew that word.

"Doa lau."

42

Behler walked into the house that had somehow begun to feel like home. Sera was just placing some food down on the table.

"Bale," just in time.

Fennix sat at the table, writing in a well-worn leather-bound book.

Behler gave a small smile and sat down. The smells of dinner made her stomach growl.

"Roasted chicken with kogum and peas," Sera said. She smiled. "Your father used to cook this for me when we first got married." She sat down. "It took me a while to get the recipe right."

They sat and ate, making small talk and chatting around all the bigger issues that were too painful or complicated.

Behler quickly figured out that Fennix's sarcasm was a tool he used to deal with the hand he'd been dealt, and she realized she'd often done the same with Mathias back in Betham – even here with Kellum since then.

When dinner was over, they both volunteered to clean up.

Her brother's energy wasn't as hostile as it had been in the Great House, so Behler decided to try to get to know him a little. "Were you writing a letter earlier?"

"Hmm?" Fennix kept his head down, lost in his own thoughts. It took him a moment for the question to register. "Oh, no...just writing. It helps me sort through all the noise."

"Noise?"

Fennix smirked. "You know...all the kak we have to deal with."

"Hmmph," Behler made a sound between a laugh and a snort. He handed her a plate he'd just washed in the basin. "How long have you known about...it?" she asked.

He shrugged. "Ama told me when I was ten. I had a tendency to...take risks, I guess. Climbing trees a bit too high, jumping off things, wandering off into the forest. I think she was hoping that by telling me, I'd be more careful. She hoped that if I knew I was destined to save the world, I would be more cautious."

Behler laughed. "No way it worked."

Her brother handed her another plate. "Nope." He laughed. "That's when she gave up and let the fates decide."

"I wish Lorna had been like that. The last time the fates decided anything for me was when I fell in a river."

"Oh yeah...when you killed the kindurbeast."

Behler looked at him, stunned. "Does everyone in this village know every vlockin' detail of my life?"

Fennix shrugged. "Don't worry...just the big stuff." He leaned over and grabbed a leftover piece of chicken and started eating it. "Ama and Warln decided to tell everyone about us last year, the day after our birthday. After that, everyone just wanted to know anything about you. When Matti or Kellum came home, they'd berate them for stories about you." He took another bite of chicken. "You've been a celebrity around here for a while now."

Behler remembered when Kellum made her put the cloak over her head that night they'd first arrived in Ardin. She groaned. "I'm sorry."

Fenn looked surprised. "For what?"

"For having to live through all that, I guess."

He shrugged. "I just went into the forest a lot." He smirked. "Sometimes a little further."

Behler remembered those one hundred paces she took past the training circle back in Betham. "Yeah, I get that."

"Don't let this freak you out, please, but I saw you a few times...before."

Behler looked at him. "Um...what?"

He shrugged again but looked a little embarrassed. "I had to know what you looked like. I *had* to see you...so I snuck over toward Betham to see if I could find you."

"And you did."

He nodded. "Yeah, it was strange. I thought I'd have to, you know, stalk the village for a while...or just sit and wait by the training circle you all had in the forest. That idea made me nervous. I was afraid Rogan...or Lorna...would find me. But once I got close to the village," his voice rose in excitement, "I could kind of feel this tug. It wasn't thaelic...it was just something pulling me. I headed south and saw you and Mathias sitting by the river...just talking."

"Yeah," Behler smiled. "We did that a lot."

"Anyway," Fennix said as he ate some leftover kogam, "Sorry I spied on you. I know that was kind of a creepy thing to do."

Behler laughed. "No, it's fine. I probably would have done the same thing if I'd known about you."

All the talk of spying made it feel like an appropriate time to ask, "Have you had any weird dreams lately?" she asked.

"Like what?"

"Bad dreams...where it feels like someone is watching you?"

Fenn put down the fork with another bite of kogum. "Have you?" Behler nodded. "And you're afraid it's Varek."

Behler felt a tug of sibling bonding at the fact her brother understood so much without her saying more. "Yes."

Fenn's expression changed. "I haven't had any dreams like that. But if you think it could be Varek, assume it is. Don't let him inside your head. If it happens again, don't be afraid...just face him and let him know you won't be intimidated."

Her brother's change in demeanor caught her off guard. "Okay. But how did you know all that?"

He shrugged again. "It must be a twin thing."

Behler took a sip of aji. "Well, now it's my turn to be a little creepy."

Fennix grinned, obviously intrigued. "Go on."

"I can only see eyes in my dream...looking at me, hating me."

"Creepy," he agreed.

"Yeah...but that's not what I mean exactly." She looked at her brother, and although his eyes were shining with a mischievous spark, she could still see them in her nightmare, cold and dead. "They look a bit like your eyes."

Every muscle in Fenn's face registered his shock. "My eyes?"

Behler nodded. "I'm not saying it's you," she said quickly.

"No, no..." He took a drink of his own aji. "I promise you it's not me. That's a bit creepier than even I'm willing to go." He smirked, trying to use humor to ease the sudden tension. Finally, he said, "Maybe they are just bad dreams from dealing with, you know, all the kak. But still...assume they're not and assume it's Varek."

He put his glass down and gently grabbed Behler's shoulders. "Assume the worst so you can prepare for it," he said in an exaggerated lowered voice.

Behler grinned. "Sounds like Lorna."

"Grampa used to say it to me. I'm sure she got it from him."

The kitchen shifted slightly around Behler as another truth fell on her. "You knew our grandparents." It was a statement, not a question.

"Yeah, I did." Fennix took a step back. His own realization landed squarely. "I'm sorry you didn't."

In that moment, they both saw pieces of themselves in each other. The bond was begun.

43

"Having the Revalars here to train with has been great," Luke said one evening at sunset as he, Fennix, and Behler were packing up to head home. Kellum had already left to visit Zola to get a few cuts cleaned up and salved and Mathias had walked with him since he'd been the one to injure Kellum in the first place.

"Did you see how hard Rafe was sparring with some of the kids today?" Behler asked. "I thought he was going to really hurt them."

"Enon held his own," Fennix chuckled. "He even drew blood on Rafe."

"He's good," she said. "And he's only twelve. Hopefully he won't have to use those skills for real any time soon."

The Revalars had been working intensely with everyone. They sparred fiercely with both the young and the old and everyone in between. They held sessions to teach maneuvers and strategies to counter Horde fighting techniques. Behler especially enjoyed learning some more hand-to-hand methods. The Revalars were a welcome addition to the training regimen she and the others had nearly perfected before the Revalars had come home.

"There's talk about training some of the younger kids on their drakas," Behler said.

"Couldn't go any worse than when you lifted Matti off the ground instead of the sandbag next to him," Fenn teased.

Behler's mouth dropped open. "Well, well..."she stammered. "He shouldn't have been standing so close to it."

Luke and Fennix looked at each other and burst into simultaneous laughter. Behler soon joined in. Finally, Luke pulled himself together enough to say, "Thank you both for letting me come along when you go find the Desharets."

Behler looked up at him and shrugged. "You're a good fighter, and I trust you. It's as simple as that."

Fennix laughed. "I mean, *I'm* letting you come along despite it all..."

Luke laughed and punched Fenn in the shoulder.

He looked back at Behler. "Still, thanks. Kellum seems to forget that I'm not a kid anymore."

Fennix scoffed. "He's always done that. Every time we came wandering in from the forest, caked in mud or all scraped up, if Kellum was here he had to make sure you knew he didn't approve."

Luke chuckled. "Yeah, he reminded me how I should be more responsible. After all, if something happened to *you*, the foretelling was doomed."

Behler imagined Kellum's trips to the village. Ardin would've been the only place he could've been himself and have friends. "Did you guys ever ask him to go with you on your little adventures?"

Luke shrugged. "He never really asked."

"He went with us a couple of times," Fennix added, a little defensively.

Behler let out a quick, silent sigh. "You guys don't know how hard it was for him in Betham. I'd hoped he at least had been able to have fun and find happiness here."

The guys looked at each other slyly. "I think he has definitely found happiness here," Fennix smirked.

Behler's cheeks flushed, but she pretended she didn't understand what her brother was getting at.

Luke laughed, but then admitted, "You're right," he said, "I should've..." he stopped mid-sentence, something behind Behler catching his attention near the kogum field. She turned to look. "Grampa!" he said loudly and began running. Behler and Fennix were right behind him.

They found Warln lying motionless right at the edge of the field.

"What's wrong with him? Is he breathing?" Behler asked.

Luke rolled his grandfather over and put his ear to the man's chest. "He's breathing."

Fennix knelt on the opposite side of Warln's body. He felt around for wounds. "I can't feel anything. There's no blood."

Luke bowed his head. "He has lidic disease," he said sadly.

"What?" Fennix sounded horrified. "Are you sure?"

Luke nodded. "Gam told us."

"What is lidic disease?" Behler asked.

"It's something some Trulars get when they get older," Fennix said. "For people like Warln...for anyone...it's torture, especially in the beginning when they are aware it's happening. You'd think a chosen people wouldn't be cursed with such a humiliating end."

"Grampa," Luke said and gently patted the man's cheek. "Can you hear me?" Warln moaned and moved a little but didn't wake up. Luke looked up at Fenn. "Can you help me get him home? I don't want anyone seeing him like this."

"Wait!" Behler said suddenly, her chest tightening. There was a sensation she couldn't describe—like something tugging something within her and pulling her toward Warln. "I think I can help."

"What?" Luke asked, desperation thick in his voice. "How?"

"I'm...I'm not sure." She couldn't explain what she was feeling. She pressed one hand to his chest and one to his forehead. A coolness surged through her arms—like a cool cloth on a feverish cheek. She felt the pull grow stronger, pulling her toward something. Then she found...*something*... inside him like a splinter too deep to pull out. Her own energy wrapped around it, holding it still and making it smaller.

Warln opened his eyes.

"What the vlock?" Luke whispered.

Behler opened her eyes to meet her brother's wide gaze. "How?" he asked.

She shook her head. "I don't really know."

"Boys. Behler." Warln said, sounding a little groggy.

"Fenn, let's get him home," Luke said quickly.

Fennix gave a quick nod. "Sure."

"Please don't tell anyone," Luke asked them both. "Not yet."

Both Fennix and Behler shook their heads. "We won't," Behler promised. "But I'll go get Kellum if you want."

Luke nodded. "Thanks."

He and Fenn helped Warln up and got under his shoulders. It looked like they were helping a man home who'd had too much firewater.

Behler looked down at her hands. Had she healed him? No, she knew she didn't have that kind of power. But she'd made him a little better, and she'd been able to feel the illness within his body. "Like Avenly's nishiri, only...different."

She looked back at the three men walking across the field. If Warln could hold on until Iskaara, maybe she could save him for good.

44

Over the next several days, Behler and Fennix both got stronger and faster. For weeks, Behler's record for the number of sandbags she could shoot out of the sky at once had been six, but a few days after the Revala arrived, she had managed to take out seven...then eight. One week after they'd arrived, she took down nine before the tenth finally hit the ground. It took two others shooting targets into the sky just to keep up with her. She was also mastering her isari stone. Not only could she command it more and more often with just a thought, but she could also do impressive things such as lifting an enormous boulder and hurling it twenty yura lengths across the field.

No one brought up what Behler had done for Warln, but then one afternoon, while sitting during a break, Kellum said, "You should try thaelic again."

"Why?"

He shrugged. "Whatever you did to help Grampa, I think it means your abilities are starting to develop even more. Have you had any dreams lately? The bad ones?"

Behler shook her head. "No. I thought maybe I was just so nervous about meeting Fenn that I kept creating those dreams on my own." She'd begun doubting her own memory of how bad the dreams had been.

"Maybe," he shrugged. "But maybe you aren't having them now because your connection to thaelic is stronger and you can block whatever or whoever it was."

It made sense. "Okay, sure," she agreed. There was no harm in trying. She closed her eyes but quickly opened them again. "I don't know who to try to talk to. I always pictured Lorna or Mat."

"Try me. I'll try too. Maybe together we can make it work."

Behler closed her eyes again and pictured an open field. At the end of the field, she pictured Kellum standing there. Kellum? she said in her thoughts. Can you hear me? Suddenly it felt like she was physically standing in the grass near the kogum field. Kellum was standing with his back to her. "Kellum," she said, and it felt like she was actually speaking the words. She reached out to touch him but stopped. Something wasn't quite right about the angle of his head in relation to his shoulders.

"Kellum?"

A low wind stirred the trees. Then a mist came in—fast and cold—curling around her ankles and rising like a living thing.

Suddenly, a raspy whisper was in her ear and all around her. It sounded like many voices speaking at once: the same as in her dream.

"I've been waiting for you, Trular," it hissed in her ear, so close that goosebumps ran down her back and up her arms.

The mist wrapped itself around Kellum and turned his body so it was facing her. Behler screamed. His eye sockets were scorched black, smoke curling from the ash that streaked his cheeks. His mouth fell open. The snake-like voices came from inside him.

Behler screamed and collapsed, closing her eyes and covering her ears.

"Behler! Bale!" Kellum was shaking her. She opened her eyes and was back in the grass next to the training fields. She still had sweat on her face from her last sparring session. "What happened?"

"I...I don't know." she said in a shaking voice. "I thought it was working, but..." she trailed off.

"It did for a second. I could feel you pulling me in, but then it just stopped. When I opened my eyes, you were hunched over and crying."

She felt her cheeks and, indeed, there were tears there.

"I, uh, I saw you in the field but then something changed. This mist came in and then...you turned around...and your eyes." she stopped, unable and unwilling to describe what she'd seen.

"I'm fine." Kellum put his arm around her shoulder. "You're freezing."

"I'm okay," she said, more to convince herself than him. She leaned into Kellum's chest, the last of her tremors fading.

"You were right," she whispered. "I can use thaelic... and Varek was waiting for me."

45

"Tonight is the night," Mathias said quietly, his voice barely louder than the splash of the falls.

Behler didn't look up. The water tugged gently at her ankles, cold and grounding.

"I know," she said.

The two of them, along with Luke, Kellum, Fennix and Meela had all taken a break from training to visit the falls. Behler sat with her feet dangling in the water.

Later that night would be the ceremony to break Lorna's bond with her stone.

"You going to be okay?" he asked.

She gave a half shrug. "Yeah."

"You know, Lorna talked to me a lot after we left Betham...more than she'd ever talked to me before."

"Really?" She looked at him. "About what?"

"Well, once she was talking about how she'd never wanted to be a mother... that had always been Sera's thing. But somehow the Anarsari had other plans for her, and she was glad she'd gotten the chance to act like yours."

Behler looked down into the water. "That doesn't sound like anything Lorna would ever say out loud." She laughed ruefully.

Mathias chuckled. "Yeah, I know...but I think she had this feeling how things were going to turn out...and I think she wanted me to tell you things she knew she wouldn't get the chance to." He picked up a flat pebble and skipped it across the water. "She regretted not being able to tell you the truth about who you are."

"Yeah, well," Behler squinted as she looked up into the sky. "I haven't quite forgiven any of you for that." She looked over at her best friend. "Yet."

They listened to the sound of the water and their friends' happy voices for a bit.

Then Mathias sighed dramatically. "Kellum is in love with you."

Behler felt as if someone had just knocked the wind out of her. "What the…? No, he's not!" she objected.

Mathias laughed. "Yeah, he is, and you know it."

Behler was so stunned she couldn't speak. Finally, she said, "I hate you."

"Maybe," he smiled, "But you love *him*."

"Matti…" she began but didn't know what else to say. Denying it felt wrong. Admitting anything was too scary.

"It's a good thing, Bale," he said and sounded much more grown up than she'd ever heard him sound. "It's a good thing for you both."

Behler looked across the water where Kellum was having a water fight with Luke. Finally, she looked back at Mathias. "I do hate you, you know?"

He smiled back at her. "You only hate me when I'm right."

"Friends. The first star of the evening has appeared," Penelope said. "Let us begin the ceremony to break the bond between Lorna Occlen and her stone."

"Can I stand next to you?" Avenly asked, slipping her hand into Behler's.

Beher smiled slightly and nodded.

Kellum, Mathias, and Luke stood nearby. Lorna's stone had been placed in the center of the training circle where everyone in the village had gathered.

"Rafe," Penelope said. "Would you begin?"

Rafe nodded. He knelt and picked up Lorna's stone. He stood and held the stone in front of him. "May the Trular who held this stone find peace. She rests now, in the fields of Shamar where the grass grows tall and the water flows clear." He held the stone closer to his face. "Stone of our ancestors, your work with Lorna Occlen is done. You have served her well. Now you must let her go." He walked over to Sera, who took the stone and kissed it then appeared to whisper something to it.

"What is she doing?" Behler asked Kellum quietly.

"She's sending a message to Lorna through the stone."

"What?" Behler looked up at him with wide eyes. "We can do that?"

Kellum smiled sadly. "It's just a custom, Bale. I don't really think the message gets delivered."

The stone glowed brightly then went dark.

"The bond is broken," Penelope announced. "May Lorna rest in Shamar with our ancestors."

Lorna rest? That was a joke.

Penelope took the stone and placed it back in the center of the circle. "Bring the other stones," she said.

Nirain and Kyra, one of the youngest Revalars, walked out each with an armful of stones. They placed them in a circle along with Lorna's former stone.

"Enon?" Penelope asked. "Are you ready for your ilari ceremony?" The boy nodded. "Step forward into the circle of stones." The boy positioned himself inside the circle. "Now speak the words."

"Together we fight. Together we are one," Enon said. "The bond between us will not be undone. I stand here for you to choose. May our bond begin."

Lorna's stone immediately glowed brightly.

"Your stone has bonded with you, Enon," Penelope said. She knelt and picked up the red stone. She smiled. "It seems this stone is eager to stay in the fight," she said as she handed it to Enon.

Behler was happy to see the stone already with someone else. It's what Lorna would have wanted.

That night, everyone stayed at the training fields to celebrate the new bonding. A bonfire was lit and casks of yulit juice and firewater were tapped.

Behler sat on a bale of hay, sipping a mixture of aji and firewater. It was both refreshingly cool and warming at the same time. The musicians from the lunafet had brought out their instruments and were playing happy, upbeat music. Behler watched as others danced and laughed while she was content to sit and listen to the joyful sounds. She was surprised when her brother fell onto the bale of hay beside her.

"So," he slurred. "Heard about our ilari ceremony?"

Behler rolled her eyes. "Unfortunately."

"All those stones fighting over you," he smirked. "Funny."

She turned and looked at him. "Funny?"

He looked at her through blurry eyes and shrugged. "Yeah. Funny."

Something about the way he was looking at her made the level-headed part of her snap. "I didn't ask for any of this. This has all been done to us, you know?"

Fennix blinked a couple times but couldn't seem to find the words he wanted to say thanks to a clouded, firewater brain.

Behler turned back to the fire. "I didn't ask for those vlocking stones to glow," she mumbled.

Fenn sighed. "I guess that was a stupid thing to say."

"Yeah, it was." Behler felt a rush of anger and frustration moving from deep within her where she'd pushed it down over and over again. She made the conscious decision to let it erupt. "You know what else was stupid? Disappearing for weeks without sending word to anyone—especially your mother—that you were safe."

Fennix's gaze drifted. "Look at it this way—if I'd died, you'd be off the hook for all this."

The flippant mention of death made something in Behler snap. Before she even knew what her hand was doing, it was making contact with her brother's cheek. A bright red handprint quickly began to appear.

Her eyes went wide as she realized what she'd done. Fenn's hand shot up to touch his cheek, his eyes as wide as hers.

"Don't joke about death," she said, fighting back hot tears.

His expression shifted. "I'm sorry," he said softly, guilt seeping in.

The initial shock of slapping her brother wore off, and all the painful emotions were right there waiting. Behler unleashed them. "You could've joined Varek, for all we knew."

He looked more stunned at those words than he had when she'd struck him. "I wouldn't do that," he said quickly. "I mean... I didn't..." His voice trailed off.

Behler wanted to say more, but the sound of her brother's voice and the sight of her handprint on his face softened her anger. They sat in silence for a few minutes. Finally, she said, "Fenn. I'm sorry." She looked down at the cup in her hand, suddenly disgusted with herself. "It's these ceremonies. And this kak." She dumped the rest of the drink into the dirt.

"I don't want to hurt anyone," he said. She wasn't even sure he'd heard her apology.

"I know," she said gently, placing her hand on his shoulder. "I know. I'm sorry."

Meela flew in from out of nowhere. "You two look like we just had a funeral." She giggled. "Oh, vlock, we just did. Sorry Bale."

Behler tried to grin. "It's okay. I was just going to find Kellum." She stood up to walk away.

"Bale, wait," Meela said, standing up and taking a step closer. Behler turned to face her. "Kellum...he's had a hard time."

"I know," Behler said.

"Just... be careful with him, okay?"

"What? Why would I need to be?"

"Because you two were here on your own for a long time. And now that Mathias is back..."

"Mathias!? Do you think...?" Mathias was like a brother to Behler. For Meela to suggest otherwise sent a queasy feeling through Behler's gut.

But Meela was already turning back around to rejoin Fennix, who still looked upset sitting on the bale of hay.

Behler suddenly wanted to get as far away from the scene as she could, so she turned on her heel and headed toward her mother's house. But, halfway there, she realized she didn't want to be there either, so she turned toward the lake instead. Once there she laid down underneath one of the many Arbirans and looked up at the night sky. The stars shone down in the veil-less sky above. She wondered if that message from Sera to Lorna actually could have gotten to Shamar somehow. Was Shamar even a real place?

"Lorna," she said as a tear fell down the side of her face toward the ground. She ached to be able to talk to her aunt. Just a few more words. What would Lorna say to her?

She curled up in the soft trellin grass next to the Arbiran and let the night sounds around her lull her to sleep. When she woke, the fire moon had moved halfway across the sky, and she could no longer hear the music coming from the training fields. She sat up and realized a small wreath of the little purple Arbiran flowers lay just beside her. She reached for it, and as soon as her fingers touched it, she heard the familiar rustling of the Arbirans' leaves around her.

"Erhana," she said, feeling the Arbirans' sympathy within the Thread. She stood reluctantly and headed for the house she now called home.

46

Aeron watched the Armigoth troops from her hiding spot in the forest. She'd watched the Horde's approach for days and continued to monitor the campsite they'd set up just north of the forest. They'd seemed to be waiting, but for what, she hadn't been sure. Rafe had sent her to watch them, though, and that's what she would do until she had better information to bring back. She'd been alone for days after her scouting partner, Uri, had moved to the west to get a better idea of how many enemy troops were ready to invade the forest.

Aeron really wished for the tug of the Deep Thread.

The Gorlogs had arrived a few days after the Horde soldiers. She thought the Horde would start moving then, but they remained.

A day later, it became clear what they all had been waiting for: the Okinars arrived. Aeron had never seen an Okinar before. The sight of *one* of them was terrifying. *Twenty* of them was like something out of a nightmare. They stood as tall as an Eastern Flinx tree – over twice as tall as the Horde guuns. Their bodies were as dense as the Gorlogs, but with more definition of sinew and muscle. They each carried a weapon with a semi-circular stone with chiseled edges on each end. The stones were attached to a large wooden handle as tall as a grown man.

Both the Horde and the Gorlogs eyed them suspiciously and kept their distance. Aeron knew she needed to get word to Ardin, but she wanted to make sure she had as much information as she could get before making the journey.

She heard movement in the forest behind her. A few moments later, she saw Uri in a tree just a few yura lengths away from her.

They used the hand signals they'd created after the Deep Thread had been broken.

Where – you? Aeron asked.

West.

Aeron could feel Uri's sarcasm even from their distant perches.

Long time, she shot back.

Uri shrugged.

Aeron motioned at the scene before them. *Huge.* She motioned toward the Okinars.

Uri nodded. *Very bad.*

The scouts watched as the Okinars stood silently. The Horde and the Gorlogs were eyeing their new comrades with both awe and trepidation.

The Okinars didn't seem to know what to do with themselves or where to go. They grew restless, bumping and shoving each other.

"Ahhhhh!" An Okinar yelled out, slashing its weapon high in the sky.

The sudden, loud, animal-like sound made everyone jump, especially Aeron and Uri.

They looked at each other, wide-eyed, then laughed silently at their own reactions.

A female Horde captain walked up to the Okinar who had made the primordial sound. Aeron assumed the bellowing giant was the Okinar leader. It appeared the captain did as well.

Aeron watched as they had a conversation. They were far enough away that she could not hear any words spoken, but she could see their body language. She was impressed by the captain's nerve; she had to give her that. The Okinar could have sliced her in two at any given moment, but the captain stood her ground.

She motioned toward the forest.

Aeron suspected she was telling the Okinars where they would be heading next.

The leader turned around and said something to his fellow Okinars.

Then they all began walking toward the treeline, only about a hundred yura lengths from where Aeron and Uri hid.

The Arbiran beneath her began to vibrate. Images rushed through her mind, too fast for her to understand. A feeling of terror nearly brought her to her knees. She glanced over at Uri whose eyes were wide. Aeron knew his Arbiran must be doing the same thing.

They're afraid, Aeron thought. The Arbirans were old, wise, and steady. She'd never felt one tremble – until now.

Soon enough, it became clear why. The Okinars began breaking trees off at their trunks. The loud cracking of wood reverberated through the forest.

Arbirans all around her began moving. Aeron thought at first they were fleeing, but they weren't running. They were heading for the Okinars. Aeron watched as the giants continued to destroy the native Garahan Forest trees, pulling some out of the ground and breaking them over their knees. But why were the Arbirans so afraid? They weren't ordinary trees. They knew something she didn't.

Then she realized the Arbiran was trembling with rage, not fear. They raged over the deaths of their native neighbors.

She gripped her draka. "Go!" she shouted to Uri. "Tell the village—the Armigoth is coming."

She touched the Tree with her palm. "I'm with you. Let's go."

The Tree swayed a bit and Aeron held on as the Arbiran pulled its roots from the ground.

Together, they headed into the fight.

47

Uri ran in the direction he thought Ardin was. Arbirans moved in all directions around him. The largest of them moved toward the Okinars and the Horde. The smallest headed away from the danger.

The changing forest was disorienting and confusing, and by sunset of the first day, Uri knew he was hopelessly lost. He looked up, hoping to see the night sky to reorient himself, but the canopy was too thick.

Uri looked around the darkened forest, trying to find at least one Arbiran who had lingered.

All he could see were native-looking trees and thick underbrush.

Uri sat down next to an amberly tree. The smell of the flowers reminded him of home, sitting next to the lake and making wreaths from fallen flowers of the different trees and Arbirans.

He slumped against the amberly tree and opened his canteen. Hopefully a little aji would help clear his head so he could figure out his next move.

"Some scout I am," he muttered. "Can't even find my way home."

He laid his draka down and illuminated the stone.

Something whizzed by his ear. He heard a small sound behind him, like a drop of water hitting the ground.

"What the..."

Something stung his cheek right under his eye.

He looked down and a small rock was sitting on his chest.

Uri was up on his feet, his isari stone flaring bright as he swept his draka around.

"Who's there?" He demanded.

"You's a Trular?"

A voice came from the undergrowth.

"Who's asking?" Uri tried to see any sign of his attacker.

"Is'a you a Trular?" The voice was more adamant this time.

"Yes, yes...I'm a Trular. Now, show yourself." Uri struggled to keep his voice steady.

Poppy stepped out of the greenery. She turned from her green, camouflaged coloring to a brown hue. She stared up at Uri.

He studied her for a moment. "Are you a...a Kribble?"

Poppy smiled her uncanny smile. "I is a Kribble. You's a lost."

"I'm not...I'm not lost," Uri said, immediately foolishly offended.

"Forest is a changin'. You's a lost. I willa help."

"How can you help?"

Poppy looked at him as if he were insane and held out her hand. "Come."

Uri stared at her for a moment, frozen with uncertainty.

"Come," Poppy repeated.

Finally, Uri reached down and took the little creature's hand. He was shocked at how soft and silky her fur was. Her palm felt like the pads on a cat's paw. "So...uh...your kind is real?" He asked, ducking leaves and branches as she led him through the dark forest.

Poppy didn't answer – just kept walking.

Uri had heard stories about Kribbles. A few had stowed away when the first Revalas had come through the danari. They had fled into the forest soon after and had helped to create the strange spookiness that native Elians had grown to fear. They were so secretive and reclusive, though, that Uri hadn't heard of anyone seeing one for years.

Uri kept walking straight into small branches and twigs as Poppy pulled him onward. "Hey, uh...can we slow down?"

"No. Gotta go fast. Trouble comin'."

"Yeah, I know," Uri said, spitting out a spider web he'd just walked through.

"A'most there," Poppy said, and Uri was pretty sure she was speaking to him like she would have a child.

Uri spent the next few minutes ducking and dodging the forest. Every time he tried to let go of the Kribble's hand, she just held on tighter.

He almost ran into her when she stopped suddenly.

"Here," she said. She took his hand and put it on the tree in front of them. He felt the familiar swirls and carvings of an Arbiran beneath his fingertips. It was the largest one Uri had ever seen.

"An Arbiran."

"Sent-i-nel," Poppy said.

Uri looked up, holding his isari stone up. "You stayed behind." It was both a statement and a question.

Poppy reached out and touched the Arbiran. The special symbols on the Tree's trunk immediately began glowing, and the tips of Poppy's fur lit with the same light.

Uri had seen the Arbirans luminesce many times. Had requested it himself when traveling. But he'd never seen this kind of luminescence. This was much brighter and contained completely in the organic etchings in the Arbiran's bark.

And the Kribble was glowing.

That was...unexpected.

Poppy removed her hand, and she immediately stopped glowing, but the Arbiran's glow continued.

A hundred yura lengths away, a soft aura began to glow.

"Go," Poppy said, pointing at the Arbiran. "Sent-i-nels willa guide you."

"Thanks...uh...Kribble."

"I'sa Poppy."

"Thanks, Poppy."

She blinked at him with her wide eyes then vanished into the forest.

Uri looked toward the soft glow ahead and began making his way to the next Arbiran.

It didn't take Aeron long to discover her isari stone had little to no effect on the Okinars. She quickly switched to her bow, but soon discovered arrows had little effect on them as well.

"Vlock," she spat.

She was unsure of what to do next.

She and the Arbiran looked on while the Okinar continued pulling trees out of the ground.

Aeron heard the captain's shrill voice from across the field. She couldn't quite make out her words, but she could tell she wasn't happy. Then she pointed right at the Arbiran Aeron was perched in.

"Those, you idiots!" The captain's voice rang out clearly.

The Okinar leader followed her gesture until, to Aeron, it felt like its eyes met hers. He raised his weapon and shouted something in a deep, bellowing yell. The language was strange and gravelly.

Every Okinar stopped and looked at their leader, then at once, all turned their heads to look toward Aeron and the Arbiran. Aeron hadn't felt true fear in a very long time. Her training for the Revala had done well to prepare her for nearly everything she had faced.

But nothing could have prepared her for the sight of twenty Okinar running toward her while she stood precariously in a Tree holding two seemingly useless weapons.

Her heart beat hard. She tried to slow her breathing so she could think better, but she was struggling. She could feel the earth vibrating from their giant, thunderous feet.

How big do you have to be to actually shake the earth just by running, she thought – then thought about how ridiculous it was to even think about that right before she was about to die. The things your brain does to deal with approaching doom.

"Stop it, kakweed." She wasn't sure if she was talking to herself, her brain, or both.

The Arbiran began vibrating more. Aeron could feel the anger moving from the Tree's bark into her own body. The anger was a good adrenaline boost and helped her mind to focus.

"What's our plan here?" she asked her foliaged friend.

Yosh-sha, the Arbiran said. Fight.

Aeron wasn't sure how they were going to do that, but she pulled her kintar out of its sheath.

It seemed to be a losing battle before it even began, but Aeron knew the Trulars owed the Arbirans so much. If she was the one to pay that, at least in part, so be it.

Just as the first Okinar got within a few of its giant steps, Aeron felt as if the Arbirans sucked in all the air around them. In the next second, an invisible wind flew out of the Arbirans in all directions. It was strong enough that it knocked people in the Horde a good twenty yura lengths backward. But more importantly, it knocked the Okinars off their feet.

Ahmei, Aeron thought. *It's their version of ahmei.*

Aeron cheered from her perch.

The Okinars had been hit hard enough that they sat stunned, but Aeron knew that wouldn't last.

"They're going to be angry now," she said to the Arbiran.

Out of the corner of his eye, she saw movement. She turned and another large Arbiran stood next to them. Just then, another stepped up to her right.

"This is more like it," Aeron smirked. She put her kintar away and grabbed her draka. She might not be able to do much, but she could leave some marks.

48

A few mornings after Lorna's ceremony, Behler found out that Enon didn't have a draka yet. Standing over her weapon's chest, she looked down at Lorna's. She'd tucked it there under a blanket because looking at it was too painful. She picked it up and took it outside.

Behler scanned the fields until she saw the younger boy. He was training with his kintar and holding his own with Kyra.

Behler approached him. "Here, Enon," she smiled, holding the draka up. "I heard you needed this."

Enon looked both reluctant and excited. "But it was your aunt's."

Behler shrugged. "She wouldn't like for it to sit around collecting dust while you don't have one. Besides, I think it would be nice to keep it with the stone it's held for so long."

Enon smiled at her. "Thank you." He gripped it tightly, and Behler had no doubt she'd made the right choice. She walked away, feeling lighter, happier, and relieved.

When she first woke up, she'd felt very reticent about seeing Meela and Fenn at the training fields, but once there, she quickly realized their memories of the night before were spotty at best. She decided the best thing to do about it all was to let it go.

The morning training passed quickly, and before she knew it, it was time for their lunch break.

"Hey," Kellum said as she walked toward him to eat. "Check out Luke." He tipped his head toward the eastern treeline. There was Luke riding Sabana. It had taken a broken arm, a bruised rib, two black eyes, and a dislocated shoulder, but he'd finally broken her.

Behler sat down and looked around the open field. She was sure nearly every Trular in Ardin was there. Some were training, some were teaching, others were just watching or tending to gardens or livestock. It was a gorgeous day, easy to pretend there wasn't a dark cloud looming a couple days' ride to the north.

Shaway hahsha.

Behler looked at Kellum. "Hm? Did you say something?"

"No."

Shaway hahsha.

Others around her stopped moving too, hearing the same thing.

"It's an Arbiran," Kellum said, standing up and looking around."

Kellum held up a finger across his lips and cocked his head to the side.

Shaway hahsha ahashuweihhh.... The last syllable lingered on the breeze.

Behler and Kellum didn't move a muscle. They each stood silent, waiting to hear more.

Instead of more whispers in the breeze, the edge of the forest started to move in a nonexistent wind.

Across the village, next to the Great House, Warln and Rafe were just preparing to head back to the training fields when the Arbirans around the lake began to move and sway. Their leaves rustled then shook.

Like a wave, the rustling began to ripple south along the edge of the lake and moved around each side of the lake until it reached them.

"What's going on?" Rafe asked. Warln understood the Arbirans more than anyone in the village.

The old man held up a hand to shush Rafe and cocked his head to the side, a mirror of his grandson across the village. The rustling grew more frantic. It created a wind that passed through the trees, and on the wind there was another sound...one that sounded like a mournful cry.

"I don't know," Warln said after a few moments. "They're scared...I think. Maybe angry."

And then every Arbiran went completely still all at once. The silence was as loud as the wind had been.

"What's happening," Behler asked, back at the training grounds. Every Trular was on their feet and staring into the forest and toward the lake.

They all watched, then, as every Arbiran they could see in the forest pulled its roots up and began walking north. The earth beneath them shook as the large Trees marched away. At the north end of the village, right at the forest's edge, a passageway formed, and all the Arbirans moved toward it.

"They're leaving us," Kellum said to Behler.

Shocked and scared Trulars began speaking frantically with each other.

But Behler had felt the pull of the Thread. She'd felt the fear and anger Warln had sensed. "Something is happening. They're not abandoning us...they have to go – fight I think," Behler said.

"Fight what?" Kellum asked.

Behler shook her head. "I don't know."

Across the village, Rafe's jaw twitched at the sight of the empty spaces around the lake. The only Arbiran that remained was the first Warln that had placed so long ago. "We're exposed," he said.

Warln shook his head. "They protected us as long as they could. Now they must protect themselves and their kind."

At the fields, Kellum asked, "What do we do now?" He watched the Arbirans march past the kogum field.

Behler looked around. She could see fear in the eyes of those who had grown accustomed to the protection the Arbirans provided.

"In Betham," she said quietly, "we never had the Arbirans. We learned to survive. We adapted. We learned to protect each other." She turned to Kellum. "We can do it again." She gestured toward the large group of Trulars nearby. "We'll show them how."

49

The Trulars who had been safely tucked away in Ardin for the longest were the jumpiest after the Arbirans left. Behler, Kellum, and Mathias quickly adapted as did the Revalars who were used to living outside the forest.

Although Behler and the others didn't do anything in particular to help ease the villagers' worries, they led by example and continued on with their day-to-day lives. That alone gave the others courage.

The sight of the eldest Arbiran was also comforting in its own bittersweet way. Behler wondered if it would be alone for the rest of its life. Would the others ever come back to the village? Would it eventually leave to find them?

Whenever she could, she'd sit quietly next to the Tree. It didn't speak to her; it simply stood stoically silent. She'd noticed Warln sitting next to it many times as well.

"Hey," Kellum walked up to her as she was packing up for the evening. "Let's go to the falls."

Behler smiled. "Okay." She tucked her canteen inside her satchel. "I'll get the others."

"Nah," Kellum shrugged and smiled shyly. "Let's just the two of us go – like the first time we went."

Behler's heart jumped in her chest, and she felt her cheeks flush. She cursed her adolescent emotions for their outright betrayal. She shrugged and nonchalantly repeated, "Okay."

They quickly readied Storm and Ciela then took off toward the falls.

As soon as they reached the clearing, she jumped off Ciela, slipped off her boots, then turned and ran for the water without waiting for Kellum. She found the rocky bank where she'd waded in before. Kellum had gotten his boots off and was running and leaping into the water just as she made it ankle deep into the pool.

He shot up out of the water. "Woooh...it's cold!" Behler laughed at him and continued to wade in slowly. "Come on! You're as slow as a slug," he teased and splashed water in her direction. "It won't seem as cold if you just jump in!"

"Oh yeah – all your squealing made that option really appealing," Behler teased and kicked water back at him. She walked in a little further and the water hit her waist. She gasped and backed up a little. "Ooosh! It's cold."

Kellum laughed. "Is there an echo out here?"

She waded in a little bit further then took a deep breath and dunked her entire body under. The cold water was a shock in all the best ways. Her warm cheeks were immediately chilled, and the crispness of the water was nearly magical.

She dunked herself down again then swam across the entire length of the pool.

"You've improved," Kellum said when she came up for air.

Behler shrugged off his comment. "It's all coming back to me." She laid back and floated, looking up at the deepening purple sky. The first star was just becoming visible. The last of the day's pillowy clouds floated directly above her in their own violet sea.

Soon the purples would turn to black and reveal the constellations that were moving closer and closer to the positions they'd be in during Iskaara.

Her mind wondered, puzzling together what might happen to her that night. Would it be big and noticeable? Or would the changes come gradually until finally she was as strong as she was supposed to be? Would there be any pain that night?

"You can see more of the sky since the Arbirans left," Kellum said, his gaze upward. She looked over at him and he was smiling gently, his eyes gently closed as he twirled his fingertips in the water. But then his face fell. "If the Armigoth had its way, we'd never see the sky again." His eyes came down to meet Behler's. "Bale, the Armigoth's cloud – or whatever it is – it's so terrible. I wasn't even under it when I saw it, but I could feel it trying to get in my head. The stronger it got, the further it could reach out."

Behler flipped and put her knees on the bottom of the pool. Her hands unintentionally mimicked Kellum's, swirling circles in the water. "It can only get in if we let it."

He shook his head. "But all those people...not *all* of them could have wanted to let it in."

"No," she stood up. Water dripped rapidly from her green luka. "I'm sure they didn't. But at some point, they forgot what was good. They forgot to hold on to that."

Kellum looked at her and she knew that everything Mathias had said about Kellum loving her was true. And what he'd said about her loving Kellum – that was true, too.

She took a step closer to him and dared to reach out for his hand. It felt so much more intentional than the first time their hands had met. "We have to hold on to what is worth fighting for."

With his free hand, he reached up and moved a wet strand of hair from her face. He let his hand linger on her cheek and Behler felt the warmth of it.

She reached up and pressed his hand into her cheek. The soft scent of yulit soap lingered on his skin—simple, clean, comforting.

The moment was completely broken as something came crashing toward them from the forest.

They moved quickly through the water and grabbed their weapons before anything broke through the treeline. Behler was taken aback when she realized she'd grabbed her draka instead of her bow.

They both stood facing the sound.

The sounds of limbs snapping and leaves crunching grew louder until a young man just a bit older than Kellum stepped into the clearing by the falls. He wore typical Elian clothes but a draka was strapped to his back.

"Who are you?" Kellum asked, his voice firm and demanding.

"Who are you?" the stranger asked in return.

"You first," Behler said quickly.

The stranger's eyes darted around, taking in their drakas and where he was. He took a deep breath and said, "I'm the Revala scout, Uri. Rafe sent me to watch the Armigoth's forces." He paused to breathe again. "I have news."

50

Behler, Kellum, and Uri rode quickly back to the village. They spotted Fennix sitting on a hay bale, whittling with the knife Kellum had returned.

"Fenn, where's Rafe?" Behler asked, breathlessly.

Fennix started to shrug—but then he spotted Uri. He stood, instantly alert. "What's going on?"

"The Armigoth has gathered its forces," Uri said. "They're tearing the forest apart to get to Ardin."

"It's why the Arbirans left," Kellum continued. "To stop them and help protect the other Arbirans."

Fenn jerked his head toward the tents. "Rafe's at the campsite."

"Let's go," Behler said.

Fennix tucked the knife in his waistband. "I'm coming with you."

Rafe was sitting at a campfire that had just gotten started. He was still fiddling with the kindling when the quartet approached him.

"Sir," Uri said as soon as he was close enough to be heard.

Rafe looked up and stood as soon as he saw the scout. "Uri. What news?"

"The forces are ready to advance. Aeron stayed behind to help the Arbirans. Sir..." he faltered. "Sir, the Okinar...they're massive. They were able to rip trees right out of the ground. Break them over their knees like that kindling you just put to the fire."

Rafe put a hand on Uri's shoulder. "I know. But they are flesh and blood just like us." He looked at Behler and Fennix. "Our time is up. You two need to leave at dawn. The children and elders as well. The Armigoth fighters will be occupied trying to get to Ardin while we are leaving it. Let's just hope Varek's dragons don't find us first." He looked at Uri. "You've given us a headstart that will save lives, Uri. Thank you."

Uri could not hide the happiness on his face. Still, he tucked in his smile and gave a quick nod. "Thank you."

Rafe looked at each of them, pausing longer on both Fennix and Behler. "Go, gather your things, say your goodbyes, and be ready to leave at first light."

Although she had hours before dawn, Behler flew through the front door and ran back to her room to pack her things. She grabbed the satchel she'd brought with her from Betham; the memory of Lorna handing it to her while standing in their tiny, worn-down house was still fresh in her memory. It had only been weeks since then, but it felt like an entirely different lifetime to her.

Maybe if she'd been able to catch up with Lorna that last night in Betham, her aunt would still be alive. *Or maybe you'd be dead too*, she thought. She pushed both thoughts out of her head and grabbed her extra canteens and an extra set of clothes. She looked at the beautiful garments in the chest. Reaching into a drawer, she grabbed another blouse with beautiful, embroidered butterflies and flowers. She'd never worn it before; it was far too pretty to wear to train in, but it felt wrong to leave it.

Everything was stuffed into her satchel as she looked around the room to see if there was anything else to bring along. The baby blanket her mother had pointed out that first night was draped over a chair. She grabbed it. There was no room in the satchel for it, but she could find room in Ciela's saddle bags.

She grabbed her canteens so she could refill them with the aji in the kitchen.

When she turned down the hallway, the sight of her brother nearly made her jump out of her skin. He was standing silently in the front room.

"Kak! You startled me," she chuckled at her own jumpiness. He turned and looked at her with a sad expression on his face. "Are you okay?"

He looked around. "I was just thinking about how I used to hate to stay inside this house." He shook his head. "Not just this house but the entire village. I would talk Luke into going to the cave or ruins...or anywhere but here. We got in trouble all the time." He smiled a little. "Now that I know I'll probably never see this place again it's just strange how much I feel I'm going to miss it."

Behler had walked down the hallway to join him in the front room. She nodded. "It's hard losing the only home you've ever known, no matter how you felt about it." She looked around the room, recalling her first night and morning in it. She was surprised how much it felt like home compared to back then. "Maybe we'll be able to come back after all this is over."

Fennix pressed his lips together as if there was something he wanted to say but simply nodded instead.

The sound of the back door opening and closing interrupted them. Sera came rushing down the hall.

"Ama," Fennix said with a start.

She stopped abruptly. "Fenn. Behler." Her eyes had been determined when she'd first looked up, on a mission to gather the things she'd need for her journey with the children and elderly. As she looked at her own children, her eyes softened. "Well," she inhaled, "here we are. It looks like we might not be together for Iskaara after all."

"We'll be fine, Ama," Fenn said.

Sera smiled. "Oh, I know that. I'm just sorry I won't be able to be with you on that special night to share it with you." She looked at Behler and her eyes immediately filled with tears. "I didn't want to miss that." Her voice cracked.

"We still have many weeks before Iskaara," Behler tried to comfort her. "We'll try to get to Riverfork before then."

Sera gently took her wrist. "No, Behler, you focus on you. Don't worry about me. I'll be okay. I'm a Revala, after all." She stood a little taller as she said the last bit. "If you make it to Riverfork before Iskaara, great...but if not, I know you two will be there for each other." She wiped her eyes. "Let's have a nice dinner before we all go our different ways in the morning."

Behler and Fennix both nodded.

That evening, they squeezed into the kitchen, cooking and laughing and sharing the space around them.

They were all well aware it might be the last time.

51

The Okinars stacked native trees in towering pyres, and the Horde lit them one by one. Aeron and the Arbirans used their powers to keep the Okinars at a distance but close to dawn on the second day of fighting, Aeron watched in dismay as the Okinars were able to surround one of the smaller of the Arbiran giants. They toppled it, and an Okinar who was carrying a rather large yulit tree as a torch touched it to the Arbiran's leaves.

Idiots. Arbirans are fireproof.

The Tree's leaves caught immediately.

"No!" Aeron yelled. "What's happening?"

Her Arbiran's leaves trembled in response. *"No more aji."*

The Trees were disconnected from the root system that allowed them to share Aji and replenish the water they needed to create it.

Aeron looked around them. "I think we need to get out of here."

"Go," the Arbiran whispered. *"Arbirans stay."*

The other Arbirans moved and formed a line with hers. Their limbs reached out for one another, intertwining. She watched as their roots dug into the earth, anchoring them. They could share what little aji they had left like this.

"Go, now. Erhana."

Aeron placed her hands on the Tree. "Erhana."

She slid down the Arbiran's smooth trunk. When her feet hit the ground, she pulled her draka out once more. At least twenty Horde guuns were standing between her and the forest.

"Hey guys, let a lady through," she smirked, and began running toward them.

Behler hadn't had the nightmare in weeks, so when it pulled her under again that night, it caught her off guard—and made her furious.

The darkness surrounded her like a cold blanket. The air was cold with moisture. She could hear the sound of dripping from somewhere, and it echoed as if she were in a huge cavern.

This wasn't the same nightmare.

"Trular." A voice came from all around her.

"Varek," Behler spat out.

A low chuckle reverberated in the room. "You know my name." He sounded pleased. "Soon we'll have to meet properly. *Sooooon*."

His voice sounded too snakelike. The sound of it made Behler cringe internally. She knew she should fear him. She knew he was completely set on killing her. But there, in her space, in her mind, he had nothing that could hurt her. "You'll have to catch me first, you son of a pig."

The voice laughed again. "Feisty," it laughed. "This is going to be fun."

"You're so brave and strong, you won't even show your face here. What are you afraid of?"

Why was she goading him?

She didn't know. All she knew was she was as angry as she'd ever been.

"You want to see me, Trular?" Varek laughed. It was a deep guttural sound. The air started spinning around her. A skeletal face came at her from the darkness. Its skin sagged and its eyes were so sunken, she couldn't quite make them out. As it quickly approached her, it opened its mouth as if to swallow her hole.

"It's a nice parlor trick, but I've seen better," Behler sneered.

She focused all her thoughts on the first solid thing that came to mind: her amulet. It took all her strength to pull her Thread out of this other place, and when she opened her eyes, she was yelling. Her body was drenched in sweat.

At first, she thought the foggy mist from thaelic had followed her into the real world. She was surrounded by a wispy cloud.

Fennix burst through the door. "Bale!"

Sera was right behind him.

"I'm okay," she said. "I'm okay. It was just a...nightmare."

Fennix sat down on the bed next to her. "No, it was Varek wasn't it?"

She looked at him. "Yes. He used thaelic."

"What is all this...fog?" Sera asked.

Her brother first looked around the room then looked closer at Behler.

"It's not fog," Fenn said. "It's steam."

Behler looked at herself, perplexed and confused. Steam was indeed rising off her arms and legs. "I was....I was really kakked-off."

Fennix smirked and laughed. "Yeah...I would say so."

Sera was confused. "You...you made the steam?"

Fennix laughed again. "Chosen ones and all that, you know." He winked at Behler. She couldn't help but smile back.

It had felt good to stand up to Varek, and whatever this steam meant...that felt like a good thing too.

52

Before the sun even began brightening the sky the next morning, Behler was leading Ciela out of the stables. The early summer morning air was pleasantly cool.

Mathias stood with his horse, Nara. He had a strange look on his face when his eyes met Behler's.

"What's going on?" she asked him.

He shrugged. "You know my father. He had to remind me what's at stake—like I don't already know."

She grabbed his shoulder. "Matti, we're going to be fine." She smiled when he looked down at her.

A tug on her luka drew her attention away from Mathias.

"Behler," Avenly said. "I made you this." She handed Behler a braided bracelet made of thin leather strips and blue beads. "Kellum said your favorite color is blue."

Behler knelt down. "It is," she smiled and slipped the bracelet on. She pulled the little girl into a hug. "Now listen, I need you to do a very important job for me, okay?" Avenly's eyes grew wide as she nodded. "I need you to help my mother get the kids safely to Riverfork."

Avenly looked a little defeated. "That's why Ama's going with her."

Behler shook her head. "This is going to take more than our mothers to get everyone safely there." She lowered her voice. "Have you seen how feeble some of the elders are?"

Avenly giggled and Behler winked at her.

"Do you have your kintar?" Behler asked. Avenly pulled it out from the sheath on her back. "Good...good." She gently took Avenly's hands in hers. "I'll see you at Riverfork, okay?"

Avenly nodded.

Kellum had snuck up behind Avenly, and she squealed when he scooped her up. "Did you pack all your important things?"

"Yes," she giggled.

"No," Kellum teased. "You forgot something very important."

"No, I got everything," Avenly insisted, still smiling at her big brother.

Kellum reached behind her back. When he brought his hand back around, he was holding a small leather sphere. "Your favorite ball."

Avenly's laughter stopped. "No, that's *your* favorite ball."

Kellum looked at the ball in his hand. "Is it? Hmm. Well," he leaned in closer. "Will you take care of it for me until we get to Riverfork. If I take it, I might lose it. You know Fenn and Matti – they've always been jealous of it. I think they might steal it," he whispered.

Avenly giggled again. "And Luke too. Luke would definitely take it."

Kellum kept his face very serious despite Behler's spontaneous grin behind Avenly. "Exactly. So can you take care of it for me?"

Avenly nodded seriously. "I will," she said solemnly.

Kellum hugged her. "Thanks, little sister. We'll see you soon, okay?"

Behler's heart cracked a little when she saw the tears rolling down Avenly's cheeks. "Okay." Her voice hitched.

Kellum tapped her nose. "Okay," he smiled. "Now, go find Ama."

Avenly ran off. Behler watched as she found her mother and fell into her arms, clinging to her waist.

A few minutes later, all of Behler and Fennix's crew were standing in a line, ready to leave.

"Hey Matti, how's Nara doing?" Fennix asked, nodding toward the gray horse.

Mathias rolled his eyes. "She's fine, Fenn. Thanks."

"Yeah?" Luke asked. "Hey Bale, have you officially met Matti's horse?"

Behler looked at them. "What the vlock are you talking about? I've seen his horse many times."

Kellum laughed. "Yeah, but have you *officially* met her?"

Behler looked at Mathis. "What the kak are they talking about?"

Mathias sighed. "I named her when I was six. Her official name is Duknara."

Behler noticed all the guys were snickering, except Mathias. "Okay, her name is Duknara."

Mathias shot every one of the guys a dirty look.

"Duknara means fartbiscuit in old Trular," Meela said, coming up behind Behler.

The entire group, aside from Mathias, burst into boisterous laughter.

"I was six!" Mathias insisted.

"And you've never changed it," Fennix pointed out.

Mathias shrugged and rubbed Nara's face. "She likes it." He leaned up and kissed her nose. Nara whinnied and chuffed happily at him.

Rafe approached them. "Trulars, I'm glad you're all in good spirits. It has been a deep honor getting to know you – even those I've known for years, these past days have been some of the happiest I can recall." He smiled crookedly. "I know that may seem strange with all that's going on, but you all have refreshed an energy in us all that's been missing. I think the Armigoth had sunken in a bit more than any of us would care to admit...but you have brought a light back to us all. I know that together we will beat back the Armigoth and prevent it from spreading through the danaris. Now go, collect the Desharets so we can end this battle. Let us find victory."

"And may victory bring us peace," the crowd around them said.

"Boys," Warln said. Kellum and Luke turned around.

"Grampa, please go to Riverfork with Sera," Kellum pleaded.

Warln nodded. "I'll help get them to Riverfork."

"And stay there," Kellum said, catching the hidden words.

Warln sighed. He pulled both boys into a hug. "Let's just get me to Riverfork before we worry about anything else." He walked over to Behler. "It's been an honor getting to know you, Trular. A true honor." He reached out and gripped her forearm with his hand. She returned the gesture.

"Stay at Riverfork," she said softly.

Warln smiled and winked. "Go out there and bring us peace."

He turned and walked away.

She knew he had no intention of staying in Riverfork but wondered if maybe he didn't really believe he'd make it that far to begin with.

She pushed away the sadness that thought brought with it and looked around at all the people staring at them. Only weeks before, she'd dreaded those strangers' eyes upon her. Now, no longer strangers, she worried which eyes she may never see again.

Don't dwell on that, she told herself.

Hopping up on Ciela, she looked from side to side. "Ready?"

Everyone nodded.

"Let's go," Fennix said.

Behler followed behind her brother, and as they passed through the archery practice field Behler remembered standing there on her first day in Ardin and how she'd felt everyone's eyes on her back, watching and waiting. She felt them all again.

Fennix stopped and turned his horse, Kina, to face the crowd. "Kinot Trulars!" he shouted, placing his right fist over his heart then raising it over his head. The other five lined up with him and each of the other five repeated Fennix's gesture. The entire Trular community then returned the gesture with fists raised into the air.

From somewhere in the crowd, a voice rang out— "Kinot Fenn! Kinot Behler!" A beat passed, and then the training field erupted.

Behler saw her mother standing quietly just in front of a wagon. She stood with her head high; the only sign she may be in distress was her clenched fists at her sides.

As the six turned and headed into the underbrush, the Trulars began chanting, "*Kinot! Kinot! Kinot!*"

Victory! Victory! Victory!

53

Aeron ran through the forest as quickly as she could. She had found the dell that led directly to the falls outside of Ardin and ran alongside the creek. She would be able to make far better time than the Armigoth forces, whenever they managed to breach the forest.

How much time could the Arbirans give them? How much time before the Arbirans fell?

She only hoped Uri had made it and that the others were already gone.

Sera had all the children sit on the bales of hay around the training circle. She'd split them into three groups so she, Nirain, and Kyra could keep an eye on their respective groups. The elders that were traveling with them were slowly gathering near the stables.

Nirain approached her, and by the look on her face, Sera knew something wasn't right.

"Warln needs to see you on the far side of the stables."

"Is something wrong?"

Nirain nodded. "Very much so."

Sera walked as quickly as she could without raising alarms with any of the gathering people whose nerves were already frazzled.

She turned to the corner to see Warln hunched over examining the underside of one of the wagons.

"What is it?" she asked.

Warln stood. "Someone has broken the axles on all the wagons. Cut them clean through."

"What!? How long will it take to replace them all?" Sera inadvertently looked at the sky as if the dragon would somehow materialize in that moment.

"That's the thing. All the spares have been cut through as well."

Sera was already working through what was to come next in her head. Thirty-two children were travelling with her to Riverfork. How long would it take them to walk that far?

"We're going to have to put all the children on horseback," Warln said. "Even the youngest – although I'm sure we adults can take turns carrying some of the smallest if need be."

"Warln…" Sera began. "How did this happen?"

He pursed his lips before he spoke. "Someone could have gotten to the village last night I suppose. An outsider. Without the Arbirans, they could find us." That explanation was far better than the alternative.

"Do we have any horses to spare…ones who can carry at least part of our load? We need supplies. Food. Water."

"Gracie can carry a hefty load. Flox can too. We do have some of the smaller wagons that the horses can pull. We'll have to leave the bakram loose to graze on their own. Can't exactly carry those on horseback and herding them would take too much time." He rubbed his hands together, dusting off some dirt. "Sera," he said quieter, and took a step forward. "I don't have to tell you the other explanation as to what happened to these wagons. We must tread carefully."

Sera looked up at him. "I've been treading carefully for years. I won't stop now."

"Has anyone seen Rafe?" Sera asked a group of Revalars who stood preparing their horses.

Zeke motioned toward Rafe's tent. "He was going to pack up his tent." He paused. "Strange that he hasn't yet."

Sera nodded then headed toward the tent.

"Rafe," she called before walking in. "Rafe?"

She opened the flap and stepped in – and gasped at the sight of Rafe's slumped body next to his cot.

"Rafe!" She moved quickly to kneel next to him. Gently, she patted his cheek. "Rafe?"

She checked for a pulse. It was there, but faint.

His lips were tinged with blue.

Sera pulled him up under his arms and flipped him onto the cot. "Rafe?" She patted his cheeks some more and held her ear close to his lips to make sure he was still breathing.

Sera stood and ran to the opening of the tent. "Quickly, come help us!" She ran back to the cot to be close to Rafe.

The group of Revalars she had just been speaking with ran to the tent.

Zeke opened the flap wide. "Captain!" He ran in and knelt next to Sera. "What's happened?"

Sera shook her head. "I don't know. I found him next to the cot." She reached for his wrist to check for a pulse again. "What...that's not possible."

Zeke looked at her questioningly. "What is it?"

Sera held up Rafe's hand to reveal four puncture wounds, arranged in an oblong diamond. The two marks on the sides were deep and wide, while the points were smaller and much more inflamed.

Zeke shook his head. "What?" He was confused. "I don't understand."

"Don't you remember history in school...this is the bite of a nitesting beetle."

"No," Zeke scoffed. "Those are from the old world. They didn't come here with the elders."

"Maybe Elium has its own version," Sera suggested.

"That we've never heard of before now?" He turned to Dax. "Do you recognize these wounds?" He pulled the boy over and had him examine the marks.

"No, sir." Dax shook his head.

"Run and get Zola," Sera instructed. "And tell her to bring the antivenom kit." She turned to Rafe. "If it is from a nitesting, we don't have much time."

Dax nodded and ran out of the tent.

54

Behler and Fenn's crew moved through the forest, led by Fenn who had traveled that way countless times. Luke, proudly riding Sabana, brought up the rear to ensure everyone stayed on track. As Fenn's compatriot, he had traveled that way nearly as many times.

"The forest is so different without the Arbirans," Fennix said, sounding melancholy. "That ridge right there leads to the ruins." He motioned toward a ridge of rocks with hundreds of thin layers stacked on top of one another. "See that black layer," he pointed. "It's a layer of ash. I think there was a giant fire sometime in the forest's history."

Mathias harrumphed. "Let's hope there's not another one anytime soon." It was an obvious allusion to the dragons and their fiery fury.

Fennix ignored the comment. "The ruins have water and shelter. We'll camp there for the night."

"This part of the forest feels pretty empty," Behler noted. "Were there a lot of Arbirans here?"

Her brother nodded. "This area was an Arbiran nursery. The younger Arbirans and Caretakers were here...away from the Armigoth and Varek."

The crew rode silently; the only sounds were those of the forest and the Trulars' horses' hooves. Behler listened to the repetitive song of a bird: three trills followed by three lower pitched ones. The bird's song was so perfectly predictable that Behler found herself almost hypnotized by it, especially with the sounds of Ciela's hooves nearly as perfectly timed.

The ground along the ridge was relatively flat compared to the surrounding terrain, but debris that had fallen from the ridge still made the going slow.

Soon, the slow rhythm of Ciela's stride and the ambient sounds had Behler's mind wandering.

And she felt the tug of the Deep Thread.

It was a gentle pull, like an invitation rather than an invasion.

She let her mind reach for the Thread and grab onto it. It felt like something within her was pulled through space, and in a matter of a second, she was standing in her old home in Betham.

She stepped toward the table where she and Lorna had eaten so many meals. Where Mathias had eaten half their food. The woodgrain felt aged and worn against her fingers, just as it had the last time she'd sat at the table.

"Hello, Bale."

Behler's breath caught in her chest. It couldn't be.

She turned toward the room that had been her makeshift bedroom.

"Lorna," she said breathlessly. A sob erupted from deep within her chest. Tears welled up in her eyes. "How?"

Lorna tilted her head to the side and smiled. "Death has some advantages."

"But thaelic..."

"Varek has no power over death, as much as he thinks he may."

Behler stood staring at her aunt. Part of her was sure she'd fallen asleep, fell off Ciela, and cracked her head open on a rock. "I...uh...made it to Ardin."

Lorna smiled. "I knew you would."

"Kellum...he helped."

Her aunt's eyes caught a wicked twinkle. "Did he, now? Kellum is quite a young man."

Behler felt her cheeks flush. How was that even possible without a real body?

"We're heading south, to the ruins and then beyond."

Lorna nodded. "To reach the Desharets."

"Yes."

"Rafe and I spoke about it before...." she trailed off.

The tears welled up in Behler's eyes again. "Lorna..." she choked on her words.

A familiar look crossed her aunt's face. "Behler, it's okay. I can help from this side in ways I never could before. Look at us now...using the Deep Thread."

"Have you talked to Sera? Fenn?"

Lorna shook her head. "No. Your Thread is the only one I could feel."

"You're not stuck...here are you?" Behler looked around the ramshackle house. After living in Ardin for six weeks, this house really felt dilapidated.

"No," Lorna laughed. "I think this is where the Thread brought us because it's where we were together. Where we were comfortable."

Behler stood straighter and met Lorna's gaze. "You could have told me."

Lorna knew what she meant without explaining any further. She nodded. "I know."

"I would have been okay if you had."

"I know that, too."

"Then why..."

"I saw what it did to Fenn. I couldn't bear to do that to you."

"Still," Behler countered, "I could have been told more than nothing...and less than the lies."

Lorna nodded. "Yes but looking back is always easier than when you're in the middle of it. I'm so sorry you had to go through the painful days of learning the truth, but I'm not sorry about the person I'm looking at today. You are strong. You're ready. That's why I could feel your Thread – our bond and your strength."

"Did you just want to say hi?" Behler asked with a bit of bite in her voice. Curiosity was starting to overcome the initial shock of seeing her deceased aunt.

Lorna laughed. "No. I need you to know something. The night I was killed...there's no way the Horde should have been able to find us. They came straight to where we were hiding, as if they knew."

Behler remembered her grandfather's words. *I don't know how the jackals got so close without us knowing.*

"What are you saying?"

"I'm saying," Lorna paused, "I think we have an Armigoth spy among us."

"Who?"

Her aunt shook her head. "I don't know, but it had to be someone who knew where we were hiding the girls."

"And who was that?"

Lorna looked her straight in the eyes. "Rafe, Rogan, Meela, Matti, and Fenn."

"No...no...none of those people would...." She shook her head as if trying to shake the words she'd just heard out of her memory. "No way."

"Bale...someone had to have told the Horde where we were."

"But why...they knew I wasn't with the girls. What would have been the point?"

But then she knew the answer without her aunt saying a word. Her heart sank as the realization settled and she knew it was true. "To kill you."

To take Lorna away from her.

Behler sat down at the table. The part of her brain that protected itself at all costs was amused that her bodiless self needed to sit at all.

Just when she felt she was finding her footing, the ground was shifting again.

55

Word about Rafe spread quickly as soon as Dax ran across the field asking everyone he saw if they'd seen Zola. He finally found her with the children, singing to them.

"Zola, we need you at Rafe's tent. Sera said to bring the antivenom kit."

The woman stood. "I'll have to get it. It's with my things in the wagons."

Together they ran to the wagons, only to find Warln emptying one of them.

"Warln – what are you doing?" Zola asked harshly.

"The wagons are busted, Zola. We're going to have to take the horses and make do with smaller wagons for our supplies."

She scanned the piles of supplies he'd already laid out on the grass.

Once she spotted her large chest full of medicines and ointments, she hurried to find the smaller satchel of antivenom bottles. "Warln," she said impatiently when she couldn't find it. "Did you see a brown satchel with a yulit flower embossed on it?"

"Er...I think so. It should be there."

Zola murmured curse words to herself that only the elder Trulars would understand. Finally, she found the satchel where it had fallen between two crates of aji water canteens.

Standing, she looked at Dax. "Let's go."

He led her to Rafe's tent. Revalars had gathered outside as if standing guard. He opened the flap and Zola walked in.

Sera looked as if she'd been crying.

When she looked up and saw Zola, the relief was evident on her face. "I think it's a nitesting beetle bite. Look." She held up Rafe's hand.

Zola knelt and took the man's hand in her own. She only took a few moments before saying, "Yes, you're correct. The inflammation here and here," she pointed at the smaller puncture wounds, "They are sure signs of a nitesting strike."

"But they aren't in Elium," Zeke insisted. He wanted to make sure they treated Rafe with the right medicine or ointment.

Zola looked at the Revala with the gaze of a woman who has lived a long life and seen a lot of things. "If you walk outside and there are puddles everywhere but not a rain cloud in sight, does that mean the rain does not exist?" She turned back to Rafe. "We must not dismiss the truth because we can't see all the facts."

Zola reached in her bag and rummaged through it. "I haven't needed this tincture for a very long time." She pulled out a vial with a deep purple liquid inside. "Hold up his head for me a bit, Sera."

Sera held Rafe's head up off the cot, and Zola gently poured a few drops of the liquid between his lips.

"He's not swallowing it."

"It's okay," Zola assured her. "His body will absorb it. It will work." She sighed. "But it will take time."

"How much time?" Zeke asked.

"A couple of hours to come to...then another hour before he's strong enough to ride or fight."

"Okay," Zeke said, seemingly okay with those numbers. "Dax!" The boy popped his head in the tent. "Go find Rogan and tell him what's happened. He's second in command and needs to know."

Dax nodded and ran off once again.

Zeke turned to Sera. "I think you should go ahead and get the children and elders out of the village. We'll take care of Rafe."

Sera knew he was right but couldn't bear the thought of leaving before Rafe woke up.

Zola reached a hand to touch Sera's arm. "I'm travelling with you. I need to stay here and make sure Rafe doesn't need another dose of the antivenom. Maybe we could send the group on ahead with Nirain and Kyra. The two of us can catch up to them rather easily."

Sera nodded, grateful for Zola's suggestion. "I'll speak with them about it."

Zola shook her head. "No, you stay with Rafe. I've done all I can for now. I'll go and speak with them."

The older woman stood and began to walk out, but before she left she turned back to Sera. "If he begins to stir, give him some aji. That will help speed his recovery. There are bottles in the satchel."

Sera smiled and nodded. "Thank you, Zola."

Zola smiled then walked out.

56

Aeron made it to the creek that eventually led into Ardin's lake. Once there, she knew it would only be a couple of hours until she reached the village.

She took a few moments to sit and rest. She took a piece of cloth that she always tied around her neck and dunked it in the water, then pressed it to her face. She repeated this a few times, then tied it back around her neck. The coolness felt good on her hot skin.

She leaned over and cupped her hands into the water, splashing some more on her face and drinking some.

Her hands were still in the water when she heard the fleshy sound of giant wings flapping.

She'd heard it before, when they'd helped those in Betham the night of the dragon attack.

She froze, her hands still in the water.

They flew right over her head.

She realized how exposed the creek had become without the Arbirans. Where once branches and leaves cloaked the ravine, there was now nothing but open sky.

The dragons were following it straight into Ardin.

She leapt to her feet and began running.

A couple of hours now felt like an eternity.

Sera and Nirain spoke quietly just outside the tent where Rafe lay on the cot.

"His pulse is stronger than it was," Sera said.

Nirain held her friend's arm gently. "It was lucky you recognized the marks from the nitesting. Not many people would have. He got the antivenom in time."

Sera gave her a crooked grin. "Yeah, all those hours of studying seem to have finally paid off."

Nirain smiled broadly. "We all have our strengths."

"Are you sure you'll be okay with the group until I can catch up?"

Nirain waved her off. "Of course. Kyra is with us and all those elders can still hold their own if need be. We'll be fine."

"Okay...just head south until you reach that ravine we used to go to as kids, then head due west. We'll catch up."

Nirain sighed. "I really wish we had the Deep Thread."

Sera nodded. "I know...but if Elians can manage without it, so can we."

Nirain's brow rose. "Good point."

"Rogan! Rogan!" Uri came running through the field. "Has anyone seen Rogan?"

"I'm here," Rogan called out.

"Come...quickly. It's the Arbiran."

Rogan – and nearly everyone else – took off running. The crowd ran around buildings and fences until they got to the bricked path and could see the Arbiran clearly. Its leaves were whipping frantically as if a violent storm was passing through.

Sera had stayed at the tent, close to Rafe. She wouldn't leave his side until he was awake. So, from where she stood, she was the first to see the incoming threat. It was still a good distance away but coming fast. It flew over the canopy, skimming the tops enough to rustle every treetop along its path. She could just make out another behind it.

She'd seen them that day when they flew over, when there were still enough Arbirans to create the veil and hide Ardin. She knew what she was looking at.

"Dragon!" she yelled. "Dragon!!"

Some of the children were still sitting on the bales of hay, waiting patiently for the grownups to return. They jumped up as soon as they heard Sera's voice.

She turned toward the tent, terrified that if she left Rafe, she'd never see him alive again. But she knew her only choice was to get the children to safety.

"Dragon!" She continued to yell as she ran to gather the youngsters. She pleaded with the Embera that her voice would carry enough that someone by the Arbiran would hear.

Dax was still helping sort the supplies Sera and the others would take on their journey.

"Dragon!" He heard Sera shout.

His blood ran cold. The memories from that night in Betham slammed into him like a hammer. His hands shook so much, he dropped the crate he was holding.

He ran around the corner to see where Sera was.

"There!" she shouted as soon as she saw him. "Tell the others, quickly Dax."

Did they even have their drakas with them? Had they already put them in their slots on the saddles?

Sera estimated they only had a few minutes before the dragons breached the village.

"Quickly, children, let's go." She gathered them up. Her mind raced where she could stow them, safe from any fires that the dragons may ignite. And then she knew, and she could have kissed Fenn for all his escapades over the years...all those times she had to go hunt him down. She looked over the group of children. "Lill," she said to the oldest in the bunch. "Do you know where the cave is just that way?" She pointed south of the village. "Fenn used to like to go there all the time." The little girl nodded. "Get everyone there. I'm going to get the other children, and we'll meet you there."

Lill nodded, accepting the task with resolute courage.

Sera looked back at the tent where Rafe lay so vulnerably. With a lump in her throat, she turned away and began to run toward the center of the village.

57

Nirain met Sera at the edge of the dirt path in front of the stables. She had somehow, miraculously, managed to keep all the children in her group together.

"Lill is taking the others to the cave where Fenn and Luke used to play," Sera said urgently.

Nirain nodded. "I'll get the rest there. Are you staying with Rafe?"

"Yes," Sera said without hesitation. "If you and Kyra can get the children there without me."

Her friend nodded. "We can. Take care of Rafe." She turned. "Children...we are going to run as fast as we can into that part of the forest...but we must stick together. Raise your hand if you know where Fenn's cave is."

A handful of the older children raised their hands.

"Everyone...look at who has their hands up. Those Trulars can lead you to the cave if anything happens."

"Like what?" four-year-old Meekah, asked.

"If I trip and slow down...something like that," Nirain smiled.

Meekah seemed okay with that answer. She nodded and sighed.

"What about our stuff?" Jos asked.

Enon put his hand on the little boy's shoulder. "We'll come back and get it after the dragons leave."

Sera saw some of the older kids glance sideways at each other.

Jos nodded, also happy with the simple answer.

Nirain clapped her hands. "Let's go. Who's going to be the first to the trees?"

The children shrieked as if they were playing a game and all took off toward the treeline.

Sera turned and nearly ran into Warln.

"The old duks are headed for the root cellar next to the greenhouse," he said. "I didn't think there'd be room in the cave...plus some of those old people are kind of crotchety. Not a good combination with a cave full of kids."

Sera smiled. "Will you join them...make sure they're safe."

Warln stared at her for a moment, his eyes twinkling. He smiled. "You're a sly woman."

Sera straightened up and gave him her best nonplussed look. "That's not an answer, Old Man."

Warln chuckled and sighed. "Yes, I'll be joining them. Just got to get a few things from the stables."

Sera nodded and smiled. "Glad to hear it." She hugged him then turned back to the tent. She pulled her draka from behind her and the isari stone flared.

The six Trulars arrived at the ruins just as the sky turned pink and orange with sunset. Behler hadn't had any expectations of what they'd find when they arrived, but she wasn't prepared for the enormity of the ancient remains.

A large domed building, covered in moss and ivy, towered above everything else. Crumbling towers flanked it on each side. At the dome's base, a gaping opening yawned, vines and thick ivy spilling across it like a curtain. It was both inviting and haunting.

"Is it safe to go inside?" Behler asked.

Fennix shrugged and he swung down from his mount. "Yeah, but it's not worth the hassle to fight all the foliage. We can just stay out here for the night."

Kina hoofed over to a wide stone basin brimming with clear water and dipped her muzzle in to drink. Fennix followed, crouching at the basin's edge to cup his hands. He wiped his mouth on his sleeve and pointed toward the treeline. "There's a spring running underground to the north. Feeds this basin year-round. If we weren't in such a rush..." He smirked faintly. "There's a little spring not far from here that's great for swims or soaks." He leaned down for another handful of water.

Behler dismounted, letting Ciela drink, but didn't approach the basin herself. Instead, she rested her hands on a large, oddly shaped stone table. Its surface was rough, pitted with age, but a low structure rose from the back—nearly swallowed by ivy and moss.

Something caught her eye. A faint glint beneath the greenery. Glass?

Frowning, she brushed a few vines aside, surprised to find such delicate material in a place this ancient.

"You okay?" Kellum's voice cut through her thoughts, startling her. She jerked back, heart thudding as she turned.

She gave a quick nod.

But she was not okay.

Kellum eyed her suspiciously but eventually went over to get some water for himself.

Behler had tried multiple times to find Sera's Thread, to warn her about the possibility of a spy. Not just anyone – Rafe. Their leader.

No. There was no way Rafe was a spy.

But she didn't really know him. Maybe he could be a spy.

323

Maybe Rafe had let the Armigoth in. Maybe he was fooling everyone.

Maybe it was Rogan.

Matti?

No way. He would never hurt Lorna.

Meela?

Fenn?

Her own brother?

She'd had her reservations about her brother…but could she really allow herself to even go down that path? They were supposed to fulfill the foretelling.

She was spiraling and she knew it.

Grabbing a canteen of aji, she took a few sips. She needed to clear her head.

"Easy on that," Meela said from beside her. "We don't know when we can get more."

"Yeah." She smiled and tried to sound casual. "I know." Meela's reminder made her feel simultaneously awkward and irritated. "I just needed a little." Why did she have to justify herself to Meela? She was the one dealing with the weight of this foretelling…the weight of the whole vlocking Anarsari.

She understood why Fenn escaped into the forest so often. The noise of everything was so loud.

A couple more sips of the aji and her mind cleared a bit. Her chest felt a little lighter.

She grabbed a hunk of bread from a saddlebag and found a quiet place to sit and eat it.

Everyone gave her space until Mathias and Kellum came and sat on a stone across from her. They didn't say a word, just ate their own quiet meal. Their silent presence was comforting and grounding and helped just as much as the aji did.

Finally, she was ready to talk.

"I found the Deep Thread on the way here," she said quietly.

Kellum and Mathias both sat up straighter.

"Did you find someone's Thread?" Kellum asked.

She nodded. "More like she found mine, but yeah."

"Who?" Mathias asked too loudly.

She motioned him to quiet down then continued. "Lorna."

Mathias and Kellum both looked at each other. "I've never heard of anyone talking to someone who...wasn't alive anymore," Mathias said hesitantly.

Kellum smiled. "There's never been someone like Behler before."

His belief in her was like an anchor for a drifting ship.

"Well," Mathias urged, "what did she say?"

"She...uh...she just said she could help us from where she is. She can use the Deep Thread and Varek can't stop her."

"Can she tell us things, like where the rest of the Revalars are or where the Horde is?" Mathias asked.

Behler shook her head. "No, I don't think so. Not yet...maybe she'll be able to in the future...maybe the longer she's there the more she'll be able to do."

She stopped and weighed her next words carefully. Mathias would never betray her or Lorna. She knew that as much as she knew anything. "She did say something about the night she died."

"What...what did she say?" Mathias asked.

325

Kellum sat quietly, letting Behler work through whatever she needed to work through before she said her next words.

"She said there was a spy that night. Someone who had to tell the Horde where she'd hidden the girls. She said there's no way they could have found them so quickly without knowing exactly where to look."

"A spy?" Kellum repeated.

Mathias nodded. "I felt something was off that night. It was like Lorna walked right into a trap."

Behler looked at him, surer than ever that he was no spy. At least not one who spied on anyone other than her.

"Who do you think it could be?" She didn't want to name any of the names Lorna had told her. Maybe there was someone else that Lorna didn't even realize who could have told the Horde.

Mathias shook his head. "I don't know. There were a few of us who knew where they were taking the girls. Apa, Meela, Fenn –" he chuckled, as if the thought of Fenn being the spy was absurd.

It probably was.

"Rafe?" His name was out of her mouth before she could stop it.

Mathias and Kellum were both taken aback.

"Of course," Mathias said. "But he wouldn't…"

"Yeah…I know," Behler said quickly.

"Bale," Kellum started softly. "Are you sure it was Lorna?"

She knew what he was getting at. The memory of the house. The feel of the wooden tabletop. Every single thing about Lorna's words.

"Yes."

Kellum nodded. Her answer was enough for him. "Then we stay alert...just like we always have."

Tears threatened to fill Behler's eyes again, only this time they were tears of relief. Kellum's belief in her – Mathias' corroboration that something was indeed off that night – she wasn't alone. She didn't have to bear the weight of it alone.

She could have hugged them both.

Instead, she smiled and took another bite of bread.

58

Warln rummaged through chests and boxes, making sure there was nothing left of value before the fire fell upon them. He knew what was coming, and it would leave little in its wake.

"Grampa!"

Warln jumped and turned. "Avenly! Why aren't you with the other children? Your mother is going to be frantic."

Tears ran down her cheeks. "There's too many people who are scared. I can feel it everywhere and I don't know what to do! I came in here because it was quieter."

Warln thought about sending her to the forest to find the others. She knew where the cave was. But he quickly realized, in her state, she may get all turned around.

"Okay, let's get out of here. We'll take the horses to the cave so your mother isn't searching for you."

"Okay." She reached up and grabbed his hand tight enough that he winced.

They smiled at each other, happy to be together.

They stepped out of the back door of the stables, and the dragons breached the village.

Behler walked over to the large basin and bent over. The air around the moving water smelled clean, just like the water at the falls. Just like the river used to.

She reached in, feeling the coolness on her fingers then her entire hand. She flinched when her hand brushed up against something very ropelike. Startled, she moved her hand around, trying to find it again.

There, she felt it.

She tried to grip it, but it was as if her hand passed right through it. She looked into the crystal-clear water. She could feel the rope, but there was nothing there.

It wasn't a rope. It was the Deep Thread somehow in a physical form.

She closed her eyes and felt her own Thread move from inside some deep part of her. It stretched until it found the Thread within the water.

The world around her shifted and she was hit with fear, anger, and an overwhelming feeling of helplessness. It all threatened to swallow her. And there was something else. Something ancient. *She* felt ancient, as if she had always been and would always be.

She could see Ardin – and she could see it in all directions, as if she had eyes on all sides of her body. Based on where everything was, she knew she was standing where the eldest Arbiran stood. The world spoke to her through her roots that furrowed through the soft soil, the past and present blending into one.

Inklings of things she felt she once knew whispered in the corners of her mind, but she couldn't focus on them. The fires blazing around the village were all she could focus on. She saw her home, still untouched, but for how long? The dragons – they flew overhead, circling, spewing fire down. And then she saw Revalars with drakas and bows fighting and running from flames.

They were still in Ardin.

Help us, the Arbiran spoke to her.

"We're coming," she said, but needed no words to communicate. She and the Arbiran were one.

The world around her shifted once more and she was standing at the basin; her hand still submerged in the cool water.

"Everyone!" She spoke with conviction. "We have to go back."

Her crew all sat up, alert but confused.

"Why?" Mathias asked.

"The others. They didn't get out, and the dragons are setting the village on fire."

"How –" Meela sputtered. "How could you know that?"

"The water," she motioned toward the basin. "It's connected to the Arbiran somehow. It showed me."

They all stared at each other for a moment.

"But Rafe..." Fenn began.

Behler's thoughts were on all those back in Ardin: the children, the elders, her mother. She'd lost enough recently, and she'd be swallowed by the shadow if she was going to lose any more without putting up a fight.

"I don't give a kak what Rafe said. I'm going back."

Her brother stared at her. A thick silence hung over the group. Then he smirked and got that familiar mischievous sparkle in his eyes. "Yeah, let's go."

No one argued.

They all had loved ones in the path of the dragons.

59

Warln watched as the dragons split up; one headed toward the buildings of the village while the other stayed on course to fly over the open field. He glanced at the horses. They were already getting spooked, but they remained steady. As soon as the dragons rained down their first streams of fire, though, the horses' animal instincts took over and they ran in the opposite direction. There was no way Warln and Avenly could get to them without putting themselves in grave danger.

Warln eyed the warming-house where the entrance to the root cellar was. It wasn't an option either. The dragons would be passing it within moments, and he couldn't risk getting caught in a stream of fire from either beast.

"Back inside, Avenly." He ushered her in then slid the door shut.

He took her and tucked her into the corner of Ciela's empty stall. When he started to leave, Avenly grabbed his hand. "Where are you going?"

"Just to get my draka. I'll be right back."

Avenly's eyes were huge, but she nodded.

Warln ran to Willa's stall and grabbed his draka and kintar. His hands had become too shaky for his bow.

Aeron ran into the village. It nearly took her breath away to see the buildings on fire, the kogum field scorched, and her fellow Revalars doing their best to defend it.

She gripped her draka and ran to join the closest group.

"Aeron," Zeke said.

"I was in the area and thought I'd stop by," she smiled, but it only lasted a moment. "The Gorlogs are just behind me a bit. I could hear them...and smell them when the wind blew just right."

"Great," Zeke said. "Just what we need."

"What's our plan?" She looked around the field. "Where's Rafe?"

"There was an incident with Rafe – he'll be fine," Zeke said quickly. "The plan is to survive at least until they can get the children out of here."

"Got it," Aeron winked. "Don't die."

Zeke shrugged. "Pretty much."

She slapped him on the back. "Good plan."

Sera watched as one of the dragons approached. When she saw it continue its course over the open field, she'd been certain it would come for the tent. It was a lone target that stood out in the empty field. Her nerves were raw and she had to focus on her breathing to stop from shaking.

Rafe lay behind her, helpless. He depended on her, and she wouldn't let him down.

She watched as the dragon inhaled so deeply that she could see its lungs expand inside its sleek chest. She and the tent were easy targets, and the dragon was about to make its strike count.

The dragon opened its gaping mouth, a flicker of flame glowing deep in its throat. Sera locked her eyes on its chest. She could see the great muscles flexing—

expanding with a slow, deliberate inhale. The air itself seemed to pause. Then came the exhale. She slammed the end of her draka into the dirt at her feet. Her isari flared to life, and a transparent dome formed over her and the tent just as the fire burst from the dragon's mouth and roared toward them.

She could feel the warmth of the fire through the shield and spreading through her draka.

The dragon pulled its body back slightly, as a bird would hover to track a mouse in the grass. Its wings pushed against the air as it blasted the dome with her fiery wrath.

Sera closed her eyes as the warmth on her hands grew hotter. "Ahhhhh!" She yelled, holding on and focusing.

After what felt like minutes, but had to be only seconds, the flames stopped. The dragon screeched in anger, but Sera heard confusion in the animal's cry as well.

Sera looked up, happy to still be standing. Her hands stung a bit from the heat in her draka, but otherwise she was unscathed. The tent as well.

Then, as if laughing at her, the second dragon screeched and prepared to breathe its own fury down. She'd been so focused on keeping herself alive that she hadn't noticed the second dragon rejoin its companion.

Just before the flames hit her isari shield again, she caught a glimpse of the first Gorlogs breaching the village across the field.

Warln sat with his draka ready to shield him and Avenly at the first sign of flames. They were sitting quietly, listening to the dragons' wings passing over the stables. When the dragon cried out, Avenly covered her ears.

They listened for more cues to tell them the dragons' locations.

"Gok alom!" A deep guttural voice came from just outside the door. Avenly started trembling.

Warln's heart sank. "Shhh. Get inside the chest," he whispered.

"Let's leave," she pleaded.

But Warln shook his head. "No. We can't." He touched her cheek, careful not to let his fear rise enough that Avenly would sense it. "It'll be okay, just hide."

Avenly climbed into the chest and Warln covered her with some blankets. He touched the back of her head through the blanket then gently shut the lid.

He made his way back to the stall door and peeked down the center aisle. Five Gorlogs were standing at the front of the building where he hadn't closed the door. Quickly, he crawled back to the chest and lifted the lid. He pulled the blanket back.

"Avenly, if the Gorlogs come in the barn, I'm going to have to leave the stall. There isn't anywhere here for me to hide and there's too many for me to fight alone."

"Grampa," she pleaded.

"Shh, shh. Hush now." He looked down and smiled at her. "I love you. I'm proud of you and your brothers. Never forget that. Always take care of each other, okay?"

She reached out. "Grampa," her little voice cracked, "don't go."

He gently placed her hand back inside the chest and leaned down to kiss her softly on the cheek. "Stay hidden. I'll be back soon." He smiled at her again and tucked the blanket back over her then silently closed the lid.

He heard the back door slide open. A Gorlog snorted and walked inside.

60

"We've got to get back to the village faster than we got here," Behler said. A feeling of urgency had taken over her.

"The ground is flat enough," Luke said, "But the rocks and debris are too dangerous for the horses to run through.

Meela's face lit up. "I have an idea. If we use our isari stones to create a shield out in front of our horses, it will push the rocks away like a plow turning over the soil."

Behler smiled. "That's brilliant, Meela. Let's try it. The path back is wide enough; we could pair up and go in twos. The two in the lead can create the shield, clearing the way for the rest."

"You and Matti were the best with the shield," Luke said.

Behler looked over at Mathias. They both shrugged and nodded. They each formed an isari shield. Behler's was a bit rounded while Mathias' was as flat as a board.

"Let's take it slowly," Fennix said. "Make sure it's going to work."

They all started out at a quick walk. To everyone's delight, the rocks and debris moved out of the way as if using a tool to clear the soil. They quickly were able to get faster and faster until finally they were at full sprints, galloping through the forest and toward the fight.

Taking turns rotating to be the two lead riders, they were able to give their isari stones rest. They reached the village a couple of hours after nightfall.

Each drew weapons as they breached the village's southern perimeter. A wall of heat hit them almost as soon as they cleared the forest. Revalars were fighting off Horde guuns and Gorlogs with coordinated isari attacks, but they were vastly outnumbered. The enemies were gaining ground.

The Gorlogs were so deformed, Behler had to look twice to see if that's really what they were. They had grown larger and stood as tall as a man sitting atop a horse. It appeared their transformation hadn't been pleasant. Tumors like the one she'd spotted on the Gorlog at the river had grown. They covered their disfigured bodies with flesh stretched so thin it had torn in some places. Their eyes reflected the light around them like a predator, and they had traded their stubby swords for large clubs with iron spiked balls at the end that would crush any man's skull like an overripe melon.

The six paused, taken aback by the scene that had unfolded before them. If their arrows had been nearly useless against Gorlog hide before, Behler knew there was no way they would do any damage now. Those glowing eyes, though, made excellent targets. She pulled an arrow from behind her back and placed it in her bow. She let it fly and watched as the first Gorlog fell just as it was getting ready to swing its giant club down. Behler loaded another arrow and quickly took out a second. Kellum and the others joined her.

At least fifteen Gorlogs fell before the six were spotted. The remaining Gorlogs started charging them.

"Split up!" Behler yelled. She, Kellum, and Luke headed across the open field while Fennix, Mathias, and Meela moved to navigate around the buildings. The Gorlogs were moving faster than their deformed bodies should've allowed, and

Behler had to let go of the reins so she could slow down the Gorlogs with a melee of arrows.

She and Luke were passing by the kogum field when a Gorlog leapt out and swiped at Luke, throwing him from Sabana. Behler saw it happening as if in slow motion. She grabbed Ciela's reins with one hand and turned her around. The Gorlog had its back to her and was raising its club to bring down on Luke who was still stunned. She slung her bow over her shoulder and grabbed the reins with both hands. Ciela dug in a little more with each step, propelling them faster and further with each stride. As Ciela passed by the Gorlog at a hair's distance, Behler leapt from her back and onto the Gorlog's. Surprised, the Gorlog spun around, trying to grab her. Its disfigured body made it so that its arms couldn't reach back far enough, so it began swinging its hammer at her instead. As soon as she felt she had a good hold, she let go of the creature's neck with her right hand and pulled her aunt's dagger from its sheath strapped to her leg. She hoped it would find its mark on her first attempt then struck where she thought the Gorlog's eye was. The dagger first hesitated as its tip hit the creature, but then the resistance gave way, and it slid sickeningly into its eye. The Gorlog cried out in pain then fell to the ground, hard, with Behler still clinging to the back of its neck. It was dead before it hit the ground.

"Luke!" Kellum had turned around and was jumping off his horse in the time it took for Behler to take the Gorlog down.

Luke got to his knees, shaken but okay. He stood up and yelled, "Bale! BEHIND YOU!"

She turned just in time to see a handful of Horde soldiers running at her. The Horde's long swords gave them an advantage over the Trulars' shorter kintars and none had grabbed their drakas from the sleeves on the sides of their horses. Without their isari stones they couldn't use their shielding command to protect them from the enemies' blades.

"CIELA!" Behler yelled. She didn't take her eyes off the Horde soldiers who were coming at them quickly. Ciela turned to come back to her, but Behler knew the horse wouldn't make it in time. "OW!" she snapped. Something had stung her right below her collar bone. She instinctively reached up to rub her chest and felt the amulet around her neck. It buzzed with energy. "AHMEI!" Behler shouted and each of the soldiers flew across the grass. Keller and Luke pulled out their bows and began taking out the enemy one by one.

Another Horde guun came running at them from the side. "SHO!" He shot up into the air. "SHUKA!" He slammed back to the ground and didn't move again.

A familiar bone-shaking shriek ripped through the air above them. Behler had heard it that night in Betham.

"Look out!" Kellum yelled.

A stream of fire came streaming downward. The underbelly of the dragon looked as if it was made of gold in the light of the blaze. The untouched section of the kogum field caught fire, and the fire raining down from the sky was relentless.

They ran back south.

The dragon cried out again, and this time her cry was answered by another. The second dragon was coming at them from the southern end of the village. Another stream of fire came raining down, setting the grass around them ablaze. The only places to go were either into the village or across the open field toward the forest, and neither were excellent options. The buildings were burning so hot that the heat made going much further into the village impossible, and they would be easy dragon prey in the open field.

"We've got to move!" Kellum yelled.

They began running toward the forest. "Ciela!" Behler called again.

The horses had been close by. Soon each was running right beside their rider. They all slowed enough so that each of the Trulars could grab on and pull themselves up into the saddle. The horses continued heading in the direction of the forest. They all realized at the same time that both dragons had circled and were waiting above the trees. Their silhouettes hovered overhead at first, and then they swooped down toward them in the open field. They opened their huge, reptilian mouths and small flames in the back of their throats ignited into two rivers of fire.

"Ciela!" Behler yelled again, but the horses had seen it and were already turning. Sabana and Storm turned and headed south, while Ciela headed north around the inferno. As soon as they were clear, she turned and ran for the forest. Once under the cover of the trees, Behler looked to her right to see if she could find Kellum and Luke, but she couldn't make out anything past the spreading flames. She jumped off Ciela and listened for any clue that the dragons had tracked her and were preparing to set the trees around her ablaze, but she heard nothing except for the crackle of the fire already on the ground. Then a Gorlog roared from somewhere within the village, and she thought she heard some human voices right after it. She needed to move and see who else was still alive and fighting. She headed south and hoped to find Kellum and Luke.

Staying just inside the forest, she moved south quickly through the underbrush until she was even with the stables. There wasn't anyone in the fields, and if Luke and Kellum had tried for the woods, she would have run into them by now. She had to try to make it back into the village proper, so keeping as low in the taller grass as she could, she ran for the stables which were still, somehow, not on fire. An overturned wagon near the stable doors made for a good place to take cover, but as she rounded the end of it, her heart sank. Nirain lay motionlessly on the ground. Behler crawled quickly to her and spotted wounds she had seen before – back in the village when Samuel had been attacked. Nirain's wounds were even worse than Sam's were. She had a large gash across her chest, and one of her shoulders looked crushed, possibly from the impact of one of those spiked balls on a Gorlog's weapon. Behler felt for a pulse. At her touch, Nirain moaned.

"Hold on. Please, just hold on." She grabbed the canteen she'd placed across her body by its leather strap. First, she poured some of the water over the gash and mangled shoulder then she poured a few drops into Nirain's mouth. Bringing the woman out of unconsciousness was the only way to save her, but it would also mean she would have to endure a lot of pain. The aji couldn't stop that much of it. Nirain moaned again, a little louder. "Nirain, do you know where the others are? Sera and the children, did you see where they went?"

She mumbled something, but Behler couldn't understand.

"What?" Behler put her ear right by her mouth.

Nirain tried to speak, but she choked and coughed instead. The woman closed her eyes and tears squeezed out from them. She was summoning all her will to speak at all.

Behler touched the woman's cheek. "It's okay. It's o..." She felt the Thread. "Nirain...can you feel that? The Thread?"

Nirain blinked her eyes. Behler took that as a yes.

Behler reached out and found Nirain's Thread. In a matter of seconds, Behler saw everything that had transpired in the village after they had left that morning.

"Vlock," she said softly. It had been a lot.

Nirain had come back to search for Avenly.

"I'll find her."

A tear rolled out of Nirain's eye and down her cheek. Behler gripped her hand. "I promise you – I will find her."

She gave a quick, high whistle and Ciela immediately emerged from the forest, running full hilt across the field to reach them.

"I'm going to need your help, Ciela." The horse chuffed softly then knelt down so that Behler didn't have to lift Nirain up as high. She was able to maneuver her enough that she could throw her leg over Ciela's saddle and hold on while the horse stood back up, but she was so hunched over, Behler wasn't sure if she'd be able to stay on. "All you have to do is hold on, Nirain. She'll get you into the forest." She looked at Ciela. "Take her to the cave...Fenn's cave." Ciela whinnied and took off. How a horse knew where Fenn's cave was, Behler didn't know – but didn't even question that Nirain would arrive there safely.

Turning, she ran to the stable doors and into the building to make sure all the horses were out of their stalls. Each stall was empty as she ran by them toward the front of the building. But something made her stop and turn back just before she reached to slide the door open. She'd caught something out of the corner of her eye in the third stall back.

Cautiously, Behler looked in. The lanterns hadn't been lit, so it was too dark to see in the stall's corners. "Aluma," Behler said softly and her stone glowed dimly.

A shape crouched in the corner. Behler gasped. Her stone flared, casting the darkness aside in one bright sweep.

"Avenly!" Behler exhaled and ran to the little girl. She knelt down and grabbed the girl's hands in her own. "Are you okay?"

Avenly was crying softly and didn't answer. Behler reached up to stroke her hair. "It's okay. It'll be..." but she stopped. Her hand was wet and sticky, and when she turned it over was shocked to see it covered in blood. "Avenly?! Are you okay?" She ran her hands all over the little girl, looking for a wound, but she couldn't find anything. "What happened?" She wiped her palms on her pants and took Avenly's face in her hands, trying to get the little girl to make eye contact. "What happened?" she repeated.

Slowly, the little girl picked up her hand from her lap. She pointed into the corner of the stall behind Behler.

Behler turned her head and looked over her shoulder. The sight she saw sent a wave of emotions that flooded her soul. "Warln," she whispered. Sadness, regret, and anger all jockeyed for position.

She wanted to look away, but she couldn't. She wanted her stone to dim, but she knew the image would haunt her even more in the darkness. She just sat there, staring at the body, so mangled it was barely recognizable. If it wasn't for his clothes, Behler may not have been able to identify him at all. She grabbed Avenly and wrapped her arm around the little girl's face, turning her away from the scene. Avenly's body melted into sobs. Finally, Behler put out her light, but she'd been right before, the image of Warln's body remained.

She would carry that image for the rest of her days.

61

Behler held tightly onto Avenly as she tried to think of their next move. It was hard to think clearly thanks to the waves of fear and sadness she felt holding on to Avenly's hand. She knew they needed to get out of the stall. Before she could think any further, they heard a ruckus outside the front of the stables.

The gurgling, guttural voices of Gorlogs carried into the building.

"Heh'a icar?"

"Po."

"Yuna! Heh!"

Did you check here?

No.

Moron! Check!

They were searching the buildings, and they were going to check the stables next. Behler squeezed Avenly's hand. "We have to move," she whispered. Avenly nodded and they began moving across the stall to the door. Avenly moved quickly, eager to put distance between herself and her grandfather's body. When they reached the stall door, Behler peeked out into the main walkway and toward the front of the building. The Gorlogs hadn't slid the door open yet, but she could hear them still arguing. She counted at least three different voices.

She slid out of the stall and pulled Avenly out with her. They moved down the walkway toward the back door but stopped as soon as they heard more Gorlog voices coming from that end as well. Backing up, Behler gently pushed Avenly into Storm's stall and shut the door.

"Latch it from the inside," Behler whispered and heard the latch click as Avenly pushed the bolt shut.

She backed up and rested against the wall on the opposite side of the walkway, not sure of what to do. She didn't have any more time to think about it before the front door slid open and a hulking silhouette was framed in the doorway. The Gorlog was so large it had to duck and turn sideways just to fit through. Two more came in behind it. Behler crouched in the dark, trying to control her breathing. She turned her head toward the other end of the building when the back door slid open and two stepped inside from that end.

"Ach te?" *Who's there?* One of the Gorlogs at the front growled.

"Ek oima ip rewnah." *It's us you fool.* One at the back growled back.

Behler's heart beat hard and her mind started to race, but she forced herself to slow down and think. Slowly – quietly – she pulled her bow from around her body. There was still enough shadow in the middle of the walkway that she could position herself without being seen; but if the Gorlogs had inherited nocturnal hunting abilities with their new eyes, she didn't have much time before they spotted her. She moved out into the walkway and placed her draka down silently, then took one last calming breath as she placed the first arrow in her bow. Those at the back were closer, so she turned herself to them first.

She set her isari stone ablaze with just the flicker of a thought. It was enough light to reflect in the Gorlog's eyes, and she'd hit her target before the other Gorlogs had even reacted to the unexpected light. The second Gorlog at the back watched his companion fall to the ground then looked up, but Behler had already reloaded and shot another arrow. It hit him square in his right eye before he'd even registered he was in danger. The Gorlogs at the front of the barn, though, had more time to react. One roared loudly and all three began moving down the walkway toward her. Luckily, the wide aisle wasn't quite wide enough for them to all come at her side-by-side, buying her a few seconds more. Behler turned as she grabbed another arrow. The Gorlog yelled out again, but its voice was cut short as Behler's arrow found its mark. The Gorlog behind him stepped over its body and kept coming, and by the time Behler pulled another arrow from behind her, it was close enough that it was lifting its club into the air and preparing to bring it down on her. She moved backwards as she released the arrow. The Gorlog made a noise like a yelp as it fell.

And then the third stepped over both the others. Behler reached back but grabbed only air. She was out of arrows.

"Kak!" she cursed at herself. She grabbed her draka then turned to run, hoping it would follow her and leave Avenly safely behind, but then she tripped over one of the Gorlog bodies at the back of the building. Her draka went flying. "Vlocking kak!" she cursed again. She turned and reached for her draka but it was just out of reach. "Uhret!" The stone went black. Silently she moved down the aisle then slid into a stall. From down the walkway, she heard a familiar sound. The Gorlog was laughing.

"I'll find you little mouse," it taunted. She heard it move past the stall where Avenly was hiding.

Behler pulled her kintar out slowly so as not to make the slightest noise.

She heard the Gorlog moving around then heard a small flint stone. It was lighting one of the lanterns hanging on a hook placed next to each stall.

"You make this fun," it teased her and chuckled deep in its throat. "I like to chase the mouse."

Its giant foot smashed in one of the stall doors on the opposite side of the walkway.

Behler tightened her grip on the kintar's handle. It made her feel a little better despite it being virtually useless. Even if she could get around that giant spiked hammer, she still couldn't do any real harm to it unless she could get to its eyes. She felt around and tried to find something that might give her an advantage.

Nothing.

But then her hands found an old rope made from bakram leather. The rope was stronger than steel.

Silently, she moved toward the stall door and looped the rope around the board between the stall's door frame and the one next door. Running the rope across the door opening, up about a yura length, she looped it through an eyelet ring that Warln had installed in every stall to tie ropes and reins to for the wild and unbroken horses. She wrapped the rope around her then tucked herself down directly opposite the doorway and held on tightly to the rope.

This is never going to work, she thought to herself, but it had to because the Gorlog was outside her stall. It lifted its lantern higher, illuminating its ugly, distorted face in the process. She would've given anything for an arrow at that moment.

It stood in the doorway, staring and grinning hideously. She stared back defiantly. That's when she saw the scar and the missing eye. It had a few new scars to match its original one.

"Hello, friend." She smirked at it brazenly. "Miss me?"

The Gorlog bared its teeth, which Behler took as an attempt at a smirk back. "I remember you from that pigsty, Betham." Its grin turned into a snarl. "I should've killed you when I had the chance."

"Funny," Behler said. "I was going to say the same thing. How'd you get those pretty new scars? Someone get upset we stole the weapons out from under you?" She smirked. "I thought they'd kill you for sure."

The Gorlog bellowed. "You!? You little runt – it was you? I spent weeks in the bowels of Kilgen because of you."

"No wonder you look like a piece of kak if that place shat you out."

The Gorlog roared in rage. It dropped the lantern and raised its hammer. Flames spilled across the floor—but it didn't flinch. It only had eyes for her. Or in its case, an *eye* for her.

It lunged into the stall, and the rope caught it right at its knees. Its disproportionate size caused it to teeter then fall over into the stall. Behler jumped up and ran over its body. It was still struggling to get up as she slid the door shut and latched it.

"Avenly!" She called out, running toward Storm's stall and grabbing her draka on her way by. The little girl was waiting for her in the doorway. "Let's go." They ran toward the front of the building, but before they got there, the Gorlog behind them kicked out the door and stepped through the spreading fire. Behler heard it and turned. She pulled an arrow from the nearest dead Gorlog and loaded it in her bow.

The fire light danced in the Gorlog's one good eye.

"Goodbye you son of pig," she said and let the arrow fly. The Gorlog fell backward into the flames.

Behler grabbed Avenly's hand again and pulled her out of the building.

62

Behler took a split second to throw her bow back across her body. She backed up against the stable wall and pulled Avenly right next to her.

"We're going to get you into the forest and to the cave. I'm going to find Sera and Rafe."

Avenly nodded, her eyes wide with fear. Behler reached down and squeezed her hand tightly. "We're going to be okay," she reassured her. Avenly gave her a weak, half smile.

Behler needed arrows. She had her isari stone and draka, but she was still most comfortable with her bow when the pressure was on.

Warln's supply! Maybe it was still there in his weapons chest.

"Did Warln get everything packed up before the attack?" she asked Avenly.

The girl shook her head. "I don't think so. Grampa was getting his weapons out of his chest. He left his bow behind. Said it was no good to him anymore."

Behler didn't even know if she could make it to the stall where he'd kept them, but she had to try.

"Wait right here. If you hear anyone coming, come back inside, okay?" Avenly nodded. "I'm just going to get some of Warln's extra gear."

She slipped back inside the building and quickly assessed the fire's progress. The flames had reached her old Gorlog buddy and its burning flesh smelled oily and foul, but its hulking mass at least was slowing down the inferno. If she moved fast, she could make it. She reached the stall and threw open the chest. Empty. Behler's heart sank. She went back out onto the center walkway and ran to the only

350

Gorlog she could get to – the one nearest the front door. Behler pulled her arrow free and then ran out the door.

"Ready?" she asked Avenly.

"Yes," Avenly whispered.

"If you see anything, squeeze my hand."

"Okay."

Behler took her hand, and Avenly clasped it with a near death grip. Behler realized that every time she touched the little girl's hand, her own heart rate sped up and she felt very nervous. Avenly's nashiri was making Behler feel the girl's terror and trauma. She took a few deep breaths and didn't let go.

They made their way along the edge of the stable wall then ran through the training fields. Behler could see the lone tent left in the field where Rafe and Sera had been in the vision Nirain had shared with her. The fires on the north end of the village were the most intense, and the flames and heat subsided slightly as they made their way toward the southern end of Ardin.

Although all the fighting was focused at the opposite end of the village, she feared there may be Armigoth forces lurking in every shadow she saw.

"I see Sera," Avenly said. "Look."

She pointed across the field at the tent. They could just barely make out Sera's silhouette against the backdrop of the tent.

"Ama," she said, a quiet joy rose up within her. Her mother was alive.

Sera stood in the opening of the tent, her eyes on the sky above watching for any sign of either dragon. The burning fires reflecting on the dragons' shiny scales were the only way she could track their movements at all. That and their occasional piercing cries that ripped through Sera's head.

She was tired. She didn't know how much longer she could keep defending the tent and Rafe. Her hands were blistered from the growing heat transferred through her draka. But she would stand and protect the man she loved.

She was haunted that she couldn't protect Brant when he needed it. If protecting Rafe meant giving her own life, so be it.

The dragons were focused on the north end and the fighting. Sera could see the occasional glint of fire off their scales.

She knew they must be biding their time until their supply of fire regenerated. She'd started counting the minutes between fiery rounds.

It was roughly four.

Behind her, a rustling from inside the tent drew her attention.

Rafe!

She spun around and stepped into the tent, taking her eyes off the sky for the first time since the dragons had arrived.

Where she'd hoped to see Rafe awake and moving, she instead found him convulsing.

"Rafe!" She fell on her knees next to him.

She didn't know what was happening. nitesting beetles were supposed to cause the victim to fall into a deep sleep until they stopped breathing. Convulsions weren't part of the symptoms...were they?

She tried to remember her lessons from so long ago. Her mind was too exhausted to even remember yesterday. Tears stung her eyes. She didn't know what to do.

Zola's bag was right next to her, though, so she reached in and grabbed the bottle of the purple liquid Zola had used earlier. She pulled the lid off. The smell was sickeningly sweet. She poured a few drops between Rafe's lips.

"Please, drink it," she whispered. "Please."

She replaced the bottle and grabbed a bottle of aji. She popped the cork out of the bottle and dropped a little aji into Rafe's mouth.

She dug through the bag, barely able to make out the labels on each bottle. She squinted in the dark, trying to read enough to find anything that might help.

Throat and Ear

Headache

Toothache

Menstrual and Labor

Bites and Stings

Lidic Disease

She grabbed the Bites and Stings and Lidic Disease bottles. She knew the bottle labeled lidic disease was for the early symptoms, which included shakes, tremors, and convulsions. She could only hope she didn't accidentally poison Rafe in the process of trying to save him.

After placing a few drops from each bottle in his mouth, all she could do was sit helplessly and watch his body twist and contort on the cot. A few excruciating moments later, his convulsions stopped. Sera put her head on his chest. The rise and fall of his breathing was one of the best things she had ever felt.

As if they'd been waiting for her eyes to be somewhere else, she heard the sound of those wings right above the tent. The shrill cry from the dragon ripped through the tent. Sera reached for her draka, but she'd dropped it when she saw Rafe convulsing.

"Noooo!" She lunged toward the opening of the tent just as she heard the sound of the flames erupting from the dragon's throat.

She wasn't going to make it.

But the flames hit an invisible dome. Unlike hers, it was blue. Sera could see its light through the tent's fabric.

She opened the tent flaps.

Behler and Avenly stood where she had been only minutes before – Behler's isari glowing brightly as it provided the shield that protected them now.

The dragon, furious to be stymied once again, forced more fire through its throat. When it saw it was not breaking through, it stopped and roared a primal cry.

The cry reminded Sera of those she'd heard mothers make when told their child was never coming home.

The dragon flew over them and over the forest.

Behler turned. Her hair was wildly falling from its knot, and she blew a piece of it out her eye. She smiled. "Hi Ama."

Sera, still on her knees, pulled Behler down and clung to her. Tears of exhaustion rolled down her cheeks.

63

Behler and Sera were still in an embrace when the tent flaps opened. "What the kak is going on here?"

Everyone looked up at the sound of his voice.

"Rafe!" Sera said.

Rafe was looking at Behler. "What are you doing here? You're supposed to be at the ruins by now."

Behler shrugged. "Matti forgot his stuffed kindurbeast. We had to come back for it." She looked around the village. "Why'd you throw a party without us?"

Rafe smirked. "So, I assume you're *all* back?"

"Wouldn't be a very good crew if we split up so soon, now, would it?"

Rafe looked at Sera. "What happened?"

"You were bitten by a nitesting beetle. You've been out of it for hours."

He looked around the village. "And missed all the fun, I see."

"And you'll miss all of it if I have any say in it," Sera said. "You nearly died. You're in no shape to fight."

"I'm okay, really." He looked at Behler. "I can't let the youngsters show me up quite yet."

Behler stood. "Someone needs to get Avenly to Fenn's cave and check on Nirain. She was injured."

Sera was reluctant to leave Rafe, but she knew he was going to fight no matter what. Her own strength was waning, and exhaustion was setting in. She looked down at Avenly. "I'll get you there. We'll check on your ama." Avenly nodded silently, her face slack and exhausted. She had gone numb, as if her little body could no longer handle all that nishiri was putting it through. Sera turned to Rafe. "Fight well so you can fight tomorrow."

Rafe kissed her on the forehead—a gesture so unexpected, it stunned Behler more than anything else that night. She had no idea Rafe and her mother were together. Her mother turned to her. "And you...maybe you should leave while you can."

Behler shook her head. "I'm not running from the Horde or the Armigoth tonight or ever again. And I'm not leaving until I know they are out of our home and our people are safe."

Sera and Rafe both smiled.

"Understood, Captain," Rafe said with a nod of salute. "But take the advice of an old duk, sometimes we run today so we can fight again tomorrow."

Behler gave him a quick nod. "Understood, Captain."

Rafe and Behler stood at the tent discussing what their next move should be.

"We're too scattered," Rafe said. "We'll never push them back like this." He looked at Behler. "We need to organize."

"Looks like most of our people are there." Behler pointed to the charred kogum field. They could see the glow of isari stones scattered throughout the area.

"Let's go," Rafe said and began running in that direction.

They had run past all the houses and were just passing the warming-house, Behler heard a familiar sound that stopped her in her tracks.

A shrill voice, carried by a growing breeze, came from the direction of the Great House.

"Where is she? I know you two were thick as thieves back in that hole, Betham."

Rafe stopped and turned to her. "What is it?"

"A Horde officer from Betham," Behler said. The sight of the vile woman beating a man bubbled up from the recesses of her memory. "Oh vlock..." Behler realized who she was talking to. "She's got Matti!"

When she met Rafe's eyes, he knew she would be no good fighting the Gorlogs while a big part of her mind was on Mathias. "Go. We'll handle the Gorlogs. You handle that."

Behler gave a resolute nod and veered toward the Great House. She ran past the laundry house and then crept quickly around the masonry until she could see the grassy area next to the Great House.

Eun stood facing a group of Trulars, lined up on their knees. Rogan and Dalen were among them. Five Horde guuns stood behind her, and a Gorlog stood at each end of the line of Trulars. In the middle of the line was Mathias.

Eun was leaning over Mathias and appeared to be saying something quietly to him, but her body language radiated frustration and anger. A tiny yelp escaped from Behler's throat when Eun suddenly hit Mathias across his face. Matti recovered quickly and stared forward.

"Tell me where she is!" Eun screamed. She looked down the line. "Mercy to anyone who tells me."

"The Armigoth doesn't show mercy," Behler murmured.

Eun waved a hand at one of the Gorlogs who immediately walked over to Mathias and hit him so hard he flew sideways off his knees.

The other Revalars continued to look defiantly forward, although Rogan looked as if he would start attacking his son's tormentors at any moment. Eun walked up to the next Revalar and started the process all over again. Behler quickly moved back behind the masonry and ran around the back of the laundry house. She crossed the dirt path and moved around the corner of the first row of homes.

Eun and the others came back into view just as Eun began shouting again. "Where is she?" she shouted. "Where is the girl you call *Behler*?" She stopped suddenly and looked toward the Great House. She paused as if she was listening to something, then nodded. "Where is her brother?"

Mathias had pulled himself up and returned to a defiant posture.

"Why couldn't you just stay down, Matti," Behler said, but she knew he would continue to rise as long as he was physically able to.

"Where are they?" the officer shrieked at Mathias. He looked past her and said nothing. "Kill him," she ordered and flicked her wrist.

The Gorlog walked over, snarling, and giving Mathias a big toothy grin. The Gorlog raised a large hammer high over its head, preparing to strike. As she watched the Gorlog's hammer rise, Behler felt a rage erupt in her like she had never felt before. Every hurt and every evil she'd endured created a pinpoint of molten fury at the center of her core.

She hissed, "Kahto!"

Both the isari stone in her draka and those in her amulet ignited in light, and in an instant, a blue beam of pure energy shot across the village. When it struck the

Gorlog, Behler could see a hole appear in the center of its chest. It looked down for a moment as if confused. The hammer, still held over its head, fell to the ground behind it. Then the Gorlog fell to its knees. Mathias rolled out of the way just in time to avoid being crushed.

Eun spun around in her direction.

Behler stood on the paved road, defiant, daring them to try to lay a finger on any of her people again.

"I think you've been looking for me," she called out.

Eun eyed her suspiciously. "You just killed one of my men."

Behler shrugged. "That's a pretty loose definition of the word *men*, don't you think? Especially now."

"Shut up, girl! What game are you playing here?"

"I thought you might be up for a trade," Behler said. "Me for them."

She saw a visible reaction from the entire line of Trulars.

"A trade? Why would you do that?"

Behler shrugged. "Take it or leave it. I'm sure Varek would understand if you let me just walk away right now."

Eun walked over to Mathias and put the point of her sword to his chest. "Drop your weapons," Eun ordered. "Your little stick with the stone first. If you try anything, I will kill him."

Behler pulled the draka from behind her and laid it on the ground, followed by her bow and kintar. She turned so that everyone could see she had no other weapon.

"Now, walk to me."

Behler walked half the distance before stopping. "I'll walk the rest of the way when you've released my people."

Eun raised her dark eyebrows. She paused again, as if listening to a voice, maybe in her head. "Very well." She turned to a Gorlog and nodded. He walked over to the large set of doors and grabbed the chain that had been placed around the door handles. He ripped the chain off and broke the doors off their hinges then pulled the doors completely out of the doorframe.

"Out!" he shouted.

Behler watched as Trulars and Elians made their way out of the building. She hadn't even realized they were there. All of them looked battle weary and confused about their sudden, apparent freedom.

"Now, walk to me," the captain repeated her order.

"The rest of them," Behler demanded, raising her chin toward those Trulars on their knees.

She met Mathias' eyes for just a split second. He was watching her closely to anticipate her next move.

Eun grunted and turned to the line. "Stand up. If any of you try anything, we'll kill you on the spot." She turned to Behler. "On. The. Spot."

Behler began to walk toward her, eyeing all the enemies as she moved. The woman's face was practically twitching with excitement.

"You will let them go." Behler said. "They will be free."

"Of course," the captain said. To Behler, she sounded too much like a snake.

She was only a few yura lengths from the captain when the woman shouted, "Take her!"

The remaining Gorlog grabbed Behler's arms roughly, and the captain walked up so her nose was nearly touching Behler's. She spoke in a low voice, "You are a foolish girl." Her bright red lips stretched over teeth that looked too white and too big for her mouth. "Bow before our master," she commanded loudly.

Behler saw a hooded figure step out of the shadows of the Great House. Varek. Dark wisps slithered around him. "He's not my master, and I will not bow."

Eun cackled. "Bow foolish girl." She raised a dark eyebrow. "Perhaps he will show you mercy." Behler held her gaze and remained silent. This just made the captain laugh again.

Behler took a deep breath. "I will not bow."

Eun leaned in so her lips were right next to Behler's ear. "You will, girl, you will," she said softly. "Just like the rest of us did." She took a step back.

"Where did you live before?" Behler asked.

The captain stopped and turned. "What?" She overemphasized the "t" so much that Behler felt spittle hit her cheek. She ignored it.

"What village? Oryn? Roan?"

"Do not try to distract me stupid girl." Eun started to walk away.

"North then. Maybe Gowan." She knew she was right when the woman's shoulders tensed just a bit at the name of the village. "Yes, it was Gowan. Did you have a family? Children?"

Eun turned to her with a look of smug pride all over her face. She stepped closer to Behler. "I *have* a family. My wife and two girls," she said. She took another step closer. "My wife works for Lord Varek in Kilgen." She smiled as if the fact made her proud. She leaned in closer and dropped her voice. She spoke directly into Behler's ear again and Behler tried not to shrink away from her hot breath. "My girls were taken when Varek came looking for *you*." She spat out the last word. "He will return them to us when...You. Are. Dead. You were a fool for showing yourself tonight." She backed away and again looked into Behler's eyes. "Summon the dragons," she commanded. Behler wasn't sure who was taking the order.

"You will not kill me today," Behler said softly and steadily. "And if you think you will ever get your wife and daughters back then *you* are the fool."

Eun laughed maniacally. "We will kill you...but not before you watch your friend die." She turned and raised her hand.

A Horde guun had stayed too close to Mathias. He drew his sword and was just ready to run Mathias through when Behler shouted, "AHMEEEI!" The Gorlog behind her flew backward. Eun was thrown nearly twenty yura lengths. Behler looked all around her, the guuns were moving in on her quickly. She saw a couple of their archers grabbing for their arrows.

"SHO!" Every enemy stopped in their tracks and rose up off the ground.

She was just ready to drop them when her body froze. Her own feet lifted up off the ground. And when she saw the cloaked figure floating toward her, a cold fear replaced her cocky bravery.

"I'm not afraid of you," she said through clenched teeth.

He said nothing, just continued to float toward her. He had raised an arm and his sleeve slipped down to reveal nothing more than thick, black smoke. A tendril slithered out toward her.

When he was a yura length from her, he stopped and in the same voice she'd heard while standing by the kogum field in the Deep Thread he said, "You should be Trular."

"From what I keep hearing, it's you who should be afraid of me," she said through clenched teeth. Varek laughed at her. "Not yet. Tonight, you are just a girl. A Trular, sure – but aren't we all?"

"You're a traitor," she spat out.

"Perhaps." He raised an arm, and Behler's heart sank as more Gorlogs stepped from the forest beyond. The tendril of smoke twisted upward and Behler rose up a bit more off the ground. "Shall I give you the same fate you gave the Gorlog? But first, let's see that stone you've been hiding." The black smoke wrapped itself around her until it slipped around her neck. It twisted around her amulet's chain and pulled it from under her shirt.

"What! What's this?" Varek sputtered as he looked at the trinket hanging on the chain.

"It's an eltip shell," she said. "Don't you know *anything*?" She sneered in her most toxic adolescent tone. Her cocky anger was returning.

Varek ripped the chain from her neck. "Your Trular arrogance is what's gotten you killed here tonight," Varek spat out. His rage was evident in the shaking of his voice. "I don't know how you've done this without a stone, but it ends now." The black tendrils moved up her body and around her throat until she couldn't breathe.

"Varek!" Fennix shouted from behind her.

Varek's attention was diverted just long to give Behler a second of advantage.

"Ahmei!" she choked out, and the cloaked figure flew backwards. Multiple arrows flew past her and went straight through the cloak which then dissipated into the air. Varek was gone. Behler's stomach jumped into her throat as her body fell back toward the ground. "Shuka!" she said, catching herself in midair then lowering herself to the ground gently.

"Behler!" Kellum's voice came from behind and above her. She jumped up and spotted her brother on the ground and Kellum in the tower. They were aiming at the oncoming Gorlogs with their bows.

Behler grabbed the chain with the shell Kellum had given her, stuffing it into the pocket in her pants. She rushed to retrieve her weapons, then she turned to run back to the tower. Just as she grabbed the first rung on the ladder to begin climbing up to join Kellum, she heard the cry of the dragons coming from over the forest.

They were coming from the north again, and the released prisoners were still gathered just outside of the building. "RUN!" She screamed and began running toward them. They all had heard the dragons' cries too and began scrambling in every direction.

"Our weapons – I saw them put them in the masonry," Dax called out.

Behler immediately turned and ran for the building. Many people from Great House were right behind her. Together, they all grabbed as many weapons as they could carry. Trulars scrambled to find their drakas, thankfully all still with their stones. As Behler was grabbing a stash of arrows, Rogan grabbed her shoulder. "You can take out their legs with a kintar to the back of their knees. Their tendons are weak."

Behler nodded. "Good to know. I've been aiming for their eyes. That works nicely, too." She handed him a bow and strapped a quiver of arrows around her own body.

"Fight well," Rogan said.

"So you can fight tomorrow," Behler responded.

They ran out into the night just as the first fiery breaths were raining down on the field to the north, outlining the Gorlogs and guuns racing toward them. With the additional light, Behler could also see that the blackness of the Armigoth had reached the village clearing. Thick wisps and tendrils just like what she'd seen with the cloaked figure were slithering from between the trees and into Ardin.

Behler turned and saw Kellum in the tower. Their eyes met for a brief moment, and then she turned and ran with Rogan and Dalen into the fray.

64

Behler took out five Gorlogs before even reaching the front line. Her sixth opponent was a Horde soldier – a man. She jabbed her bow into his gut and drew her kintar to take him down. She felt the blade slide through the man's flesh and her stomach turned. It was the first person she'd ever killed, at least in hand to hand. She had no idea if any of the guuns had survived their fall.

An arrow hissed past her and took out another soldier. Judging by its angle, it had come from the tower.

The dragons circled overhead waiting for their reservoir of fire to return.

After a while, it seemed that the Revala was finally gaining ground, but then a loud crashing sound came from within the forest followed by a deep, guttural roar. Behler looked, and with the flames lighting up enough of the landscape, she could see treetops moving as if something huge was coming through. She turned to the tower. Kellum had seen it too and was already aiming his next arrow. Luke stood next to him, a mirror image of his brother.

The last tree parted and a giant walked out of the forest. It was covered in chain maille from its shoulders to its feet. A helmet covered its huge head, revealing only its face which was painted with dark markings. It carried a weapon with two semi-circular stones with chiseled edges. They were attached to a large wooden handle perfect for making sweeping, slicing arcs. Strangely, with all its armor and weaponry, it wore no shoes.

"Okinars?" Behler asked.

"Yes – and avoid their blades," Rogan said. "They're betilans, and their edges are razor sharp and covered in a deadly poison."

"Avoid the scary sharp things. Got it." Behler grabbed her bow and began a melee of arrows at the giant, trying in vain to find a chink in the armor.

The giant swept its weapon across the body, slicing through the air and flesh alike. So far, it had only hit Gorlogs, and it didn't seem to care. Behler saw more treetops behind it moving and swaying. More of those giants would reveal themselves soon.

"Rogan!" she shouted. When he looked at her, she pointed to the forest just as two more giants burst through the treeline.

"Revalars, retreat and regroup!" Rafe bellowed from behind Behler.

She turned and ran, looking for Kellum in the tower as she did. He was still taking aim at the Okinar. She searched the area for Mathias, but she couldn't find him.

She flared her isari, knowing he had to be close by. He'd been right behind her and Rogan when they'd left the warming house.

There he was. She spotted his blond hair. But he was crouching and holding his side. She ran to him. "Come on Matti. We have to get out of here."

"I can't walk," he said. His right foot was twisted to the side, the ankle obviously broken badly. There was a large gash on his side, not to mention all the bruises and cuts he'd received from the Gorlog during his time with Eun.

"Then I'll carry you," she said and heaved him up from the ground. His blond hair, darkened by crusted blood, fell into his eyes as his head lolled about.

"You can't carry me, Bale."

"Sure, I can," she insisted. "Sho," she said and Mathias' feet left the ground. He looked at her out of the corner of his eye and actually smirked a little at her. "Impressed?" she asked.

"Not as much as when you put a hole through that Gorlog's chest," he chuckled.

"That wasn't even my best work of the night," Behler smirked, but then her mouth turned into a line and a crease formed over her eyes. "I got the Gorlog that attacked Sam that night."

Matti's expression matched hers. "Good."

When they had reached the watchtower, Mathias came to rest gently on the ground while Behler supported most of his weight with her body. "Kellum!" she shouted up. "Kellum, we're leaving."

Kellum and Luke quickly descended the ladder, and each touched Mathias' shoulder reassuringly when they reached the ground. He leaned heavily on Behler for support but reached out to grip first Kellum's forearm then Luke's.

"Where's Meela and Fenn?" Behler asked.

Before anyone could answer, the giants near the masonry roared and sliced with their betilans. This time, there were only Horde guuns around for them to take out and half a dozen went flying.

A young female Revalar ran up to Behler and her partial crew. "Hey all, I'm Aeron...nice to meet you. We'll get to know each other later. Right now, we need to get out of here. There's more of them coming."

"We'll help Matti," Kellum said, moving to support Mathias' weight from the other side. He motioned to Luke for him to take Behler's spot. She moved out of the way, careful to avoid Mathias' injuries. The sky was just beginning to turn gray as morning approached.

Behler's hand was resting on the ladder as the boys got into position to help Mathias. She felt a giant thud reverberate through the entire structure. It shook a couple more times. She looked up toward the platform and there, staring down at her, was the dragon from Betham. Their eyes met, and for a moment, Behler could swear she felt a tug of The Deep Thread. An aching grief tore through her, just like the one she'd felt the night she'd learned of Lorna's death.

The stone around the dragon's neck flared, and the grief was instantly gone.

The dragon cried out its ear-piercing cry, and Behler and the others immediately covered their ears and shrank down in agony.

"Fire incoming!" Luke yelled. They all could see the flicker of flame glowing within the dragon's mouth.

"Hold!" Behler shouted. She held up her draka and the isari shield formed just before the flames reached them. The fire curved around them as if they were inside a giant, invisible bowl. They stared at the flames – an arms-length from them all. Behler looked around at them. "Pretty neat, huh?"

"Gah!" Aeron laughed. "I love being a Trular!"

The dragon held her flame only to see the five still standing unharmed. She cried out and began her fiery onslaught once more. When she saw they remained unharmed, she rose upward with two powerful wingbeats. She swung around and reared back and tried to attack them with her giant hind claws, but those too bounced off the shield. She cried out in utter frustration and rage. Behler thought she would attack again, but in the next second, her entire body froze except her beating wings. She looked to the east, where the sun was just rising over the horizon.

Her body shifted away from them, and she cried out again, but instead of the angry shriek from before, these were three short, high-pitched trills.

The second dragon rose above the treeline and returned its own three-trilled response. They both rose up higher and scanned the eastern skies. Each of the dragons made the three trills again then immediately took off north. Behler and the others looked to see if they could see what could have possibly scared them away, but the only thing they could make out in the sky was a flock of birds. In the scant light of the brand-new morning, it was hard to judge how far away they were, but then the light changed as the sun continued to rise.

Luke made a whistling sound through his teeth. "Those are some big-ass birds."

"Is there something else you forgot to tell me, guys?" Behler asked.

Luke, Mathias, and Kellum all said "No," at the same time as they all continued to stare at the approaching birds.

"I have no idea what this is," Kellum added.

Aeron looked at them like they were all a little dense. "Those are the Cawree," she said. When they all looked at her, still clueless, she added. "The Cawree Bird clan from the Eastern Coast?" She looked at them for a moment before sighing. "You all need to brush up on your Elium history."

Luke pointed. "The hawk in the lead has a human rider."

The flock glided silently over the treeline and then the leader called something out. The birds separated and went directly for the Okinar giants. In teams of two, they slashed and tore at the chain maille while also avoiding the slicing betilans. Their talons were able to grip at the rings of the chains. The birds ripped away at the armor. Behler cringed as she watched an Okinar slice at a snow-white owl.

Blood immediately colored the bird's body. The large bird cried out and began struggling to stay in the air. A second bird flew up and gripped the Okinar's arm. Behler gasped as she watched the bird tear the arm away as if it were a piece of cooked meat. The Okinar roared and fell in a heap. The snowy owl flew away, still struggling to stay airborne, until it landed near the lake and away from the fighting. A hawk soon landed near it and started tending to its wounds.

Revala archers were taking the opportunity to target the unarmored giants. Behler saw an Okinar stumbling backwards who already had half-a-dozen arrows lodged in its body. She looked at Kellum, then Luke, then Aeron who gave her a quick nod. They sat Mathias down gently against one of the tower's supports then took off to rejoin the fight.

"Yeah, guys..." Mathias called out to them. "I'll be...I'm good." He grabbed his draka and scooted underneath the tower, hoping the shadows would keep him hidden.

65

With the arrival of the Cawree, the Gorlogs and Horde fled into the forest, but the Okinar giants refused to flee. They continued swinging their betilans, trying to make contact with anything they could. The Okinar who had stumbled backwards with so many arrows protruding out of his chest had regained his footing and was once again moving toward them.

"Behler – look!" Kellum was pointed to their left where the trees were beginning to sway just as the others had. "Another one's coming."

The hawks and owls were in a frenzy clawing and tearing at the Okinars' armor and flesh.

As if there wasn't enough chaos, thunder ripped through the sky and the clouds released torrents of water. Rafe came running up to them, blood from a large cut on his cheek already beginning to mix with the falling rain.

"We've got to get closer," he shouted to them. "We've got to knock them off their feet while the Cawree have them distracted. We'll need to move fast. We need the horses."

Kellum gave a loud, short whistle and Storm came running. Each of the other Trulars whistled to their horses, and soon all five horses were running across the field from different directions. Ciela and Sabana came from the field near the stables. Rafe's horse was right behind them.

Lightning cracked and lit up the sky.

"We're going to make an indari wall," Rafe said.

"What is that?" Behler asked.

"It's like an isari shield, only it extends to make a wall. It will extend from each of us. But we have to focus on keeping it going. One break and the wall may fail."

Behler looked at Kellum and Luke and all three started laughing.

Rafe looked confused. "What...what is it?"

"We made one to get back here quickly," Behler said. "We just didn't know it had a name."

"Good," Rafe said as he pulled himself up on his horse, Vala. His isari stone immediately began to glow. "We're going to knock those jackals on their asses."

Behler looked at Aeron. "Wanna ride?" She reached her hand down.

Aeron smiled. "Thought you'd never ask." She grasped Behler's hand and pulled herself up to sit behind her.

Rafe looked out across the field. "Let's ride."

They took off, making their way around the outskirts of the fighting. The hawks were still ripping and tearing at the Okinars.

"Indari ja!" Rafe cried out. A chain of light first reached from his stone to Behler' stone, and then to Kellum's stone. Soon, each of them was connected by a bright beam of light. They all readied their bows.

The Okinar nearest them had seen them coming and had pulled a long spear from behind its back and was just preparing to hurl it.

"Look out!" Aeron yelled.

"Don't stop moving forward," Rafe called out.

The spear flew at them, striking the wall between Behler and Kellum as if hitting a wall made of solid stone. It hovered in the air for a few moments before gravity finally overcame momentum and pulled the spear down to the ground.

Behler could see the weapon was roughly as long as a horse and looked about as thick as a man's leg. The tip on it was barbed, making removal possibly lethal to any victim who managed to survive an initial strike, something no human could ever hope to do.

They were quickly approaching the giant who was preparing to slice at them with its betilan, but a hawk swooped down and began clawing at the arm and hand holding the chiseled blades. Kellum took advantage of the distraction and aimed an arrow at the fleshy side of the giant, just below the arm which was raised trying to strike down the hawk. As soon as he released the first arrow, he grabbed another and took aim again.

Behler grabbed an arrow of her own and took aim at the Okinar's throat. She released the arrow and watched as it found its mark. The giant grabbed the arrow and ripped it out, tossing it aside as if it were a little more than a stinging hornet. Kellum shot another, hitting the creature in its shoulder. The Okinar looked at the arrow then looked back at the Trulars racing toward it. Behler saw it smile. The hawk was still flying around the giant, trying to get a clear angle to tear at its armor, but the Okinar turned and with one lucky swat of its hand, made contact with the hawk and the bird went sailing across the sky. Behler lost track of where it landed. The Okinar looked back and locked eyes with her. Its snarling smile was filled with sharp, jagged teeth. It began spinning the betilan in the air by a leather rope attached to the handle, and the blade was gaining momentum with every revolution.

All those riding with her were bombarding the giant with arrow after arrow, but it didn't react to the volley at all. Instead, it kept its eyes locked on Behler and continued to twirl its betilan through the air. Behler could hear the *whoosh...whoosh...whoosh* as the blade spun.

"Keep going!" Rafe yelled.

The Okinar's face resembled a human's, but its eyes were more like a bear's. They were small, but she took aim anyway. She let the arrow loose, but the creature saw it coming and lowered its head just enough so that the arrow glanced off its helmet.

"Kak!" she grunted in frustration.

The Okinar began running toward them, spinning its blade as it came. An owl grabbed at it, trying to stop it or slow it down, but the giant shook it off and continued running.

"Stay with me!" Rafe called out to the others. "The wall has to hold!"

Another hawk flew at the giant. It timed its flight perfectly, knocking the betilan from the Okinar's grip. The giant faltered but then regained its balance. It hesitated and turned, trying to locate its weapon.

"Indari ja!" Rafe yelled loudly, trying to fortify the wall.

"Indari ja!" Behler and Kellum shouted.

"Indari ja!" Fennix shouted from behind them. Behler looked and saw her brother riding up to join them.

The indari wall extended itself to Fennix's isari stone just before the Okinar slammed into the wall of light between Rafe and Behler. For a moment the Okinar was frozen, stunned by the impact. Its feet dug deep ruts in the ground as it was pushed backwards while Behler and the others continued moving forward. Then the giant began back-peddling, desperately trying in vain to find any kind of traction, but the more it struggled, the more off balance it became.

Behler couldn't be sure if the giant simply gave up or if it actually lost its balance, but a moment later, it fell. The wall pushed the Okinar along the ground and its body twisted and crumbled over itself until it looked more like a rag doll rolling over and over on the ground instead of anything with bone and cartilage.

Time slowed for Behler. She thought of Warln's crumpled body back in the stables, his only company the dead Gorlogs.

"Uhret," she said softly. The light between her and Rafe immediately vanished. The giant tumbled a few more yura lengths then stopped and lay motionless in a big heap. Behler watched over her shoulder for a few seconds to make sure it wasn't getting up. "Indari ja!" The wall reappeared.

"Look!" Kellum shouted and motioned behind them. Another Okinar stared at them, its shoulders heaving in rage at the sight of its fallen comrade. One of the large spears was lodged in the ground next to it. It reached over and pulled it out with one swift tug and aimed at them.

"Look out!" Behler cried.

The group split down the middle, and the wall between them vanished. The spear flew past and dug itself back into the ground.

Behler wiped the rain out of her eyes.

"It's coming!" Aeron shouted, watching the Okinar over her shoulder.

The giant was giving chase, and as fast as the Gorlogs were, the Okinar was faster. Its shoeless feet meant that it could sink its toes into the softening earth each time it landed, allowing it to dig in even more and propel itself more with each step.

She saw the spear lodged in the ground and had an idea. She turned Ciela back and headed straight for the spear and straight at the Okinar who was racing toward it. Kellum saw what she was going for and turned Storm around, he looked over and saw Fennix had already done the same.

"Sho!" Behler yelled, focusing on the spear.

The Okinar was getting close to the spear, and she thought it may reach it before they did.

The spear wiggled a bit.

"Sho!" She repeated.

"Sho!" Aeron said from behind her.

It wiggled again, more this time.

Behler could see the light from her amulet shining on Ciela's mane. "Ready?" Behler asked Aeron.

"Always."

She looked over at Fenn and Kellum. They nodded.

"SHO!" they all shouted together.

The spear wrenched itself free and hovered above the ground. "AHMEI!" The weapon spun around and hurtled itself at the Okinar. Behler saw its strange bear-eyes register surprise as it watched its own weapon barreling down upon it, and that moment of hesitation was its death. The head of the spear hit the giant square in the chest and knocked the giant back with so much force that when it fell, the spear stood at a steep angle, lodged in the ground once again. The Okinar hovered, skewered, just above the ground.

Kellum caught up to Behler and Aeron, and together with Fennix and Meela they turned their sights on the next closest giant, but as soon as the indari wall formed between them, the giant backed away. It stared at them for a few moments, and Behler could see it working out its options.

"Gobda!" the giant called out then immediately backed up into the trees. It kept its eyes locked on Behler and Fennix as it retreated; its lips turned up in an angry snarl, then it turned and was gone. The dark mist that had been slithering into the village retreated back into the trees.

Moments later, Rafe rode up to join them. Fennix scanned the treeline. "Those things gave up all of a sudden."

"I think we spooked them," Rafe said. He looked around the village. "This wasn't a full attack. Varek wanted to see how strong we are...how strong you two have become." He looked over at the impaled giant. "He got a good show, but we paid the price," he looked around at the ruined village and the injured or dead. The rain had nearly completely put out the fire.

Overhead, the surviving birds were circling. The leader landed and the others followed, forming a semicircle behind it.

"We couldn't have done it if the Cawree hadn't shown up when they did," Aeron said as they watched the rider hop down off the lead bird. "We're lucky she went for them."

Behler squinted. There was something very familiar about the rider. The woman looked older but moved with the nimble fluidity of a much younger person. And then she pushed a gray strand of hair behind her ear and Behler knew. She'd seen her do it countless times in Betham in just the same way.

"Tilda," Behler said breathlessly.

The woman looked up, saw Behler and smiled.

66

Rafe walked toward Tilda. He approached her then crossed his arm over his chest and knelt on one knee with his head bowed. All the Trulars who were standing did the same while the Elians looked around confused. Behler could understand how they felt. Kellum and the others on the horses crossed their arms over their chests and bowed their heads. Feeling awkward, Behler did the same, watching out of the corner of her eye so she'd know what to do next.

When she looked up, Tilda had her hand on Rafe's head.

He stood. "You have done well, Rafe," Tilda said. All the other Trulars stood as Rafe and Tilda began walking toward Behler and Fennix.

Behler jumped off Ciela.

Tilda smiled happily. "Behler."

Overcome by happiness to see the woman, Behler took a step forward and embraced her tightly. She heard a few people gasp and murmur behind her, so she let go of Tilda, feeling embarrassed over what was obviously an infraction of Trular customs.

Tilda chuckled and the sound was like tinkling glass. "It's okay. They simply aren't used to people greeting me in such a way."

"I'm sorry," Behler said.

"Don't be. As the governing leader of our people, maybe I should make that an official greeting." She looked around at all the others who had gathered nearby. "We need to search for the injured while we still may be able to help them."

Behler looked toward the stables. Her heart ached for the man who lay inside.

She hoped she would be able to tell Kellum and Luke before anyone else did, so she tried to make her way to them, but Dax stopped her.

"Behler," he said shyly, and she realized she'd never heard him say her name before. "There's a guun in the field. He's injured."

"Okay," Behler said, unsure of what Dax was trying to say.

"He's...uh...we know him – or I know him at least – Lucias, from the village, er Betham. He's the man whose wife passed away from the fever awhile back and he never quite recovered."

"I know him, Dax," Behler said quietly. "I used to play with his dog, Kinti." She smiled at the memory of the sweet pup that also happened to be a complete bonehead. "What are you saying?" she asked gently.

Dax scratched his head. "It's just that...he...he seems like Lucius." His cheeks were breaking out in a smattering of fiery red blotches.

"He seems like Lucius?" She repeated. "What do you mean, exactly?"

Dax swallowed and willfully got his nerves under control. He looked her square in the eye. "He's not like the Horde guuns, anymore. He's Lucius again."

The realization of what Dax was saying finally struck Behler squarely in the face. "Show me," she said, her voice sharp with urgency.

Dax nodded and turned. He ran across the field, dodging bodies of Horde guuns, Okinars, and a few Trulars. Soon, he stopped and knelt over the body of a guun in brown grunt clothing.

Behler gasped. She turned to find the guard tower where they'd left Mathias before returning to the fight then turned back to Dax and the man on the ground. She was almost certain it was the man she'd stabbed with her kintar.

She fell to her knees. "Lucius?" She tapped his cheek gently. "Lucius, can you hear me?"

He opened his eyes, and there he was: the kind man who had always had an extra sweet biscuit to give her and his dog, Kinti. "Sorry, lass, no sweets for you today."

Behler smiled while tears spilled out of her eyes. "Lucius, I'm sorry. I didn't know it was you." She looked up at Dax. She nearly ripped the canteen strap as she fought to get it from around her neck. "Lucius," she rushed and she opened the lid. "You have to drink this."

Dax looked at her, eyes wide. "It won't work for Elians."

"Why not?" Behler asked. "Who says? Have you ever tried any?" He shook his head. "Our bodies look pretty much like your bodies...maybe it will work. Maybe no one has ever tried."

She held Lucius' head up and helped him to drink the rest of the aji in her canteen. He spilled a lot of it, but a good portion of it went down his throat.

Behler ripped the sleeve off her luka, so much like Kellum had ripped his that night of the attack on Betham. She held the cloth over Lucius' wound.

"Behler, I'm sorry," Lucius said. "It was me...but it wasn't. I felt as if I were trapped in my body – all the good things about me that is. Every hateful thought or meanness I ever dealt out, it all came back and it ruled me. It made me want to hurt everyone and to see everyone as devastated as I felt.

The luka was quickly becoming saturated with Lucius' blood. "Dax, do you see Zola anywhere?"

He stood and scanned the field. Her bright purple luka and wild frizzy hair would make her easy to spot, but he soon knelt back down and shook his head. "I don't."

"I don't think the aji is working." She grew angry. Why wouldn't the aji work for an Elian? Didn't all creatures deserve a chance to be healed...to feel that darkness lift a bit...just to catch a break when they needed it most?

Lucius' eyes were closed. "Lucius!" she shouted, lightly hitting his cheeks again. She threw her head down on his chest to listen for a heartbeat, and that's when she felt the Thread from the aji. She sensed it moving through his body, searching for what it needed to do but unable to navigate in a non-Trular system.

She lifted her head and looked at Lucius and Dax again. "We must be the same," she whispered.

Placing her hands on Lucius' chest, she reached for the aji's Thread. She found it, but it wasn't quite the same. It felt weaker – lost. She guided it, unsure how, letting it search for wounds within Lucius—both the ones she could see and the ones she couldn't. Her skin prickled as the Thread brushed against something buried deeper. Something cold. Something wrong.

It was there, hiding – the darkness of the Armigoth. A shadow curled tight within him, weak but alive in its own way. She felt a humming vibrating within it.

Get out of this man, she thought, though she didn't believe it could hear her. But then a chill crept across her fingers, and her breath hitched. She felt it stir. And somehow, impossibly—she knew it could feel her too.

This wasn't like the Armigoth she'd seen slithering across the forest or blotting out the skies over Ardin. It was part of it, but... smaller. A remnant. A shard of the greater whole, lurking in Lucius' blood like a wounded predator waiting for strength to return.

For an instant, she swore she heard faint clicking—tiny, chittering sounds at the edge of hearing, like insects crawling across glass. The echo vanished before she could focus on it, leaving only the wrongness pressing against her senses.

"No," Behler said aloud, her voice sharper than she intended. Dax flinched at her side.

A strong grip on her wrist pulled her mind back to the field and Lucius' physical body. His eyes were open again, glistening with the deepest sorrow and regret.

"Behler," his voice cracked like thin ice. "I can feel what you're doing. Please...let me go."

"Lucius, I think I can help. I can feel where the aji needs to go."

He shook his head. "I've done things I can never forget. I could spend my whole life trying to make it right and never come even close." His voice grew weaker as he spoke. "And I can still feel the darkness inside me just waiting – and I can't go back to that. I just can't..." A tear slipped from the corner of his eye. His grip on her wrist tightened – desperate, yet gentle. "Please, let me go find Martha and Kinti. They are waiting for me." He swallowed. "Please, let me have peace."

Tears flowed from both Behler's and Dax's eyes. "Lucius, stay...we can fight together," Behler pleaded. "We can help you keep the darkness at bay."

But he shook his head again. "It will haunt me. Every day. Lurking. Waiting." His gaze darted from her to Dax, then back again. "Tell them all... tell them I was me in the end. Whoever's left... please, tell them I'm sorry."

One last tear slipped down his cheek as his eyelids fluttered shut—this time for good.

"Lucius!" Behler cried. She reached back in and found the aji's Thread, but there was no longer any living paths for it to take.

Something was still chittering right at the edge of her senses, though, and it didn't feel like anything she'd ever known before. Whatever it was, it wasn't life – but it wasn't death. It was something else.

She lifted her gaze to Dax. "The people these guuns once were...they're still there – inside them." She looked around the field at all the dead. When her eyes came to rest on Lucius once again, she whispered, "I think I could have saved him."

"Bale," Dax finally said, taking her wrists off Lucius' chest. "Don't you see what he did?"

She shook her head. "No...what do you mean?"

"He distracted you so you couldn't save him." He looked down at the man lying peacefully in the grass. "All he wanted was peace and to be with Martha and Kinti."

Behler wiped tears off her cheeks, sniffling. "I hope he found them all."

67

Behler and Dax moved through the field, searching for any other survivors. By midmorning, searchers had found two surviving guuns and seven injured Revalars, including Meela who had got separated from Fennix and Mathias soon after the crew had joined the fight.

All could be saved, but there was great discussion on what to do with the guuns. There were no surviving Gorlogs or Okinars – probably because it took so much force to take them down at all.

"It's our duty to help them," Rogan argued.

"But what do we do with them after that?" Henry posed, his voice strained with concern and trepidation.

The group continued to discuss this while Behler left to mull over just exactly what had happened with Lucius in the field. She'd sensed that darkness still lingering, but it was distant and weak, as if it were a wounded predator hiding – the most dangerous kind of predator. Was it safe to believe the guuns could recover from the Armigoth's infestation?

She'd wandered through the rows of houses, each with varying degrees of fire damage. Soon enough, she was standing in front of her own. It felt like so long ago she'd stood in that same spot and saw her mother for the first time.

The front of the house looked undamaged. She walked up the front steps and opened the door. She could see light coming through the roof over the loft where a fire had caught, but it hadn't seemed to spread much.

Echoes of voices played in her mind. Sera's eagerness to welcome her back. Kellum's reassuring words. Avenly's youthful excitement. Her brother's willingness to open up to her.

She looked over at the chair where she'd sat and learned about the foretelling. It had seemed an impossible thing back then, that she would become something more than others around her. It was silly then. But now, after finding the Deep Thread more than once, after helping Warln when he was sick, and nearly helping Lucius – something was happening to her.

She walked down the hall toward her room. The sight of the large tub in the bathing room caught her eye and she stepped in. She ran her fingers over the hammered metal edge. It had been such a luxury to bathe in such a way. Would she ever do so again?

She turned to walk out but caught a glimpse of herself in the mirror. Her face was covered in soot, mud, and dried blood streaked from the earlier rain. She noticed her bare arm and remembered tearing her sleeve to try to help Lucius.

Grabbing a small basin, she primed the water from the spigot and filled it with cool water. Cupping her hands, she splashed her face and scrubbed. A square of yulit soap still lay on the table. She picked it up and lathered it up in her hands, then scrubbed her face some more.

"You missed a spot," Kellum said from the doorway.

"Kak!" she yelled, jumping back and nearly spilling the basin of water.

Fennix peeked around the corner. "Wow...you're jumpy."

"Gah! Don't sneak up on people! Ugh – kakweeds!"

Fenn laughed, but Kellum looked sincerely sorry for scaring her. He walked in and grabbed a towel, then gently wiped at a place on her cheek. He smiled. "You really did miss a spot."

"I'm going to grab a few more canteens for aji," her brother said. "I'll be in the kitchen."

Behler heard his footsteps move away from the bathing room. She let Kellum continue to wipe at her face. He dipped the towel in the water and brought it back up to her cheek.

"Kellum," she said but didn't know what she wanted to say after that. A flood of words was buried somewhere within her, bundled up and as elusive as the Thread.

He smiled. "I know," he said. He wiped a spot from her forehead, then knelt and gently kissed the spot.

"Thank you," she said softly. "For everything since Betham." She hesitated. "For everything you've *ever* done for me."

His hand slid to the back of her neck, thumb resting by her ear. "Bale, you don't have to thank me." He swallowed and gave his crooked smile. "I'll always be here for you. I always was."

Before she could think twice, she kissed him. For a fleeting moment she felt Kellum's Thread. In that split second, she felt his love for her. It was warm and comforting, and it made her feel safe.

She drew her Thread back and broke the kiss. The silence that followed felt strange.

Kellum held her face for a moment longer before letting go.

"I think I'll get another luka from my room," she said quietly, holding her sleeveless arm up as if he hadn't noticed it before. "Come with me?"

He nodded.

As she dug through her clothing, Kellum sat down on her bed. "We can't find Grampa. You didn't see him when you were searching the field did you?"

Her heart sank. With everything that had happened with Lucius, her mind had set the memory of Warln aside. Her face must have said everything Kellum needed to know.

"Where?" His voice was tight with emotion.

Behler stood up so she could better look him in the eye. "He died protecting Avenly."

Kellum gave a sad smile. "Where did you find him?" he asked again.

Behler didn't want to tell him out of fear he would go and try to find his body, but she couldn't keep it from him forever. "In the stables – but Kellum – don't go. The others will take care of him."

There were no tears in Kellum's eyes, but his voice was thick when he spoke. "He wasn't going to let the disease take him. He wouldn't want just anyone to see him at his most vulnerable."

"I'll go," Fennix said from the doorway. "Sorry," he grimaced, "I was just going to my room and I heard. Kellum, I'll take care of your grandfather."

Kellum looked at him for a moment then nodded. "Thanks, Fenn." He turned to Behler. "Luke's in the Great House with Matti. I need to go tell him. Gam's probably there, too."

Behler nodded. "I'll come with you." She grabbed a couple of lukas and closed her armoire drawer. "Let's go."

When Behler and Kellum arrived at the Great House, Tilda stood in the doorway speaking to a couple of the elders. She smiled when she saw the two younger Trulars approaching and said goodbye to the others.

Behler studied the older woman for a moment. "When you confronted that Gorlog in Betham...the night of the depot raid – you were watching me?"

The woman laughed. "Just a watchful observer." She put an arm around Behler's shoulder. "There's some people who've been asking for you."

Tilda led Behler and the others into the hall. The room was filled with makeshift beds that held Trulars and Elians with varying degrees of wounds. She saw Zola tending to an injured Revalar. Sillar was at another bed helping Nirain who was still in bad shape but looking better.

"There," Tilda pointed. Mathias was leaning up and talking to Luke. Meela was in the bed next to him, her eyes closed, resting.

Behler and Kellum made their way to them, navigating around beds and people. Behler hugged Mathias.

"Ow!" He winced.

"Oh, sorry," she grimaced. "Sorry." She stood back and looked him over. He had a bandage tightly wrapped around his ribs and another around his ankle. His broken arm was resting in a sling, and a nasty bruise was just turning dark purple on the entire left half of his face. The deeper cuts had already been cleaned up and salved.

"You scared me back there."

Mathias gave a small, crooked grin. "You should see the other guy. He's half the Gorlog he once was."

She laughed softly, but her eyes still burned. "Just don't make a habit of it." She looked at his ankle. "Can you walk on that?"

Mathias raised his cup of aji and drank it down. "Soon enough."

Tilda nodded. "He'll be fine by the time you all land. Meela, too."

Behler looked over at Meela whose arm was in a sling. Penelope was stitching up a gash on her forehead. But then Tilda's statement registered fully, and Behler's head snapped to look at her. "Land?"

Tilda grinned. "I'll be outside."

Behler looked at Mathias. "What does that mean?"

He shrugged. "She talks in riddles a lot. Listen, how did you make those Horde guuns float back there without your stone?"

Behler smiled and unhooked her taakin. She reached inside her luka and pulled out the amulet that was stowed in the small pocket sewn into a seam of her shirt. "Varek obviously didn't pay attention to the differences in our clothing when he used to wear it," she sneered wickedly.

Mathias laughed then grabbed his side. "Ow!" He chuckled a little more. "Let me just rest this ankle a bit more. I'll be out in just a bit."

Kellum had been standing back a bit, but when Behler stood to leave, he quickly said, "Luke, can we talk outside for a minute."

Luke's gaze shifted from one of Kellum's eyes to the other then back again. "Sure," he said. He turned to Mathias. "See you out there."

Mathias nodded and they each grasped the other's forearm.

391

As soon as Luke and Kellum were gone, Mathias looked at her. "What's going on? Is it Warln?"

Behler cocked her chin. "How did you know?"

"Sillar was looking for him earlier. Some of the elders told her he never made it into the root cellar."

Behler's mouth turned down. "No, he was in the stables. I found him. The Gorlogs. He was protecting Avenly from them."

Mathias frowned. "It's better than lidic disease, I guess."

Behler shook her head quickly. "No...Matti...I think I could have helped him even more than I did in the field that day. I just needed more time."

It was Mathias' turn to shake his head. "Bale, he died the way he wanted...and he died protecting a kid he loved very much."

"I guess," she sighed. She looked around the room. Revalars were drinking aji, getting patched up, getting tonics and medicines from Zola. So much effort to save the Trulars. Didn't Elians who had succumbed to the Armigoth deserve as much effort. "I'll see you out there, Matti."

She hurried back through the maze of the makeshift triage to find Tilda again.

She found her speaking with Rafe outside. They looked at her as she approached them with what must have looked like extreme urgency.

"Behler, what's wrong?" Tilda asked in her light, tinkling voice.

"Don't harm the guuns, please," she pleaded.

"Harm them? What do you mean?" Tilda questioned.

"Whatever you're going to do with them...or to them...please, just don't hurt them."

"We don't know what kind of danger they pose." Rafe's voice was raspier than usual. "We've been discussing it at length."

"They may be able to communicate with Varek," Tilda suggested. "That could be very dangerous."

"Please, just listen. There was a...a guun on the field. He was injured and I gave him aji. I could feel the Deep Thread of the aji when it was traveling through his body. I could feel traces of the Armigoth, but it was small and weak. I...I think I could have killed it and helped him....helped *Lucius*, Tilda."

Tilda's brow crinkled for just a moment. Lucius had been her friend.

Finally, she said, "I believe that is a very likely possibility – that those infected can be helped. The Armigoth is like a disease...and very lethal one no doubt...but even the deadliest of diseases can sometimes be defeated with the right medications or tonics."

Rafe was not convinced. "But like many diseases, it could be dangerous to others until it's cured."

"Then keep those captured separated...isolated," Behler suggested – thinking quickly on the fly. "Leave them with guards – like the prisons where we're heading. Leave guards to make sure they don't pose a threat. A Revalar and some Elians should be enough...at least for those we have here in Ardin now."

Rafe scratched at his beard. "We could use the root cellar as a kind of holding cell, and we could spare a couple Revalars to guard them."

Tilda gave a quick clap. "It's settled. Rafe, make it so." She turned to Behler. "It's more important than ever for the Desharets to join us in our fight. You must make it to the Anover Mountains before Varek sends his minions to release the Sulimar." Her voice continued – steady to match her gaze. "We can't say what you

393

and Fenn will face in the coming days. We don't know what either of you will become. But know this, we must walk through the darkness to find the light. We must face evil to remind it of the power in the light." She took Behler's hands in her own. "You've always been stronger than you think. But strength isn't just in what you can fight—it's in what you can carry and still keep going."

Rafe rested his hand on the handle of his sheathed kintar and shifted his weight to one foot. "The Okinars have marked all of us. Once you've killed one of their own, they will hold the vendetta for life. We need you to travel quickly so you can outrun the Okinars and the rest of Varek's forces."

Tilda let go of Behler's hands and crossed her arms over her chest, a stance she took whenever imparting something of importance. "We can't afford a delay, so we believe you should travel...a little differently." She looked up at the circling Cawree overhead who were aiding in the search effort while also watching the forest and skies. "Our friends have already agreed to help. They will take you south of the forest, just past the river. Unfortunately, asking them to take you further would be a huge insult to them, but they have agreed to keep a couple of their best fliers close by if you run into trouble."

"And what about our horses?" Behler asked. "Will we go on foot once the Cawree leave us?"

Tilda smiled broadly. "Oh no. You'll have your horses. Our friends will get them there for you. Now, go gather your group so you can be off."

Behler found Kellum and Luke speaking quietly around the corner of the building. She hated to interrupt but knew time wouldn't wait for their grief.

"It's time to go," she said gently.

The boys both turned to her. "Okay," Kellum said, nodding.

"Yeah," Luke nodded. "Let's get out of here."

Behler felt the need to ease the tension. She gave a little smirk. "I hope neither of you are afraid of heights."

"What?" Kellum asked, confused.

She chuckled. "You'll see."

She turned and began walking back toward the field where their rides were waiting.

68

As Behler, Kellum, and Luke rounded the building, they ran into Fennix who was helping Mathias walk with a pretty substantial limp. Meela was right behind them.

"Are you sure you're okay?" Behler asked Mathias.

He shrugged. "I'm okay to sit on a horse for a couple days."

Behler laughed. "That's...uh...not how we're traveling for the first bit of our journey."

"What?" Mathias asked.

Fennix laughed, obviously already aware of their mode of transport.

"Hey!" Aeron called from a good twenty yura lengths away.

Everyone turned and watched as she ran up to them.

"So...uh...I was thinking maybe I'd go with you all," she said, uncharacteristically awkwardly. "Rafe gave me the okay. He's going to have Dax running scout now with Uri."

Behler smiled. She'd seen what Aeron could do with a bow, and having another female in the crew would be good. "Hope you're not afraid of heights," she quipped. It was her new favorite joke.

"Why do you keep saying that?" Kellum asked, growing amusingly concerned.

Behler laughed and led them to where the Cawree were waiting.

Tilda greeted them. "This is Eru," Tilda said after she'd led Behler's small group to the Cawree leader.

"Greetings, Trulars," the hawk said. Behler jumped a little, not expecting it to be able to speak with such a clear voice.

"Hello," Behler said. The others uttered their greetings. Eru wore a helmet and across the forehead was a symbol Behler had seen before.

"The symbol on your headpiece, what does it mean?" she asked.

"It is the symbol of all Cawree," he answered simply then looked around.

Eru studied Behler and Fennix then turned his gaze to the others standing behind them. "Seven travelers. And you all have horses?"

Aeron cleared her throat and looked at Behler with a sheepish grin. "My horse hasn't made it back to Ardin yet," she said as if embarrassed by her horse's absence. "Granite is a kakweed of a horse, really. Love him to death...but, yeah – he's a pain in the ass."

Behler laughed. "We'll figure it out," she said.

"We will take you to where the river comes from the forest," Eru continued. "We will leave you there, but..." he turned his head and looked over his shoulder, "Balta will stay close by and alert the rest of us if you need our assistance any further."

"We are so grateful for your help, Eru," Tilda said. She bowed her head deeply and stretched her arms out wide. Eru returned her gesture, his wings spreading magnificently.

"You helped us when our kind was in need," Eru said.

Tilda looked at Behler and Fenn, then back to Eru. "Protecting this group means everything to us."

"And to us as well," Eru agreed. "The darkness draws nearer to our lands every day." He turned and spoke in a strange language, and fourteen raptors stepped forward. He turned back to the Trulars. "I know it is customary for your kind to say goodbyes before a journey. Please go ahead with that and we will be off."

As if waiting for a cue, Avenly ran up to Behler. "Aeron can use Cake if she needs a horse." She looked down at her feet. "Sorry I was listening."

Behler smiled. "Don't be sorry. That is so kind of you to offer to let Aeron ride Cake, but I think you and Cake are going to need each other, don't you?"

Avenly looked at her with huge, sad eyes. "Maybe."

Behler knelt and put her arm around Avenly's waist. A strand of hair clung to the tears on Avenly's cheek, and Behler gently tucked it behind her ear. "Do you think it would be okay if Aeron rode Willa?"

Behler felt a surge of grief and joy as it raced through Avenly's little body. Tears spilled out of her eyes. "Yes, I think that would be good."

Behler smiled and hugged her. "Warln would be happy to know Willa is going on such a big adventure."

Avenly threw herself into Behler's arms. "Please be safe," she said, her voice muffled in Behler's neck. "And keep my brothers safe. Don't let anything happen to them. I love them so much."

"I'll protect them, I promise." She smiled. "I'm pretty fond of them too."

Avenly pulled back and looked into Behler's eyes. Despite her tears, she smiled. "I know." She leaned over and gave Behler a quick kiss on the cheek then grabbed her wrist and kissed the bracelet she'd given her earlier. Then she ran to Kellum who scooped her up in his arms.

Rafe had gathered more canteens and a resupply of weapons for each of them. He handed them out. When he got to Behler and Fennix he said, "When you reach the prison, ask for Riv just as we discussed. Tell him who you are and what happened here. He will make sure the other Desharets come."

The twins nodded, each taking turns gripping Rafe's forearm to say goodbye.

Sera was the last to walk up to the twins. She smiled. There was little they could say to each other that they didn't know. She touched each of their cheeks. "Take care of each other and your friends."

"We will, Ama," Fennix said.

"We will," Behler echoed. When Sera walked away, Behler took the opportunity to turn to her brother. "Did you find Warln's body?" Her voice was barely more than a whisper.

"Yes, the stables are really damaged, but a lot of the fire was held back by a Gorlog's body. Warln's body wasn't burned." His jaw tensed and a crease formed above his eyes. Behler knew he was remembering the image of Warln's body. "You were right to not let Kellum go see him. It wasn't good."

Behler nodded and softly said, "I know." She smiled the smile people use when everything is terrible, and everyone knows it. "Thanks for going to take care of it."

"Kellum's my friend. It was my duty to him."

Eru stood tall and began speaking again. "You all will ride the smaller Cawree." He turned and began speaking in the Cawree language again. Seven of the smaller birds walked toward them.

"How do we stay on?" Behler asked.

"You can hold our feathers," Eru said. "It won't hurt us. Trust yourself and trust the Cawree whom you ride." He stepped aside. "Choose the Cawree you wish to ride."

Behler walked up to the hawk Eru had called Balta. "Hello," she said. She bowed her head and stretched her arms in respect, hoping that copying Tilda's gesture was appropriate.

"Hello." The hawk's voice wasn't as deep as Eru's. "I am Balta."

"I'm Behler. Thank you for helping us on our journey."

Balta bowed his head but said nothing. His wings appeared iridescent in the light of the sun as it finally began to break through the overcast sky. They altered from brown to red to auburn.

"How should I...climb up?" she asked

Balta lowered his wing, making somewhat of a ramp for Behler to shimmy up. She was surprised by how soft and silky his feathers were. "Hold on. It won't hurt."

"Okay." The others were climbing up on their raptors' backs. "What about the horses? How are you going to move them?" Behler asked.

"The others will carry them."

"Carry them?"

"Yes, they will be fine. They will not be hurt at all. Ready?"

Behler looked at her mother, Rafe, and Tilda one last time. "Ready."

Balta didn't give her time to rethink her answer. He spread his wings and Behler felt his body lower just a bit before he pushed off the ground. She instinctively grabbed handfuls of feathers tightly as she felt her body rock from one side to the other, trying to find a center of balance.

The ground dropped further beneath them as Balta began his flight by heading north. Behler saw the Armigoth's black cloud looming over the forest. It had retreated and loomed many liyura lengths north of the village again. Balta turned back and flew over the village, revealing the haunting charred remains. Smoke was still rising from most of the eastern side of the lake

Behler watched as the seven larger hawks and owls flew down and grabbed each of their horses in their large talons. Ciela gave a startled whinny but quickly calmed. Watching her horse relax mid-air, Behler couldn't help but laugh—Ciela looked far more at ease in the hawk's talons than she felt perched on its back.

Everyone on the ground had their eyes fixed to the skies. Behler looked back over her right shoulder at Kellum. He was riding a large owl with feathers that made it appear as if it had horns.

She turned back forward. Beneath her, the tops of the trees flew past them in a blur. The sun had finally won its own battle with the clouds and was beginning to warm the air and the world around her. Balta's shadow raced over the canopy of Gaharan Forest.

Ahead she could just make out the peaks of the Anover Mountain range where they would find the Desharets. The distance between the edge of the forest and the mountains was vast, and the journey to find them would be far. It would be difficult, she knew, and the list of those who wanted them dead just continued to grow, but as she looked around at the Cawree flying gracefully through the sky, she realized their list of allies had grown too.

If they could stay alive, maybe they stood a chance.

They were the chosen ones and all.

Epilogue
The Foretelling

Zol sat alone beside the crackling fire she'd built before dusk. The cold night air pressed against her thick, slate-colored skin, but the heavy fur wrapped around her shoulders held most of it at bay. She relished the solitude—just as all Desharets did.

Far to the east lay the lands of the Trulars. She would steer clear, not out of fear or animosity, but respect. She had no reason to fear them, nor to seek them. They were guardians—protectors not just of Arda, but of something vaster, something her people rarely spoke of. The Trulars' work stretched beyond the boundaries Zol had ever dared to cross.

The day had been long. She'd tracked a herd of long-haired elk along the river and thought, perhaps, tomorrow she might finally take one. Her eyes drifted half-shut, lulled by the fire's warmth and the low chorus of crooner bugs in the grass.

A presence at the edge of her firelight brought her back to alertness. Eyes watched her from the shadows, faintly aglow.

She watched in silence, still as stone. Likely just a curious wolf, or a forest cat drawn by the scent of something left behind.

"Zol," came a voice—gentle, clear, and unmistakably from the shadows. "Do not be afraid."

Zol scoffed. "Afraid? Of what?"

The figure stepped into the light: a fox—but not quite. It had markings that shimmered strangely across its sides and forehead.

"I am Mowgwhy," it said. "And I bring a message."

"A message? For me? What message could a fox have for a Desharet?"

"Not for you alone. For this world and all others. The people to the east will one day find a land of two moons—one like fire, the other like rain. Under their light, when they cross the sky as one, two children shall be born. They will grow in power beyond anything the Ansarsari has ever known."

Zol squinted at the creature. "Then go tell them yourself."

"Your people have been chosen to deliver this message. You are truth-sayers, and we wish for you to be part of this journey."

"And where is this land with two moons?"

"When the time is right, they will find it. The twins will be born beneath the moons, and when those moons rise again together and walk the sky as one, their true strength will awaken. But they must be wary – the bond these twins will share must be tested. If one twin dies after the moons have walked the sky, the other shall inherit the powers of both moons."

Zol frowned. "Why tell me this?"

"Because your people will one day become guardians, too. When the Trulars find the land of two moons, the Desharets must go with them."

Zol laughed aloud. "My people are content. We do not go chasing omens."

"If you do not go, the Armigoth will consume this land, and all others."

Zol leaned forward, narrowing her eyes. "And how do I know you are not some little trickster creature?"

The fox smiled—an unsettling thing on a fox's face. "Your kind knows the truth when it hears it. You know I speak it now. Go. You will be rewarded for your trouble."

"They won't listen to me."

"They will because a Desharet does not waste her breath without reason. The Trulars will know that."

And with that, Mowgwhy vanished into smoke.

Zol grumbled, annoyed at the errand she knew she would now undertake. But still, she slept soundly that night. When morning came, she found a large herd of elk drinking from the river near her camp—perhaps the fox's reward already paid.

She took down two, cleaned them, and packed the meat. Then, with little more than a backward glance, she began the long walk east.

Don't miss the next book in the

Trular Series.

The Trular Chronicles

Book Two: Shadows Between

Sometimes survival demands the choice you fear

the most.

The truth lies between the shadows.

Coming Soon

www.ingramcontent.com/pod-product-compliance
Lightning Source LLC
Chambersburg PA
CBHW020011120726
47903CB00004B/1233